December 2

MW00780991

Best Wishes

P. McCree Thornton

The Star Spangled Son

By
P. McCree Thornton

ISBN 0-7414-6486-1
Library of Congress Control Number: 2011922597

Printed in the United States of America

Published March 2011

INFINITY PUBLISHING
1094 New DeHaven Street, Suite 100
West Conshohocken, PA 19428-2713
Toll-free (877) BUY BOOK
Local Phone (610) 941-9999
Fax (610) 941-9959
Info@buybooksontheweb.com
www.buybooksontheweb.com

TABLE OF CONTENTS

The Star Spangled Son is a work of fiction in the historical setting of the Vietnam War. It contains some errors of fact. Times and places of specific circumstances in actual military operations, and naval communication procedures have been distorted in order to suit the story. All persons and events in the naval squadrons are imaginary. Any resemblance to persons or events is coincidental. The squadrons VR-89 and VC-110 never existed. The general obscenity of naval talk has been minimized and has gone almost wholly unrecorded. That which remains is considered necessary where occurring.

P. McCree Thornton

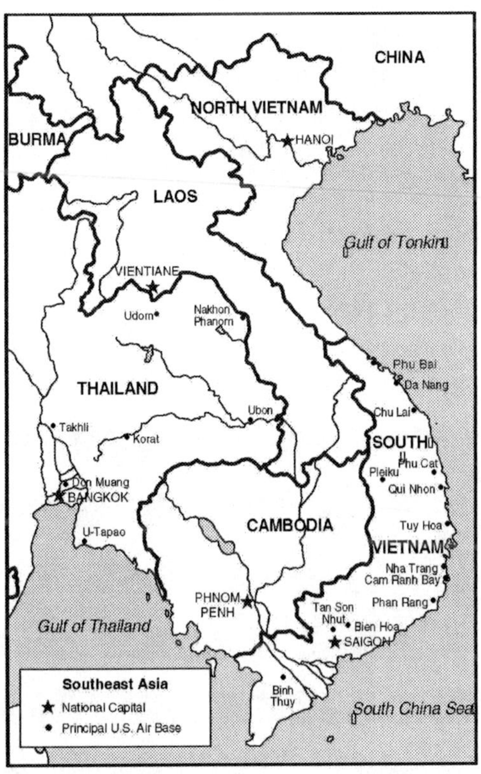

This tale is dedicated to my amazing wife, Kathleen, an American Patriot in every sense of the word. She epitomizes the meaning of wife, best friend and mother. Without her encouragement, assistance and vast patience, this book would not have been possible. The story is also dedicated to all the men and women who served in Vietnam and Southeast Asia during those troubled war years. In particular, this work is dedicated to all those men and women who have died in the service of the United States of America, not only during the Vietnam conflict, but in all wars throughout our country's history.

Acknowledgements

I must express my profound gratitude to Ed Egan, my good friend and a valiant Marine who flew many combat missions as a helicopter pilot in Vietnam. Ed's dialogue and counsel have been invaluable to the completion of this parable.

And not least, I want to thank my lifelong friend, Wayne Simmons, an accomplished author and artist in his own right, for his unwavering friendship, his commentary and advice which goes beyond measure.

Chapter 1

Bud Cotter

Hawaii - January 1967

Ensign Toland M. (Bud) Cotter, US Navy felt a welcomed rush of balmy air when the stewardess opened the cabin door of the American Airlines Boeing 707 at Honolulu International Airport. The trip out from Los Angeles had seemed longer than the Renaissance. He had been seated in the first class section next to an obese bleached blonde of perhaps forty who talked and ate non-stop. The woman was bedecked with gaudy turquoise jewelry and wore perfume so obnoxious that Bud had developed a headache because of the sickening odor. In case the young ensign may wish to call on her, the woman offered a phone number scribbled onto a piece of paper smudged with a chocolate fingerprint.

He avoided the Hawaiian lei line and flagged a cab at the airport entrance. A squat grinning Hawaiian cabbie wearing an oversize flowery shirt loaded the baggage and drove off out of town. The trip to Barbers Point Naval Air Station was pleasant and uneventful as the cabbie drove skillfully through Pearl City, Waipahu, Ewa and past vast fields of pineapple and sugar cane.

The base was sprawling, shady and cool. Palm, yellow ginger, orchid, bougainvillea and hibiscus dominated the landscape. Slowly twirling sprinklers were scattered about manicured lawns giving the base a garden like appearance. The driver dropped Bud at the Bachelor Officer Quarters, commonly known as the BOQ, and drove happily away after receiving a generous tip.

Bud was pleasantly surprised when he walked into his assigned quarters on the second floor of the BOQ. His room was not a room at all, but a two-bedroom suite connected by a common sitting area. Both bedrooms were unoccupied, and for the time being at least, he would have the place to himself. Fragrant breezes cooled the suite through screened louvered windows, and there was a magnificent view of distant jagged mountains covered with tropical greenery set against a backdrop of towering white clouds. He selected the bedroom on the right and dumped his gear onto the bed. Compared to the austere quarters he had shared with other cadets while in flight training at Pensacola, these accommodations were nothing short of luxurious. Bud unpacked his suitcases, shaved and took a shower in his own private bath.

Dressed in fresh pressed khakis, he grabbed the large envelope containing his orders and records and set out walking along quiet palm lined streets in search of the VR 89 hangar. Located at mid-field, he had no difficulty identifying the squadron where phalanxes of large four engine aircraft were parked in neat rows out on the tarmac. Inside a gigantic hangar, Bud was directed to the squadron Admin Office by a pot bellied, cigar-chewing Chief Petty Officer who had a voice like a frog.

The Admin Office was bright, spotless and airy. A neat friendly Yeoman First Class wearing summer whites greeted Bud.

“We’ve been expecting you, Ensign Cotter,” the yeoman said as he stamped Bud’s orders. “If you’ll have a seat, sir, Lieutenant Cross will be with you in just a few minutes.”

Five minutes later a trim, crew cut Lieutenant appeared from an inner office and extended a hand to Bud. “Welcome to Hawaii, Cotter. I’m John Cross the Squadron Admin Officer.”

“Glad to meet you, sir. It’s great to be here.”

“How was your trip out from the mainland?”

“Fine, sir: no problems.”

"Good. Let's go into my office. There's been a change in your orders."

Entirely astounded at this revelation, the young ensign blurted, "Change. What change, sir?"

Lieutenant Cross sat down and motioned to Bud to take a seat in a yellow wooden chair at the side of the desk. The Admin Officer opened a manila bound folder. "It appears that there was a SNAFU at the bureau with your orders to us. Three days ago we received revised orders reassigning you to squadron VC-110. They're located over on the west end of the field," Cross said, grinning, "It looks like you'll be flying A-1 Skyraiders, Cotter."

"Yes, sir." Bud attempted to picture a Skyraider. He was sure he'd read about this aircraft at one time or another. It seemed that a Skyraider might be a small single seat attack jet. Or was that a Skyhawk? He couldn't remember exactly, but whatever it was, it had to better than flying transports, which in Bud's salty view was an assignment for idiots. Upon receiving his orders to VR-89, Bud had been bitterly disappointed that he would not be flying jets. Having graduated fourth in his class at Pensacola, he expected to be ordered to a fighter squadron where he would realize his dream of becoming a fighter pilot.

"Cotter, you're just starting out in your naval career," Cross said in a fatherly tone, "so let me give you some friendly advice. You need to understand up front that those guys over at one ten are, well, a different breed. Give yourself time to learn the drill over there and don't do anything out of line."

"I'm not sure that I understand what you mean, sir."

"Let me put it this way. Commander John J. Ferguson is the Skipper over at VC 110. He's one of the best combat skippers in the Navy, but a lot of people think that he runs a rodeo over there. They seem to always be in the middle of some kind of controversy: safety stand downs, disputes with the FAA, issues with the Air Force and Air National Guard, disregard for NATOPS procedures, I could go on. So what I'm telling you is this, while you're just starting out in your career, take your time and do things by the book, like you were taught at Pensacola. Don't let those cowboys over there get you into trouble."

"I think I see what you mean. Thanks for the advice, sir. I'll remember it."

"Good. Okay. Here are your orders, good luck, Cotter."

Chapter 2

VC-110

Bud declined Cross's offer to be driven to his new squadron and walked the two miles along the flight line road to the hangars of VC-110. Out on the tarmac sat a conglomeration of propeller driven aircraft. Most were large single engine machines resembling World War II fighter aircraft. There were eight or ten twin-engine propeller aircraft of various types, none of which Bud could readily identify. Some of the aircraft were painted in jungle camouflage, others were standard navy gray, and a few were orange and white designating these as training aircraft. One disappointing thing, he did not see a jet anywhere among these aircraft.

Inside a massive hangar identified as B, several aircraft in various stages of disassembly sat surrounded by stanchions, maintenance equipment and toolboxes. The place was quiet as a church and there was no one around. Bud wandered around in the hangar until he came across a lone sailor sitting in an office pecking at a senile Royal typewriter.

"Excuse me," Bud said, clearing his throat, "can you tell me where I can find the OOD (Officer of the Deck)?"

The sailor called over his shoulder without turning around. "If he's around, he'll be in Flight Ops over in hangar Alpha."

"Okay, thanks." Walking to hangar A, Bud pondered over a viable reason to justify why a Duty Officer might not be around.

He found the Flight Ops spaces inside Hangar Alpha. Like Hangar Bravo, Alpha was also deserted and silent. A sailor in frayed dungarees wearing a Cleveland Indians baseball cap sat with his feet propped on a desk. He was watching a John Wayne Western on a small black and white TV. The sailor did not move or even acknowledge that Bud had entered the room.

“Excuse me,” said Bud timidly, “could you tell me where I can find the OOD?”

Without taking his eyes off the TV, the sailor replied, “He ain’t here.”

“Do you know where he is?”

“He went to his girl friend’s place to get some chow and a piece of tail.”

The impertinent response astonished Bud. He thought the sailor should be brought up short, but he wasn’t sure of his ground. “Any idea when he might be back?”

“Dunno, probably tomorrow morning.”

“Jesus,” Bud muttered under his breath. Then louder, with a glint of impatience in his voice, “Well, is anyone around who can stamp my orders and get me checked in?”

This motivated the sailor to take a long swig from a green Coke bottle, yawn wide as a cat, and for the first time turn to observe Bud. “You must be a nugget.”

“I’m a new officer, if that’s what you mean.”

“That’s what I mean.” He yawned again, very wide, so wide that Bud could see the fillings in the sailor’s teeth. “I’m JOOD today,” the sailor said while stretching, “you can leave your stuff here with me. I’ll take care of it.”

Bud had no intention of leaving his orders and records with this sloven. He was appalled that the OOD had gone off base and left this recalcitrant in charge. He wasn’t sure that this supposed Junior Officer Of The Deck was even a Petty Officer. Recounting Lieutenant Cross’s earlier cautions, Bud decided not to push the issue further. “No thanks. I’ll come back in the morning.”

"Okay, whatever," the sailor replied and returned to his movie.

When Bud arrived at VC-110 the next morning, the place was bustling with activity. Out on the tarmac props were turning and big radial engines were rumbling as plane captains warmed the engines and checked the systems for the morning flight. Flight Operations was a frenzy of pilots in flight gear, officers and chiefs in khakis and sailors in blue work dungarees. Teletype machines clacked noisily printing weather and flight planning information onto coarse yellow paper, and there were shouts, oaths, blasphemies and one recurring four letter word that seemed to fill the air.

The young pilot gawked at big Plexiglas boards marked with aircraft numbers: the status of the aircraft and the names of pilots; all written with yellow grease pencil and being continuously updated by sailors wearing sound powered headsets. Another big board listed names of instructors and students slated for the day's training flights. To Bud's eye, it seemed a scene of complete chaos and confusion.

He found the Duty Officer's desk and presented his orders. The Duty Officer, a short stout Lieutenant jg (junior grade) wearing an olive green flight suit festooned with squadron patches took the envelope. He had bristly black hair and stubby hairy fingers. A leather nametag on his flight suit identified the pilot as LTJG C.R. Cozort.

"Welcome aboard, Cotter." Cozort extended a hand.

"Thanks," said Bud taking Cozort's hand. "I was here yesterday, but there was no one around."

"Yeah, we were on a safety stand down."

"Why were you on a safety stand down?"

"Day before yesterday Chicken Wing accidentally shot a chunk of rudder off an Air Force C-123 tow plane, caused kind of a panic if you know what I mean."

"Was anyone hurt?"

"Naw, the crew made it back to Hickham okay. But the word is some Air Force General was real pissed and raised hell over at COMFAIRHAWAII. Skipper had to call a safety stand down to cover our ass."

"I thought a lot of intensive training went on during a safety stand down. It was a major deal at Pensacola."

Cozort grinned, "Everything's a major deal at Pensacola, Cotter. You've got to forget all that Mickey Mouse stuff. Things are different out here in the fleet, especially in this outfit. The Skipper says there's no better place to think about safety than on the beach or the golf course."

"Unbelievable," Bud muttered wagging his head.

Cozort grinned knowingly. "Skipper will want to see you right away. Come on. I'll take you up there."

The Commanding Officer and Executive Officer offices were located on the second deck of the hangar. Painted on the glass of an outer door, big gold letters on a dark blue background read, COMMANDING OFFICER. On the next door was painted EXECUTIVE OFFICER. Cozort opened the CO's door and glanced at Bud.

"Wait here, Cotter." Cozort walked past a yeoman seated at a desk and went directly into the CO's office without knocking. Feeling peculiarly self-conscious, Bud studied framed pictures of aircraft and aircraft carriers hung on the walls. The yeoman read the sports page of the Honolulu morning paper and totally ignored him. Three minutes later, Cozort appeared. "Okay, Cotter, you can go ahead in. See you around. Maybe we can have a beer sometime."

"Yeah, that would be great. Thanks, Cozort."

Commander John J. "Jack" Ferguson, call sign "Big Dog," sat at his desk holding a short non-filter cigarette between yellowed nicotine stained fingers as he read through Bud's file. He appeared rumpled and fractious, as though he had been at his desk since dawn. Tall and lanky, Ferguson featured bony cheeks, a Marine Corps haircut, bushy black eyebrows and startling black hollows around sunken eyes. On the CO's disheveled desktop was an ashtray made from a cut down brass five-inch gun shell. It was gummy brown with cigarette tar and heaped with butts. The office reeked of cigarette smoke, fresh paint and floor wax. A metal louvered window behind Ferguson's desk appeared not to have been opened in years. An ancient oscillating fan mounted on the wall stirred the ghastly miasma from end of the room to the other. Bud wondered why the CO didn't open the window and allow some fresh air to come in.

Ferguson stopped reading the file and looked up at Bud who was standing nervously in front of the CO's desk.

"Welcome aboard VC-110, Cotter." Ferguson extended a long bony hand across the desk. "Sit down, Lad."

"Thank you, sir."

"Now that's something you can knock off right now," Ferguson said sharply, peering at Bud. "You will address me as Skipper, not sir, understood?"

"Yes, Skipper."

Ferguson turned a page of Bud's file. His eyebrows went to maximum elevation. "Fourth in your class at Pensacola is goddamn impressive, Cotter! Whose punch bowl did you piss in to get dumped into this outfit? Did you request recips?"

"No, sir, I mean no, Skipper. I requested jets, VF on my dream sheet but I was ordered to VR-89, but when I got in yesterday they said the Bureau had changed my orders to VC-110."

"Hell, I need pilots; that's why you're here, Cotter. Christ, we lost six pilots on the sixty-five WestPac, and the bureau has been slow as hell to replace people. We're supposed to deploy WestPac again in October, and even with you here I'm short four pilots. So you're gonna have to bust your ass to get qualified and trained up. VC-110 is a composite squadron. Do you understand the mission of a VC squadron, Cotter?"

"No, skipper, not really."

"Briefly, we fly several types of aircraft, in our case, all recips. We execute various missions that are assigned to us by Commander Fleet Air Hawaii or COMFAIRHAWAII for short. We may have birds up doing target towing for the fleet or the Hawaii Air Guard. We fly anti-sub and anti-ship patrols. We work with the Coast Guard on search and rescue missions in Hawaiian waters. We fly close air support missions for the marines training in the islands. Bottom line, Cotter, we have to do it all and we do it damn well too. Our pilots are probably the most versatile in the navy and marine corps because every pilot has to be checked out and proficient in a variety of aircraft. You may be flying anti-sub patrol today, and tomorrow you may be assigned to fly close air support for marines training in jungle warfare. The next day you may be towing target sleeves or flying a SAR (search and rescue) mission." Ferguson paused and lit a Camel. He cast a hard look at the young pilot. "So I gather you expected the bureau to order you to a VF squadron, didn't you, lad?"

"Well, yes I did."

"Everybody wants to be a fighter jock, Cotter, and very few ever make it. You had better get used to the fact that your ass is in the junkyard navy now. The newest aircraft we have was built in 1953. Our job is to keep all the equipment airworthy and to complete any and all mission assignments. That means we are constantly training and maintaining the highest levels of proficiency. I will not tolerate crybabies with a negative attitude in my squadron. I expect you to bust your ass at all times no matter what we assign you to do. Is that clear?"

Swallowing hard, Bud replied, "Yes, Skipper."

"Got any tail wheel time, Cotter?"

"Maybe five hundred hours."

"What about multi-engine time?"

"I have a couple of hundred hours in a Lockheed twelve."

"Where the hell did you get time in a Lockheed twelve, Lad? Christ, I didn't know there were any of those birds still flying."

"It was my dad's company plane until he bought a business jet. He still uses the old Lockheed occasionally for short trips or vacations."

"What kind of company does your old man run?"

"He owns a communications company; it's a radio and TV station."

"Did your old man fly military?"

"No, actually he doesn't fly. A couple of guys who work for him do the flying."

"I see. Well with your experience, you should be ahead of the game. Some of these idiots around here could ground-loop a goddamn pickup truck. Coffee, Cotter?"

"No thanks."

The phone on Ferguson's desk rang. He scowled, pressed a lighted button with impatient motions and picked up the receiver. "Ferguson speaking, what is it now?____ Okay, I've got it. Call the line shack and tell them to preflight one of the S-2's, and listen, find Mad Dog and tell him I want him to handle this. Tell him orders are to harass the son of a bitch until the can (destroyer) gets out there. And one more thing, tell him a new pilot, Ensign Cotter is going to fly with him. What? I don't give a goddamn if he's in bad mood today! Those are his orders, and you tell Mad Dog for me that I'd better not hear any crap about this either!" He slammed down the receiver and muttered, "goddamn Mad Dog thinks he's some kind of goddamn prima donna around here."

Ferguson scribbled on a piece of paper and said, "Okay, Cotter, take this chit over to the parachute loft and draw your flight gear. They'll give you anything you want. After you've done that, find Red Lead back in Aviation Stores. He'll get you squared away with your survival gear and set you up with a locker. Now here's the situation. Half an hour ago, a P-3 crew reported that they think they have located a Soviet sub off Molokai. The sonar operators on the P-3 think it may be a Golf Class boat with ballistics on board. Orders have come down from CINCPAC; they want us to harass the sub until the can gets out there. You'll fly with Mad Dog and get yourself some first day OJT."

Ferguson gulped muddy coffee from a crock mug. "Oh, and one other thing, Cotter, when you're not out flying, I expect you to have your nose in a NATOPS manual. I want you checked out in all the squadron birds and be qualified Hawaiian and Midway local within 90 days. Questions, Lad?"

Head spinning, Bud said, "Ah well, where do I find, Mad Dog?"

"He'll be down in Flight Ops in a few minutes. You'll spot him right away. He's one of our four Marine Corps pilots. He looks like a gorilla and he doesn't like ensigns or second lieutenants. He's also one of the most experienced pilots in the squadron. If you keep your eyes and ears open and your mouth shut, you'll learn a lot from him. If you piss him off, he'll stomp your guts out. Now, get your ass out of here and get busy."

To expedite things, a sailor was assigned to drive Bud around in a gray navy pickup truck. Bud was taken to the parachute loft where he drew his flight gear. He was then delivered to hangar Alpha and introduced to Red Lead, an auburn headed second class Aviation Storekeeper who wore a magnificent handle bar mustache. Red Lead supervised the procurement and stowage of aircrew gear and was the supply guru everybody went to for extra gear and for favors. Red Lead had Bud sign for a locker, a helmet, an oxygen mask, a parachute, an inflatable Mae West life vest. Their last stop was at the squadron armory where Bud signed for a .38 caliber Smith & Wesson revolver with holster and a bandolier of ammunition.

Chapter 3

First Flight

Mad Dog was a Marine Corps Captain and a veteran of an earlier WestPac (Western Pacific) deployment. He hunkered over a large table in flight planning writing on a green form. Mad Dog stood an intimidating six feet one inch tall, was broad, burly and had dark hair cut Marine Corps high and tight. His muscular body seemed to be almost bursting out of his flight suit. Two well-worn black leather bandoliers crisscrossed his chest supporting two rows of fat .45 caliber cartridges. A nickel plated Colt Government .45 pistol was tucked into a black leather holster and hung on his waist at a slant. He had a sheathed stiletto knife strapped handle down to the bicep of his left arm. The hulking Mad Dog had the coldest, most frightening eyes Bud had ever seen.

When Mad Dog finished with the form, Bud introduced himself. "My name is Cotter. The Skipper assigned me to fly with you today."

Mad Dog cast a murderous glance toward Bud and said nothing. He picked up his gear and walked out of the building onto the tarmac. Thoroughly intimidated, and not knowing what else to do, a meek and frightened Ensign Cotter picked up his bag and hurriedly followed Mad Dog to the aircraft.

The S-2E was a stubby nose Grumman twin-engine propeller aircraft painted gray. Oil dripped into catch pans set under the breather tube of each engine and the bulky engine cowlings were adorned with grease and oily handprints. A sailor in a greasy green flight suit appeared from behind the left wheel well holding a fuel sampling tube in his hand. Mad Dog said, "Everything checked out Cracker Jack?"

Cracker Jack was nineteen, pimply, matchstick skinny and had black hair cut in a flat top. He was assigned as the combination plane captain and air-crewman.

The sailor surveyed Bud. "All checked out, Mr. Otis. Who's he?"

"A nugget."

Cracker Jack instantly discounted Bud Cotter's physical existence and resumed the pre flight briefing. "Oil in both mills is up to temperature. Mag drop is 75 on both engines; twenty sounding charges in the torpedo bay. Fuel topped off in mains and auxiliaries. That friggin' right strut seal is still leaking though. I thought AIMD was supposed to get the friggin' thing fixed."

Mad Dog squatted and peered up into the wheel well at the right strut. "What's the extension on the strut?"

"Fourteen, that's in spec."

"Well, if it's in spec, why are you whining to me about it," Mad Dog snapped, "if it's still leaking, write it up again."

Mad Dog climbed into the airplane, went forward and wedged himself into the right seat and promptly lit a cigar. Puzzled at Mad Dog sitting in the right seat, which is normally where the copilot sits, Bud pointed to the left seat and asked in a hesitant tone, "Ah, you want me to take the left seat?"

Mad Dog slowly turned and stared at Bud for a very long five seconds, and then slowly turned away without uttering a word. Not knowing what else to do, Bud carefully squeezed into the left seat and began to strap in. He was aghast that Mad Dog was smoking in the airplane, but he was too frightened to object. The cockpit was hot and stuffy and rapidly filling with choking cigar smoke; Bud steeled the nerve to reach overhead and open a square window hatch above his head and the side window next to his seat. Afraid to touch anything else, Bud sat motionless and glanced around the cockpit.

The interior of the old S-2 was well-worn, bare aluminum or green zinc trichromate primer showed through in many places. The throttle, mixture and prop control levers were on the overhead, a configuration Bud had not seen before. The instrumentation seemed relatively standard and the radio equipment was easily accessible at the center of the instrument panel. Suddenly and without warning, Mad Dog roughly dropped a thick leather bound checklist into Bud's lap. Mad Dog then pointed to the master switches on the overhead panel and said, "Masters on." Bud raised the red switch covers and engaged the switches. A rainbow of colored lights suddenly illuminated all over the cockpit, radios hissed and the gyros began to noisily wind up. Nervously, Bud began flipping through the pages of the checklist until he found the pre-start section. He heard the rear hatch close as Cracker Jack climbed into the aircraft. Mad Dog plugged his helmet headset into the jacks on the side panel; seeing this, Bud did the same. Cracker Jack called over the IC, "Station one standing-by, checklist complete."

Mad Dog responded, "Okay, Cracker Jack."

Realizing that he wasn't going to get any instruction or help from Mad Dog, Bud began to carefully and methodically go through the checklist. Just like he had been taught at Pensacola, he verbally announced each step of the checklist once he had located the proper switch, lever or instrument. During this process, Mad Dog puffed the cigar and thumbed through a tattered Playboy magazine that he pulled from a map rack on the bulkhead.

When Bud was finally ready to start number one engine, he said to Mad Dog, "Pre-start checklist complete. Ready to start engines."

Mad Dog was admiring the centerfold photo of the magazine and ignored him. Bud waited half a minute and hesitantly repeated himself, “Sir, pre-start checklist complete. Ready to start engines.” Mad Dog slowly turned toward Bud with a thoroughly sarcastic expression. “Well start the engines, or do you expect me to do it for you?”

“No sir.”

Through his side window, Bud called to a sailor who was lolling on a yellow start cart next to the engine.

Bud made a whirling motion with his hand and shouted, “Generator on, ready to start number one.” The sailor rose, yawned, stretched and attempted to start the generator cart. Several times the engine failed to start, and each time the sailor commented on the failure with spectacular obscenities, some words Bud had never before heard. Once the cart started amid a billowing cloud of grayish-white smoke, the sailor went to stand next to the big exhaust stack of number one engine and held the nozzle of a large CO2 fire extinguisher a few inches from the orifice of the stack. “Clear number one prop,” Bud shouted. The sailor gave him a thumb up sign. Bud engaged the starter switch and the big three-blade prop began to slowly rotate. He pressed the primer switch and allowed the prop to rotate nine blades as instructed by the checklist; then he moved the magneto switch to the both position. The engine belched fire and a cloud of thick white smoke, and stuttered into life.

When number one engine had settled into a smooth throaty idle, the sailor walked around to the number two engine and pointed the CO2 nozzle at the exhaust stack. Bud repeated the procedure with number two engine. He was gaining confidence and proud of himself having successfully started up an aircraft he knew absolutely nothing about. In a skewed sort of way, he was beginning to enjoy this bizarre experience despite the presence of the scary brute, Mad Dog.

The sailor shut down and disconnected the start cart and moved to a position forward of the airplane. He began to make hand signals, each of which Bud acknowledged by cycling the flaps and each of the control surfaces. Once all the control checks were completed, Bud held the brakes and signaled for the chocks to be pulled.

"Startup and pre-taxi check lists complete," he said glancing at Mad Dog.

Mad Dog depressed the transmit button on his control yoke. "Ground, Zephyr one two at west ramp, taxi."

"Zephyr one two, cleared to runway four left. Squawk 0643."

"Taxi four left. Squawk 0643." Mad Dog pointed at the IFF transponder. Bud twisted the knobs to 0643 and pressed "IDENT".

Mad Dog motioned forward and said, "Let's go."

Bud released the brakes and the S-2 began to slowly roll ahead. Being cautious, Bud experimented with the brakes and nose wheel steering. He cracked the overhead throttles and the airplane began to gradually gather speed. By following the taxiway signs, he easily located runway four left. There, he methodically went through the checklist until both engines and all the aircraft systems were checked. Mad Dog talked to the tower.

"Tower, Zephyr one two ready to roll on four left."

"Zephyr one two, check flaps down. Traffic is a C-118 on downwind for four right. Cleared for takeoff, runway four left. Maintain runway heading. Climb and maintain three thousand, contact Honolulu departure one two four one."

"Roger. Flaps down, runway heading and maintain three thousand. Call departure one two four one and we have the one eighteen on downwind."

Mad Dog motioned to the runway with his cigar, and as he did so, ashes fell onto the top of the instrument panel. Bud taxied into position on the centerline carefully following the checklist. He held the brakes, set the gyro and brought the engines quickly to full power and released the brakes. The airplane leapt forward. The airspeed reached 80 knots very rapidly and it was passing through 90 knots when he eased back on the control yoke. The old S-2 rotated on its main wheels and literally jumped into the air. Rapidly rolling in forward elevator trim, Bud brought the nose down, raised the landing gear and flaps and struggled to maintain 130 knots on the climb to three thousand. Reading rapidly from the checklist, he set the RPM and reduced the manifold pressures into the green arc as indicated by the checklist. The quickness and responsiveness of the old airplane amazed him. He managed to hold a heading of 040 and remembered to ease into the assigned altitude of 3,000 feet. When he had the airplane level at three thousand, he adjusted the cowl flaps, oil cooler flaps and set the props and RPM to cruise setting as stated in the checklist manual. The airspeed indicator read 190 knots.

"Departure, Navy Zephyr one two at three thousand direct to Molokai VORTAC for Orion vector."

"Navy Zephyr one two, maintain three thousand, cleared direct to Molokai VORTAC. Frequency change approved. Good day."

"Roger. Maintain three thousand to Molokai. See you later."

Mad Dog tuned the Nav radio to Molokai VORTAC. He pointed to the OBS on the instrument. Bud made a gentle standard rate turn to heading 095. The needle centered on a To heading and the DME read 93 miles.

They passed Diamond Head and crossed into Kaiwi Channel. When they reached the Molokai VORTAC, Mad Dog contacted the TACCO aboard the P-3 on a secure frequency. Using radials off the VORTAC, the TACCO directed the S-2 to the area in Kalohi Channel where the submerged Russian sub was being tracked by the P-3 Orion with sonobuoys.

"Cracker Jack, stay awake back there," Mad Dog said, "we're coming up on the smoke visuals from the P-3."

"Roger."

Minutes later, a few miles ahead of the S-2 four thin columns of white smoke appeared on the surface of the azure sea. "I've got the airplane," Mad Dog said. He took the controls and aligned the S-2 on the row of smoke pods the P-3 had just then deployed.

"Cracker Jack, opening torpedo bay doors, standby to deploy four sounding charges on the count, set depth at two five zero feet."

"Doors coming open, standing by, set four charges at two five zero feet," came the reply.

Peering at the smoke pods, Mad Dog slowed the S-2 to 140 knots.

"Standby to deploy #1 charge;" ten seconds later the smoke passed under the nose of the aircraft.

"Three, two, one, deploy one."

"One deployed," came an instant answer.

Five seconds later, "three, two, one, deploy two."

"Two's away."

A sounding charge was deployed at each of the four smoke pods. The four cylinders of explosive began falling in a line roughly parallel with the Russian sub. The submarine would move into the path of the charges as they drifted to a depth of 250 feet whereupon they would explode. The explosive would do no major damage to the sub, but it would create deafening and terrifying noises inside the submarine. Four of these charges exploding in close proximity to a sub would hopefully accomplish two purposes: first, it will let the submarine captain know that his boat has been located, and secondly: these nearby explosions straddling the submarine would very likely intimidate the captain and crew into believing they were actually being depth charged. Sounding charges were designed to create an intensely high volume sound that passive sonar could track at some distance as it resonated off submerged vessels. Up close, the charge created a deafening explosion and a noticeable pressure wave.

Mad Dog wheeled the old S-2 around in a tight turn. The smoke pods were now off their port quarter. Suddenly small boils of white froth began appearing on the surface of the sea near each of the smoke pods. As a spectator, Bud watched all this with awe and fascination. They continued to circle the area for several minutes until Mad Dog said, "Here he comes, Cracker Jack, standby with your cameras."

"I've got him."

Bud had no idea what Mad Dog and Cracker Jack were talking about. Then suddenly, a thousand yards beyond the smoke pods a massive shadow began to form under the azure surface of the sea. It was the Soviet sub coming to the surface! What a sight! He had never seen a submarine except in pictures.

Mad Dog said to Bud, "You've got the airplane. Circle the sub while Cracker Jack gets photos. One four zero knots."

The submarine broke the surface of the sea in an enormous cloud of spray and foam. Seconds after the conning tower had broached the surface, Bud could see a hatch open and men began to scurry out of it. Within half a minute, a dozen men were on deck, some peering at the S-2 through binoculars while others began to break out deck guns.

"Hurry up back there, Cracker Jack. The Russkis are breaking out their 23's."

"Almost done, Mr. Otis."

Pangs of alarm shot through Bud Cotter's viscera. He hadn't imagined in his wildest dreams that he could possibly be in a situation where he would actually be shot at out here a few miles off Hawaii. This was almost surreal.

"Will they really shoot at us?" Bud said.

Mad Dog ignored the question.

Cracker Jack shouted through the IC, "Okay. Let's get the hell out of here!"

In a cool blasé tone, Mad Dog said, "Head two four five."

Bud rolled the S-2 around in a sixty-degree bank and headed away from the sub. During the turn, he saw the Russian sailors swinging the turrets of the anti aircraft guns toward the aircraft. He thought, "Those bastards are going to shoot at us."

"Tin can off Laau Point, coming hard," Cracker Jack announced.

"I see him," said Mad Dog."

Mad Dog switched the stand-by UHF radio to a new frequency and depressed the transmit button.

"Red Rooster, Zephyr One. Sub appears to be diving at your eleven o'clock, about eight miles."

"Zephyr One, roger, we have visual, sonar and radar contact. Thanks guys, good work."

"Roger. Zephyr One departing the area."

Bud steered a heading of 245 degrees and climbed the aircraft to three thousand feet as instructed by Mad Dog. A few minutes later, as the East Coast of Oahu was coming into view, Cracker Jack's voice hissed on the IC: "Mr. Otis, how about swinging over the nudie beach on the north shore before we go in."

"Not today".

“Aw, sir, come on. We ain’t seen all them fine naked babes in the longest time.”

“I said no, goddamn it!” Crackerjack thereupon began to curse, blaspheme and kick his parachute pack which lay on the deck. Bud was certain that Mad Dog would castigate the sailor for such language and conduct, but the marine took no notice whatsoever. He lit a fresh cigar and began to study a well worn National Geographic magazine he had found among the navigational charts.

Bud flew the airplane back to Barbers Point. Mad Dog ordered him to communicate with approach control and the tower by unceremoniously dumping the approach plates into this lap. Taxiing to the VC-110 ramp, Bud was singularly proud of himself after making the approach and landing without assistance or a word from Mad Dog.

During the debrief session Ferguson walked into the room. “How’d it go, Mad Dog?”

“We laid four charges right on top of that pig boat. She was a Golf Class, no doubt about that. He surfaced and broke out some of his deck 23’s and waved them around. When he saw the Walker coming at him at flank speed he crash dived.”

“Did Cracker Jack get the photos?”

“Affirmative, he should have some good shots. We hung in close for the photo run. Maybe the photo lab boys can blow up the pictures and identify the skipper of that pig boat.”

“Maybe so, CINCPAC (Commander-in-Chief Pacific) seems to be all excited about this Russian boat. They’re sending out a small task group of cruisers and cans to chase him back to Vladivostok

Ferguson turned to Bud. “How’d it go Cotter?”

Bud glanced at Mad Dog. “Fine, Skipper.”

"Good. Okay, Cotter. Tomorrow morning I want you to meet with the XO after muster, and then I want you to report to Buck Farley down in training. He'll get you set up for your physical and flight physiology and get you started on your qualification training."

"Aye, aye, skipper."

Mad Dog walked into Ferguson's office and flopped into an armchair next to the squadron XO, Lieutenant Commander Sonny Miles, call sign "Zorro." Miles was a trim six foot aviator and wore a steel gray flight suit festooned with a leather nametag and two large squadron patches. He looked, moved and talked like a fighter pilot. For years, Sonny Miles had been thoroughly frustrated that the bureau ignored his numerous requests for transfer to jet training.

"Okay, Mad Dog," said Ferguson snapping shut his Zippo after lighting a Camel. "What about this new kid, Cotter."

"No problem, he'll be okay."

"You think so, do you?"

"He was thorough, methodical and cool. My hazing didn't seem to faze him a damn bit. He greased that Stoof onto the runway like he had been flying one forever."

"He was fourth in his class at Pensacola," said Ferguson. "No reason he shouldn't be in a VF Squadron since that's what he requested. He's not very happy about being ordered to us. So I want his attitude and performance monitored."

The XO said, "Think he's going to be a problem, Skipper?"

"Hard to call, you never know about these kids they send us right out of Pensacola. Every goddamn one of them thinks he ought to be flying F-4 Phantoms."

"Cotter will be okay," Mad Dog said. "He's the first nugget I've ever had who took the initiative and flew that Stoof despite my bullshit. Don't worry about him, he'll be fine."

Miles said, “Fourth in his class, was he Academy?”

“Negative,” Ferguson said, “he came through NROTC. He went to school at Vanderbilt. I think it’s somewhere in Tennessee, isn’t it?”

“Yeah, it’s in Nashville,” Mad Dog said, puffing his cigar, “worse football team in the SEC.”

“Oh, yeah,” Miles said, grinning and reaching to poke Mad Dog with a forefinger. It just so happens, big boy, that Vandy beat your precious Alabama last year.”

Mad Dog bristled. “Everybody knows that was a fluke….nothing but a freak accident! No way could a pansy-ass school like Vanderbilt ever beat the Bear and his Crimson Tide unless it was an absolute freak accident!”

“You people are giving me gas,” Ferguson snorted. “I don’t have time for all this bullshit.” He dashed his cigarette. “I’m hungry. Let’s go over to the club and get a beer and a sandwich.”

When Bud returned to his room, he found that the Hawaiian Bell telephone man had installed the telephone he had requested. He showered, changed into shorts and a tee shirt, picked up the phone and called June Chandler. It was 11 p.m. in Nashville, but he decided to risk waking her. He needed very much to hear her voice. Luckily, June was still up studying and they talked for nearly an hour. Bud described Hawaii, his adventure with the Soviet submarine and the flight with Mad Dog and Cracker Jack. June astonished Bud by telling him she was thinking of flying to Hawaii after she graduated and had taken the Tennessee State Board Teacher Examination. This was unexpected news. He and June Chandler had met during his Christmas leave between flight school and his coming to Hawaii. Their relationship had been purely on the up and up. June was conservatively Catholic and quite straight laced. All contact had been limited to long kisses and necking in automobiles. Now June was hinting that she may fly to Hawaii. Bud wondered if her uncompromising attitude could be softening. After some thought he doubted it, but then one never knew about women, but on the other hand, Bud Cotter was probably as naïve about women as any young man could possibly be.

Chapter 4

Old School Flying

During the next three months, Ensign Bud Cotter underwent a fast-paced training curriculum involving a combination of classroom and flight instruction each day of the week except Sunday. The Training Officer, Lieutenant Buck Farley assigned Bud to Chief Warrant Officer Bobby Davidson, call sign, "Boats," who became his instructor and mentor.

CWO Davidson had risen through ranks as an enlisted pilot flying seaplanes, patrol bombers and transports. Short and stout, with a face creased from years of smoking and sun, Boats Davidson was a hard flying, hard drinking, hard living officer, but most of all he was a pilot's pilot. At one time or another since 1942, Boats Davidson had flown practically every type of propeller driven aircraft in the Navy's inventory logging over twenty thousand hours flying time. He had the distinction of holding the Navy's all time record of over two thousand five hundred carrier traps, a phenomenal achievement of skill, survivability and luck.

Bud's training began in the twin engine Beechcraft SNB, the Navy version of the Air Force C-45. Known irreverently in naval aviation circles as the "Bug Smasher," the SNB was an excellent multi engine and instrument training platform. It was also a handful on the ground being a notorious machine for ground loops in crosswinds. Following two weeks flying this machine with Boats Davidson as instructor, Bud passed the phase check ride and moved into the Grumman S-2 Tracker, the aircraft he had flown with Mad Dog on that memorable first day with the squadron. He studied diligently and mastered this airplane quite quickly. Designed as a carrier based anti-submarine warfare and patrol aircraft, the S-2 was a powerful and versatile weapons platform, yet it was docile and relatively easy to fly, at least Bud thought so. He completed twenty field carrier traps in the S-2 at the

Marine Corps Air Station at Kaneohe Bay located on the Eastern side of the island of Oahu. Having done that, he passed the phase check ride and became qualified as pilot in command in the Grumman S-2 Tracker.

The final and most exciting phase of his training came when he moved into the formidable Douglas A1-H sometimes identified as the AD-6 Skyraider. Over the years, the Douglas Skyraider had been modified by the Navy to fulfill a wide variety of missions. Some of the versions included its use as an Attack Dive Bomber, All-Weather Attack Bomber, Radar Counter-Measures Aircraft, Airborne Early Warning, Anti-Submarine, Photo Reconnaissance and Target Towing Aircraft. This was a brute of an airplane, powered by a powerful 18 cylinder Wright Cyclone R-3350-26WD engine that produced 2,800 horsepower. The Skyraider had a cruising speed of 260 knots and a maximum sustained speed 410 knots. It could get low and slow to hug the terrain below enemy radar and deliver up to four tons of ordnance onto bad guys. In addition to hauling all this ordnance, the Skyraider was an effective ground strafing weapon being equipped with six M-3 20 millimeter cannon, three in each wing. These weapons alone could take out a tank, a small ship or annihilate a battalion of infantry.

Bud's training in the Skyraider began with Boats Davidson in a multi-seat version, the AD-5. Sitting in a side by side configuration, the instructor could work directly with the student. To Bud, the big Skyraider was initially somewhat intimidating. The cockpit sat very high off the ground and the big Wright engine coupled with the thirteen foot four blade prop generated a high level of P Factor along with a healthy dose of engine torque. This compelled the beast to yaw left when the power was brought up on the take off roll. If the pilot neglected to set the rudder trim properly and be particularly alert when bringing up the power, this P factor/torque tendency could generate a remarkably exciting off-runway (or off-flight deck) event especially if there was a cross wind from the left.

Following four weeks of intensive instruction in the AD-5, and following a sign off by Boats Davidson and a demanding NATOPS phase check ride with Farley, Bud was listed as qualified in the Skyraider. Now Bud thought, he would begin flying the single seat A1-H and preparing for gunnery, weapons and carrier qualifications, but as he was beginning to learn, things in the Navy did not always go according to his plan. He admitted to himself that he did enjoy flying the squadron aircraft, but he came into the navy to fly jets and train as a fighter pilot. Surely he wasn't going to have to spend his naval career in a flying circus like VC-110

Chapter 5

Engines & Airframes

The day after Bud was signed off in the Skyraider, he was summoned to the XO's office. The squadron Engineering Division Officer, Lieutenant Commander Mike "Dusty" McCall was in the office drinking coffee with Sonny Miles when Bud walked in.

"Congratulations getting qualified local so quickly," Miles said, motioning Bud to the coffee mess.

"Thanks, sir….. Morning Mister McCall."

"Morning, Cotter." Mike McCall stood an unassuming five feet six inches tall. Early on, he had been christened with the nickname and radio call sign, "Dusty." Dusty, an ellipsis for "Blow Dusty," meant because he was short, every time he had gas a small cloud of dust would blow up from the ground. Dusty was good natured about it however, and in no way harbored a small man complex.

Bud removed a cup from a dispenser on the wall, poured coffee from the Silex and sat in a chair next to McCall.

"Say, Cotter," Miles said, "didn't you major in engineering at school?"

"No sir, I was a physics major."

"Physics, huh? Well, that's close enough. Look, Cotter. Dusty here needs help down in AIMD, so I'm assigning you to his division."

This was not what Ensign Bud Cotter wanted to hear. He had convinced himself that he was going to be flying. Now he was being dumped into the Maintenance Department. He knew absolutely nothing about maintenance or engines other than the bits and pieces he'd picked up during flight training.

"I don't want to seem un-cooperative sir," Bud said, "but I have no experience in maintenance or engineering."

"Don't sweat it, Cotter," McCall said affably, "what I need you to do is help Camp and Cozort with the test hops. We'll teach you everything you need to know before we send you up to Flight Eval and Testing."

Immediately after the meeting, Dusty McCall led a very disenchanted Bud Cotter down to the power plant shop and introduced him to Chief Aviation Machinists Mate, William "Wild Bill" Story. Chief Story was somewhat of a legend in the Navy. He had begun his career in 1939 as a Seaman Apprentice and was later appointed to Aviation Machinist School then located in Pensacola. Throughout the years, the Chief had gained an uncanny in-depth knowledge of the Wright and Pratt Whitney radial engines. Scuttlebutt had it that Wild Bill had been born in the Pratt Whitney plant and had been baptized by a priest with holy water and anointed with engine oil. One thing for certain, Chief Story was undoubtedly the Navy's foremost expert on these engines.

"Okay Ensign Cotter," Chief Story said in his gravel-like voice, here's the engine manual on the Wright R-3350-26WD. Use that office over there where it's quiet. Study the manual until you think you've got it down. There's a test section in the appendix. Let me know when you can pass the sample test in the book; then we'll see if you're ready for the standard exam on the engine. Questions, Ensign?"

The manual contained 1,841 pages of information and mechanical drawings. Bud confidently accepted the bulky five pound manual from the grinning Chief and scurried off into the office. He thought that if really applied himself, he would master the information in a couple of days.

In fact, Bud studied and struggled in excess of one week before he could pass even the sample quiz on the big Wright engine. He found that he needed to spend long hours in the engine shop with the mechanics watching these skilled sailors disassemble, repair and overhaul these engines. They encouraged him to assist and he gained valuable hands on experience in this manner. Even then, he developed only a fundamental working knowledge of this intricate power plant that was indeed an engineering marvel, precision as the workings of the finest clock, yet capable of operating reliably under the most demanding conditions and abuse.

Satisfied and secretly impressed with Bud's score of 100% on the difficult written exam, Chief Story handed Bud an armload of manuals relating to the big Hartzell propeller and all its multifarious obscurities. He spent the next four weeks in the prop shop working with the mechanics. At the end of that time, he could intelligently discuss things like: propeller lift component, blade dynamics, blade balancing, planetary gears, governors and gear reduction units; but best of all, he had once again been allowed to turn wrenches and operate equipment while performing hands on training in the shop.

During the final phase of training, Chief Story assigned Bud to the airframe, electrical and hydraulic shops. Here he spent the next month learning about airframes and the electrical and hydraulic systems of the Skyraider, the S-2 and the SNB. Hot, sweaty and dirty each day after hours laboring with the mechanics, Bud steadily grew in his working knowledge of the squadron aircraft.

After 12 weeks of this diligent study and hands on training, Chief Story walked into Dusty McCall's office and declared, "That Ensign Cotter is a regular goddamn Einstein." As a result of the Chief's remarks, two significant events occurred: the first: Dusty McCall placed Bud on the schedule to begin flying test hops, and secondly: Bud now had his squadron name and radio call sign, "Einstein."

On a bright fragrant Hawaiian Monday morning in late April, Bud was introduced to his new boss, Senior Lieutenant Buster Camp, call sign "Lone Ranger". Camp was from Italy, Texas and both his father and grandfather had served as Texas Rangers making Buster's call sign practically automatic.

Lieutenant Camp was in charge of the Flight Evaluation & Testing section of AIMD. Up until now, he and his lone assistant, LTJG C.R. Cozort call sign, "Wizard" were the only pilots assigned to test fly the aircraft after maintenance work was completed. Due to the large number of aircraft perpetually waiting to be tested, Camp and Cozort were constantly behindhand. Many times, when things got really stacked up Camp would ask his boss, Dusty McCall for help. Dusty would in turn ask Miles. Sometimes they would get some extra help for a couple of days, sometimes not. It all depended upon what was going on with flight operations. By overhearing the conversations among the other pilots, Bud discerned that the majority of them viewed flying test hops as an activity for "nuggets" and "shitbirds," therefore, flying test hops was viewed as being far below the dignity and good form of the regular pilots.

The post maintenance flight check or PMFC shack held four ancient wooden desks, a number of gray metal file cabinets, a scattering of wooden chairs, sundry VHF and UHF radios and an obnoxiously noisy 1940's era teletype machine. Several Playboy centerfolds were taped onto one wall and a large area chart of Hawaiian airspace dominated another wall. There was a metal coffee urn and monogrammed crock mugs sitting on a small rickety-looking table.

"Well Cotter, to get you started off right, I've got something for you from the Skipper." Camp handed Bud a set of silver bars. "You made jay-gee (Lieutenant Junior Grade) on the ALNAV that just came out. Congratulations." Camp shook Bud's hand.

"Hey, thanks," Bud grinned, happily surprised.

"Good going," said Cozort shaking Bud's hand. "There's a big raise that comes with those bars you know." They laughed, and to celebrate the occasion Cozort opened a green box of freshly baked doughnuts.

"Skipper would have given you the bars himself," Camp said, "but he and the XO are at a three day conference at COMNAVAIRPAC in San Diego."

Camp, Cozort and Bud spent the next two hours reviewing the procedures and protocols relating to test flying the aircraft. Referring to the Local Area Chart, Camp gave an overview of the MOA test area where all test flights were conducted. Each morning the trio would meet at 0700 and discuss the work orders for each aircraft and formulate a plan. Then each of them would proceed to begin their individual first hop of the day. Normally, operational flights in multi engine aircraft were staffed by two pilots, but due to the shortage of pilots, a qualified maintenance crew chief or plane captain would ride in the co-pilot seat and assist the pilot.

Because of the large backlog of aircraft awaiting a test hop, workdays were twelve hours, Monday through Saturday. After each flight, there was a period of detailed paperwork to be completed along with engine and airframe logs that had to be signed off.

Bud's initial flights were stressful but went without any major incident. Following an established NATOPS protocol, he methodically completed each step on the check sheets as he tested the aircraft engine, systems and controls. As a beginner, he averaged only two test hops per day, and by the end of the first week he was dead tired but had gained a generous boost of self-confidence in his ability to handle the various aircraft. And too, he now understood the value and importance of the shop training he had received under the supervision of Chief Story. Bud's understanding of engines, airframes and systems even though limited, had already helped him resolve a couple of thorny in-flight operational problems.

Chapter 6

Ensign Shug Early

Returning to his room on an evening in late May after a particularly hot and sweaty day of flying, Bud was surprised to find that the other bedroom in his suite was jumbled with luggage and flight bags. Across the unmade bed lay a prone snoring figure wearing only skivvies, his hairy stomach rising above the elastic band of the shorts each time he breathed. The solidarity of having the suite all to himself these past months had been a pleasure. Now the presence of this snoring interloper brought about a forceful twinge of selfish disappointment.

He went into his room, stripped off the dirty sweat streaked flight suit and went into the shower. When he came out and was drying himself, he heard the new man bustling around in the other stateroom. Eventually the stranger stepped out into the sitting area. When he saw Bud, his face brightened and he stepped into Bud's room.

"Hello, there friend," the fellow said, extending a hand to Bud. "Robert E. Lee Early, but everybody calls me Shug, I got that name because my mama says I am sweet as sugar."

"Bud Cotter, Early, glad to meet you."

Wavy sandy-red hair flowed straight back on the top and sides of Shug Early's head. Laughing azure eyes offset an aristocratic face and a fleshy mouth. His square dimpled chin suggested strength in a modest five foot ten inch frame.

"Did you just get in today?"

"Yeah, and son am I beat. Flew all last night and half of today. Started out in Charleston, laid over in Saint Louis for a few hours, and then I ended up in Seattle. I had to wait there half the night until they could get me on a flight. Well, finally I got a ride out of SeaTac to Honolulu on Continental. Son, I had myself a fine farewell party two nights ago."

"Is Charleston your hometown?"

"Yeah, that's right. People say we are old Charleston blue-bloods, but that's a lot of shinola. My great grandfather is General Jubal Early, the Confederate General. Our family roots are in Virginia. My grandfather moved to Charleston in the 1920's."

"What squadron did you get?"

"They didn't give me a squadron. I suppose they figure that I tore up enough stuff during flight school at Pensacola. I'm attached to staff at COMFAIR HAWAII. I guess the Admiral has his headquarters somewhere on the base."

"Yeah, it's over on the east side, next to the golf course."

"The golf course! Hot damn, now that is good news, son. Just so happens my clubs are downstairs in the gear locker. Say, Cotter, I'll bet you're a golfer."

Bud scowled. "I used to be. I haven't shot a round since I've been here. Christ, I haven't been off base since I've been here. All I do is work."

"Not good, son, not good, we're gonna have to do something about that. Say," Shug said with a toothy grin, "I met these two fine ladies on the flight out from SeaTac. Seems as though they're new to the Island and I'll bet they sure would like to be shown around. What say we oblige? Just so happens I have a phone number handy over there on my dresser."

"I don't think so, but thanks anyway, Early. I don't have time for socializing. We work twelve on and twelve off, sometimes more. That's just the way it is."

"You working Sundays too, son?"

"Well, no, not normally. That's usually when I catch up on my laundry and stuff like that."

"Well, son, don't you worry about a thing. Ole Shug will take care of everything. Plan on taking yourself a day off this Sunday in the company of pretty little lady."

"Well, I don't know. I'm not too big on blind dates. Who are these girls anyway?"

"They're civilian nurses. They've been hired by the Department of Defense to work at Tripler Army Hospital over in town. Don't worry, son, you'll love 'em. Nature's been good to both of them, if you know what I mean, heh, heh, heh." He sauntered off into his room whistling.

Shug Early and Bud Cotter drove into Honolulu in an enormous 1964 Lincoln Continental. Shug had borrowed the sprawling vehicle from a Navy doctor he had become friendly with and whom had the duty on Sunday. Sandra Blosser and Phyllis Day waited for them at their small rented bungalow located a few blocks from Tripler Army Hospital. Bud was paired with Phyllis Day simply because Sandra Blosser got into the front seat with Shug.

The couples attended a party on the base at Pearl Harbor in the lavish home of Admiral Louis Stokes, CINCPACFLEET. Through contacts he had made at COMFAIR HAWAII, Shug Early had arranged an invitation to the party. Many of the guests were in the presence of an admiral for the first time and therefore closely guarded their manners. After a few drinks however, things began to loosen up and the party began to get underway. Shug Early brazenly sat at the Admiral's baby grand piano and played a few timid notes. Hearing this, the Admiral immediately perked up. "What! Who's that at the piano? Whoever it is, let's have a song there, Lad!" Shug grinned and began to skillfully play Cole Porter's, *All of You*. The party gained momentum as the liquor flowed and Shug rolled through a seemingly endless repertoire of popular songs and a few pieces from Broadway musicals. The Admiral and his wife were enormously pleased. "Marge," the Admiral exclaimed, "this is the best damn party ever! Somebody give me a cigarette."

The evening ended with a hilarious all hands sing along rendition of, *Who Hit Annie in the Fanny With a Flounder*.

"By George, Matt," the Admiral said to his Chief of Staff. "These young aviators do bring some life into things. I want you to invite them back again, and often!"

As Bud, Shug and the nurses were leaving, Captain Mason slipped Shug his business card. "Call me next week. And I want to thank you ladies and gentlemen on behalf of Admiral and Mrs. Stokes. This did a world of good for the Admiral. He needed a break like this."

"I had a really good time tonight," Phyllis said, looking up into Bud's face as the couple stood on the front walk of the nurse's bungalow. Slightly five feet three inches tall, Phyllis was blonde with dark wondering eyes. To Bud's eye, Phyllis was sexy and cute, not elegant and fashionable like June Chandler, but he liked the way Phyllis projected her feminism in an enticingly unconscious manner.

"I'm glad you enjoyed the party," said Bud, "it was kind of different wasn't it?"

"It sure was. I've never been around an admiral before. And Shug Early, wow! He's the life of the party playing the piano and singing."

"Yeah, he's quite a character, that's for sure."

"Listen, I don't want you to think I'm rude. I'd invite you in, but we've just arrived and the place is still a huge mess."

"That's not a problem at all," he said glancing at his watch. "I understand completely. I've got to be up at 0500 anyway."

She smiled. "Well, good night then."

"Good night, Phyllis."

On the second Monday in June, Bud was instructed to report to Lieutenant Commander Buck Farley in the Flight Training section. Now that Bud had logged in excess of one hundred hours in the Skyraider, he would begin gunnery training and field carrier landings in preparation for the upcoming October WestPac deployment. Each Monday, Wednesday and Friday, Bud would be assigned a training mission involving either gunnery on the range on Kahoolawe Island or field carrier landings at Kaneohe.

This training, added to his regular duties of flying test hops was a welcome diversion for Bud. He assiduously studied the gunnery and weapons manuals each night in his room. He marveled at the variety of weapons that the Skyraider could carry and deliver. He also enjoyed performing field carrier traps in preparation for live Carquals (Carrier Qualifications) which would begin sometime in July.. This was a particularly intense time for Bud. He pushed himself hard and strove to excel in every aspect of his training. All this work and training left him little time for social activities, but he did maintain the weekly phone calls to June Chandler, otherwise his off days were devoted to the study of combat tactics, ordnance and gunnery.

It was on a hot sunny Wednesday in late June when Bud finished his last test hop of the day very early in the afternoon. The trio of Camp, Cozort and Cotter had finally overcome the backlog of aircraft awaiting a test flight, and he was not scheduled for a training flight that evening. Bud went to his room, showered and changed into shorts, a golf shirt and brown leather deck shoes. He decided that the time had come to get off the base once in a while and he wanted to buy a car. Chief Story had told him about an impeccably maintained 1953 Buick Convertible that was for sale by a Chief over at squadron VP-67 who was retiring and going back to the mainland. Bud contacted the Chief and when he saw the car, it was love at first sight.

"Son, this is one fine automobile," sang Shug Early. "Why the women will be chasing us from every direction just begging for a ride in this baby!"

Simonizing the already gleaming car late that evening in the back lot of the BOQ, Bud admitted to himself that even though he wasn't flying fighters, flying the Skyraider and performing test hops was probably a valuable learning experience for him. He decided to view this as his year in the wilderness. He expected that after a year had passed, he could manage a transfer to jet training. After all, there was a war on, and scuttlebutt had it that a lot of fighter pilots were being lost in Vietnam.

Chapter 7

Phyllis Day

"Big doings, Son, big doings; I got us lined up for another bash at the Admiral's place this weekend." Shug Early blew into Bud's room with a handful of mail he had picked up in the BOQ lobby. "Saturday night at 1900, son, get yourself a set of whites to the laundry, got to look sharp for the old man and the ladies. Word is that admirals are gonna be there thick as fleas on a Black and Tan, great way to make some valuable contacts, son. It's who you know in this man's Navy that counts."

"I've got to work Saturday," Bud complained as he shuffled through letters from his sister, his mother and June Chandler.

"Don't worry, son. The party doesn't start till 1900. Besides, it isn't everyday you get invited to CINCPACFLEET's house. I've already got the gals lined up. Get off your duff and get dressed, son. You can read your love letters later. Let's ride over to the A&W and get one of those big burger plates and a root beer. I'm starvin."

"Why are you making date arrangements without asking me, Lad? Besides that, I don't even know if Phyllis wants to go out with me again."

"Sure she does, son. She thinks you're hot stuff. Sandra told me so. You just never worry about ole Shug's social arrangements. I'll never steer you wrong, son. Come on now, son, put your drawers on, I'm starvin."

Thanks to Shug Early's prowess with the piano and an endless supply of Mai Tai and liquor from the bar, the Admiral's party was a sensational hit with all the guests. CINCPAC himself, Admiral Sharp and his wife dropped by for a drink. They gleefully joined in on a riotous and risqué sing-along of Shug's invention, *If You Knew What The Gnu*

Knew. The party disbanded around ten-thirty when Shug finished with the admiral's favorite, *Who Hit Annie in the Fanny with a Flounder* followed by several salty and boisterous encores.

Shug and Sandra left the Admiral's house with another couple to see the late show at Don Ho's nightclub on Waikiki. Alone with Phyllis in the big Buick convertible, Bud said: "Anything special that you would like to do?"

"You know what," she said eagerly. "It's such a beautiful evening. I'd like to get an ice cream and take a drive to a pretty place."

They bought Hawaiian sherbet compote in cones at a stall on Waikiki and drove out Highway 72 in search of a suitably "pretty place." When they reached Kawaiho Point, a spit of land jutting into the Pacific Ocean on the southeast coast of Oahu, Bud pulled off the road and parked the car. Here this night nature painted one of her most romantic displays of rising moon, reef, gentle surf and flowery perfumed breezes.

"Oh, this is so incredibly beautiful," Phyllis breathed. "Why....it's...it's like something out of the film South Pacific. I can almost see Mitzi Ganor standing here."

"Yeah, this is really nice. I'm glad we found it."

"I'd like to take a walk. Can we?"

"Sure."

They strolled along precipices of the point and came upon a path that led to the beach of a horseshoe cove below.

"Let's go wading," Phyllis said girlishly.

"Okay."

On the beach they removed their shoes and waded in the warm surf enjoying the sand and water against their feet.

"This is so unbelievable," said Phyllis, looking out to sea. "One month ago I could never have imagined myself in

Hawaii of all places, and surrounded by this much beauty. It's just mind-boggling. Thank you for bringing me here tonight, Bud." She turned and kissed him tenderly, and for a brief moment her body seemed to dissolve deliciously into his.

"You don't have to thank me," he said, feeling an exhilarating and unexpected pulse of emotion.

"I wanted to kiss you, and please don't think I'm forward or trashy, because I'm not."

"Don't be silly. I don't think you're trashy."

They waded in the surf holding hands, and after sitting on the beach for a long while watching the surf break across the reef, the couple made their way back to the car. There they sat barefoot in the front seat and gazed at the sea, moon and stars. After a while, Phyllis laid her head on Bud's shoulder.

"Is it okay if I do this?"

"Of course it's okay."

They sat in silence for a while, absorbing the magnificence of the evening. "You've never really told me anything about yourself," Phyllis said, "What do you do in the Navy?"

"Most of the time I fly airplanes. When I'm not out flying, I do paperwork."

"What kind of airplanes, jets?"

"I wish. No, I fly different types of propeller aircraft after maintenance work has been done to them. It's my job to make sure everything works like it's supposed to."

"Is it a dangerous job?"

"No. It's pretty safe and non eventful, but I enjoy the flying."

"Do you like the Navy?"

"It's okay. I'd like it a lot better if I could fly jets."

"Shug Early says they call you Einstein because you're so intelligent, pretty impressive stuff."

"Shug Early has a very big mouth," Bud sneered. "Einstein is my radio call sign, which I hate by the way. Somebody gave me that call sign because I happened to get a good score on an exam about engines, that's all."

"If you hate your call sign why don't you change it to something else?"

Bud chuckled cynically. "You don't understand. It doesn't work like that. Once you've been given a call sign, it's as permanent as a tattoo. It's one of those idiotic traditions of the Navy. Everybody has a nickname that is also his call sign, and everything is abbreviated in the Navy, that's something else that gets on my nerves. Aside from the profanity which is unbelievable, the Navy has a whole other sub-language you have to learn. For example, a wall isn't a wall, it's a bulkhead. The ceiling is the overhead. The floor is the deck. A door is a hatch. Stairs are a ladder. Junk food is called geedunk. A bed is called the rack. Underwear is skivvies. I could go on; it's just the way it is in the Navy."

She sat quietly for a time gazing out to sea. "Do you have a girl friend?"

"Yes."

Phyllis sat up with a start. "Oh.......Really?"

"Well,... yeah."

"Here in Hawaii?"

"No. Back home in Nashville."

She allowed this revelation to digest for a few moments. "I see, tell me about her."

"Okay, well.....Let's see.....Her name is June Chandler. She's a teacher, 4th grade I think. We met in December while I was home on Christmas leave. We dated a few times and we've been writing since I came out here in January. I usually call her once a week. That's about it."

Phyllis shifted her body so that she could see his face clearly in the moonlight. "Are you in love with her?"

He sat back and slowly shook his head with a mystified grin. "You certainly are direct."

"Yes, I suppose that I am: one of my many shortcomings. You don't have to answer the question if you don't want to."

Bud regarded her inquisitively. He wasn't sure why she would ask him such a question. In a naïve lightning estimate of the situation he said, "I don't mind answering the question. I like June a lot. We've become very good friends. She's a very nice and upstanding girl. We had some great times together, but I can't honestly say that I'm in love with her. We really only knew each other four weeks before I had to fly out here. There wasn't time enough for our relationship to develop much beyond a friendship."

"Time enough," Phyllis blurted. "Ha! People meet, fall in love and even get married on the same day. It happens all the time."

"Well maybe that happens to some people, but I certainly don't fit into that category."

"Hmm….. What do you think your friend June would say if she knew you were here with me tonight?"

"I don't know. I have no idea what she'd say. You'd have to ask her."

"I don't have to ask her. I already know the answer. She would want to claw my eyes out."

Bud laughed. "I don't think June would feel like that."

Phyllis patted his cheek affectionately. "Oh you pretty sailor. I can see that you don't understand women very well at all, not at all."

Phyllis fell silent and put her head back onto his shoulder. She stared at the moon for a long while. "Wow, it sure is beautiful here. This is so romantic, isn't it?"

"Yes, it is." After a very long pause, Bud said, "So, what about you? Do you have a boy friend?"

"No, no one. I seem to have a really lousy track record when it comes to relationships. I should qualify as the Queen of Broken Hearts. I have this odd propensity for making bad choices I'm afraid, or maybe I'm the bad choice, I don't know."

"I doubt very seriously that you are the problem," Bud said in a tone of compassion. "I'm sorry that you've been hurt. It seems as though people hurt one another too much these days."

"Tell me," she said, turning to look into his face.

On an impulse he kissed her, a long luxurious passionate kiss. When they parted, she whispered. "I was beginning to think you were never going to get around to this." She grasped his neck and pulled him to herself. The kiss lingered, and lingered. She opened her mouth, tongues darted and the kiss suddenly became fiery, desperate and breathless with fervor. Finally, she pushed him away. "We've got to stop this for God sake," she panted.

He looked wonderingly into her eyes. "Do you really want to stop?"

"No damn it, I don't want to stop, but we have to. This just isn't right. I...I...I mean, we hardly know each other. This isn't me. I don't do this sort of thing despite what you may think. This moon, this place, and you........especially you! I'm letting myself get carried away. I can't allow this to happen. I can't! I won't!"

He swept her up in a crushing embrace and kissed her hard. She melted in his arms. When her head fell back against the seat, he began to softly kiss her neck and her throat. "Oh, God, Bud," she gasped, "don't do this to me. Please don't do this to me."

His heart galloped. Testosterone surged wildly through his entire being. Reckless, unheeded he knew that he was on the verge of taking this too far. Her panting words of refusal had no teeth. She was his for the taking and it was driving him mad, but a glimmer of sanity was rising from somewhere deep inside his lust-fogged brain. He let her go and fought to regain his composure. His hands trembled as he twisted the key in the ignition and started the engine. "We have got to get the hell out of here, right now!"

Phyllis clung to him as they drove along the highway toward Honolulu. She was beginning to get to him, really get to him, and he wasn't sure if he should like it or not. Phyllis was dreadfully desirable, too much so in fact. Bud suspected that she had experience with sexual matters. He on the other hand had none. This thought led him to suppose that this may be something he should worry about. Now being able to think more clearly, he realized that he would have to be very careful with this vivacious little angel of mercy. He needed to take his time with her and not allow himself to foolishly become involved in a mess. Then it occurred to him, what about June? This could get complicated and quite nasty if not properly managed. He didn't need any drama in his life. He had to stay focused on preparing himself for the WestPac deployment in the fall. What he needed he decided, was a relationship geared for maximum fun and minimum entanglement.

Chapter 8

Learning To Kill

The radio in Bud's room purred a Haydn quartet as he lay on the bed in skivvies deep into a delightfully tranquil Sunday afternoon nap. A copy of *The Old Curiosity Shop* sprawled obliquely across his chest and a gentle pleasant breeze filtered through the screens and shutters.

"Wake up, son wake up, big news, big news." Shug Early barged into the room and began poking at Bud's leg. "Get up and put your britches on, son. COMFAIR Hawaii staff is piling aboard Constellation next week. Looks like ole Shug is finally gonna get some sea pay. Admiral wants to observe the Connie's work-ups and ORI (Operational Readiness Inspection)."

Bud jadedly sat up on the edge of his bed, mussed, cross and yawning. There were red streaks across his face from creases in the pillow. "What the hell is the matter with you coming in here waking me up? I don't give a crap about your sea pay."

"You will when you hear the rest of this, son. I got the information fresh off the Op Order half an hour ago. You VC-110 boys are gonna be doin' your carquals on the Connie while we're out there."

"How did you get access to operational orders like that?"

"Now son, you know that I've been Assistant Comm Officer for over a month now. I see everything that comes across the skeds and out of the coding machines. The radio boys always keep me posted on the good stuff that comes in. Now, the way I have it figured son, in addition to your regular flight pay, you'll be gettin' sea pay plus hazardous duty pay. Nice fat check next month, son."

"Well, that doesn't necessarily mean anything for me," Bud replied, yawning, "all I do is fly test hops. I get to practice gunnery and field carrier traps once in a while, but I've never flown an actual training mission in a section or a division. Camp told me the other day that he thinks him and Cozort and I might stay here when the squadron deploys West Pac."

"Why would they leave you guys here?"

Bud shrugged. "I don't know. Somebody has to look after things here. Maybe that is the reason."

"Maybe so, I hadn't thought of that. Hells bells, son. If that's the case, you ought to be tickled pink about staying here in sunny Hawaii. Sure beats going to Nam. Just in case you haven't heard, son, people shoot at you over there. And don't forget about Phyllis," he grinned and dropped his voice, "I hear she's really crazy about you, son."

The remark generated an emotive spark of interest, but Bud didn't want to be obvious about it. He thought it would be crafty to appear indifferent. Bud was relatively certain that anything he said regarding Phyllis would get back to her via a Shug-Sandra pipeline.

"I don't know why she'd be crazy about me," he said in a matter of fact tone, "I've just been a convenient date until she meets somebody, that's all." He stood, yawned and stretched. "I'm hungry. I think I'll get dressed and go over to the Chief's Club and get a sandwich. Wanna come along?"

"Absolutely, this boy is starved. Let me get changed and I'll be right with you, son."

Shug Early's information about the VC-110 carquals was completely accurate. The next morning, Commander Jack Ferguson held a meeting with all pilots in the Squadron Ready Room. He briefed them on the schedule and announced new division and section assignments. Bud was happily surprised, shocked in fact, to hear that he was being shifted out of PMFC and reassigned to Section #1 of Division #4. After the briefing was finished, he eagerly read down the Division/Section listings posted on the ready room bulletin board. When he got to his name, his heart dropped. A knot formed in his guts as the implications of his new assignment gradually spread through him. He was Mad Dog's new wingman.

Muscles bulging ominously in impeccably starched and pressed Marine Corps summer uniform, Mad Dog glared at Bud with a horrible scowl and a nasty down turned banana mouth. He wagged his head signaling pure and total disgust. "Holy Mother of God! What did I do to deserve this? What's your call sign, Maggot?"

"Einstein."

"Einstein! Well, hear this, Einstein," Mad Dog snapped, "as my wingman you will remember this, and don't you ever forget it. Unless you're asked a question, there are only two possible things I should ever hear coming out of your pie hole: one is, Mad Dog, you're on fire, and two is, I'll take the ugly chick. Got it?"

"I've got it."

"You'd better have it, Einstein." Mad Dog pulled a thick blue bound folder from a slot in a massive wooden case where training manuals and operation orders were staged for distribution to the pilots.

"Take this folder and study it," Mad Dog snapped. "It's everything you need to know about our field carrier schedule this week and our carquals next week. The ship's call signs, frequencies, traffic patterns, approach plates and the ship's GCA. Memorize it. I do not intend to fly out to the carrier and generate some kind of ungodly cluster-fuck because you have your head up your ass and are not following procedure. Understood?"

"Understood."

"You screw up just one iota, Einstein, and your ass'll be right back running test hops with those other two shitbirds. Got that, Maggot?"

"I've got it."

"JJ will be your Plane Captain. From this second forward, four zero nine is your aircraft. You will treat and handle that aircraft like it is your wife because that is the only pussy you are going to get until this training period is over. Questions?"

"None."

"Be in the Ready Room with your gear at 0600 tomorrow."

Mad Dog stalked out of room leaving Bud incensed with humiliation. "He's nothing but a big overgrown immature bully," Bud seethed, "getting his jollies debasing a junior officer just because he's senior and because he's such a big brute marine. The egotistical boor, the Prussian, the asshole!"

Bud walked out onto the tarmac and located A1-H number 409. Goliath-like in its Navy gray paint scheme, this awesome machine was his to fly, to care for, and maybe someday to wield as an instrument of death. No doubt it would carry him thousands of miles across vast expanses of the Pacific and into adventures he could not yet begin to imagine. As he walked around the airplane touching its aluminum skin, he began to feel the bizarre bond that can inexplicably develop between man and an inanimate machine. Standing in front of the aircraft, he marveled at the great blades of the propeller and the spotlessly clean Wright engine that awaited only a touch from his fingertip to bring it into thunderous life.

Sitting in the cockpit it was all so familiar, but now somehow different. This was his cockpit now, his private little world of gauges, switches, levers and radios. He cherished this place, the array of instrumentation, the controls, the smells, the way he fit perfectly into the seat. Everything had its place and was in a perfect order. It was here, strapped snuggly to the seat that his mind and body would become one with this remarkable weapon. It wasn't a jet, but now, somehow that didn't matter.

He studied diligently, going over and over the data Mad Dog had given him until he knew it intimately. As wingman to Mad Dog, Bud struggled mightily during the first weeks of training, but he managed to stay in position and he made no major errors. Mad Dog was a demanding and uncompromising Division Leader. He had zero tolerance for sloppiness or errors in the air. Heeding the hulking Mad Dog's introductory instructions, Bud said nothing on the ground or on the radio unless asked. In the air, Bud maintained his position at Mad Dog's four o'clock and at a hair-raising six foot separation that Mad Dog demanded as a routine. This required intense concentration at all times, and initially this close quarter flying was highly stressful and exhausting for him. Eventually though, after several weeks, he became accustomed to flying in such close proximity and began to regard it as normal.

Call signs Chicken Wing and Fat Back were the pilots in Section #2 of Mad Dog's Division 4. Being the most experienced pilot of the pair and a veteran of the 1965-66 West Pac deployment, Chicken Wing, another marine, flew number one position as section leader. Having come out of the PMFC shack the nugget Einstein was considered inexperienced and untrustworthy and therefore regarded askance by the other pilots.

Unbeknown to anyone except Ferguson and Miles, Mad Dog had specifically requested Bud as his wingman. Throughout the months that Bud was performing test hops, Mad Dog had been quietly following the young pilot's progress. He was impressed with Bud's accuracy and thoroughness. He noticed too, Bud's natural skill when handling the various squadron aircraft. It amused even the austere Mad Dog to see Bud fly the ILS approach at BP (Barbers Point) inverted just for the sake of doing it the hard way, and the young Einstein always requested the crosswind runway when he was flying a tail wheel SNB or a Skyraider. Such a mind-set conformed to Mad Dog's perception of what a good pilot is made of. Mad Dog usually got the best of the young inexperienced pilots to fly as his wingman. These young pilots he could mold and hone their flying and gunnery skills to razor sharp proficiency.

Mad Dog had seen war in Vietnam. Too many times he had experienced firsthand the mortal fear of combat in the air. So many friends and buddies were gone, fallen to earth, unable to escape the tumbling fireball in which they were trapped. Even now, Mad Dog could feel the dread and fear of those night traps in monsoon weather. Desperately struggling to find the flight deck in the midst of incessant lightening and driving rain, sometimes bathed in Saint Elmo's fire, the airplane would be buffeting and bouncing wildly in vicious turbulence. All alone, pulses of vertigo coming and going, flying the gauges, hoping like hell the guy on the ship's GCA knows his stuff. And if that wasn't enough, there were times when you had to do it in a shot up airplane, maybe wounded and bleeding yourself. And it wasn't just something you did once or twice. It is nine months of living with death that could come with a cold cat shot, a hit by a SAM, Triple A fire, a lucky hit by small arms or crashing a flight deck barrier. Every minute of everyday you're in that airplane you can feel the cold breath of death on your neck. Mad Dog knew these things and he knew that the only way to survive was by training, training and training some more, to be as sharp and proficient as humanly possible, to fly as a team, to cover each other and never ever leave your wingman. Mad Dog knew this was their only hope for survival when they went to Vietnam.

During field carrier traps at Kaneohe, Bud excelled ranking ninth in the overall squadron standings. When they began the series of carrier qualifications aboard the USS Constellation, Bud fared even better and scored seventh in the squadron standings. This performance, Bud felt, vindicated him as the squadron nugget. He took great personal pride in the fact that his “greenie board” scores exceeded those of many of the most experienced pilots. Bud began to notice a shift in the attitude of the other pilots. They were friendlier and began to include him in conversation and ready room banter.

Bud’s success, however, had no effect on Mad Dog or on his attitude. He ignored the “greenie board” scores and he was consistent in his no slack treatment of Bud. In fact, Bud was adjusting to Mad Dog and his obdurate ways, although his dislike of the man was no less intense. The hard-core Marine Corps drill instructor manner no longer vexed him as it had initially. It had become an unpleasant way of life and Bud went quietly about his flying understanding that this is just the way things were. He knew that sooner or later an opportunity would arise that would allow him to escape from the infamous “Mad Dog Division,” but for now, he would just have to suck it up and deal with it.

Carrier flying is taught and is executed by conformance to a set of numbers and standards. These factors include such things as airspeed, aircraft weight, angle of attack, attitude, wind and so forth. But there is another factor, unwritten, yet just as important and that is a carrier pilot’s instinct. Early on, Bud had begun to acquire the critical ‘seat of the pants’ feel and judgment, the instinct that makes a conventional carrier pilot an exceptional carrier pilot. He set himself a goal to rise into the top five in the squadron standings. This was a lofty goal indeed, one that would put him in a class with pilots such as Boats Davidson, Ferguson, Miles and Mad Dog. Most of all, he intended to exceed Mad Dog on the greenie board scores. He could think of nothing else in life that would bring him more pleasure or greater personal satisfaction than to silence this harrying antagonist’s mouth.

The day and night carqual period completed, the squadron returned to Barbers Point to begin an intensive training regimen that included concentrated close air support training with Marine Corps infantry. They spent long arduous days and nights perfecting the techniques of flying close air fire support for the marine infantry and for rescue aircraft searching for down aircrew. The pilots spent innumerable hours working with Air Force and Marine Corps Forward Air Controllers (FAC's) preparing for the days ahead when life and death for troops or air crew stranded on the ground would depend on the close coordination between the FAC and the pilots of the Skyraiders.

The versatility of the A1-H truly amazed Bud as he learned to manage and deliver the wide variety of ordnance that the Skyraider could carry. On the range at Kahoolawe, he hit targets with high explosive bombs, fiery napalm, white phosphorus and cluster bombs. He fired rockets, fired the six 20 mm cannon and Boats Davidson taught him the waning art of skipping a five hundred bomb across the water. He labored hard and was developing into a highly skilled naval aviator. Unconsciously, he was learning and perfecting the art of killing, although it seemed to him more like a grand boy's game being played with magnificent toys. The deadliness of what he was doing meant little to him, for it had yet to permeate his soul. Here in Hawaii, far from war, it was really just marvelous adventure and amusement to enjoy.

Chapter 9

A Virgin in Paradise

Shug Early jauntily bounded down the quarter deck gangway of the USS Constellation as she lay tied to Ten-Ten dock in Pearl Harbor. On the pier, Bud Cotter had been waiting for his friend. He still marveled at the sheer enormity of the ship. Gazing aft where the tails of F-4 Phantom Fighters extended over the edge of the flight deck, Bud had begun to mentally relive the moments of his first trap aboard this magnificent ship. It came to him as clearly as if it were actually happening once again.

On down wind, he had dispersed to a separation of one mile behind Mad Dog. Running through the checklist he set the prop into low pitch, dropped the gear and flaps and held the airplane at 120 knots until Mad Dog turned across the ship's wake on the base leg. When the Landing Signal Officer or LSO called Bud to turn base, Mad Dog had a green light and was about to cross the round-out of the flight deck. Nose up, bleeding off airspeed to 110 knots: he backed off the power a few inches of manifold. Everything was just like the field carrier approaches at Kaneohe except now, the runway was moving through the sea and away from him at 15 knots. The Skyraider was sensitive to his every movement, the big Wright engine purred steadily as the airplane settled gently toward the ship. The LSO talked to Bud on the radio.

"Einstein, call the ball."

Bud could see the red-orange meatball clearly. It was centered in the green bars exactly where it ought to be. He was on center line and on glide path.

"Einstein has the ball," Bud radioed.

The green light went on, he had a clear deck. The sudden burble of turbulence from the ship's island structure surprised him, the airplane rolled a little: he had forgotten to anticipate that distraction. He resisted the impulse to add power to compensate for the turbulence. The meatball floated a tiny bit as he went high for a brief second and settled back to center. The Skyraider crossed the round-out and floated serenely onto the flight deck to a three-point touchdown. He had learned to hold it off by nursing the power slightly so he wouldn't slam it down like most guys did. Stick full back into his gut to keep the tail down and prevent a hook bolter, throttle forward to full power until he felt the arresting cable stopping the airplane.

The LSO turned to his assistant who stood on the platform behind him. "Four zero nine. Okay three." An okay meant that the Landing Signal Officer gave Bud a perfect score. Three meant that he trapped number three wire, the preferred arresting cable.

A plane handler wearing a blue shirt ran across the flight deck, disengaged the cable from the tail hook and began to make a whirling signal with his arm. This signaled the arresting gear operator to retract the cable. A flight deck director in yellow shirt and helmet was signaling to Bud. Bud flipped the "up hook" switch and retracted the tail hook. The yellow shirt directed him forward and handed him off to another yellow shirt farther down the deck. They were fast taxiing him up to the port catapult on the bow. He taxied up to the catapult and held the brakes on signal from another yellow shirt. He could feel the catapult crew connecting the harness and hold back coupling to the airplane. Bud was going over his emergency egress plan in case he got a cold cat shot or the engine failed. Then he quickly ran through his checklist: flaps set, prop set, cowl flaps set, speed board retracted, fuel pumps on, oil pressure okay, gyro set, no trouble lights. Good to go. Now Bud watched the Catapult Officer known as the shooter. He stood erect working his right hand at the wrist holding up two fingers. Bud brought up the power, quickly re-checked the magnetos and scanned the panel. Good board, no trouble lights. He signaled thumbs up and flipped a quick salute to the shooter. The shooter nodded, took a quick clearing look around, went down on one knee and pointed forward with a sweeping motion of his arm. Bud put his head back against the seat rest. Two seconds later, wham! Gee force nailed him against the seat and immobilized him. The big Skyraider was hurled down the track of the catapult and out over the sea. Clear of the catapult, Bud let go of the handhold bar with his left hand and put it on the throttle quadrant. He moved the stick forward a fraction to help the elevator trim to bring the nose down. Speed 100 knots and increasing, sweet engine pulling hard, climbing well, no trouble lights. Roll into a standard rate turn to the left to get clear of the ship's path. He slapped the landing gear handle to the UP position and began retracting the flaps. Climbing on the cross wind leg, he looked around then turned down wind and leveled the airplane at 1500 feet. He picked up Mad Dog out in front of him and prepared to set up for his second trap. He remembered thinking, "At this moment, in this time and in this place, I can think of nothing I'd rather be doing more."

These pleasant thoughts were broken by the familiar voice of Shug Early. "Son," said Shug handing Bud one of his hefty flight bags, "What a time! What a time! I got tons of great pictures of you flying that Skyraider, son. Word is you tore 'em up on the greeny board scores."

Bud frowned. "I didn't do all that well on my night traps. I had two fairs and one of those was a dusk pinkie that I should have aced."

"Don't try and pull that modest routine with ole Shug, son. I saw the greenie board. Seventh in the squadron, and you a nugget! Outstanding! It's the talk of the ready rooms!"

"Huh," Bud grunted, "I'll bet it is."

Shug let the subject drop. "The Connie is one hell of a ship isn't she? I was lost half the time I was aboard. Great chow though. Played the wardroom piano a few times for the Admiral and the Captain. Made some good contacts son, could come in real handy. You never know about those things."

They walked through the gate at the end of the pier and out into the sprawling parking lot. Bud said, "I got your message. What's all this about going over to Kauai for the weekend?"

Shug's face brightened. "Oh yeah, son, now that's what having contacts will do for you. It just so happens that Captain Locke, he's our Chief of Staff, has a house over on Kauai. He says he and his wife hardly ever get to go over there and he'd appreciate us using it just to check on things for him."

"Hey, well that does sound great," Bud said enthusiastically. "It would be nice to get away from here for a few days. Kauai, huh? Maybe the Skipper will let us use one of the SNB's to fly over there."

"Yeah, great idea, son, say, let's invite the girls. I'll bet they'd love to go."

Bud's face darkened and he became wary. "Well, I don't know about that. I feel kind of awkward taking women over there. I don't know. The Captain may not like it."

"Son, don't be such an old fuddy-duddy. This is 1967. Besides, the house has four bedrooms if that's what you're worried about. Everything will be all prim and proper for you, and I'll clear it with the Captain, no problem, son."

"Well, I don't know. Let me think about it."

"Okay son. Think while you drive. I've got a dinner date with Sandra tonight."

"When are you going to buy yourself a car, anyway?"

"It just so happens that I ordered a new Triumph Roadster, a fine little two-seater. I bought it the day before we went out on the ORI. It should be in from the states in the next couple of weeks."

"Hey, that's great! What color?"

"Fire engine red, with wire wheels, sharp, son, mighty sharp," he grinned happily.

"You and Sandra seem to have hit it off real well," Bud said as he steered the Buick towards Nimitz Gate.

"Yeah, we kind of clicked from the very beginning. We have a lot in common, you know. Both our daddy's are politicians."

"I didn't know your daddy was a politician."

"Oh, yeah, daddy's been in Congress for the last eighteen years. Sandra's daddy is Senator George Blosser of Missouri."

"I guess you do have a lot in common," Bud said as a marine snapped to rigid attention, saluted and waved him through Nimitz Gate.

"What about you and Phyllis, son?"

"The way my schedule has been, I haven't had time to go out. I call her once in a while. She's busy with her work and I'm always out flying. There's just never time."

"Well, son, a weekend away will do both of you good. Got to kick back and relax once in awhile."

Bud arranged with Ferguson to use one of the SNB's for a weekend of "proficiency training". Phyllis sat in the right seat next to him on the flight from Oahu to Lihue Field on Kauai, a beautiful jaunt across ninety miles of sunny cloud flecked skies and smiling turquoise seas.

They rented a Ford convertible at the airport and drove north up the coast toward Hanalei. The Captain's house was a long low bungalow nestled among thick palm, hibiscus, ginger and fern. The house faced Hanalei Bay, the location where the picture South Pacific had been filmed. This fact was not lost on Phyllis and Sandra. They were completely awestruck by the house and the tropical magnificence of the island. The couples spent the afternoon exploring the nearby light house and village and walking on the beach at Hanalei. When they returned to the house late that afternoon, Shug said, "Let's do dinner at the Coco Palms. They have a great menu and a fine wine list."

The Coco Palms Hotel sat amid acres of coconut palms where a 19th Century coconut plantation had once operated. Surrounded by tropical gardens, streams and ponds, the hotel appeared to be a natural part of this breath taking landscape. When they had finished a sumptuous dessert of haupia served with strong Kona coffee, the couples returned to the Locke house.

Bud opened a bottle of chilled California Chardonnay and brought it to the table on the lanai. Shug and Sandra walked slowly down the beach arm in arm into a spectacular Pacific sunset.

"I hope you like this chardonnay," Bud said, pouring wine.

Smiling, Phyllis picked up her glass and they toasted. "Here's to a great weekend," Bud said.

"This is absolutely incredible, Bud. This place is like a fabulous dream. I just can't get over this. Wow, this wine is wonderful by the way."

"I'm glad you like it. Yeah, this is really a nice place," he said looking out across the bay. "Ole Shug really came through this time. It was sure generous of Captain Locke to let us use the place."

Phyllis smiled sweetly. "Shug Early will become a politician just like his father. You wait and see."

"I believe that," Bud said and sipped wine. "Want to take a walk on the beach?"

"If you don't mind," she grinned impishly, "I'd rather stay here, drink this wine and enjoy having you all alone to myself."

"I don't understand you, Phyllis. I'm never around to spend time with you because I have to work so much. I'm surprised you want to spend time with me at all. I'm sure you have many other opportunities."

She smiled a little self-consciously, "Working in a hospital full of men I do get hit on pretty often. They're nice guys generally. A few are obvious pigs. Most of them are just kids away from home for the first time, lonesome, scared, suffering with horrible wounds and very homesick. I try to be nice to them, and if I have to, I try very hard to let them down without hurting their feelings." She paused and sipped wine. "You on the other hand, sailor boy, happen to have become quite special to me. That's why I go home at night dog tired hoping that you'll call. Sometimes I can't stand it anymore and I'll call your room. Shug Early usually answers your phone and tells me you're out on another night flight to Midway or to some place I've never heard of. I take my shower and iron my uniform for the next day. Sometimes I watch TV or write a letter to my mother, but mostly I sit there and think about you until I fall sleep. Then I wake up in the morning and do it all over again. Sounds silly and kind of dull, doesn't it?"

He leaned forward and kissed her tenderly. "Phyllis, I believe that is the nicest thing any girl has ever said to me."

"Ha! Well, you just wait until I have a few more glasses of this wine," she twittered. "I may say things to you that will shock us both."

"Really," he grinned. "Let me refill your glass." They both giggled.

Phyllis turned to him and said in a more serious note, “The Navy is very demanding on you, isn’t it?”

He thought a minute, and said, “Well yeah it is, but it has to be that way. We’re getting ready to deploy to Southeast Asia this fall and we have to be as proficient as possible. Too many people can get killed if we make an error.”

“Are you worried about going to Vietnam?”

“Worried? Not too much about my personal safety. I’m most concerned about being prepared, about being as proficient as I possibly can be. The worse thing I can imagine is to get over there and have somebody get hurt or killed because I’m all screwed up and don’t know where I am or know what’s going on.”

“I see the results of the war everyday at Tripler,” Phyllis said. “It’s so heart breaking to see those guys come in all shot up, mangled by mines and booby traps, loaded with infection and diseases no one has heard of. When Sandra and I took this job, we didn’t really understand what it is really all about. Now that we’re here, it’s been a revelation for us.”

“Is it that bad?”

“I mean after a while you’ve seen so much of it, there’s not too much left that will shock you.”

“What exactly do you do at the hospital?”

“Sandra and I are surgical nurses. We work in the OR.”

“Sounds gruesome.”

“Not really. We have the opportunity to observe some very talented surgeons. Most of them specialized in reconstructive surgery, emergency and trauma medicine.”

“My best buddy back home is a doctor. He specialized in emergency room medicine. He says it is the most exciting, challenging and rewarding area of medicine to be involved in.”

"He's right about that."

Bud rose and retrieved another bottle of chilled wine from the refrigerator, removed the cork and poured.

"This wine is fabulous," Phyllis said, swirling the amber liquid in her glass.

"I'm glad you're enjoying it," Bud said. "There's plenty more in the fridge. I bought a whole case at the wine mess at BP."

"Are you going to get me drunk and take advantage of me?"

Bud laughed. "Well, actually, I was hoping you'd get drunk and take advantage of me first."

"I just might do it, sailor boy!"

They tittered happily, having become giddy from the wine. Phyllis grinned wickedly at him as he poured more wine. "You devil you, I definitely love this wine, and it's all your fault."

He just smiled and said nothing. She was so intolerably lovely and desirable. He simply wanted to gaze at her and allow himself to absorb her extraordinary femme fatale.

The couple fell silent as they sat absorbing the magnificence of Hanalei Bay. It was Phyllis who broke the quiet.

"I've not been completely candid with you," she said.

"About what?"

"About us."

"What about us? Is there someone else?"

"No there isn't anyone else, silly. I'm not a tramp you know."

"Of course you're not. I've never thought that."

"This wine is really getting to me. I may say some things that I really shouldn't."

"You can say whatever you want, Phyllis."

"You don't understand, Sweetie," she said and patted his cheek. "You are so wonderfully naïve. You have no idea about the effect you have on me, do you?"

Bud grunted a startled kind of laugh. "No, I guess not. Actually, I don't know what you're talking about."

Phyllis placed a delicate hand on his face and kissed him. "I know you don't. That's what I'm talking about."

He sat back, uncomprehending and blinked at her. "Okay."

She gazed into his face and smiled sweetly. "I'll probably regret this, but I've got to say it. I've been in love with you since that night we drove out to Kawaiho Point." She hesitated and put her head back, looking up at the stars in thought: "no......no, that's not really true. Actually I fell in love with you that first evening at the Admiral's party, but I wouldn't....I couldn't admit it, even to myself. I couldn't admit it because I was scared, afraid to let my feelings go. Now I have succumbed to these irrepressible feelings for you, and once again find myself involved in yet another romantic fiasco, one sided this time, and definitely of my own doing. You may recall me telling you that I have a habit of making bad romantic decisions."

He stood, took her hands and lifted her out of the chair. "You haven't made a bad decision this time," he whispered. He wreathed her in an inescapable embrace and kissed her with great passion. The ardor deepened, and the emotions of the moment fashioned a dangerous mélange with the wine and swept them away.

The fever embrace was broken by the sounds of Sandra and Shug coming up the beach walk laughing and talking in low tones. The couple disappeared inside the bungalow without noticing Phyllis and Bud.

Gasping, Phyllis said, “Every time you kiss me, I just go all to pieces. I’ve never been affected like this before.”

He made a deep sigh, trying to compose himself a little, “I don’t know why, but I’m glad.”

He pulled her into himself and kissed her again. When they separated, Bud gazed into her face and softly said, “I think I am in love with you, Phyllis.”

Suddenly tears welled in her eyes. “Oh, Bud, you don’t know how desperately I’ve wanted to hear you say that.”

He held her face in his hands and wiped the tears away with his thumbs. “I’ve never said that to a girl before. Until now, I never really knew what it is to be in love.”

“Are you sure it’s not the wine talking?”

“It’s not the wine.” He took a folded handkerchief from his back pocket and gave it to her.

“Thank you.” She daubed at her eyes. “You probably think I’m a neurotic crying drunk,” she sniffed.

“I think you’re the most incredible woman I’ve ever known, Phyllis.”

“Oh, God, I love you, Bud Cotter.”

He kissed her again and then said, “Let’s sit on the swing. I’ll bring the wine.”

They sat on a white slat swing near the edge of the seawall. He put his arm around her and they intermittently kissed, whispered words of love and drank wine. And as the wine flowed, his boldness increased. Deep into a fiery kiss, he amazed himself by touching her firm breasts. She moaned in her throat and did not resist. This emboldened him more, and with trembling hands he began to unbutton her blouse.

“Let’s go into the house,” Phyllis whispered, “I want to make love with you.”

He straightened, appearing flustered. “Phyllis, I….I don’t….Well, you see…..”

She smiled knowingly, “It’s okay, Baby. I’m on birth control. I have been ever since…..well, never mind. You don’t have to worry about that.”

He appeared even more startled. “I hadn’t even thought of that.”

Phyllis chortled at his unsullied discomfiture. “What is it then, Baby, what’s the matter?”

“I….will you promise not to laugh at me?”

“Why, of course,” she said in a reassuring tone. Phyllis had no idea what he could be talking about.

“I’m a virgin.”

Her mouth dropped open. “You’re what! You’re kidding,” she whispered not knowing whether to be amused or shocked. “Oh, my word, I would never have imagined. How can that be? You’re so gorgeous, so desirably innocent.”

“It’s true. I’ve never been with a woman….because, well…. for a lot of reasons……. mostly because I’ve never been in love with anyone before now.”

She threw her arms around his neck and kissed him. “Don’t worry about anything,” she whispered softly, “we’re in love, and nothing else matters.”

He surrendered his virginity with a great deal of enthusiasm and zeal, spurred on by the wine and by Phyllis’s breathless proclamations of love and ecstasy. Some time later, replete and exhausted, entwined in each other’s arms, they slept.

Chapter 10

Jealous Women

"Your golf clubs came in today." Shug walked into Bud's room and dropped a yellow custody slip onto the desk. "Thompson has 'em down in the vault. How about a round this afternoon before the club house closes?"

"Man, I'd love to, "Bud said as he unzipped his sweaty flight suit, "but there's no way I can play today, Lad. We're flying a night op at 1830. Besides, I need some time on the driving range and putting greens. Christ, I haven't hit a golf ball in a year."

"Shute, son, the best place to practice is on the course. You'll be right back in the groove after you've played a few holes."

"No way am I going to do that and embarrass myself more than I usually do."

"What's your handicap, son?"

"Uh.....Well, I really don't have a handicap." Bud didn't want to admit that he had been a two time All-American at Vanderbilt.

"Well, it doesn't matter. Lots of fine courses on this island, son, we need to take advantage of it as much as we can."

"How's your new car running?"

"Sweet as a Singer sewing machine, Sandra loves it. We're having a big time running here and there and everywhere in it."

"You two spend almost every evening together, getting serious, Lad?"

Shug grinned bashfully. "Well now, son serious is all relative isn't it? Can't rush into anything, you know."

"Yeah, I know," Bud grinned.

"How about you and Phyllis, son?"

Bud uttered a nervous laugh. "I haven't been able to see her since we got back from Kauai. We're going out this weekend if the Skipper doesn't schedule weekend flight ops again."

"Gettin' serious, son?"

"Well, I don't know. I guess maybe you could say we're going steady."

"Fine, fine. Nice arrangement for the both of you. Phyllis is a fine little lady, and has she flipped over you buddy boy. Sandra says you are all that she talks about. Even wrote to her mama and told her about you."

"Yeah, she's really something," Bud grinned. "Wrote to her mama, huh? She hasn't mentioned that."

"Say, I've never asked you, son. Who is that pretty thing in that picture on the desk there? Is that your sister?"

"No. Her name is June Chandler. She's a friend of mine back home."

"Friend, huh, what kind of friend, son?"

Bud shot a nervous glance at Shug. "You're meddling now, Lad."

"Ohhhh, ah, ha, I see, son."

"What the hell is that supposed to mean?" Bud snapped testily.

"Well, if you and Phyllis are an item now, and you're friendly with this fine looking filly, sooner or later somebody's gonna get real upset. These ladies don't handle competition very well, son."

"Phyllis knows about June Chandler. We talked about that a long time ago."

"Does Phyllis know you have a picture of your female friend here in your room? You don't have a picture of Phyllis. If she caught wind of that, things could get real nasty, son."

Bud whirled around and stuck a finger in the middle of Shug's chest. "Early, don't start any crap like that with me," he snarled, "I'll whip your cream puff ass if you do."

Shug couldn't restrain himself and started laughing. "Son, I believe you'd try," he laughed, "I believe you would."

Bud couldn't stay angry at his friend and he started laughing. "Don't get on my nerves today, Lad. I don't need any more grief than I have already. I've got to deal with that asshole Mad Dog half the night."

Commander Jack Ferguson was driving his squadron hard. He kept them in the air day and night pushing them to attain peak levels of proficiency in navigation, instrument flying, gunnery and airmanship. He knew from hard experience that their ultimate survival in Southeast Asia depended on their ability to operate under a multiplicity of combat and emergency situations. The unorthodox Skipper had his pilots flying day and night training missions in support of Marine infantry and coordinating air strikes and target acquisition techniques with FAC pilots. They flew long range missions throughout the Hawaiian chain of islands as far northwest as Midway where a Marine Brigade was running amphibious assault training, and as far south as Johnston Atoll which lay 850 miles south of Hawaii. It was an intense time and to Bud, the pace seemed to become almost desperate as the West Pac deployment grew nearer.

Phyllis flung herself at Bud when he came to the front door of the nurse's bungalow late on Friday afternoon. "Oh, God I've missed you," she breathed when they parted from an eager kiss.

"I've missed you too."

With Phyllis nuzzled next to him, Bud drove the Buick across the island to the north shore. He pulled into a small hotel on Waimea Bay where he had made reservations. Their room was on the top floor, very airy and tropical with a spacious open balcony facing the sea.

Near midnight, satiated and depleted after impassioned ravenous love making, the young lovers showered together and after they were scantily dressed, went to sit on the balcony. They sat on a rattan couch with flowery cushions drinking California Pinot Noir gazing at the moonlit Pacific. Rustling palm fronds and the thud of big North Shore waves pounding onto the beach added the finishing brush strokes to this wonderfully romantic setting.

"I never realized that I could be this happy and this much in love," Phyllis said softly. "I love you with all my heart."

"I love you, Sweetheart, very, very much."

"I know. I can tell. You treat me like a queen, and I don't deserve it."

He touched her chin and gently turned her to face him. "You deserve a lot better than me. I feel really bad that I have to work so much."

"Baby, I'll take you whenever the navy will let me have you. You are definitely worth the wait."

He sipped wine and looked out to sea. "Could I have a picture of you to put in my room?"

"Why yes, of course, and I want one of you."

"Phyllis, I want you to know that I used to have a picture of June Chandler on my desk, but I put it away."

Phyllis flushed jealously and twisted to observe him. "I hope you threw it in the trash. Have you broken up with her?"

"Well, no. I mean there's nothing to break up about. I told you before, we are just friends. I don't feel that I have to explain anything to her."

"Are you afraid to tell her about me?"

"No, of course not. It's just that, well, I don't feel it's really necessary."

Phyllis said adamantly and with a look of fiery jealously that even the naïve Bud Cotter could read. "It is necessary, Baby. It is very necessary. You have to tell her. You have to do this for me."

"You're really serious about this."

"You're damn right I am, Baby. I won't allow anyone, especially another female to come between us, ever!"

"Okay, if it's that important to you. I'll call her first thing after work on Monday."

"It's that important. Thank you, Baby. I needed to hear that." She paused and drank wine, then said: "You may as well know this from the very beginning, Baby. I'm very jealous when it comes to you and other women."

"I understand, Sweetheart. I'm glad you care for me enough to feel that way."

"You are my dreams come true, Bud Cotter. I'll do whatever it takes to hold onto you."

Bud rose from the couch. "I almost forgot about something," he said. He went to his flight bag and retrieved a small nicely wrapped box with a gold bow. When he returned to the couch, he handed the box to Phyllis.

"Here, this is something I want you to have."

Her eyes illuminated. "What is it?"

"Open it."

Phyllis tore away the ribbon and paper and removed the top from the square box. Inside, resting in a purple velvet liner was a heavy 24 carat gold Herringbone necklace.

“Oh my goodness, Bud, this is so beautiful! I can’t believe you did this, oh my God!”

He took the necklace from her trembling hands, unfastened the clasp and put it around her neck. Phyllis touched the heavy gold chain with delicate fingers and began to weep.

“Oh, Bud, I’ve never had anything so beautiful. I’ve never had anything like this before. You are so unbelievably incredible. I love you so much.” She jumped up to observe herself in a mirror.

“I’m glad you like it, Sweetheart.”

“I love it. I’ll cherish it forever.”

She pushed him back on the couch, threw herself on top of him and began kissing him, and in a while, they were once again lost in scorching frantic passion.

Nashville - August 1967

June Chandler spent two days in her bed. She had developed a massive migraine headache brought on by a shocking phone call from Hawaii. She hadn’t worried when Bud Cotter’s weekly phone calls had become somewhat less frequent over the past couple of months. He had been telling her and she had innocently believed him that the Navy was keeping him very busy training for the upcoming WestPac. Now, it was clearly obvious, he was indeed being kept busy, but not entirely by the navy.

The anger, the pain, the jealously and the frustration had truly overwhelmed her. When the full impact of what Bud Cotter was telling her finally penetrated her consciousness, she had hung up on him. She sat in her room and wept for hours until the horrifying agony of the migraine set upon her. The pain was so intense that she vomited until her stomach was voided. Her vision came and went, and she could not bear to have a light on in the room.

Despite June's weak protests, her concerned parents took her to the emergency room at Vanderbilt Hospital. There, she was examined and treated by Bud's old boyhood chum, Doctor Caldwell Kreer now a staff physician at Vanderbilt.

"Doctor Kreer," June whispered after she had been given an injection of powerful medication, "I'm afraid that I'm not very good at receiving bad news."

"Did you lose a family member?"

"No, I'm afraid that I've received a devastating phone call from a man whom I thought loved me." She began to weep.

"I'm sorry to hear that, June. Now listen, you must try not to dwell on it, it will only make things worse. The DHE I've given you should begin to bring you relief very soon. When the pain has decreased significantly, we'll remove the IV and let you go home. You will probably sleep for at least twenty-four hours. When you wake up, the migraine should be gone completely."

"Thank you, Doctor Kreer." She attempted a brave smile.

"Do you get these migraine headaches often?"

"No, not all that often, but never before has one been this intense."

Caldwell nodded thoughtfully. Listen, June. I'd like you to do a follow up visit with one of our staff neurologists, Lee Greenwald. I think he can help you with your migraines. Call my office next week I'll see that you get an appointment with him."

"I will. Thank you, Doctor Kreer, and God bless you."

"Okay June, now just try to relax and you should be feeling much better within the hour."

The next day, exhausted and bedraggled, June was recovered from the hideous migraine. She could think more clearly and objectively now and decided that maybe, just maybe, all was not lost between Bud Cotter and herself. Being nearly five thousand miles away from him put her at a huge disadvantage. She knew that from Nashville, she could not possibly compete with that wicked little trollop who had her talons entangled in Bud Cotter's heartstrings. June Chandler was profoundly in love with Bud Cotter, and unless she could do something to salvage their relationship, she knew that all would be soon lost between them. Gritting her teeth, she avowed to herself that she wasn't about to roll over and give up this easily. She would think of something.

Chapter 11

The Storm

7 August 1967 was a hot sunny afternoon on Tern Island, French Frigate Shoals located 488 miles northwest of Barbers Point, Hawaii. Second Class Aerographers Mate, Jim Reed, a Coast Guard weather observer on Tern Island, stood outside the small weather shack twirling a wet bulb thermometer. The barometric pressure had been slowly falling during the past twelve hours, the wind was picking up and shifting from southwesterly to easterly and high clouds were moving in from the east-southeast. Reed knew these were signs of a coming tropical storm system. Fleet Weather Central at Pearl Harbor had issued a Tropical Storm Warning for Midway Island and the northwest Hawaiian atolls.

Aerographer Reed looked up at the spinning anemometer mounted near the top of the LORAN transmitting tower. From experience, Reed estimated that the wind was now a sustained 20 knots with occasional higher gusts. White caps were beginning to lap against the coral runway riprap. An hour ago, while taking the last hourly observation, Reed had watched a flight of Navy Skyraiders pass over the field heading in the direction of Midway. Reed thought it was a good thing that no aircraft were scheduled into Tern Island this evening because it was going to get a lot worse as the storm moved closer. Reed read the wet bulb temperature from the mercury thermometer, jotted the numbers on a pad and went inside to finish his hourly observation.

Two hundred and fifty miles northwest of French Frigate Shoals, two divisions, comprised of eight aircraft of VC-110 Skyraiders, headed northwest toward Midway Island. Bud Cotter was in his usual number two position off Mad Dog's starboard wing. From their altitude of 10,500 feet, the pilots were enjoying a thirty-five knot quartering tail wind and a fabulous view of sparsely spaced Northern Hawaiian atolls.

To provide the needed range to reach Midway, and to provide a comfortable margin of fuel reserve, the aircraft were equipped with auxiliary fuel tanks mounted under each wing of the aircraft. The training assignment for today was simple enough: execute a 1200 mile dead reckoning navigation flight, in formation, from Barbers Point to Midway Island, refuel at Midway, and execute a formation night flight back to Barbers Point. The pilots were aware that the weather was worsening and that they would be flying against an increasingly brisk wind and into stormy skies on the return trip to Oahu, but for now it was a fine ride in their splendid magic carpets made of aluminum and steel.

At Midway, while the aircraft were being refueled and serviced, the pilots went to chow in the base Flight Suit Mess. The surface winds had increased to a sustained thirty knots but the landing at Midway had been an easy one, almost directly into the wind.

The sky was high overcast at 20,000 feet when they departed Midway at 1940 Hawaiian time. Darkness would come early this night. The Skyraiders climbed into a forty-knot wind, rising quickly but their forward progress was slowed considerably. The seas around Midway were building and white capping. Small plumes of spray were whipping off the white caps as the storm gained momentum and slowly crawled northwestward.

Flying at eighteen thousand feet to stay under the lowering overcast, the Skyraiders pushed southeastward at a ground speed of only 220 knots. “At this rate,” Bud thought to himself, “it’ll be after midnight when we get back to BP.” He switched on his penlight and pointed it at a wallet size photo of Phyllis that he kept taped to the instrument panel. He smiled underneath his oxygen mask and said aloud, “I love you, Sweetheart.”

And indeed, he was very much in love with Phyllis Day. She was truly his first real love. Oh, there had been crushes and infatuations during high school and college but this, this was something all together different. When he was with Phyllis, he felt completely happy and contented. To Bud, Phyllis was the ideal woman for him. Very intelligent, she had a wonderfully bubbly personality and a softhearted compassionate spirit, and she was so feminine and delicate. He was crazy about her figure and her shapely, well-proportioned legs and ankles. She had a perfect figure for her five foot three inch frame, not too much bust, but just enough for his taste. Bud smiled happily, nature had definitely blessed this girl, yet she was in no way vain about it and that made her all the more alluring.

He was sure too, that Phyllis had a dark side. He knew she was very jealous of other women, and there were things in her past that she had not yet shared with him, unpleasant things that had hurt her deeply. He would show her true love, true affection and be a caring and faithful partner.

Bud had been toying with the idea of asking Phyllis to marry him. He was convinced that she was the woman to share his life with. Although they had only known each other for a few months, he was confident that they were totally compatible. He snickered to himself and muttered aloud, “We’re definitely compatible in the sack.” Phyllis had tenderly, lovingly and eagerly transformed his innocent virginity that night on Kauai. She was the perfect woman to have his first sex with, and she made it all the more euphoric for him as she experienced her own shattering climatic rapture.

He decided that he should begin to look at engagement rings when he had some time to browse the jewelry section of the Base Exchange, and then, when the time was right, he would make his proposal and present the ring to her.

“Einstein, tuck it in! What the hell are you doing over there?” The loathsome boom of Mad Dog’s voice blasting through the radio headset jolted Bud’s thoughts. He had drifted out of place by a few feet and subsequently drew the nasty snarl from Mad Dog. Bud slipped the airplane back into position. He felt his face flushing and he seethed. “What a pain in the ass!”

For the uninitiated, it is difficult to imagine darkness more black and all encompassing than is a cloudy night sky over the sea. Yet the pilots of VC-110 were accustomed to flying in these conditions. Their world became the cockpit bathed in a dim, soft red glow of instrument lights. Outside the canopy was total and absolute darkness except for a tiny white tail light on the aircraft ahead. The array of instruments was their eyes to the world; the radios were their voice and ears. After all the months of training, night flying had become a completely normal event for these pilots flying high above the wind-whipped Pacific.

On Tern Island, the Coast Guardsmen sat in their recreation room playing cribbage, bridge, shooting pool and listening to a Honolulu radio station. There was no TV here. The Shoals were far out of range for the Honolulu television stations, but a new movie came in twice each week on the mail plane from Pearl.

The storm was approaching very quickly now. The wind had increased to gale force and occasionally whistled and moaned through the buildings and radio masts. A few minutes before 2000 local time, Aerographer Reed rose wearily and made the windy trek to the weather shack for the 2000 observation. He would continue to do this every hour until midnight when Petty Officer Peterson would relieve him. The two weathermen worked twelve on and twelve off seven days a week. Working long hours made the time pass a little quicker out here on this desolate atoll. It was a lonely and solitary life here, almost a monastic one that these men lived.

Aerographer Reed read the anemometer wind speed and direction indicators: 050 degrees at 38 knots sustained. It was going to be one hell of a blow tonight. He wondered if the tidal surge would push seawater across the reef and onto the runway again. Last fall, a force two hurricane flooded the entire atoll including the runway with over six inches of water. Christ, what a mess that had been. They didn't have hot chow for over a week until a supply barge arrived from Pearl. Reed looked at the big brass aneroid barometer and whistled: 29.45 inches of mercury and falling. The UHF radio crackled and hissed when a nearby bolt of lightning struck the water out near the boat channel. Reed glanced up at the radio, "Nobody will be out flying in this stuff tonight," he said to himself.

Across the horizon and directly in the path of the flight of Skyraiders, billowing cumulus blinked with lightening. The turbulence had increased dramatically, the big Skyraiders jumped and bounced in the wind making it extremely difficult to hold formation. Finally, even the uncompromising Mad Dog conceded that it had become too dangerous to fly tight formation.

"Division four," Mad Dog transmitted, "disperse formation to two zero feet." Bud, Chicken Wing and Fat Back opened up the gap in the formation. Division 3, led by Boats Davidson had opened formation a few minutes earlier. Using the LORAN, Bud calculated that they were about one hundred and ten miles northwest of French Frigate Shoals. That figured to a ground speed of only 190 knots. They were barely moving forward. Well, at least he could relax a little now that they were dispersed in a reasonable manner for this turbulence.

His thoughts once again drifted to Phyllis. Maybe he shouldn't be so hasty with the prospect of marriage. After all, he really didn't know a lot of details about Phyllis, things like her church affiliation if she had one. He was Catholic, although admittedly not a very good one. But if they were going to be married, they really should do it in a Catholic church with a priest officiating. What if Phyllis objected to this? It could become an issue and what about the children?

They would most definitely have to be raised Catholic. Then there was this business with her taking birth control pills. He wondered about that. Bud thought that he remembered reading something about the Pope saying that Catholics shouldn't use birth control but, he wondered, if Phyllis is not a Catholic, would that make any difference? And religion was just one thing, there were other issues, like her career and his career, going to Vietnam in October, money, her family, his family. Suddenly it seemed that a marriage proposal carried with it a lot of complication. He needed to think about it some more, but in the meantime he would enjoy being in love with Phyllis and spending as much time with her as his job would allow.

His thoughts were broken by an almost indiscernible thump. Through the control stick it felt like a slight buffet, not the same feeling turbulence created in the controls. His eyes rapidly scanned the engine instruments. He had a green board. The steady sound of the engine had not changed and there was no change in the feel of the controls. What could it have been? Something like this had not happened to him before. He waited and listened. He wondered if possibly he could have hit a bird caught in the storm. Yes, of course! He decided that he had probably hit an Albatross. Those things are all over these islands and atolls by the thousands. He felt better and relaxed again, a bird strike certainly would not damage a big sturdy Skyraider.

The young pilot's mouth was dry. He felt around the right side of his seat and located his canteen. He took a long drink of the tepid water. He wished it was iced water, but at least it was wet. He was twisting the cap back onto the canteen when a red trouble light suddenly illuminated. LOW OIL PRESSURE. "Now what," he thought. He stuffed the canteen away and ran his eyes to the oil pressure gauge. It had dropped from 60 to 28 PSI. He tapped the glass face of the gauge with a forefinger. "Jesus!" He fingered the radio transmit button on the control stick.

"Mad Dog, Einstein is losing oil pressure. Pressure is two eight PSI."

"Division Four," Mad Dog radioed, "go to guard on 243.00," and then he transmitted: "Coast Guard Station at Tern Island, this is navy strawberry one leader."

The radio hissed. Bud looked up to see cloud to cloud lightening jumping in front of them. Half a minute went by with no response.

Mad Dog called again. This time he received an answer.

"Strawberry one, this is Coast Guard station at Tern Island, go ahead."

"Coast Guard, strawberry one is declaring an emergency. Aircraft losing oil pressure, approximately six zero miles northwest of you. Anticipate emergency landing at your location."

"Roger strawberry one. Advise your progress. Current weather is thunderstorm in progress with heavy rain, ceiling estimated 600 feet, winds 040 at 46 with gusts to 53, visibility estimated at three quarter mile, altimeter two niner three four."

"Roger, Coast Guard, we will guard this frequency and advise our progress."

Bud set his altimeter to 29.34. The oil pressure fell to 20 PSI. The big Wright engine continued to run smoothly. Bud began to wonder if possibly the oil pressure instrument had failed and the oil pressure in the engine was really okay. His eyes shifted to the oil temperature gauge. It was touching the red arc of the instrument. His eyes jumped to the cylinder head temperature, it too was nearing the red arc. No chance that the gauges had failed. He was in big trouble.

"Mad Dog, my oil and cylinder head temps are almost in the red. I'm backing off on the power and jettisoning the auxiliaries."

"Roger, Einstein. I'll fly wing on you. Chicken Wing and Fat Back, form up on Boats and follow him home."

"Roger."

Bud reduced the power to forty inches of manifold. The oil pressure seemed to stabilize at 15 PSI. He knew that soon the engine would begin to heat up dramatically from lack of lubrication. After that, it would be only a matter of minutes until the engine would seize up. He switched on his penlight and methodically went through the emergency checklist. His eyes went to the LORAN, 42 miles from the Shoal. A quick mental calculation, he had to keep flying another fourteen minutes to make the field. Then the question would be how to get the airplane on the ground in a gusting 60 knot wind. Fear was spreading to every cell of his body.

"Flatten it out a little, Einstein," Mad Dog Radioed, "try to maintain altitude as long as you can. What's your oil pressure now?"

"One five PSI and steady: temperatures are all in the red."

"Einstein, do you have your oil cooler cowl flap full open?"

"Affirmative, emergency checklist is completed."

As the minutes passed, the sound of the big Wright engine began to change. Bud noticed a slight vibration that wasn't there before. He now expected that at any moment the engine was going to seize. He fingered his Mae West vest and felt for the inflation lanyards. He must remember to extract the inflatable raft under his seat pack. This was going to be nasty. He touched the canopy emergency release lever. Once he was in the water, he didn't have time to be fumbling around searching for the emergency egress stuff. It had to go smoothly and quickly, before the airplane sank in the storm. He felt really rotten about losing this airplane. He had formed a bond with this great machine. If he didn't make the runway it would be like losing a good friend.

"Two zero miles," Mad Dog radioed. The turbulence was terrific. They had entered a thunderstorm. Heavy rain and pellets of hail hammered the aircraft and a bolt of lightning suddenly exploded very close off to the left. Bud raised his eyes toward heaven and said a Hail Mary. It was the only prayer he could think of. The airplane suddenly snapped to the left in a terrific gust of turbulence, he fought it back to level and backed off on the throttle a little more. Now there was definitely a steady vibration being transmitted through the control stick to his hand. He expected the engine to stop at any second. He thought about Phyllis and his family. "Surely I'm not going to die like this."

The Coast Guardsmen on Tern Island had donned their foul weather gear and were preparing the big Sikorsky H-3 helo (helicopter) for a rescue mission. These guys were professionals. They had performed rescues in weather like this before. They would keep the helo tied down as long as possible. The runway lights had been switched on as well as every outdoor light on the tiny atoll. The wind was gusting, moaning and driving the heavy rain in quasi-horizontal sheets. The sea had risen above fifteen feet and now, row after row of towering waves marched in from the northeast and slammed into the reef.

"Twelve miles," Mad Dog radioed.

"Roger." Bud went through the emergency checklist once again. As he fought the turbulence, he was completely focused on egress from the aircraft. At the last possible moment, he planned to turn into the wind. That would slow the airplane to almost a stand still. He knew he could not hold the airplane on the runway in a cross wind like this. He would have to make a wheels up water landing as close to the field as possible. The down side was that he would be landing directly into the seas. He had no idea how high the waves were, but he knew that they must be huge. If things worked out, he might make the lagoon next to the runway, the waves should be much lower inside the reef. He could try and cut across the seas at a forty-five degree angle. He remembered someone saying in one of the ready room lectures that this was the best thing to do if you could pull it off, but in a sixty or seventy knot wind? "Why does this stuff happen to me," he said aloud to himself.

The engine continued to run but the vibration had increased significantly. He was amazed that the engine could function under these conditions, a tribute to its skilled makers. He knew the moving internal parts were being fried in the heat.

He said another Hail Mary and took Phyllis's picture off the instrument panel and stuffed it into a pocket. The airplane jolted severely as a vicious wind shear slammed the Skyraider and thrust it toward the sea. The instrument lights blinked off then came back on. He flashed his pen light on the DC breaker panel. None of the breakers had tripped. Outside the canopy was total blackness. The airplane jumped again in another slashing down draft. A quick glance at the altimeter, he was down to three thousand. The airspeed indicator read 160 knots.

"Three miles," Mad Dog radioed. "No visual on the field."

Bud looked outside hoping for a glimpse of the airfield. "Another minute, Cotter," he said to himself out loud, "and we'll make the field."

At that instant the airplane shuddered and then there was silence. His heart jumped into his throat. He tried to speak but for a few seconds he couldn't.

"Engine out," he radioed, "maintaining this heading to one thousand."

"Roger, Einstein, turn on your landing lights."

Bud complied. The powerful landing lights illuminated the driving rain and mist creating blank opaqueness. It was almost as though things were happening in slow motion. He was amazed at how calm he was, scared yes, but calm. He concentrated on the altimeter. As the needles dropped below the one thousand mark, Bud began a turn to the left to align the airplane directly into the wind."

"Turning left into the wind," he transmitted calmly.

"Strawberry one, this is Coast Guard at Tern Island. Wind zero four five at six zero, altimeter 29.39."

"Roger, thank you," Mad Dog answered. "Einstein, remember the release link on the PK-2 Pararaft when you need it."

"Roger."

Turned into the wind, the airspeed indicator read ninety knots, but the airplane was making less than 30 knots forward ground speed. Like a giant glider it floated on the wind slightly nose down. Bud's eyes were glued to the compass. He stopped the turn on the heading of zero four five. He should be directly into the wind now. A snap glance at the altimeter: six hundred feet. He slowly shook his head in frustration. "Why me?" He said another Hail Mary while he watched the needles of the altimeter drop to one hundred feet. He looked out across the wing root. The landing lights revealed a world of spraying frothy white water not far below, all else was complete blackness.

The Skyraider struck the first wave hard and bounced back into the air. Bud pulled the stick all the way back and kicked the left rudder in an attempt to get across the waves at an angle. The heavy machine wallowed momentarily and dropped into a trough between two towering waves. It hit with a horrific impact that snapped Bud's head forward into the gun sight. He saw stars and was dazed for several seconds, but luckily his helmet had absorbed most of the impact. He could feel the airplane floating and bobbing on the angry sea, but why was he was hanging in the straps? At that instant, the horror filled realization hit him, the airplane was inverted. He frantically ripped off his oxygen mask and radio connections. Still strapped into the seat, he reached for the emergency canopy release and desperately jerked it although it moved quite easily. The air pressure of inside the canopy created a wild hiss of air and bubbles. Water began to rapidly flood the cockpit, and at that moment Bud Cotter believed he was going to die.

In wet suffocating total blackness, he struggled not to panic. He felt for the seat harness release and freed himself. Stay calm, stay calm. He had to swim down and away like he had done so many times in the training tank at BP, but this was different, appallingly different. He swam downward several strokes burdened by the parachute seat pack and the PK-2 Pararaft raft package. Very quickly he hit the bottom of the sea floor. He swam a few strokes to clear the aircraft. He found the inflation lanyard on his life vest and jerked it. The vest inflated and began to carry him toward the surface. He had no idea how far under the sea he was but he had to breathe! He began to exhale a little at a time. "Don't panic! Don't panic! You'll be on the surface in a few seconds." He felt as though he was being tossed about in a colossal struggle between wind and waves. Abruptly he bobbed on the surface. He gasped and took in desperate breaths of delicious air; then he was under water again as a massive wave crashed over him. He fought frantically against the force of the water. The Mae West brought him to the surface once again. Desperately he felt for the life raft pack and pulled the handle. The raft began to slowly inflate and unfold. Bud could not see it in the darkness, but he could feel the raft inflating. When it was nearly inflated, a gust of wind seized the raft and almost wrenched the safety cord off the raft. Another wave crashed over him, and once again he was submerged under the angry sea. When the wave had passed, he wasn't sure if he had surfaced or if he were still submerged. Nothing could be better than a deep breath of wonderfully fresh air in his lungs. Another vicious wave tossed him high in air and then rolled him under tons of water.

The panic and terror gradually began to leave him. Illogically, he felt contented and very peaceful. He gripped the pararaft with one hand and worked to shed the bulky parachute seat pack. His last conscious thoughts were of Phyllis and his family and the smell of fresh mowed grass, honeysuckle and Magnolia blooms, and finally he thought to himself, "This must be what it feels like to die."

Mad Dog landed at Barbers Point at 0210. Ferguson and a group of officers stood on the ramp waiting for him. Mad Dog had circled the area where Bud Cotter had gone down. He dropped flares into the storm hoping to locate Cotter's aircraft. Apparently the Skyraider sunk almost immediately. The marine pilot loitered in the area until the Coast Guard helo arrived, and because of his fuel state, and because there was no 115/145 Avgas available on the island, Mad Dog was forced to depart for Barbers Point.

The storm reached its peak and the seas were mountainous. There was no sign of Bud Cotter or of his aircraft. The Coast Guard H-3 executed a methodical search of the area using flares and spotlights until they were forced to return to the atoll to refuel. They held little hope that the pilot had survived. The emergency locator transmitter that all pilots carry in their life vest was not transmitting a signal. Not a good sign. They waited until daylight to resume the search. Aerographer Reed assured them that the worst of the storm would be past by 0500, but the weather would remain stormy and rainy well into the next day.

Bad news travels fast, especially in the Navy. At 0400, Shug Early was shaken out of a sound sleep by Fat Back and told about the loss of Bud Cotter.

"Don't call his folks," Fat Back said, "the Skipper will take care of the official notifications, but somebody probably ought to tell his girl friend."

Sitting on the edge of his bed in shock, Shug sadly said, "I'll take care of it. Jesus, this is going to kill her. Are yall sure he didn't make it?"

"Nothing is certain, but it doesn't look good for him. No signs of a raft, no emergency locator signal, no flares. The Coast Guard helo searched the area for over three hours. It's just too damn bad. Officially they'll list him as missing for now, but that's just a formality. It doesn't mean anything."

"Yeah, I know what you mean." Shug stood. "Thanks for coming by, Fat Back."

Fat Back looked at the floor. "Yeah, Cotter is a really good guy. Everybody likes him. He's a damn good pilot too. Maybe he'll be okay. All we can do is hope."

The two officers shook hands and shared a look like people do during a sad shocking moment. "See you around, Early. We'll let you know if there's any news."

When Sandra told her about Bud, Phyllis remained calm for a few minutes, but as the realization fully penetrated her mind, she became hysterical. Shug hurriedly drove Bud's Buick to the bungalow to be with the women. Later in the morning, Phyllis fell into a shock-like state. She said nothing and refused to be consoled. Shug and Sandra remained with her throughout the day and that night, making futile attempts to compel Phyllis to eat and drink.

Chapter 12

Missing and Presumed Lost

Jack Ferguson and his staff were mounting a full scale search plan to try and locate their down pilot. There could be no better search and rescue, SAR training for the squadron than doing it under actual conditions. In conjunction with the Coast Guard helo crew at the Tern Island station, a relay system of Skyraiders and S-2's was set up whereas four aircraft equipped for long range search operations would search an assigned area off French Frigate Shoal. The search would gradually spread outward in a 180 degree arc to the west, the direction it was assumed that the wind and waves would have taken a raft or a man in life vest.

For two long intensive days, they searched the seas off French Frigate Shoals and as far northwest as Maro Reef. On the morning of the second day, the Coast Guard H-3 helo found the Skyraider. The seas had calmed and the sand had settled in the shallow waters inside the reef. The aircraft lay in twenty feet of water one half mile north of Tern Island. The dark outline of the aircraft was clearly visible against the reef. Two hours after the Skyraider was located, one of the squadron S-2's located an orange inflatable raft adrift approximately forty-five miles west of the Shoal. The H-3 was dispatched to retrieve the raft. The round inflatable vessel was empty. Clearly stenciled on the raft was the designation VC-110. None of the pararaft's pouches or compartments that contained survival gear had been opened.

Ferguson & Miles flew a modified S-2 from Barbers Point to Tern Island. Mad Dog, Chicken Wing and Cracker Jack rode in the passenger seats. It was a solemn flight. The possibility that the body of Bud Cotter was still inside or very near the aircraft was on everyone's mind.

"We've got a dive team headed out there now," Coast Guard Lieutenant, Rick Daniel said to Ferguson. "We spotted the aircraft at 0940 this morning. If you like we can take the H-3 out there so you can take a look."

The divers verified the tail number of the aircraft. It was number four zero nine. The squadron designation VC-110 was clearly stenciled on the empennage. They reported that the aircraft was resting inverted on the reef and that the canopy was open and the cockpit was empty.

"There are several possibilities," Ferguson said to LT. Daniel. I have to assume that Cotter was able to egress the aircraft before it sank and did inflate his Mae West. Based on that assumption he will be floating on the sea regardless of whether he is dead or alive. We will continue to fly SAR missions in the west one eighty out to seventy-five miles. Based the raft's position, I don't see much chance that our pilot would have drifted any further than that."

"I agree," Daniel said. "We will continue to patrol with the H-3 and assist in whatever ways that we can. Your crews are welcomed to use our facilities."

"Thanks, Lieutenant."

10 AUGUST 1967.........0047Z

TO: MR. NORMAN COTTER

FROM: COMMANDING OFFICER, VC-110. NAS BARBERS POINT, HAWAII.

SUBJECT: LTJG TOLAND M. COTTER

THE COMMANDING OFFICER, VC-110 REGRETS TO INFORM YOU THAT YOUR SON LTJG TOLAND M. COTTER IS MISSING AND PRESUMED LOST AT SEA. ON 7 AUGUST 1967 AT APPROXIMATELY 2140 LOCAL HAWAIIAN TIME, LTJG COTTER'S AIRCRAFT EXPERIENCED ENGINE FAILURE DURING A NIGHT TRAINING MISSION IN THE VICINITY OF TERN

ISLAND, FRENCH FRIGATE SHOAL, HAWAII. SEARCH AND RESCUE EFFORTS ARE CONTINUING BY NAVY AND COAST GUARD AIR AND SEA UNITS. ANY CHANGE IN LTJG COTTER'S STATUS WILL BE COMMUNICATED TO YOU IMMEDIATELY.

COMMANDER J.C.FERGUSON, COMMANDING OFFICER, VC-110

The Radiogram, delivered by a Marine messenger was a hammer blow to Norman Cotter. Having been the Commanding Officer of the destroyer USS Jacob Rogers during the latter part of WWII, Norman Cotter knew exactly what the message implied. His son was presumed dead and the Navy would not spend an inordinate amount of time looking for him beyond the three days they had already.

Being a highly disciplined man, Norman Cotter's mind cleared quickly. He left his office in the studio and went home to be with his wife and daughter. That afternoon Norman called his old friend and fellow destroyer skipper, Admiral Sharp, Commander in Chief Pacific. The admiral was aware of the down pilot but did not know this was Norman Cotter's son. With CINCPAC now involved, a series of events quickly took place and a full-scale effort was put into place to locate the missing pilot. After the Admiral had been fully briefed on the situation, he believed that it was most likely that the young Cotter had drowned in the storm. And as did Ferguson, the Admiral and his staff concluded that the body must be floating somewhere out in that vast area of the Pacific. Finding a floating immobile man in the ocean is a nearly impossible task, but in CINCPAC's view, doing the impossible is standard performance for the United States Navy.

LPH USS Princeton, a converted WWII aircraft carrier and four destroyer escorts were dispatched from Pearl Harbor to conduct SAR exercises in the area off French Frigate Shoals. The Princeton's helicopter air groups would fly dawn to dusk

SAR missions as an adjunct to the ship's ORI (operational readiness inspection), which was scheduled to begin the following day.

On the afternoon of 12 August, Norman and Millie Cotter arrived at Honolulu International Airport accompanied by their daughter Bernadette and June Chandler. They would stay in the VIP quarters on the base at Pearl Harbor as guests of Admiral Sharp.

Chapter 13

Bernadette Cotter

Bernadette Cotter returned to her parent's home in mid June following two years of university studies abroad. The experience of studying in Europe left her indelibly imbued with the genius of the European masters of music, art and philosophy. Her purely American predilection toward the world had changed dramatically. Bernadette grasped the reality that America was not the cultural center of the world. Nearly all that had been accomplished in America had sprung from the ideas and teachings of European descendents: the Italians, the English, the French, the Germans, the Spaniards, the Poles and the Russians. These were the immigrants who came to the United States during the centuries following Columbus, Desoto and Ponce De Leon. Bernadette returned to Nashville an ardent advocate of expanded liberal thinking possessing the capacity to objectively examine social, religious and political matters on much broader plane. Her youthful frivolous idealism had been tempered and had matured in Europe.

One thing Bernadette did not bring back to America was her virginity. Entangled in the libertine attitudes of European culture, she had embarked upon a sordid love affair with a charismatic Austrian cellist. Bernadette possessed birth control tablets, but she was absent minded about such things and often neglected to take them. Predictably the dreadful day arrived when a gray bespectacled obstetrician announced that she had indeed killed the rabbit. Her Austrian lover disappeared, abandoning Bernadette to deal with her situation alone. The calamity induced her to seek an abortion, which in the end only appended her emotional devastation. She dared not turn to her conservative devoutly Catholic parents for support. She believed her mother would be mildly supportive but she feared that her father would disown her completely.

Contrary to the pro-life teachings of the Catholic Church, Bernadette firmly supported the popular free choice philosophy embraced by much of 1960's society. Women's rights and equality were a dominating factor in the ideals that she so zealously embraced. She firmly believed that a woman had the right to choose abortion as a means of avoiding an unintended pregnancy. Bernadette could not imagine herself unmarried and burdened with a fatherless child. Such an appalling embarrassment and humiliation would be intolerable for her, and she believed, for her family. Irresponsible and immoral behavior could be expected of public school girls, but in Bernadette's social class such circumstances were perfectly out of the question.

Once she had exercised her right of having the pregnancy terminated, she found herself ridden by devastating guilt. Had she destroyed a Mozart, a Bach, an Einstein, a Prime Minister, or a President? She would never know. Desperately seeking peace for her tormented soul, she became isolated and began to drink heavily. Her studies and her music suffered. She lost weight and her pretty features became gaunt and drawn. She left her flat in the evenings only for an occasional meal at a small cafe. Fearing that Bernadette may be tottering on the edge of suicide, her closest protégés persuaded her to see a doctor in Vienna who convinced Bernadette to undergo gestalt therapy in a convent hospital. Under the care of a brilliant Austrian psychiatrist, Sister Marta Von Rundstedt of the Sisters of Mercy, Bernadette responded favorably regaining her self-worth and confidence. It was during this delicate emotionally charged turning point that she came to truly recognize the deep attachment she had for her family and surprisingly for the Church. As a result of her therapy, Bernadette decided to return to her parent's home. She would return to Belmont

University School of Music to begin work on a Masters degree.

Exhausted after her European ordeal, Bernadette spent her time in Nashville relaxing, playing the piano and violin and renewing relationships with family and friends. Here at last, she realized the contentment and happiness that had so ardently eluded her in Europe.

Bernadette paralleled her mother's features in many ways: shoulder length hair, quick dark eyes, clear fair skin and a slightly up-turned nose. She was endowed with her father's prominent chin, and not the least his shrewd intelligence and sharp tongue. She possessed a modest figure which annoyed her greatly, yet most men considered her sexy and alluring. One resulting aftershock of her libidinous European whirlwind was a cultivated taste for musically talented men. Yet, she also found great fascination in men of adventure. Bernadette decided that men who were musically inclined and yet intrepid in nature would be much more to her taste. Having never met such a man, she wondered if such man really did exist. He would be profoundly fascinating and a true rarity within her world of art and music.

Mercurial romantic predilections aside, Bernadette's foremost ambitions were simply to enjoy her family, her friends, and above all her music. Possibly she would teach or even conduct someday; then again, she may marry a lavishly rich magnate and live in extravagant splendor on the French Riviera. Perhaps she would remain in her parent's home, composing classical symphonies and playing her music, withering into a rich wrinkled old maid. Bernadette's genius with piano and violin coupled with her remarkable retention of entire symphonies seemed almost beyond human capability to many people. To Bernadette, these gifts were simply inherent, a natural talent not unlike impressionists and writers who are masters of their crafts.

She had begun to seriously play the piano at age three, finding sonorous gratification in the works of Chopin. She was introduced to the violin at age five, a difficult instrument that she adroitly mastered in a year. At age 10 she was playing a rare Stradivarius violin purchased by her father in Saltsburg. At sixteen, she was presented with another Stradivarius after winning the European violin competition in Munich, and as a college freshman, Bernadette stunned the music world by becoming the first non European to win the International Frédéric Chopin piano competition in Warsaw.

Bernadette Cotter had become widely recognized as the eminent prodigy in the world of classical music. Fiercely independent, she created a great deal of controversy, haughty huffing and indignation when she declined an open offer to attend the Julliard School in New York City. Bernadette was universally quoted as saying, "New York is a filthy and vulgar place inhabited by equally vulgar and rude people. I have no intention of casting my pearls before those swine." Outside New York City, this posture only served to enhance her reputation as a plucky, autonomous prodigy.

Her graduate studies at Belmont would begin in September and it was with great anticipation that she looked forward to the return to academia. There, cloaked in the very substance of symphonic genesis, her euphonious essence would delve deeply into the genius of the grand masters, concurrently questioning, tutoring and creating. When asked by a prominent music critic why she insisted upon studying at Belmont rather than at one of the more "highly recognized" schools of music, Bernadette replied, "Contrary to the insistence of many self-aggrandizing snoots, thought, literacy and art are not confined to the elitist institutions of the east coast."

Bernadette was amused and considered it adventuresome that her brother Bud had become a naval aviator despite the loud and adamant protests of their father. Contrasted to her amusement with her brother's defiance, Bernadette fervently opposed the US involvement in Vietnam. During her second year at Belmont, Bernadette had become active in a group of pacifist young Republicans whose political ideals paralleled her own. After refusing to report for the draft, the leader of the group was carted off to jail by the FBI. Bernadette and her friends picketed the jail and within the hour, they too were behind bars charged with disturbing the peace and illegal picketing. Refusing bail and legal representation, Bernadette spent five miserable days in the Nashville women's detention center surrounded by dreadfully wicked and savage women. Unwavering in her convictions, she took her own defense in court. Bernadette's fiery idealistic oratory in the Nashville courtroom resulted in a contempt of court charge, and she spent another two days in jail. No longer able to tolerate her revolting cell mates, nor the hideous jail meals of fried bologna, eggs and gravy, Bernadette bitterly conceded defeat and allowed her father's attorney, John P. Harper to handle her next court appearance. Arriving home, trembling with fear, Bernadette faced her father across the massive desk in his library. Mr. Cotter was surprisingly calm. "Well, young lady, did you learn anything from your experience?"

"Yes, I did, daddy. I learned there is no such thing as liberty and justice in this country."

Mr. Cotter puffed on a fat Partagas cigar and regarded his only daughter. "Of course there is liberty and justice baby daughter, but in order to benefit from it you have to work within the system, not against it. No matter what you think of the democratic process, the establishment, or whatever you young people are calling it nowadays, you're not going to change or control it by childish conduct in the street. If you want the system changed, you must get yourself involved in the political process, either directly by getting yourself elected to office or indirectly by forming strong political allies. You'll never get anything changed by making a spectacle of yourself on the street or in a court room, baby girl."

"Daddy, Bill Foster is going to prison because he opposes that lunatic war in Vietnam! It's not right! We can't allow the government to control our lives like this!"

"Bill Foster is in jail because he chose to violate Federal law by not reporting for military induction, not because he opposes the Vietnam War. If he had worked within the system and appealed his case, he wouldn't be in jail. But he's young and idealistic and he stood his ground to uphold his convictions. Now he's in a world of trouble."

"But daddy. . . ."

Mr. Cotter threw up his hand. "Baby Girl, I'm not going to debate this with you any longer. Having your youthful ideals and convictions is fine, but from now on, you will work within the system. I will not tolerate you making a public spectacle of yourself again. Your little episode created a very poor reflection on this family as well as on the employees of WLVX and I won't have it! Is that understood?"

Bernadette burst into tears. "Yes, daddy, I'm sorry."

Mr. Cotter rose, walked around the desk, hugged his daughter and kissed her forehead.

"You're my baby girl and I love you." Mr. Cotter walked out of the library. He never again mentioned the incident to his daughter.

In typical brother-sister fashion, Bud and Bernadette had been antagonistic toward one another throughout their childhood years. She had always viewed her brother as an impetuous mama's boy, but now, with the disaster of her brother missing at sea, the image of her older sibling was forever changed. It was in that instant, through tears of fearful sorrow for her lost brother that Bernadette realized Bud was not the spoiled brainy brat she grew up with, but he had indeed become a man, and to her, now a hero.

Chapter 14

Conflict and Recovery

Japanese fishing trawler number 38, the Eitoku Maru plowed through sunny Pacific waters at a position of 168 degrees west longitude and 25 degrees north latitude near the Gardner Pinnacles. Her captain, Isoruku Inomata paced the wheelhouse puffing an American cigarette and wondering how to solve three big problems. His first problem was his position. Having been caught in the storm, his ship had become separated from her two sister trawlers, the Fumi Maru and the Sanko Maru. His second problem was much worse. His radio antenna had been swept away in the heavy seas and he couldn't communicate by radio. So far, his crew was having no luck repairing the antenna. They needed two isolators and a coil and there were none on board. The crew was working hard to improvise, but thus far they were being frustrated by the lack of parts. The Captain's morning star shot placed him in American territorial waters where it was illegal for Japanese to fish. Under the fisheries accord between Japan and the United States, the waters east of longitude 165 west in the Hawaiian chain were off limits to commercial fishing. But his first two problems paled in comparison to his third problem: What was he going to do with the American they had rescued during the storm?

The helmsman had spotted the orange raft on 9 August just after daylight. The seas were running 35 feet and the wind was at force two. As the Eitoku Maru approached the raft, the crew observed a man wearing a life vest lying inside the raft, apparently unconscious. It had been very difficult, but Captain Inomata's vast ship handling skills and seamanship had prevailed and they dragged the delirious, barely conscious man aboard the trawler. The crewmen stripped the American, put him into a bunk and covered him with wool blankets. He mumbled and moaned but none of the Japanese crew understood English. Hours later, the American sat up and appeared to be dazed and frightened. They gave him hot strong tea from a wooden cup. He nodded thanks and fell back onto the bed. He slept for nearly 30 hours.

Bud Cotter slowly awoke in a confined darkened stateroom of the Eitoku Maru. For an instant, he wondered if he were dead. He was so weak that he could barely raise his arms. He had swallowed a lot of seawater and his guts were revolting in painful knots. When he did move, it was painful and very tiring. He could hear the muffled sound of powerful diesel engines and he could feel the pitching of the trawler as it plowed through the sea. Gradually the events of the crash and the storm began to seep from his memory. The impact had been unbelievable. The egress from the inverted cockpit in total blackness was a hideous ordeal, worse than any nightmare. He had no idea how he had managed to get into the raft. Once again he moved to be sure that he was indeed alive. He didn't know where he was, but someone had plucked him from the storm and was caring for him. He mustered all his strength and called out, "Hello…Hello there."

A dim light was switched on and a small oriental man with bristly black hair came to the bunk and bowed. He spoke Japanese which Bud could not understand. The young pilot slowly swung his feet out of the bunk and sat up. Every cell of his body was atrophied and he ached terribly. He smiled at the little man and said, "Do you speak English?" The fisherman bowed, said something unintelligible and left the room. Moments later the man returned accompanied by another oriental man. It was immediately obvious to Bud that this man was in charge. Although Bud had no idea what he was saying, the man spoke with an air of authority. The man bowed and shook Bud's hand. Slowly and painfully, Bud slid out of the bunk and stood, holding tightly onto the chain that supported the bunk. He was naked and in a moment, another man brought his clean dry skivvies and flight suit into the room.

Bud ravenously ate a bowl of cooked rice and fish and drank hot tea. His benefactors were amused as he fumbled with chopsticks, but he managed to scoop up the food and every bite he took seemed to bring more strength to his battered body.

After several hours of worry and deliberation, Captain Inomata made his decision. Bud was assisted to the chart-house on the bridge where the Captain had a map of the Hawaiian waters spread open on the chart table. Using a pencil, the Captain pointed to Pearl Harbor and gave Bud a questioning look. Bud nodded. The Captain studied the map a moment. He picked up a set of dividers and measured the distance from his present position to Pearl. He mumbled something in Japanese to another man who shook his head and pointed to French Frigate Shoal. The Captain took the pencil and circled Tern Island, the atoll where the Coast Guard station and airfield was located. He looked at Bud, and although he spoke no Japanese, Bud understood that the Captain intended to take him there.

During the day as she moved toward French Frigate Shoals, helicopters from the Princeton flew around the Eitoku Maru. Using semaphore and blinker lights, Captain Inomata's signalmen attempted to communicate with the aircraft, but these attempts were apparently unsuccessful. Then at 1940 local Hawaiian time, a small Coast Guard pilot vessel appeared on the horizon and after signaling by blinker light, the pilot boat led the trawler to the boat channel and on to the pier. As a gesture of goodwill and appreciation for the rescue and care of LTJG Cotter, the Coast Guard technicians provided parts and assisted in the repair of the Eitoku Maru's radio equipment

When Ferguson received word that Bud had been rescued, Boats Davidson and Mad Dog flew out to Tern Island in a squadron S-2 to bring Bud to Pearl Harbor.

Arriving back in Oahu, Mad Dog landed the S-2 on Sand Island Naval Air Station in Pearl Harbor. Bud Cotter was transferred from the S-2 onto a waiting Navy helicopter which immediately air lifted him across the harbor to the Naval Medical Facility. Following an extensive examination, the doctors declared that LTJG Cotter suffered from exhaustion and a mild concussion where his head had struck the gun sight when the Skyraider had impacted the sea. The diagnosis also included notations about the young pilot having swallowed a great deal of seawater and dehydration due to retching and vomiting. The staff doctors concluded their examinations and testing and recommended another twenty-four hours of hospital observation followed by twenty days of rest. Earlier that morning the CINCPAC Chief of Staff telephoned the Head Surgeon, Captain Langer and directed that LTJG Cotter be billeted in a private room.

Phyllis Day rushed into the room and sat on the edge of the bed grasping Bud tightly. "Oh, Bud, I love you so much. Thank God you're safe!" She began to cry and clung desperately to him. The Cotter family observed this scene, as did a fierily jealous June Chandler. Earlier in the day Shug Early had introduced Phyllis to the Cotter family. June Chandler and Phyllis were also introduced. The two women appraised each other circumspectly and shared a cool handshake.

"It's nice to finally meet you," Phyllis said in a pleasant but insincere tone. "Bud speaks so highly of you."

June considered Phyllis warily. She deplored the fact that Phyllis was petite, pretty and very feminine. No wonder Bud Cotter had been attracted to her! June Chandler correctly perceived that Phyllis's words were nothing more than phony verbiage and automatically disliked her. She would never trust this woman, and why should she? After all, they were in direct competition for the affections of Bud Cotter, and at this point the little bimbo certainly had the upper hand. "This is not the kind of woman," June thought, "that Bud Cotter needs or deserves. Undoubtedly she's a conniving manipulative little tart who's taking advantage of a very naïve and wonderful man." Despite her quiet and reserved personality, June Chandler possessed a harsh and even malevolent side, and although it was not her nature, she was confident that she could play hardball with any woman, and this was just the time to do it.

"Bud is a really wonderful guy," June said. "It was terribly shocking to hear about his accident. Thank God he's going to be okay."

"Yes, it's been a nightmare for everyone," Phyllis replied.

"Especially for his family, his parents and sister were devastated when they thought he was lost."

"And how did you feel?" Phyllis said with raised inquisitive eyebrows.

June looked Phyllis in the eye. "I was devastated to think he may have been killed. I am very much in love with him."

Phyllis was jolted as though a hammer had hit her. So it is true! June Chandler considers the relationship to be much more than friendship! Struggling to recover and not allow her shock to be obvious, Phyllis said, "Can we go somewhere and talk in private?"

"Very well," June replied with a curt smile, "there are tables on the terraces outside this building. How would that be?"

"Fine."

The two women faced off across a circular wooden table under a large shade tree. Without the courtesy of asking Phyllis, and as a sign of not being intimidated, June took out cigarettes and lit one. She turned her head to exhale, being careful not to allow the smoke to drift toward her rival.

June looked directly at Phyllis. "So, what do you wish to discuss?"

Phyllis returned June Chandler's stare. This was a beautiful and unfortunately, a sophisticated and elegant woman, and it was becoming obvious that she was not going to be a push-over. Phyllis took some comfort in the fact that Bud Cotter insisted that he was not in love with June Chandler, but Phyllis reminded herself that the demarcation between friendship and love could be a very thin line indeed. Inwardly, Phyllis felt panic. This woman was a formidable rival. Given the opportunity, she could easily sway Bud Cotter's heart, and that Phyllis could not and would not allow.

"Well, isn't it obvious? We have a mutual situation, don't we? We are in love with the same man."

June drew deeply on the cigarette. "Yes, we do have a dilemma, and you may as well know this up front, I don't believe that he doesn't have strong feelings for me."

"In what way are you and Bud committed?"

"Committed?" June pursed her lips. "Unfortunately there's no ring on my finger if that's what you mean."

"Have you slept with him?"

June peered at Phyllis with shiny combative eyes. "That's none of your business. You have some nerve asking me a question like that."

"When it comes to Bud Cotter, I have a great deal of nerve Miss Chandler."

"Just for the record, I never slept with him. Our relationship was not like that. Have you slept with him?"

Phyllis hesitated. "I should tell you that it is none of your business, but I won't. Yes, I've slept with him. Several times as a matter of fact, several wonderful heavenly times."

June faltered and nearly dropped her cigarette. A red haze of jealously swept through her. She was deeply hurt by this news, but she recovered quickly.

“I don’t believe you,” June said forcefully.

“I don’t care if you believe me or not, Miss Chandler. I am very much in love with Bud Cotter and he is in love with me. He called you a few weeks ago and told you about our relationship.”

“Yes, he called.”

“Then why do you persist in this pursuit of him?”

“I told you, because I am in love with him. I am not prepared to concede our relationship on the merit of one phone call. He and I spent several fabulous weeks getting to know one another over his Christmas leave. I find it gratifying to say that we did so without sleeping together. He respected me and my virginity and I his. Our relationship was clear and pure. Not based on lust and the vulgarity of fornication.”

Phyllis bristled. Her face became deeply flushed. “Are you insinuating that our relationship is vulgar or trashy?”

“What else do you expect me to think?”

Phyllis clenched her fists on the table. “Bud Cotter and I have nothing to be ashamed of. We are deeply in love. There is nothing dirty or vulgar about our relationship.”

“I don’t see an engagement ring on your left hand. I wonder how serious he really is with you.”

Phyllis jumped up with a venomous glare in her eye. “God-damn you, June Chandler! You stay away from him! I’ve never loved anyone in my life as I love him! And now I have finally found the one true love I have always hoped and prayed for! I don’t intend to allow you or anyone else to interfere with our relationship! He will ask me to marry him in his own good time! I'm prepared to wait as long as it takes. I warn you. Stay away from him!"

June hesitated, concerned that Phyllis may be capable of physical violence, but she steeled herself and looked Phyllis directly in the eye. "That is not going to happen Miss Day," she said calmly, "not until I see Bud Cotter's ring on your hand. Until then, I have no intention of giving up on him. So you'd better get used to that idea." June rose and stubbed the cigarette with the toe of her shoe. "I see no further point to this discussion." June rose from the table and walked into the building.

Phyllis sat at the table and wept bitterly. She hated June Chandler. The wicked, wicked bitch! It was as though Satan himself had risen to ruin her life through this beautiful wicked witch. She truly loved Bud Cotter with all her being. He had become a part of her very soul. She could not bear to lose him. It would be the end, the very end if he deserted her for June Chandler!

When told that his family had arrived from Nashville, Bud was astonished. The presence of June Chandler was an even more startling revelation. He was very tired and fatigued and he didn't need a jealous female calamity to erupt between June and Phyllis. Never would he have imagined that his parents and sister would show up with June Chandler. He wasn't even sure how they learned about the crash. When the Cotter's left Bud's room, June Chandler audaciously stayed behind. Phyllis was sitting on the edge of the bed holding his hand and talking to him.

"Bud," June said sweetly, "I'd like to talk to you, alone if you don't mind."

Phyllis stood and glared hatefully. Her tone was calm, but possessive and assertive. "Anything you have to say to him, you can say in front of me. We have no secrets between us."

June ignored Phyllis and addressed Bud as though he were the only person in the room. "I can come back some other time if you'd rather."

Bud laid his head back on the pillow and groaned inwardly. He still couldn't get over the fact that June Chandler had come all the way out here from Nashville. He had no idea that her feelings for him were really that serious. He was in love with Phyllis. Why couldn't June understand that? She had hung up on him when he told her about Phyllis. How much more straightforward could he have been?

"Okay, June." He looked at Phyllis and squeezed her hand. "Give us just a few minutes, will you Sweetheart?" Phyllis swelled with jealously glaring at June. "No! I don't want her near you!"

"Please trust me, Phyllis," Bud said in his best bedroom voice. "I promise there will be no secrets."

Flushing crimson, Phyllis jerked her hand away from his and stormed out of the room.

"Well, that's not so good," Bud sighed. He turned his head slowly to look at June. "Thanks for coming all the way out here, June. I'd be lying if I didn't tell you how surprised I was to hear that you came."

June went to him, took his hand in hers and bent to kiss him tenderly. The time for reserved polite talk was past. This may well be her last chance to get a toehold with Bud Cotter. "I'm here for two reasons: Most important is because I am very much in love with you, Bud Cotter. I'm here because I love you and need you in my life. I'll do whatever you ask of me. If it means surrendering my virginity before marriage, it's yours. Whatever it takes, Darling."

He sat up straight in the bed. "Jesus, June! I had no idea that you felt this way. In all the months we have known each other, we never talked about anything like this. How was I supposed to know?"

"I guess that in some ways I am nearly as naïve as you are, Bud. I should have told you how I felt, but I was afraid. Now I'm telling you these things because I am losing you. I am so much in love with you that it hurts me. I would marry you today if you asked me."

"Jesus Christ, June! You've never been like this before! What has happened to you?"

"Phyllis Day is what has happened to me. She has become my nemesis."

"Phyllis and I are in love. I thought you understood that."

"What I understand is that you and she are involved in a perfidious relationship. I can't tell you how hurtful and disappointing it is to learn that you have been sleeping with her."

"Who told you that?"

"Phyllis."

He slowly wagged his head. "Jesus."

"I am not convinced that you are truly in love with her. I suspect much of what you regard as love is really lustful desire."

"That's not true."

"Are you sure? How can you be really certain, Bud?"

"June, this is an amazingly bizarre conversation. What do you want from me?"

"I want you to say that you have some feelings for me. I want you to say that there is a chance, even a slight chance for us. I want you to say that you will promise me that you won't do anything rash until you've had time to think about us and this whole issue."

"Rash! What is that supposed to mean?"

"I'm talking about you not asking Phyllis to marry you before you go to Vietnam in October."

"Who said anything about getting married? Phyllis and I have never discussed marriage."

June was swept with a huge wave of relief. At least he and Phyllis weren't yet to that point. "Please Bud. Please be sure you know what your heart really and truly wants. Please consider what is best for you and for your future. Don't allow the passion of sex to sway your good judgment. Please!"

"You know, June. You and I had a great time together after we met. Everything has always been above board with us, and we didn't make any commitments one way or the other. We both knew that I was leaving and coming out here. When you told me that you were thinking of coming to Hawaii after your state boards, I was really excited. I thought that would be our chance to pick up where we left off, but you never mentioned it again. Then I met Phyllis. Nothing happened at first. It was probably two, maybe three months before anything serious began to happen. I didn't feel guilty because I considered you and me to be good friends. It never occurred to me that you had feelings like this for me. I would never do anything to purposely hurt you, June. I never dreamed that you would react the way you did. Phyllis says I am the most naïve man she's ever met. Maybe she's right. But you need understand, June, I am in love with Phyllis. It has nothing to do with sex."

These words penetrated into June Chandler's very soul. He really was in love with Phyllis. June burst into tears and ran out of the room.

Phyllis watched June Chandler rush by with tears streaming across her face. She understood, and for a fleeting instant, Phyllis could almost feel sorry for her. She too, had been deeply hurt in the past. Phyllis ran into the room and threw herself at Bud. "Oh, Baby, I love you more than life itself."

He caressed her pretty oval face in his hands. "I love you, Sweetheart. More than you'll ever know."

Throughout the day, a steady string of visitors, mostly VC-110 pilots and personnel visited Bud at the hospital. Ferguson arrived around noon and was invited to lunch with the Cotter's.

Late that afternoon Bud was astounded when Mad Dog walked into the room.

"How's it going, Einstein?"

"Okay, just waiting to get my release out of here."

"Any idea when they'll let you go?"

"No, no one has told me anything."

Mad Dog appeared hesitant for a moment. "Look, Einstein. I, ah, well I want you to know that I'm goddamn glad that you made it. You may be the best wingman I've ever had, and well, hurry up and get your ass back to the squadron."

Bud couldn't believe what he was hearing. It took him a few seconds to respond. "Thanks, Mad Dog. I appreciate it."

Mad Dog grinned. Bud wasn't sure if he had ever seen Mad Dog smile. "Yeah, well, Einstein, your biggest problem is that you're not a marine, but I want to buy a few drinks after you get out of here anyway."

Bud grinned with one side of his mouth. "Okay, sounds good."

Mad Dog fumbled with his cover, "Well, we've got a night op scheduled, so I better get going. See you around, Einstein"

"Okay. See you, and thanks."

Bud was discharged from the hospital the following afternoon. Shug Early brought the Buick to the hospital and drove Bud and Phyllis to the VIP quarters where the Cotters had arranged a dinner party. The house staff situated the back lanai and garden for the event. Admiral Sharp and other senior officers would be attending.

Bernadette, Bud and Phyllis sat at a white glass top wicker table sipping drinks. “Well, oh brother of mine,” said Bernadette as she held a cocktail in one hand and a cigarette in the other, “You certainly have a propensity for drama: Crashing an airplane into the teeth of a storm. Drifting aimlessly in a raft and being rescued by the Japanese. You couldn’t write a screenplay adventure any better than this.”

“It was just a freak accident,” Bud said.

“It was a nightmare at home. Everybody but daddy had given you up for dead. Don’t you ever do something like this again, your family and poor Phyllis couldn’t handle it.”

“The thought of losing you is inconceivable,” Phyllis said and kissed his cheek. His face flushed. He was uncomfortable having Phyllis be so demonstrative around his family. She clutched him constantly. When they were together she did everything for him. Her love and devotion were clearly obvious to everyone.

Bernadette accepted a second Mai Tai from a smiling Filipino steward.

“These things are really great,” she smiled and sipped the drink.

“Well, don’t get smashed and embarrass Daddy. A lot of his Navy buddies including Admiral Sharp are coming tonight.”

“Don’t be a bore, Brother. And oh my God, Daddy wants me to play for these people tonight. I wonder how many sailors got a hernia moving that nine foot Bosendorfer Grand out here on the lanai.”

“You’re going to play?” Phyllis said enthusiastically, “I’ve been hoping you would. Bud has told me so much about your music.”

"Ha!" Bernadette threw her head back and laughed. "Phyllis, Hun, you are such a darling. My brother is really a troll. Don't say I didn't warn you."

Phyllis grinned sweetly and hugged Bud's arm.

Bernadette cast a sly glance at her brother. "So big brother, when can we expect an announcement?"

"What are you talking about?"

"Yours and Phyllis's engagement, of course."

Phyllis and Bud glanced at each other and flushed. "Don't get on my nerves, Bernadette." He said to Phyllis, "Did I forget to mention that my sister has a big mouth?"

"Oh, Bud, she's just teasing you," Phyllis said sweetly.

"No I'm not," Bernadette said and drank Mai Tai, "you two are perfect for one another. I've never seen two people more in love. Daddy thinks Phyllis is the best thing since Merlot."

Bud stared at his sister with cold murderous eyes. "Knock it off, Bernadette."

"Okay, I'll shut up, Big Brother……for now anyway." She began to paw through her purse. "I thought that I had another pack of cigarettes in here. Darn it!" She looked at Phyllis, "do you have cigarette, Hun?"

"No I'm sorry, I don't smoke."

Bud flagged a steward and asked him to get a pack of cigarettes for Bernadette.

"Thanks, Brother, always the gentleman. By the way, Vice President and Mrs. Nixon were in Nashville recently. They were asking about you. We met them for dinner at the Colemere Club, and of course we had to sit through an incredibly boring after dinner speech. Talk about a drag. After that he made more speeches at the Capitol and at Maxwell House. I thought I was going to lose my mind."

Phyllis was flabbergasted. "Bud, you know Vice President Nixon?"

"Well, yeah."

"Oh, my God, Baby. You never told me that!"

"Well actually the Nixon's are friends of the parents. The Vice President served with Daddy in the South Pacific during the war."

"Wow. Do you think I'll get to meet him someday?"

"Sure. If he comes to Hawaii, I'll introduce you."

"Brother, you haven't told me what to play for these admirals."

Bud appeared thoughtful. "Play something lively like, "*The Turkish March* or *Strauss* and maybe something from a musical. No Bach fugues or heavy Beethoven."

"Okay," she teased, "How about Anchors Aweigh fortissimo?"

"Negative, that's one of Shug Early's specialties after everybody gets drunk."

The dinner guests began arriving around 1830. CINCPAC and Deputy CINCPAC, Rear Admiral Stokes arrived in a long black Lincoln with four star flags fluttering on the front bumper. A marine wearing summer dress blues hopped out of the vehicle, opened doors and snapped to rigid attention as the admirals and their wives exited the vehicle.

Shug Early sat at the massive Bosendorfer grand piano and began to play Scott Joplin tunes. Bernadette took her drink and went to sit next to him.

"You're really good, Shug. Bud told me that you played. Where did you go to music school?"

He laughed and said, "I went to music school in my parent's living room. Mama started me with piano lessons when I was six or seven. I hated playing and practicing until I found out that the girls loved to hear me play rock and roll. I learned by default I guess. I just play for fun and at parties. No one notices all my mistakes after they've had a few drinks. Thanks for the compliment though. Coming from you it means a lot."

"No, I'm serious. You play very well. Have you ever considered serious study?"

Shug grinned, "No, that's not my thing. Jerry Lee Lewis, Little Richard and Fats Domino are my heroes."

Bernadette laughed. "Can I play along with you? I love Scott Joplin."

Shug grinned happily. "Sure! It'll be fun."

The Admirals were formally introduced to the guests and shook hands making polite chatty conversation. A covey of navy stewards clad in white smocks and black pants hovered everywhere to serve the officers and guests.

"Well, Lieutenant," Admiral Sharp said to Bud, "you had quite a time out there. Jack Ferguson's report indicated that the aircraft was inverted and you had to make an underwater egress."

"That's correct, Admiral, it was a pretty nasty situation. If not for the outstanding training we've received, I probably would have drowned."

"You know, Lieutenant, I had COMNAVAIRPAC and his people do some checking around. We've not had a successful inverted night egress at sea, and in heavy seas at that. How about doing a synopsis on your episode? I believe that it would be a great training benefit for our fleet pilots."

"I will be happy to do that, sir."

"Fine, Lieutenant." The Admiral turned to Norman Cotter. "Fine lad you've got here Norman. I know you and Millie are proud of him."

Norman Cotter smiled proudly. "Yes, Grant we certainly are."

Admiral Stokes said to Bud, "Thinking of making the Navy a career, son? We need bright young officers like you. You'd be doing the Navy a disservice if you left active duty."

Realizing this was a moment for political correctness, Bud replied, "A naval career is a very attractive option, Admiral. I've definitely been thinking about it."

"Good, good, son, we World War Two officers will be retiring soon. There will be tremendous opportunities for capable young officers such as you."

"Your dad tells me that you were a two time All American on the Vanderbilt golf team," Admiral Sharp said, "How about joining me for a round sometime?"

"I'd be honored, Admiral, anytime," Bud lied. He had no desire to get involved with CINCPAC. He had heard stories about all the political sniping and intrigues that went on in that hierarchy of the navy.

"Very well, son, we'll be giving you a call in the near future."

After several more minutes of polite small talk, Bud managed to escape from the Admirals and his father. He hated being involved with his father's big shot cronies.

Later in the evening, while the coffee and desert were being served, Bernadette sat down at the gleaming Bosendorfer. She began with a Strauss waltz; *A Walk in the Vienna Woods*, faded into Mozart's peppy but complex *Turkish March* and finished with pieces from Vivaldi's *Four Seasons*. She then invited Shug Early to sit and play duets with her. They livened up the crowd as Bernadette and Shug adroitly played and sang rock and roll and Boogie-Woogie. The lively music coupled with an open bar spurred many guests to cast aside polite reservations and they began to dance.

The guests had swelled to well over fifty people. Mostly CINCPAC staff and CO's of local Naval commands. The majority of officers were accompanied by wives or girl friends who wore summery dresses appropriate to an admiral's cocktail dinner party. Bernadette, not being accustomed to military social gatherings, was amused to note that the pecking order of the women was in direct proportion to the rank of their husband or escort. Bernadette noticed too, that this circumstance generated many snobbish appraisals regarding the other women's taste in fashion.

Phyllis and Bud dined with the Cotters and the Admirals. Within the hierarchy of the navy this was indeed significant. The young junior grade Lieutenant sitting at the CINCPAC table drew considerable attention from many senior officers. Those politically astute career ladder climbers made a mental note of LTJG Bud Cotter. This young lieutenant could possibly be a most valuable tool to be utilized on the road to future promotion.

Around 2300 Bud excused himself and went to bed in the VIP house. The dinner had been a strain and he desperately needed to sleep. Phyllis saw him off to bed with sweet kisses and mutterings of love. When Phyllis returned to the lanai, she sat and talked with Mrs. Cotter and the admiral's wives until all the guests had gone.

Next morning, rested and much refreshed, Bud showered and dressed in khaki shorts and a blue golf shirt. Now that the issue with June Chandler was apparently resolved, he could relax and enjoy his family with Phyllis at his side.

He went downstairs in search of coffee. A steward directed him to the back lanai where his parents were breakfasting.

Sitting with his parents, drinking coffee and eating an English muffin was June Chandler.

Mrs. Cotter smiled at her son. "Bud," his mother called as he approached the table, "come and sit with us."

He sat down and took and cup and saucer. A steward immediately filled it.

"Cream and sugar, sir?"

"No, thank you, black."

The steward disappeared into the house.

Bud said, "So, June, did you enjoy the dinner party last night?"

"Oh, yes, it was very pleasant. I met some very interesting people."

"Are you staying here?"

"Yes, your mother was gracious enough to let me stay here."

"Oh, Lord, yes," Mrs. Cotter said, "The house has eight bedrooms. There's plenty of room for everyone."

Bud felt his stomach rolling into knots. A feeling of heavy dread spread throughout him like a pall. This was going to be a nightmare. Phyllis had spent the night as a guest in Bernadette's suite. She would be down soon, and if she saw him sitting here at the table with June Chandler all hell would break loose. His brain scrambled for a solution. He couldn't just get up and leave without a viable excuse. He glanced at his father who puffed on a cigar and read the Honolulu morning edition tactfully staying out of the conversation. It was humiliating having this soap opera go on right under his parent's noses. His mother wasn't helping things by including June Chandler in everything. He longed to just get away from all this and go back to his squadron.

Bud finished his coffee in silence and excused himself. It was Saturday and Shug, always a late sleeper should be asleep in his room. Bud went into the house and dialed Shug's room at the BOQ. No answer. He left a message at the BOQ desk for Shug to call him. He called the nurse's bungalow. Sandra sleepily answered the phone.

"Sandra, is Shug there?"

"No he's not here Bud. I don't know where he is." She began to cry.

"What's the matter, Sandra. Why are you crying?"

"It's nothing. Goodbye, Bud." She hung up the phone.

Bernadette and Phyllis appeared on the lanai around 1030. When Phyllis saw June Chandler sitting in a wide rattan chair smoking and talking to Mrs. Cotter, she hesitated, scarlet streaks of jealousy pulsed through her. She glanced at Bernadette.

"What do you suppose she's doing here?"

"I know that she's here on business with Daddy. Something about a hotel he's building."

"A hotel, isn't she a teacher?"

"She is, or was. All I know is that daddy has hired her to work for him. I'm not sure what it's all about. Daddy hasn't talked about it and neither has June."

Phyllis sat at a circular glass top table with her back to June Chandler. Bud came out of the house and sat next to Phyllis. A steward poured juice for him.

Phyllis ate fruit and toast. After a while, she sat back and said to Bud.

"Did you sleep well, Baby?"

"Yeah, I feel a lot better today."

"I'm glad." After a pause, Phyllis said, "What is she still doing here?"

"Evidently the parents invited her to stay here while they are in town. I can't control that."

"I know what the bitch is doing and I'm going to put a stop to it once and for all."

"Phyllis, don't make a scene in front of the parents."

She gave him a wry smile and kissed his cheek. "Why I wouldn't dream of it, Baby."

"Phyllis, I'm asking you as nicely as I can. Please don't start any trouble."

"Don't worry, Baby. I won't embarrass you or your family."

Bernadette chimed in. "Let Phyllis handle this her way, Brother. Isn't it nice having two beautiful women fighting over you?"

"Shut up, Bernadette."

Bernadette frowned. "How nasty, big brother, you've hurt my feelings."

"Knock it off, Bernadette! I'm in no mood for your sarcasm this morning." He cast his sister a fierce threatening look, one that she remembered from childhood after she had tattled to her father about something Bud had done.

"Well!" She said in a counterfeit huff. "I'm going to sit with Mama and June and have a cigarette. The atmosphere here is getting a little, shall we say, noxious."

"Baby, I am going to settle this business with June Chandler, today if possible."

"What are you going to do, Phyllis? What can you possibly say to her that will convince her to go away?"

"I'll have a talk with her and reason with her. I'm hoping we can reach an understanding. As far as I am concerned, she's here for one purpose and one purpose only, and that is to try and take you away from me."

"Phyllis, Sweetheart, that's not going to happen. I don't have those kinds of feelings for her. You know that."

"I truly believe that, Baby. And I intend to keep it that way. Please, Baby. You'll just have to trust me on this one. You're so innocent and so naïve, and I love you all the more because of it. Let me handle this my way."

"Well, okay, just don't do anything rash or impulsive."

Shug called a few minutes before noon. "Where the hell have you been, lad?"

"Ah, hem, well I had some things to do. I got your message, what's going on?"

"I need you to get our clubs and come over here and pick me up. I've got to get away from this circus."

"Okay, son, I'll be there in forty-five minutes."

Bud seethed over the drama of having June Chandler and his family here in Hawaii. What a damn mess! He could not believe that he was actually trapped in the middle of such a fiasco and in full view of his parents, his sister and his friends!

Mrs. Sarah Cotter harbored mixed feelings about her son and Phyllis Day. She was highly pleased with Phyllis's obvious loyalty to Bud. As far as Millie knew, Phyllis was the first girl that Bud had ever been really serious about. Yet Mrs. Cotter felt disappointment in regard to her son's broken relationship with June Chandler. In many ways, the two young women were complete opposites. Phyllis was vivacious, demonstrative and loving, but she obviously came from a blue-collar family background. Although acceptably educated with a Bachelor degree in nursing, Phyllis lacked the poise, grace and reserved sophistication of June Chandler. Mrs. Cotter was accustomed to associating with highly sophisticated people of wealth, good breeding and high position. Her son had chosen a girl far below his social class and this rather troubled Mrs. Cotter. She could not picture Phyllis Day aptly fitting into the high social circles of politics, wealth and the arts. She resolved not to be condescending with Phyllis, but doing so would be a serious challenge.

Norman Cotter on the other hand, viewed Phyllis as a potential opportunity to draw his son off active duty and into the family business. There was nothing like the responsibility of a young bride and family to get a young man's priorities in line. Especially a young man married to an assertive and strong-willed woman that Norman perceived Phyllis Day to be. Her social class was irrelevant to Norman. Phyllis obviously would be a good wife to his son and that is all that really mattered. Yes, Norman thought, Phyllis would have a great deal of influence over the decisions his son would make. He began to develop a mental plan in which he would subtly manipulate Phyllis's thinking where over time, she would bring his son into the flourishing Cotter Communications Company.

Chapter 15

Decisions

Norman Cotter and his son sat on the shady lanai sipping iced tea from tall sweating glasses. They had finished a round of golf with Shug Early at Kaneohe and were relaxing before dinner. Phyllis and Bernadette were off shopping in Honolulu and Mrs. Cotter and June Chandler were attending a charity reception with Mrs. Sharp and the wives of several Flag Officers at the Waialae Country Club.

"Alton Jeffers is flying out here on Thursday," Mr. Cotter said to Bud. "We'll be wrapping up the contract on the land for our hotel down on Waikiki."

Bud's mouth dropped open, "Hotel, what hotel?"

Mr. Cotter was toasting a big Partagas cigar. "Cotter Communications has purchased eleven acres of beach front on Waikiki. We'll begin construction on the hotel and resort in November."

"How long have you been planning this?"

"Oh, it's been in the works for a couple of years. Everything has finally come to fruition and we're ready to move ahead."

Bud was astounded. He knew that Cotter Communications was a prosperous company, but he had no idea that this kind of money was involved. "You must be talking a couple of million dollars."

"Four and one half million...puff..puff...puff...puff. It's going to be the largest operation on the beach. We're going after a five star rating."

"This is impressive, Daddy."

"There's a lot to do. Alton will manage the construction phase and be involved in hiring a manager. I've hired your friend June Chandler to be Director of Personnel and Training. She's going to handle the initial staffing of the hotel."

"June Chandler? I thought she was teaching."

"Evidently she's changed her mind. She learned about the hotel from your mother and came to me with a request that I hire her in some administrative capacity. She will be moving out here this fall."

"This fall, you do move fast!" Bud considered the fact that June Chandler was going to living in Honolulu. He thought, "Phyllis will go ballistic when she hears about this".

"The hotel will be twenty stories. The entire top floor will be a Presidential suite," Mr. Cotter went on, "the outside grounds will provide gazebos for private meetings, weddings and luaus. We'll also have a covered concert hall. The architects who did Disneyland in California are doing the design work."

"Have you decided on a name for the place?"

"Yes, it's already registered. It will be the Wai Momi Hotel. Wai Momi means water of pearl in Hawaiian."

"Well, that's great Daddy. Sounds like this will be a profitable thing."

"It had better be, four and a half million is a lot of money. With the tourism increase in Hawaii, we anticipate being booked at a minimum level of 89% at all times."

"It's smart to diversify," Bud observed.

"That's the general idea and we need the tax breaks too."

Bud picked up a cigar from his father's cigar case. He trimmed the end and toasted it with the big butane lighter. When he had lighted the cigar, he signaled to one of the stewards.

"Yes, sir?"

"Please bring out a bottle of brandy and two snifters."

"Yes Lieutenant." The prim Filipino nodded and disappeared into the house.

Norman puffed the Partagas and viewed his son. The elder Cotter knew that Bud was going to be offered a reassignment to CINCPAC staff. The crash at sea in the storm and his son's subsequent loss had pushed Norman Cotter beyond restraint. If there was any way to prevent it, he had no intention of allowing his son to become cannon fodder in that asinine war in Indo China. Norman felt certain that his son possessed the political savvy not to refuse such an opportunity. Plus, it would offer him the chance to remain in Hawaii with Phyllis Day. Norman knew that he was indirectly meddling in his son's personal life, but there was simply too much at stake. Norman justified his actions by the fact that this was not a World War where the country was struggling for survival. No, his son was not going to die in that stinking malaria infested country in support of that Cowboy in the White House and a grossly corrupt South Vietnamese government. No way.

When the Phyllis and Bernadette returned from shopping, Phyllis ran across the lanai to Bud, threw her arms around his neck and kissed him. His face flushed with embarrassment as his father sipped brandy and observed the affectionate scene. Although there had been no talk of an engagement, Norman Cotter's instincts told him that this effervescent little beauty would soon have his son's ring on her finger. Once married, she would become the greatest influence in her husband's life. Therefore Norman decided, once the engagement was formally announced, he would begin to slowly form a special alliance with Phyllis. He decided that the best way to begin was to bring her around very gradually. Obviously she was no dummy, and he didn't want her to suspect in the slightest way that he would be taking her on one of his famous guided discoveries. The end result would be that Phyllis's influence would steer her husband out of the navy and straight into the Cotter family business.

That evening rare thunderstorms formed in the mountains above Honolulu, it was raining periodically over the harbor as the winds moved the storms across the southern side of the island. The stewards served dinner in the formal dining room. June Chandler and Phyllis sat at opposite ends of the long table and ignored one another. Bud noticed that Phyllis was unusually quiet at dinner. He assumed that she must be tired from the day of shopping. The dinner conversation revolved around the Wai Momi Hotel project, and Norman made the announcement of June Chandler's new position as Director of Personnel and Training.

Full of scallops, abalone and shrimp, Bud and Phyllis excused themselves and walked out onto the lanai. It had stopped raining.

"Let's take a drive," Phyllis said. "I want to be alone with you, and it's such a beautiful evening."

"Okay. I'll get the car."

With the top up, Bud drove out highway 93 to Makaha where he parked the car at a place overlooking Pokai Bay.

"This is a gorgeous place," Phyllis said, "let's walk on the beach."

"Okay." Bud took a large blanket from the trunk and spread it under a clump of thick palm. The couple kicked off their shoes and walked hand in hand along the beach. After a long silence, Phyllis said, "June Chandler and I had a talk this morning."

"You did? Tell me about it."

"Well, we were very civil. There were no harsh words. She dropped a bomb on me, and well, I kind of dropped one on her."

"What kind of bomb? What are you talking about?"

"She told me about your father hiring her and that she would be moving out here in November."

"Oh, so you knew about that before Daddy announced it at dinner."

"Yes, I knew about it and I don't like it. It scares me that she is going to be living here so close to you. How convenient that she manipulated her way to Honolulu. It's no coincidence, you know. I hate it!"

"Phyllis, Sweetheart. It doesn't make any difference. She'll be living downtown. We'll never see her. Besides, I'm going to be in WestPac for at least ten months."

"Ten months," Phyllis repeated reflectively, "a lot of things can happen in ten months."

"What are you talking about?"

"I'm talking about you being away so long. I don't know how I'll manage without you, Baby. I'll be lost without you."

"You'll be fine, Sweetheart. You have your work to keep you occupied and Sandra will be there if you need her."

"You make it sound so simple and nicely packaged. I'm sorry, but I don't share your optimism."

"What can I do to make it easier for you, for us?"

"Don't go to Vietnam. Stay here with me."

"You know I can't do that. Besides, the navy doesn't work that way."

"The truth is you would go even if they said you could stay here. That's how you are."

Bud said nothing. A long silence ensued as the couple stood looking out at the reflection of the moon across the sea.

"What bomb did you drop on June Chandler?"

Phyllis turned away from him. "Oh, it's not really important, just woman talk."

Her grasped her shoulder and gently turned her around. "Yes it is important, Phyllis. Tell me what went on."

She looked at him with big wondering eyes and she began to cry.

"Phyllis, what's the matter with you? Why are you crying?"

She sniffed, "Oh, this is so stupid. It's nothing really, let's just forget it."

"No, we're not going to forget it! What is it that you don't want to tell me, Phyllis? I thought we didn't have secrets between us."

Her bottom lip trembled when she looked at him. "I told her that I missed my period this month."

He stared at her, his face reflecting incomprehension. "Why would you tell her something like that?"

Phyllis touched his face with her hand. "Oh, God, Baby, you are so innocent, and I love you so very very much. When a woman misses a period, it usually means that she's pregnant."

Bud took a step back. His face went blank as a fish. The impact of what Phyllis had said slowly absorbed into his brain.

"But what about those pills you take?"

"This isn't supposed to happen while I'm on birth control. I talked to one of the GYN doctors at work. A very low percentage of women, less than one percent can and do get pregnant even though they are on the pill. The doctor told me not to worry, that it is probably just a simple hormonal adjustment my body is making. If I miss another period, he wants to see me."

His head was swirling through the horrifying repercussions of her announcement. He felt panicky inside. What was he, what were they going to do?

Phyllis sensed his inner turmoil. "Listen, it's okay, baby, nothing is your fault. If I am pregnant, it's my problem to deal with. I'll have the pregnancy terminated and that'll be the end of it."

"What! No you won't! That's murder, Phyllis! You're talking about murdering our child!"

"Oh, God, Bud Cotter, do you have to be so Catholic!" She broke down and began to cry. "Can't you understand? I don't want you to feel like you are being trapped or forced into anything. I'm not ready for the responsibility of raising a baby, especially alone. Oh, this is all my fault."

"No it isn't. It's nobody's fault, Phyllis, and I would never abandon you or our child."

He was beginning to think clearer now. His mind was racing through contingencies.

"How do you find out if you really are pregnant?"

"I have to go to the doctor and have a test done. It takes a few days for the lab to get the results. I haven't done it because I'm so afraid of what the outcome will be."

"Okay," Bud said with conviction. "First things first: you have the test done and when we get the results, we'll decide what to do from there. Does that sound like a reasonable first step?"

"Oh, Bud." She threw her arms around him and wept.

Bud didn't sleep very well that night. He was up early the next morning and sat glumly on the lanai sipping coffee. June Chandler appeared and sat across the table from him. A steward poured coffee and juice for her.

"You look tired," she said.

"Yeah, I didn't sleep much. I have a lot on my mind right now."

"I assume Phyllis told you."

He looked at June, "Yeah, she told me."

"I'm sorry, Bud, for you, for Phyllis, and for me."

"I suppose you predicted this would happen," he said with a note of sarcasm.

"No, actually it never occurred to me that something like this would happen. If she's been on the pill for any length of time, there is a high probability that she isn't pregnant. Regardless, I do believe that Phyllis is manipulating you and taking advantage of your inexperience."

He shook his head. "I don't believe that. I'm convinced that she is sincere. I may be naïve about some things, but I'm not stupid."

"She has every reason to do so. You are heir to a large fortune. Someday you and Bernadette will inherit Cotter Communications whether you want it or not."

Bud wrinkled his mouth in disgust, "June that is a shitty thing to say. For your information, Phyllis knew absolutely nothing about the family business until this week. We never talked about it, not once."

"Under the circumstances, I find that incredibly hard to believe."

"Well, it's true. It doesn't make any difference whether you believe it or not."

"Are you going to marry her?"

"Someday, if she'll have me."

"Oh, she'll have you. You don't have to worry about that."

"I had planned to ask her when I got back from WestPac. If she's pregnant I'll have to ask her sooner."

"Did it occur to you that she may have gotten pregnant intentionally?"

Bud snapped a fierce look at June. "I don't believe that! If she is pregnant, she wants to have an abortion."

"She told you that?"

"Yes, and I had a fit. Killing a baby is murder as far as I'm concerned."

"But Phyllis doesn't agree with that?"

"I don't think she believes that terminating a pregnancy is murder. The issue never came up until last night."

"A lot of women, including some very misguided Catholics, believe that abortion is simply a convenient method of birth control."

"What do you believe?"

"I agree with you. I believe that aborting a normal pregnancy as a method of birth control is murder. There may be extenuating circumstances that could possibility justify a woman having an abortion, but whatever the case it amounts to killing a baby."

A steward appeared and asked if the couple was ready for breakfast. Both declined and had their coffee cups refilled.

"So have you said anything to Mama or Bernadette about this?"

"Of course not, Bud. It's not my place to get involved. I'm out of the picture now. That's what I came out here to tell you. I'm flying back to Nashville this morning. I won't be back to Honolulu until November."

"Listen, June. I really do appreciate you coming out here. I'm truly sorry that I've hurt you. I didn't know how you really felt. Maybe I should have been aware, but I wasn't. I'm sorry if your trip was ruined."

She smiled, "Actually it's been quite productive. Your father has given me a wonderful opportunity. Who knows, maybe someday things will be different. We'll just have to wait and see." She rose from the table. "Well, goodbye, Bud. I wish you and Phyllis all the best." She withdrew into the house.

"Sorry I had to call you in while you're on sick leave, Cotter," Jack Ferguson motioned Bud to a chair. "Have a seat."

"What's going on, Skipper?"

"You have an appointment with CINCPAC."

"CINCPAC!"

"That's right, Lad, here." Ferguson handed the envelope to Bud.

Bud's eyes scanned the orders. "CINCPAC Staff, what the hell is this?"

"It's orders for you to report to CINCPAC Operations Officer."

Bud's face suddenly glowed crimson, and his hands began to tremble. He jumped out of the chair and began to pace in front of Ferguson's desk. "Goddamn it! This is bullshit! What the hell is going on?"

"I think it's bullshit too, Cotter, but orders are orders. You don't have a choice."

"Yes I do. I can resign my commission and get out of this chicken-shit Navy!"

Ferguson allowed the insubordination to pass. He patiently waited while Bud paced back and forth. "Okay, Lad, sit down and let's get rational."

Bud dropped into the chair. "I know my old man had something to do with this. This makes me want to puke!"

Ferguson lit a Camel and sat back in his chair. "What's your old man got to do with this?"

Bud answered through gritted teeth. "My daddy and Admiral Sharp are big buddies from the war, and I guarantee you that my old man talked the Admiral into this to keep me from going WestPac. I know it as well as I'm sitting here, goddamn it!" He struck his fist on the arm of the chair.

"He'd have to be a Congressman or a Senator to have that kind of pull, Lad."

"You don't know my father, Skipper. He knows everybody who's anybody and he gets things done. He may have had Vice President Nixon involved for all I know."

Ferguson's eyebrows signaled astonishment. "He knows Nixon?"

"Yeah, and a lot of other people too."

"Jesus, Lad."

"You see what I'm up against, Skipper?"

The Commanding Officer understood. He sympathized with his young officer but there was nothing to be done. He didn't have a lot of time to waste.

"You've got two options," Ferguson said sharply. "You can show up at CINCPAC as ordered or you can submit a letter of resignation. You've got twenty-four hours to decide. Report back to me at 0900 tomorrow, questions?"

"No, Skipper." Ferguson's sudden all business manner shook Bud out of his red curtain of anger.

"Okay, that's it, Cotter. I've got a lot of work to do."

Bud left Ferguson's office and went straight to a downtown jewelry store where he bought a diamond engagement ring. He put the velvet covered box in his pocket. He was waiting for Phyllis when she came out of the hospital at the end of her shift. She slid onto the front seat next him and kissed him lovingly.

“Baby, this is a wonderful surprise.”

“Things have changed. We have to talk.”

“What do you mean things have changed? Is it something that will affect us?”

“It affects everything. I received instructions today to report to CINCPAC.”

“Oh. Well what does that mean, Baby?”

“We can talk about it over dinner. I’ve reserved a suite at the Queens Surf.”

“Wonderful! Take me home so I can change and pack a bag.”

When they finished dinner, the couple sat on the balcony overlooking Waikiki. Tourists and local surfers were scattered along the beachfront, walking, swimming, sun bathing and surfing in the gentle waves. Hawaiian steel guitar music floated serenely through the palms from hidden speakers. Bud remembered staying in this garish but elegant hotel with his parents when he was very young.

Bud tasted brandy and said, “Did you have the test done today?”

“Yes. It’ll be a few days before we have the result.”

“We’ve got to make some heavy decisions, Phyllis. I can’t make them alone. I need your help.”

“Of course, Baby. What can I do?”

“I’ve got two options as far as the Navy goes. There is a good possibility that I’m going to be reassigned to CINCPAC staff. So, I can accept the job or I can submit a letter of resignation.”

“What do you want to do?”

"I came into the Navy to fly. I can see that flying jets isn't going to happen. Accepting a job at CINCPAC will land me behind a desk. I'll be a flunky running errands for the admiral. That's not how I intend to spend my naval career."

"What will you do if you resign your commission?"

"I don't know. Maybe I'll go fly for the airlines."

"Would that be so bad?"

"It's not what I want to do for the rest of my life."

"What do you want to do?"

He looked at her as though she had said something particularly silly. "I don't know. I've thought about going back to school and get a Doctorate in physics. Then I could teach or do research."

Phyllis drank wine and studied his face. She loved this man so deeply and she wanted desperately to be part of his life, to be his partner, his wife. She didn't care what career path he chose just as long as they could be together.

"I think," Phyllis said hesitantly, "that you should go to the appointment at CINCPAC. At least give it a chance and see what the job is all about. If it evolves into something you can't tolerate, then you can always resign and do something else."

"I don't guess that I have a lot of options at the moment." He looked at her and gently kissed her. "Okay, Sweetheart, that's what I'll do. I've got a lot of time and effort invested in the navy, and the navy has a lot of time and money invested in me. I guess I can give it a shot. No doubt this is exactly the way the old man had it played."

"What makes you think that your father caused this?"

"Because of the timing, I'm not due for orders. All this just popped up out of the blue after I crashed up at French Frigate

Shoals. Daddy and Admiral Sharp are very close friends. To me it's obvious what happened."

"If your father did do this, he did it to protect you, because he loves you."

"Maybe so, but my father has no goddamn business meddling in my life! All he cares about is getting me into the family business, and that's not going to happen!"

They sat silent for a while. Bud poured more brandy into the snifter, sampled it and said to her. "Since it appears that I'm going to working here at CINCPAC, I want to know how you feel about us getting a place together. I'd like to get out of BOQ living and maybe rent a small house. What do you think?"

"Oh, my God, Bud. Are you serious?"

"Very."

She appeared perplexed and out of sorts, "But what about Sandra? She can't afford the whole rent for the house. I can't just desert her."

"I'm sure Shug Early will take care of your half. He practically lives over there now."

Phyllis hesitated and looked down into her lap. "No he doesn't, Baby, not anymore. I haven't told you yet, but Sandra and Shug have broken up. She told me at work this morning."

"Broken up! Why that's fantastic! I don't believe it!"

"There's really only one way to say this, Baby. It seems as though Shug and your sister Bernadette have become an item."

"What! You're kidding me, Phyllis!"

"Baby, I wish I were."

"He's out of his goddamn mind! Bernadette changes boyfriends about as often as people change their socks. He's an idiot! Wait until I get my hands on him!"

"Sandra is devastated. She feels thrown, betrayed and cheap. She is a very hurt and angry woman right now. I understand her feelings completely."

Bud was wagging his head, "I guess she is devastated. How could she not be? I just can't believe that Shug Early could be this stupid! I would expect this from Bernadette but not Shug. He and Sandra were practically engaged weren't they?"

"Yes, and she is still head over heels in love with him. I don't know what she's going to do now."

"Jesus Christ, that stupid son of a bitch!"

"I wish you wouldn't talk like that, Baby."

Suddenly he became contrite. "I'm sorry, Sweetheart. This is just so unbelievable. I just can't believe he would do something this reckless."

Phyllis said, "I should have known something was going on that night at the dinner party because Shug didn't bring Sandra. I thought it was odd that Sandra wasn't there with Shug. I remember thinking that maybe she didn't feel well or maybe she had been called into work. After I told you good night, I went back out on the lanai. Shug and Bernadette were not there. I didn't think anything about it. After that, I noticed Bernadette and Shug together on a couple of other occasions. They appeared innocent enough, sitting and talking or playing piano. Since they like to entertain and play the piano together, I had no reason to suspect anything was going on. Boy was I gullible."

Bud just shook his head slowly. He didn't want to believe it. It was almost too fantastic to grasp. He was convinced that

Bernadette was the culprit here. He knew how flighty and fickle she could be, especially with men.

"Well, this complicates us getting a place together, doesn't it? We can't leave Sandra hanging with a house and rent that she can't afford."

"I know, Baby."

"Then we'll wait. Sandra needs you now. If you moved out now, it might put her over the edge. Once she is better, we can start looking for a place, and maybe you and Sandra could find another girl to move in with her."

They sat silent for a while and watched the people on the beach.

Then it occurred to Bud the main reason that he had brought Phyllis here. He reached into his pocket and withdrew the box containing Phyllis's engagement ring. He opened the box and removed the ring. He slid the ring onto her left hand. "I want you to marry me, Phyllis."

She gasped and held her chest. Her eyes sparkled with awe and wonder. Then tears burst forth and she began to shed tears. He held her, and waited for her to stop weeping. He lovingly stroked her hair and face.

"I love you, Sweetheart. I want to be with you for the rest of my life."

Phyllis sat up straight and faced him. She took a Kleenex from a box on the table and wiped her eyes. She took the ring off her finger and admired it.

"This is the most wonderful moment of my life, Bud. Oh, I can't get over how incredibly beautiful this ring is." She wiped her nose and looked at him, not smiling.

"I'm sorry, Baby, but I can't accept this, not now."

His mouth fell open. "What! Why can't you? Don't you want us to be married?"

"I want to marry you more than you can possibly imagine, but this isn't right. You're doing this because you know I might be pregnant."

"Look, Phyllis. I intended to wait until I got back from WestPac to ask you. I didn't want to go to Vietnam and get killed and leave you hanging. But now things have changed. It looks like I'll be staying here, so there's no reason why we shouldn't get engaged and get married. I want to marry you pregnant or not."

She crushed him with a loving embrace and burst into tears again. When she had composed herself, she gave the ring to him. Bud took it and put it back on her finger.
"Will you marry me, Sweetheart?"
"Yes! Oh, God yes! I love you so much!" She began kissing him, her hands slipped under his shirt and began to roam and soon the couple fell onto the bed and became lost in a fervid erotic passion.

Chapter 16

WESTPAC

Captain Ridley Remington, CINCPAC Operations Officer began his naval career as a seaman apprentice in 1947. At age twenty-one as a Second Class Petty Officer, Remington applied for and was accepted to the US Naval Academy at Annapolis. Upon graduation, Ensign Remington went to sea as a line officer. Throughout the years he rose to command the heavy cruisers Portland and Chicago and later on, Cruiser Division Seven. He had a reputation as a tough no-nonsense naval officer. He was considered to be one of the toughest disciplinarians in the Pacific Fleet.

The young pilot waited outside Captain Remington's office. He arrived ten minutes early for his 0900 appointment. The Captain's yeoman, a husky mannish WAVE in summer whites greeted Bud, offered him coffee and directed him to have a seat. The Captain kept him waiting until 0910. When the Captain signaled with a buzzer, the WAVE rose and opened the door for Bud.

"Captain Remington will see you now, Lieutenant," she said with a curt smile.

"Thank you."

The Captains office was bright, cluttered with brass nautical ornaments and adorned with sea paintings in heavy frames, most of which Bud thought were paintings of battleships and cruisers. The Captain sat behind a massive mahogany desk with a large black pipe clenched between his teeth. Captain Remington's gray crew cut hair receded deeply at the brow above bushy black and gray eyebrows. He had thin lips, a mouth like a pencil line and steel gray, penetrating eyes. The Captain was quite intimidating as the young officer stood nervously in front of his desk.

"Have a seat, Lieutenant," Remington said without looking up. He was reading Bud's service record. On his desk were stacks of file folders and official papers. It appeared that the Captain had been working for several hours.

"Thank you, sir."

Without preamble, the Operations Officer said, "Your report on the egress from your aircraft in heavy seas was excellent, Lieutenant. CINCPAC has directed COMNAVAIRPAC to disseminate the report and to develop a plan to utilize this information in a new fleet-wide training syllabus."

"Thank you, sir."

The Captain shifted in his chair and peered at the young officer. "Now, Lieutenant Cotter, I've been directed by Admiral Sharp to offer you the option of accepting a staff position here at CINCPAC. You would be detached from VC-110 and reassigned as personal flag assistant to CINC-PAC. This is a highly coveted position because it practically guarantees quick promotion up the career ladder. Given this unusual levity, I'll ask you, will you accept this staff position or do you prefer to remain in your present position with your squadron?"

Without hesitation, Bud said, "I'd like to remain with my squadron, sir."

Remington's bushy eyebrows went to full elevation. Sparks and a volcanic cloud of smoke rose out of the Captain's pipe. He stared at the young officer and pulled the pipe out of his mouth.

"Lieutenant, CINCPAC himself has spent a great deal of time and effort arranging this opportunity for you. Be advised that refusing such an offer could have far reaching career repercussions. This is an unheard of opportunity for a junior officer. This billet is normally staffed by an O-4."

Unwavering, Bud returned the Captain's eye. "Captain, I understand completely, however sir, I feel that I must respectfully decline the admiral's most generous offer for two reasons: First, I do not want to deprive a more deserving officer the opportunity to serve in this position. A position that I believe, I have not merited on my own accord. Second, and most important to me, I want to serve the Navy by putting to use all of the extensive training that I have received. Captain Remington, with all due respect, sir, please convey my sincere gratitude to the admiral for offering me this opportunity."

The captain sat back and regarded the young officer for several moments. "Very well, Lieutenant. I will advise the admiral of your decision. I admire your courage and your sense of duty. Frankly speaking, if I were in your position I suspect I would do the same thing." The Captain closed Bud's folder and placed it into a basket. "You will receive orders to return to VC-110 within the next few days. In the meantime, you will check in with my yeoman by telephone each morning at 0800." Remington looked straight at Bud, "Any questions, Lieutenant?"

"No, sir."

Remington returned the pipe to his mouth and turned his attention to the papers on his desk. "Good day, Lieutenant."

"Thank you, sir"

Phyllis was watching TV and waiting for Bud to return from his appointment. Throughout the morning, she worried over Bud's appointment at CINCPAC. She desperately wanted him to stay here in Honolulu, but she knew in her heart that he wanted to fly and that he would be unhappy working for the admiral. When she heard Bud walk through the door, she jumped off the rattan couch and ran to him.

"Oh, my, God, Baby. I've been on pins and needles. Tell me what happened."

Bud began to describe the interview with Captain Remington. "The bottom line is, Sweetheart, they gave me a choice: work at CINCPAC or return to VC-110. I couldn't believe it. I tell you what Sweetheart, I feel like a huge load has been lifted off me. I'm going back to the squadron where I belong."

Tears rose into her eyes and Phyllis began to softly weep as he held her. He understood that she wanted him to stay here, but that was impossible, unthinkable to him. By accepting a soft staff position, he would be betraying his squadron mates, his country and most of all, himself.

"I know you have to go back. I'll go along with anything you decide," she sniffed. "I love you so much, Baby. If you are not happy with what you are doing, I wouldn't be happy either. I will never come between you and your work. I will always support the career that you choose."

"Sweetheart, I love you very very much."

The couple walked hand in hand along the beach at Waikiki. They remained in the hotel suite until Bud received his orders to return to VC-110. During this time, Bud drove Phyllis to work and retrieved her at the end of each day. The young couple spent long hours making love and making plans for the time and place of their wedding. They decided it would best to wait until Bud returned from WestPac in June of 1968. It would be a magnificent wedding. Their families and friends would attend a grand celebration with the island of Oahu as the backdrop. In the event that Phyllis is pregnant, then they would marry right away in a private ceremony.

Three days later two significant things took place in the lives of Bud Cotter and Phyllis Day. He received his orders to VC-110 and Phyllis received the lab report. She was not pregnant.

The couple checked out of the hotel. As they had discussed, Phyllis would remain in the house with Sandra and Bud would return to the BOQ. While Bud was on the WestPac deployment, Phyllis would find a suitable apartment or small house for Bud and herself. This would allow plenty of time for Sandra to find a compatible housemate.

"Now, son," Shug Early said backing away with hands turned flat towards Bud, "don't start a fight before you've heard the whole story."

"I can't believe this shit, Early, and with my sister! What the hell is the matter with you?"

"First of all," Shug said nervously, "Bernadette and I didn't do anything wrong. We didn't have sex or anything like that, I swear. We just hit it off real well because we have a lot in common, especially music and our Southern backgrounds, that kind of shinola, you know."

"Okay, so you two hit it off. What about, Sandra? You dumped her like she's a tramp who meant nothing to you. Phyllis says Sandra damn near had a nervous breakdown."

"You need to understand, son, Sandra and I have been having a lot of problems lately. I broke it off with her the night before I met Bernadette. Meeting Bernadette had nothing to do with the break-up with Sandra. She's been putting a real squeeze on me to get married. She tries to be in control of everything. She doesn't like it when I play golf. She doesn't want me to go anywhere if she's not along. She even calls me at work to check on me. Son, I just can't deal with living with a woman who wants to dominate my life like that."

There was a long pause, "Okay, I can understand all that, but what about you and Bernadette? What kind of relationship do you have with her?"

"I told you already that everything is on the up and up. We didn't sleep together, so you can quit fretting over that. It's like this, son. Bernadette is going back to school and work on a doctorate. She'll be in Nashville living at home and I'll be here or maybe in a squadron where I can fly. We're going to write to each other and make telephone calls and see how things work out."

"What did you mean when you said that you may be in a squadron? You're on COMFAIR Hawaii staff. I thought you loved the job."

"I do love it, but after rooming here with you and after listening to you talk about flying all the time, and then going out on the Connie for Carquals, well, I finally realized that even though I barely scraped through flight school, I want to fly."

"Have you requested orders?"

Shug grinned. "The same day we got the word that you had been picked up, and I asked for orders to VC-110. I know you guys are short of pilots. Captain Locke said that he would help me all he could. I talked to your skipper, Jack Ferguson. He said he'd be glad to have me. So I'm hoping that maybe I have a chance. Now it's all up to the bureau."

"Jesus, lad, you do realize that we're deploying WestPac in a few weeks, don't you? If you get orders, you'll never get qualified in time."

"Ferguson told me that if I get orders to VC-110 he would get me checked out in the Skyraider one way or another. He said that he would use me as the squadron utility and ferry pilot at Danang."

"Shug, you have surprised the hell out of me. I thought you just wanted to stay here in Hawaii and play golf and sit on your duff. Well, lad, I hope all this works out for you. It would be great to have you in the squadron, and that way I can keep track of what you and my sister are up to."

"I have only the most honorable of intentions with your sister."

"Bullshit," Bud grinned, "let's go get a beer and a pizza."

Lieutenant Commander Tom "Popcorn" Seckman had recently been elevated to the position of VC-110 Training Officer and Chief NATOPS Check Pilot. He had a humped nose, sugar bowl ears and bristly brown hair. He looked like someone who would be found behind a team of mules in a cornfield rather than at the controls of naval aircraft. Seckman came from rural Indiana. His family was in the popcorn business and owned a small processing plant south of Terre Haute at Vigo, Indiana. Tom Seckman planned to be a career Naval Officer, and like Bud he had no desire to become involved in his family's business.

"Glad to have you back Cotter," Seckman grinned and extended a hand. Bud always liked Seckman and now he had even more reason to like him.

"Thanks, sir," Bud said gratefully.

"Call me, Tom, I like to keep things informal around here."

"Okay, Tom."

"Okay, here's the deal," said Seckman, "I've got you scheduled to begin flying with me tomorrow morning. We'll get you re-current on carquals and up to speed on procedure for carrier ops on Yankee and Dixie Stations. As you know, we're running short on pilots. Now the squadron has evolved into a situation where we have more aircraft than we have trained people to fly them." Seckman sat back in his chair. "We're at the bottom of the personnel list when it comes to getting replacement pilots. The VC squadrons suck hind tit behind everybody. It's like the Bureau forgets we are even out here. Problem is the workload doesn't change. That's why they formed the Danang Detachment, because the attrition rate is expected to be high."

"Why do we expect a high attrition rate?"

"Mostly because our assignments will be SAR and close air support. The bad guys have a lot of 23mm and 37mm AA weapons. They are mobile and easy to conceal. A gunner who really knows what he's doing can cut a low flying Skyraider in half with one of those new Russian rapid fire 23's." Seckman took out a pack of gum and offered Bud a stick. "Gum?"

"No thanks."

The training officer peered at Bud. "By the way, Cotter, I've been meaning to ask you, how the hell did you get out of that inverted bird up at Tern Island?"

"A lot of luck, and using all the training we've had. The main thing was that all the emergency stuff worked. I still don't know how I got into the raft."

Seckman smirked knowingly. "Yeah, I know what you mean, Cotter. Getting into one of those rafts is like trying to catch a greased pig."

"Yeah, that's for sure," Bud laughed.

Chapter 17

Danang, South Vietnam

The waters of the Han River have been Danang's fortune and its misery. In the 19th century, the city was the nation's most important port, and that very accessibility inspired the French to invade in 1858, renaming the city Tourane. The beaches of Danang drew foreign invaders again a century later, when the first wave of American marines came ashore at Red Beach in 1965 to establish an airfield. Danang's nearby beaches became a recreational retreat for recuperating or relaxing soldiers who came to R&R stations such as China Beach.

The Navy took formal control of the I Corps logistic establishment on 15 October 1965, when it established Naval Support Activity, Danang. The logistic establishment at Danang functioned with growing efficiency by mid-1968 as it built new port and shore facilities. Seabees, initially using materials pre-stocked long before the war in Advanced Base Functional Component packages, constructed three deep-draft piers for oceangoing ships, two 300-foot wooden piers, an LST causeway, and the Bridge Cargo Complex that consisted of a 1,600-foot-long wharf, 300,000 cubic feet of refrigerated storage space, and 500,000 square feet of covered storage space. Amphibious fuel lines were laid along the sea floor to storage tanks ashore at Red Beach north of the city, and at the Navy-Marine air facility at Marble Mountain to the south.

Finally, the harsh Northeast Monsoon made cargo operations at Danang and throughout I Corps hazardous and difficult during the winter months. From 1966 to 1968, however, new resources and management procedures dramatically improved the situation. By July 1968 the Naval Support Activity handled 350,000 tons of cargo each month for the 200,000 allied troops in I Corps. Danang had become the largest fuel complex in South Vietnam capable of holding over 500,000 barrels.

The station hospital begun in 1965 had treated over 21,000 casualties, 44,000 non-combat patients, and one million outpatients flowing in from the hostile and disease-ridden I Corps environment.

USS Hornet CVS-12 departed Pearl Harbor on 3 October 1967. Three hours later, as Diamond Head faded on the distant horizon, twenty-five A1-H Skyraiders of VC-110 trapped aboard her flight deck. Hornet transited the vast Pacific and made a port call in Yokouska, Japan where she officially relieved the USS Bennington CVS- 20.

Hornet departed Yokouska on 11 October, transited Western Pacific waters and steamed into the South China Sea. On the morning of 18 October the aircraft of VC-110 flew off to their new home at Danang Airfield. The Skyraiders were directed to a section of the field known as Area Sierra. The following day, VC-110 ground support personnel and equipment arrived at Danang from Hawaii aboard three giant C-141 Air Force transport aircraft. The next two weeks were intense and a frenzy of long hot and humid days as the squadron organized itself and became accustomed to the routine at Danang. Squadron aircraft were staged inside individual revetments to protect them from incoming mortar and rocket attacks. As the squadron awaited orders to begin its training and familiarization schedule, the maintenance crews worked feverishly to prepare the aircraft for combat operations.

"Man," Bud complained to Sonny Miles, "this place is hotter than the hubs of hell." The two officers were sitting in the squadron operations Quonset hut studying charts of I Corps. Ceiling fans slowly rotated above moving the oppressive air providing little cooling.

"Yeah, this heat and humidity is brutal. The word from the weather guys is that it will cool off in the next few weeks.

Even if it doesn't, the skipper has Red Lead and his crew of cumshaw pirates on a mission to appropriate air conditioners for our Quonsets."

"You know what makes the heat and humidity so bad," said Bud "is this sitting around doing nothing, when are we going to start flying something besides training and test hops?"

"I don't know," Miles said as he lit a cigar, "typical Navy hurry up and wait. They haul us all the way out here from BP and when we get here, we sit on our ass. The Skipper's in a meeting over at base ops now, he thinks the meeting may be related to activating the squadron."

"Well, I hope so. This sitting around is no good."

Ferguson returned from his meeting at operations at 1530. He called a meeting of all officers and chiefs in the ready room Quonset hut.

"Okay, people, here's the straight skinny. We are going to begin flying training and familiarization sorties three days from now."

A cheer went up. This was the news they had been waiting for. Everyone agreed that it's better to get shot at than to rot in the heat and humidity.

"Okay, okay, knock it off," Ferguson said as he stubbed a cigarette. "We will be flying training familiarization missions for the next two weeks. This is to get everybody oriented with the areas where we will be operating. We will be in contact with Marine FAC's and coordinate simulated SAR and ground support missions. We will also receive vectors and intercept information from CATTC, E-1B's out over the gulf. Questions?"

Seckman spoke up. "Skipper, what happens if we get incoming AA fire?"

"While we're training, orders are to call in fast movers from the carriers to take care of the situation. Nobody does any firing. We are not yet familiar enough with area to try and do any ground support fire. If the Marines call for an air strike, the carriers will have to handle it."

That night they received their first taste of real shooting. VC (Viet Cong) guerrillas fired mortar and rockets into the base. The men scrambled into sandbagged bunkers, some of them in their skivvies, some who had been in the shower were naked except for flip flops. The fire was sporadic and lasted about ten minutes. The firing stopped when Marine Cobra helos got off the ground and began dropping flares over suspected areas. All of the new hands, Bud Cotter included, were badly scared. The reality that they were in a shooting war fell upon them like a pall.

17 November 1967, VC-110 was released from a training status and ordered to begin conducting combat operations. Ferguson pushed the squadron hard and the ground crews were getting a real workout refueling and rearming the Skyraiders two and sometimes three times per day. The pilots were gaining valuable experience, and they now knew the area from Danang to the DMZ, and the areas around the marine airstrip and combat base at Khe Sanh. They were also introduced to a very hot area known as the A Shau Valley.

Upon his return to VC-110 from temporary duty at CINCPAC, Bud Cotter had re-qualified in the Skyraider. Thanks to Tom "Popcorn" Seckman, Bud's re-qualification was basically a mere formality. Shortly before the squadron deployed to Hornet, Ferguson and Miles agreed to elevate Bud to section leader of Division 2. This assignment took him out of the Mad Dog division. Being elevated to section leader is a big step in a pilot's life. Bud now had a wingman, a young ensign named Jerry "Too Tall" Fletcher. The pair was a good match from the beginning and the two pilots quickly became friends. Too Tall was eager and enthusiastic and he worked hard. Bud patiently tutored the six foot two inch pilot who grew up in Cairo Illinois, a small farming community located near the convergence of the Ohio and Mississippi Rivers.

The annual Northwest monsoon was beginning to form as warm moist air moved up from the Indian Ocean spreading across Southeast Asia. Billowing cumulus formed and moved along the hills and mountains and spilled out over the Gulf of Tonkin. The squadron aircraft flew several SAR missions the first few days after they were released to combat duty. Mainly they provided top cover for SAR helos operating in I Corps. They assisted in the rescue of a number of downed pilots who had experienced battle damage or mechanical failure forcing them to egress their aircraft.

Thanksgiving Day dinner brought turkey, dressing and all the trimmings for the squadron. And with the good food came a longing to be home with family and friends. The officers and men of VC-110 dined together in the squadron mess hall. This was not unusual but rather the norm. Ferguson insisted that there would be no special officer's mess. The officers ate with the enlisted men in the same chow hall, and too, the officers and men shared the recreational facilities. A few of the officers, especially the two newly arrived non-flying ensigns who were Annapolis men, resented and grumbled over this integration of commissioned and enlisted personnel, but neither of them had the courage to challenge Ferguson.

Bud sat at a table eating his holiday dinner with Too Tall and PO3 JJ Searcy who was Bud's plane captain. A senior Chief Petty officer, new to the squadron dined with them also. Chief Bob Bradley, known as Pee Wee had arrived from East Coast duty at NAS Oceana, Virginia. Pee Wee worked with Chief Story sharing the demanding responsibilities of running AIMD, the squadron maintenance division.

Bud pushed his plate away, sat back and lit a cigar. Outside the long wooden mess hall it was raining hard, occasional bolts of lightning crackled and boomed as a line of thunderstorms passed across Danang and out into the sea.

"That was a fine dinner," Bud remarked, "the boys did a great job."

"We're lucky to get a stand down for today because of this weather," JJ said, "kind of gives everybody a chance to wind down a little."

"Yeah, no kidding," Bud replied, "We all needed a break. This flying two and three sorties a day is rough on everybody."

"I sure do miss being at home though," JJ said. "The holidays always make me a little homesick. My dad and my brothers and me always went deer hunting on Thanksgiving morning."

Too Tall lit a cigarette with a monogrammed lighter. "You know," he said, "back home daddy and my brothers and me always went goose hunting on Thanksgiving morning. Most of time we'd be back home by noon, Mama and Granny and my sisters would be cooking dinner, turkey and pies and all. The house always smelled really good, you know, like home is supposed to smell on Thanksgiving or Christmas."

Bud left the mess hall and ran two blocks through the rain to his room in the Q hut. Like everyone else, he was lonesome, and the dinner conversation about home and family made him feel even more melancholy. He missed Phyllis terribly. He wondered what she was doing on her Thanksgiving Day in Hawaii. He took out writing paper and pen and wrote to her:

November 22, 1967

My Love,

Today is Thanksgiving and I cannot truly express in words how much I miss you. These long weeks since we last parted have been really difficult because of the loneliness. As I sit here gazing at your picture, I wonder if I should have taken the job at CINCPAC, but I know that I could not live with myself if I had. This place, this country and this war are becoming more and more ingrained into our very being. The heat, the humidity, the long hours flying are becoming routine, and in an odd sense almost normal. We have justified our existence by assisting in the rescue of eleven pilots so far. Actually it's pretty boring around here, not at all what I was expecting. Mostly life is a dreary cycle of flying, sitting around and sleeping. Most of all, I spend the idle hours thinking of you. I daydream a lot about our wedding and how wonderful it will be having the families and friends with us in Hawaii. It will be the beginning of our lifetime of happiness together. There is nothing more important in my world than being married to you.

I love you and I miss you very very much. I want to hold you in my arms and kiss you and make love to you. I want us to be together and never again separated. I've been doing some thinking about life after the Navy. I'll tell you about it in another letter.

I Love you, Sweetheart, Bud

Four days following Thanksgiving Day, Bud was summoned to the Catholic Chaplain's office. The priest, solemn faced and sympathetic, held a Red Cross telegram in his hand. Phyllis had been killed in an auto accident. At first Bud was bewildered and completely shocked; then, as the truth penetrated into his mind and soul, he sat down in a chair and cried. It was the first time we had wept since he was a child.

That evening he managed to get a call through to his father in Nashville. Norman Cotter told his son that Phyllis's family was having her body flown to Topeka, Kansas, Phyllis's home town. The arrangements were not yet finalized. Norman told his son that he would notify him as quickly as the Day's called him.

Chapter 18

Doctor Whitefield

It was mid December and raining when a lonely and depressed Bud Cotter walked into the Officers Club at the Navy piers. He had been told that this club was quiet and somewhat cultured, not like that wild-ass Gunfighters O Club where loud music, shouting drunks and fights were the nightly norm. The club was crowded with officers, mostly naval officers wearing summer whites. The Maitre D flagged a waiter who led Bud to his table. Soft Tony Matola guitar Jazz floated throughout the club and Bud was pleasantly surprised to find a wine list lying on the table. Reviewing the list, he noted the selections were heavy on French vintages with California wines being listed on the back pages. A wine steward appeared and Bud ordered a bottle of California Pinot Noir.

While Bud sipped iced water and waited for the wine, a woman Bud guessed to be in her mid-twenties walked into the dining area and began surveying the tables. Moments later, the Maitre D approached the woman and with apologies, handed her a note. She read the note and chirped her disappointment. The person she was supposed to meet for dinner was unable to come, and worse, the person had neglected to make a reservation. The woman asked the Maitre D if he had a table for her. Once again he apologized and told the woman that there would be at least a one hour wait.

Overhearing this exchange, Bud decided to offer the woman the empty chair at his table. He stood. "Madam," he said, "I could not help but overhear your conversation with the Maitre D. You are welcome to sit here and dine with me." He indicated the chair with an open palm. The woman gave him a look appropriate to a fresh doorman. "Thank you, no, Lieutenant. I'm not here to be picked up."

Officers at surrounding tables smirked and exchanged glances intently observing the scene with amused curiosity.

Bud flushed, quite annoyed with the woman's attitude. "Madam, you'll do well not to flatter yourself," he said curtly, "I am not here to try and pickup you or anyone else. When I overheard your situation, I thought that offering a seat at my table was a decent thing to do. If you want to wait an hour, it makes no difference to me." He turned and sat down. The woman appeared to be entirely startled. She glowered at him, her eyes blazing with disbelief and astonishment. She hesitated, and said in a softer tone, "I do appreciate your offer, Lieutenant. It's just that I hear so many cheap pick up lines that it is difficult for me not to suspect a man's motives."

"Thank you, but it's not necessary to explain yourself," Bud replied, quite indifferently. He busied himself with the menu.

Obviously embarrassed the woman said, "I'm not very comfortable doing this, but I suppose that under the circumstances I will accept your offer, if of course, it is still open."

"Certainly it is." Bud stood and the Maitre D pulled the chair for her.

The woman nodded to the Maitre D, "Thank you." She adjusted her chair and said to Bud, "Please understand, Lieutenant that I will pay for my dinner."

"Why of course," he said. "I've ordered a bottle of Pinot Noir. I'll be happy to share it with you."

"Thank you, Lieutenant. I will pay for half."

Bud looked the woman directly in the eye. "No you won't. I ordered the wine and I'll pay for it."

"Lieutenant, I will not be put into a position that could possibly be construed as my being indebted to you."

Bud stared at her with a mystified grin. "Madam, what is your problem?"

"I told you, Lieutenant, I won't be indebted to you. You may have expectations of me that I cannot and will not deliver."

"Lady, I have no idea why you are talking this way. I have no expectations of you now or at anytime. For your information, I lost my fiancée two weeks ago. She was killed."

The woman's face immediately transformed from suspicion to sympathy. "Oh, Lieutenant, I'm so sorry. This makes me feel terrible."

"It's okay. You had no way of knowing about my situation."

The waiter appeared and poured iced water for the woman. Bud said to him, "Please bring the lady a wine glass." The waiter bowed, "of course, sir."

"By the way, my name is Bud Cotter."

She gave him quick guilty self-conscious smile. "My name is Margo Whitefield."

"Nice to meet you, Margo, is Margo a moniker for Margaret?"

"Marguerite."

"Beautiful name."

"Thank you. It's French. It was my great grandmother's name."

"Are you a naval officer?"

"No, I'm a civilian."

"You are? What in the world are you doing here?"

Margo looked at him and hesitated. "I am a medical doctor. I work in the Naval Hospital."

"Oh, really, well, I should address you as Doctor Whitefield."

"That won't be necessary. When I'm not working, I don't get hung up on titles. Margo will be fine."

The wine steward appeared and placed a wine glass in front of the doctor. He displayed the bottle for Bud's approval, a California Franciscan 1963 vintage.

"Very good, thank you."

The steward went about de-corking the bottle and pouring a small amount in Bud's glass. He nosed the bouquet, then swirled the wine looking at its leg. Finally he tasted the wine. The Pinot Noir was excellent. He nodded and smiled at the steward. The steward then poured wine for the couple.

"I see by your wings that you are a naval aviator," Margo said, "are you a fighter pilot? This Pinot Noir is very good."

"Yes it is, isn't it? No I'm not a fighter pilot. I fly propeller driven attack aircraft."

"Isn't that the same thing?"

Bud smirked. "Not exactly, fighter pilots fly jets high and fast. We fly low and slow. Primarily we provide suppression fire so that a rescue helicopter can get to a down pilot."

"I see. It sounds like hazardous work."

"It can be I suppose, but then it's nothing compared to the guys who fly downtown every day."

"Downtown?"

"Over Hanoi or Haiphong: in North Vietnam."

"Oh, I see. You know, Lieutenant Cotter," she said after a pause, "pardon me for saying this, but you really don't seem to fit the typical mold of navy or marine pilots I'm accustomed to."

Bud grinned. "As a matter of fact, you don't look a lot like an MD." Margo possessed lustrous auburn hair tucked into a French roll. She was quite pretty Bud thought, although she wore little makeup and she dressed conservatively in black pleated pants and a satiny white blouse.

"If I don't look like a doctor, what do you think I look like?"

Bud appeared pensive, "Oh, I don't know, maybe a business woman or an English teacher, something like that."

Margo appeared surprised. "Well that's a pleasant switch. You should hear some of the lines I get."

"I take it you must get a lot of come-on's."

"Since I've been here, yes."

The waiter came to the table and asked if they had made their meal selections. Margo asked for chicken cordon bleu. Bud asked for a thick rib eye.

"You'll die of arterial blockage eating like that," she said with a shadow of a smile.

"I might die tomorrow out over that stinking jungle. It's all relative."

Margo laughed. "Well, you've got a point there."

He poured wine into her near empty glass and refilled his own.

"Tell me," Margo said, "what happened to your fiancée?"

Bud sipped wine and straightened in his chair. "She was coming home from work. She was a civilian RN at Tripler Army Hospital in Honolulu. A large truck loaded with sugar cane lost its brakes and came barreling downhill through a red light. Phyllis couldn't see him coming because it was a blind corner with tall bushes that blocked the view. She was killed instantly." His bottom lip began to tremble. He sipped wine in an attempt to hide his emotions.

"I am so sorry, Lieutenant. This must really be difficult for you, especially being so isolated over here."

He sat with a faraway look in his eyes. "I never knew it was possible to feel such pain."

After a pause she said, "Did you go to the funeral?"

"No, I couldn't get transportation to Kansas in time for the funeral. Her family had her body brought back to Topeka, Kansas. They have a family burial plot there."

"That's really a shame, Lieutenant."

"My parents and sister flew up there for the funeral. It's probably better that it worked out this way. I don't think I could have handled seeing her in that casket." Tears welled in his eyes. He jumped up and turned away from her. "Please excuse me." He scurried off to the men's lavatory.

Margo Whitefield felt a great deal of sincere sympathy for him. She knew full well the devastation of losing a loved one. She had experienced the accidental death of her eldest brother when a tractor rolled over on him. Margo now realized too that Bud Cotter posed no threat to her. Strangely, he was like none of the pilots she had met, an arrogant horde of self-proclaimed hot shots who thought they were God's gift to women. Most were nothing but vulgar animals that wanted only to get her into bed. She knew all about those kinds of men and she genuinely loathed them. Oddly enough tonight, here was a guy who appeared to be much different, and he was grieving. She wasn't going to let her guard down, but she was relatively certain that Bud Cotter had no inappropriate ambitions toward her.

"Sorry about that," Bud said as he sat down at the table with reddened eyes.

"It's okay. I understand completely."

"So," he said changing the subject, "where did you go to medical school?"

"I went to Baylor Medical in Houston."

"A highly regarded school, are you from Texas?"

"No, I'm from Montana. Near a little town called Big Timber. It's in south central, Montana. I did my undergraduate course work at the University of Montana."

"Well, congratulations. I have some idea how hard you had to work to become a Doctor of Medicine. My best buddy back home is a doctor. He specialized in emergency medicine."

"What a coincidence," she said, "emergency medicine is my specialty also."

"So, how did you end up in Vietnam as a civilian?"

"After I finished my residency, I attempted to pursue a naval commission. Very quickly I learned that the Navy does not commission female doctors. A rather bizarre attitude, don't you think?"

"That is bizarre. I assumed the navy commissioned both men and women doctors. Actually, it is something I've never really thought about."

"Anyway, I wanted to serve the country, you know, help with the war effort in some capacity. So I signed a two year contract to come here. The Navy is perfectly willing to accept me as a female civilian doctor. They pay me a small fortune completely tax free, strange, very strange."

"Well, the Navy does a lot of strange things. You wouldn't believe some of the stuff that goes on in my world."

"Where did you go to school?"

"I went to Vanderbilt in Nashville, Tennessee. That's my home town."

"Vanderbilt, a very good school, their medical school is one of the finest in the country. Since you are an aviator, I suppose you majored in some type of engineering?"

"No, actually my major was physics, math was my minor."

"Physics and math," she exclaimed, "you certainly don't look like an egghead physicist to me."

"Sorry to disappoint you," he grinned self consciously, "you are having dinner with a genuine physics nerd, and I may as well confess all: Most of the time I listen to classical music, and I read Dickens, Thackeray, Kipling and Wouk for relaxation."

"A cultured rocket scientist and an aviator," she chortled, "that's truly a peculiar combination. The few physicists whom I've known seem to exist in some kind of mathematical postulating nirvana, most of them can hardly drive a car and here you are a naval aviator."

"Bud laughed. "Actually, I'm pretty normal, most of the time anyway. It just that, well, physics and math come easy to me. It was the path of least resistance to get me through college."

"Did you play sports?"

"Yeah, I played golf on the school team."

She sat back, her expression blending curiosity and amazement. "With your obvious cultured background and education, how in God's name did you get involved in naval aviation?"

"Oh, I learned to fly when I was a kid. We have an airstrip on our farm and I learned to fly in an old Travel-Air bi-plane that belongs to my grandfather. He taught me to fly. He'd let me solo around the farm when I was twelve. Later on, when I was old enough to get a license, my flight instructor, John Douglas who had been a navy fighter pilot during World War Two and Korea, told me stories about the Navy and all the stuff that he had done. I guess he was the catalyst that brought me to naval aviation, that plus Vanderbilt has Navy ROTC."

The dinner was served by two waiters and accompanied by much pomp and bowing. During the meal, the conversation lagged and focused mostly on Margo's work at the hospital. When they had finished eating, Bud said, "May I ask you a personal question?"

A shadow of suspicion crossed her face. "You'll have to ask first and then I'll let you know."

"Okay, well, I'm curious to know, as apprehensive as you seem to be about the men around here, why did you decide to have dinner with me?"

Margo stared at him, searching his face for a few moments. "For two reasons, I guess: the first reason is because you referred to me as madam, a very rare sign of etiquette that I am certainly not accustomed to. Obviously you are not some typical run of the mill sailor flyboy. The second reason, and probably the main reason, is because you very quickly put me in my place by telling me not to flatter myself. No one, no man has ever turned the tables and brought me up short like that. It was a shock to my system."

"Sorry," he said, a little embarrassed.

"Don't be," she said, "I had it coming. I was out of line speaking to you the way I did. My issue is that I get so many cheap come-ons that are so blatantly a hustle, that well, I find it impossible not to suspect a man's intentions, and as you could see, I can be rather boorish about it." She hesitated and appeared to be gathering her thoughts. "This is probably more information than I should share, but I'll tell you anyway. By nature, I am a very private person. I'm not the type of personality who reaches out to other people, except when I am practicing medicine of course, and that is strictly on a professional level. Conversely, I don't care to have people, especially strange men, reaching out to me, and no, I'm not lesbian if that's what you're thinking. I don't make a lot of friends by being this way, but the few friends I do have are very fine people that I can trust."

Bud drank wine and regarded her. He surmised that she was introverted and possibly borderline paranoid, especially about men and possibly about people in general.

"I think I understand," he said, "you put up kind of a safety net as a means of protecting yourself. The other thing that I perceive is that when guys approach you, you're aware that your femme fatale is the attraction, not you as an intelligent and gifted person."

Margo gave him a small dismal smile. "You've read me well. Among your other talents, you seem to be quite perceptive. Please understand I do not see myself as a beauty queen by any means, passable looks yes, but nothing more."

"I'm afraid that you underestimate yourself in that regard. Your appearance is clearly the main reason many men approach you like they do. And, I don't believe that I am perceptive at all. Phyllis used to tell me that I am probably the most naïve person in the world."

"Tell me this, if my appearance, my being a woman isn't the reason you offered me this chair, why did you ask me to join you?"

"Under the circumstances, I would have offered the chair to anyone, female or male. I was educated that way by my parents. It is the right thing to do. It's simply a question of good manners."

She tilted her head and blinked at him. "You know, I really do believe you would have offered that chair to any stranger."

"Of course I would have. I have nothing to gain by deceiving you about my motives. After tonight it is highly unlikely that we will ever see each other again."

"Yes, you're right of course."

"Well," Bud said, "are you having desert?"

"No, but I think I'd like coffee."

He flagged the waiter. "Please bring coffee for the lady and a snifter of cognac for me. Courvoisier if you have it."

The waiter bowed, "Very good, sir."

When the coffee and cognac were served, Bud said, "I think I'd like a cigar with my Courvoisier. Will you bring your coffee and join me on the veranda?"

A full look of suspicion masked her face, gradually relaxing as she fought off her native distrust. "I shouldn't. I really should be going. It's getting late and I have to work early tomorrow morning."

He nodded. "Me too, I have to fly early in the morning. I'll be leaving as soon as I finish the cognac."

She peered at him as though she were formulating some form of an analysis. After several moments she said, "Well, okay. I suppose that I can have coffee with you."

They moved to the veranda and found an empty table overlooking the harbor. Bud prepared and lighted a Partagas cigar.

"Do you smoke often?" Margo asked.

"Two or three cigars a week, I guess. I don't inhale the smoke, not much of it anyway. If I do inhale, I get sick."

"Why do you smoke if you don't inhale it?"

"Mostly because I enjoy the taste, cognac and cigars complement one another. My daddy smokes cigars. He taught me that a man can enjoy a fine cigar with brandy or cognac without inhaling."

"Oh, I see."

"Does my smoking offend you?"

"No, I think cigars and pipes are rather masculine in a skewed sort way."

"I assumed that since you are a physician you would object to smoking."

She smiled without showing teeth, "I didn't say that I approved of smoking. I merely meant to infer that your smoking a cigar doesn't offend me."

They were silent for a while. Looking out across the harbor they watched two slowly patrolling PBR gunboats. Occasionally one of the boats switched on a powerful spotlight to illuminate an object.

Margo broke the silence. "Lieutenant, when you're out flying, do you worry about getting shot down?"

"I did at first. I was really scared on the first few missions. After a while though, the 'it will never happen to me' mentality kicks in. What I worry about most is accidentally hitting our own guys. I cannot think of a worse scenario. And please call me Bud. Like you, I'm not a stickler about titles."

"Okay, Bud it is. How long will your squadron be here at Danang? Do you know?"

"We're scheduled to be here until June of next year. If nothing changes, we go back to our home base at Barbers Point in Hawaii."

The waiter appeared and handed Bud the check. Bud reviewed the check and said to the waiter, "I believe you neglected to charge me for the wine."

The waiter smiled and made a head motion in the direction of the dining area, "The three gentlemen who sat at the table next to you insisted on paying for your wine."

"They did? Who are they?"

"Other naval officers, sir, they didn't offer their names."

"I see. Hmm, well, that was certainly good of them. I'll have to go inside and thank them."

The waiter said, "I'm afraid they have already left, sir."

"Oh, I see. Well, it was good of them." Bud took some bills from his wallet and gave them to the waiter.

When the waiter was gone, Margo reached for her purse and said, "How much do I owe you, Bud?"

"Nothing, this one is on me."

"Oh, no, you can't do that, we agreed."

He held up his hand and tilted his head gesturing her to be silent. "Next time you can pay, and you don't owe me a damn thing. No expectations as you put it."

"Don't be ridiculous, Lieutenant, there will not be a next time and you know it! I don't like this! Not one bit! It's not what we agreed to do. Here, take this money, I insist."

"All I can say, Doctor Whitefield, is that you're going to have to suck it up and get over it."

She protested again but became silent when the waiter returned with Bud's change. He peeled off some bills and tipped the waiters.

"Well, I've got to get back," he said, "May I give you a lift? I've got a jeep outside."

"Thank you, no. I couldn't possibly do that. I'll call for the van."

Bud shook his head and gave her a look of complete frustration. "Jesus, Doctor, give it up. I'm going right by the hospital. It's absurd for you to wait around all alone while they get a van over here." He stood and gently pulled the chair for her. "Let's go, Doctor Whitefield."

She stared at him. "I can't believe that I am actually doing this."

"It won't hurt a bit," he grinned. "That's you doctors always tell your patients."

The circuitous ride across the base was accomplished mostly in silence. In the far distance, flares illuminated the night sky. Over the noise of the jeep's engine, Bud said, "Looks like the Marines are slugging it out with Charlie on Monkey Mountain. I hope it goes our way."

"Yes, so do I, it is so heartbreaking to see the terrible wounds when they bring us patients out of the field. It is all so tragic, so unnecessary."

Margo directed him to stop at a peaked roof building one block from the hospital. She got out of the jeep. "Thank you for the dinner and the ride, Bud. Take care when you're out there flying."

He smiled. "Okay, you're welcomed, Margo. It has been good meeting you. Goodbye now."

He put the jeep in gear and drove away.

The next day around 1600, Ferguson summoned Bud to his office. Low Rider and Mad Dog slouched in cushioned chairs in the now air-conditioned space smoking cigars. The two officers exchanged an amused glance when Bud walked in.

"You want to see me, Skipper?"

"That's affirmative Cotter," Ferguson said as he snapped the big Zippo shut and drew deeply on a Camel. "How much goddamn trouble can you cause in one night?"

"What are you talking about, Skipper?"

"I'll tell you what I'm talking about. Thanks to you and this magical attraction you seem to have over women, VC-110 has been dubbed 'The Poontangers.' It's all over the god-damn base!"

"The Poontangers," Bud blurted, "Skipper, what are you talking about?"

“Horseshit, Cotter, you know goddamn well what I’m talking about. The scuttlebutt on the street all over Danang is that you nailed the Virgin Ice Doctor last night.”

“What! Skipper, what are you talking about?”

Ferguson smirked. Look Cotter, you were seen in the Navy Pier O Club last night with that red head woman doctor from the hospital over here. Is that right or do I have bad information?”

“That’s right. We sat at the same table and had dinner, that’s all.”

“No, that’s not all. You were also seen coming out of her quarters last night around 2230.”

“No, that’s not true. I dropped her off in front of her quarters. I never got out of the jeep.”

Ferguson took another long drag on his cigarette. “Well scuttlebutt has it that you did. So now those fools over at the Gunfighters Club are having the Danang Poontang Award Plaque, the one that hangs on the wall behind the bar, engraved with VC-110 and yesterday’s date. VF-96 has had the Poontang plaque until now. They got it after one of their pilots knocked up a British Admiral’s daughter in Singapore. Now thanks to you, we have the honor and privilege of being the recipients of this prestigious award.”

“I don’t believe this,” Bud said, “who’s feeding you all this bullshit anyway?”

“Hell, Cotter, I’ve heard from three different Skippers today. They called to congratulate me. Jesus H. Christ! I’m trying to run a squadron here! I don’t have time for bullshit like this!”

“Skipper, I didn’t do anything with that woman,” Bud said defensively, “we had our dinner together, and that happened only because whoever she was supposed to meet there for dinner didn't show up. So I offered her the empty place at my table. That's all there is to it."

Ferguson exhaled smoke through his nostrils and picked a fragment of tobacco from his lower lip. "Get this through your head, Cotter. Ten thousand horny sailors and Marines have been after that royal prime stuff since she got here eight months ago. Nobody has even made it to first base with her. Then you come waltzing in and her goddamn panties hit the deck."

Maddog and Sonny broke into guffaws. Ferguson smirked and pointed a finger at Bud. "Cotter, you've now got a rep to uphold. Everybody thinks that you've done the impossible, that you have nailed the Virgin Ice Doctor."

"Skipper, you know damn well none of this crap is true," Bud said scowling, "I hope this doesn't get back to Doctor Whitefield, I wouldn't want her to be humiliated or embarrassed by all this stupid shit"

"It doesn't make a damn what I think," Ferguson snapped, "What matters is that every swinging dick on this base believes it. You've become an overnight celebrity, Cotter. And don't worry about her finding out about this. Unless she starts hanging around the Gunfighters Club, she'll never know the difference."

"Well, I can guarantee that she'll never set foot into that dump. The woman is absolutely paranoid about the men around here. She really believes that all any man wants from her is to get into her pants."

"Well she's so right about that," Mad Dog, sneered. "I'd give a months pay to see her naked. Hell, I'd give two months pay to have her sit on my face."

Everyone, including Bud fell rolling into laughter.

"Okay," Cotter, Ferguson said as he began to shuffle through a pile of papers on his desk, "the main reason I called you in here is because I've got a job for you. Intel is saying that SEAL teams and Marine recon are reporting a lot of new traffic in the A Shau Valley area. Some analysts think Charlie may be setting up additional base camps in preparation for a big offensive in the south. As you know, the A Shau Valley is inside our operating area so we are responsible for interdicting anything the bad guys may be doing. I want you and Too Tall to spend the next couple of days doing a full photo recon of the A Shau. Concentrate on interdiction points, the choke points where we can do the most damage when Charlie tries to sneak through the Valley. You'll probably take some AA fire. Reports are that Charlie has set up 23 and 37 millimeter stuff and hidden them along the ridges. Remember, you're out there to get photos, so no John Wayne strafing runs. Tell Chief Story to have the camera pods rigged on your birds. And we'll need some night stuff too. Tell the chief that he'll have to borrow the infrared camera pods from the Air Force people on the north end. I'll call the skipper down there and get it set up. Okay that's it Cotter, any questions?"

Bud shook his head, "No, I don't think so."

"Okay, Hot Nuts, get your ass out of here."

Chapter 19

A Shau Valley

Located in I Corps, the A Shau Valley is located in Vietnam's, Thua Thien province west of the city of Hue along the border with Laos. The A Shau Valley runs roughly parallel with two mountain ranges. The Valley was one of two strong holds for the communists. The other strong hold was the U Minh Forest. Both of these strong holds were considered by Charlie to be his personal territory. The Rao Lao River flowed through the valley and three abandoned airfields were spread along the valley floor. At the Southern end of the valley was an abandoned Special Forces Camp that had been overrun in March 1966. Once Charlie had taken the camp, the A Shau Valley became the strongest enemy base in South Vietnam. The VC garrisoned 5000 to 6000 troops in the area, and as Einstein Cotter and Too Tall Fletcher were about to learn, portions of the valley were protected by a complex of interlocking anti-aircraft batteries.

The two pilots left Danang at 0640 and turned to a heading that quickly positioned them at the southern end of valley, but low clouds and fog covered most of the mountains and valley. Flying at 10,000 feet they dead reckoned the length of the valley which was blanketed by low cloud its entire length. They returned to Danang to wait for better weather.

Later that afternoon, Bud received an advisory from VC-110 air ops. A FAC pilot reported broken clouds at six thousand feet in the Valley. Bud and Too Tall were in the air within the hour. Crossing the south end of the valley, they could see the abandoned Special Forces camp. Flying a northerly heading at fifty-five hundred feet, they followed the Rao Lao until they came to the first "choke point" at Dong So. Here the mountains created a narrow neck on either side of the river.

"Too Tall," Bud radioed, "standby to start cameras, on my count."

"Roger, Einstein."

"Mark, three, two, one."

"Engaged," Too Tall radioed.

The two Skyraiders began photographing from nearly six thousand feet.

As they passed over Lo Doi, about half way through the choke point, anti aircraft suddenly erupted on both sides of the Valley. White-orange balls of AA floated towards the two aircraft.

"Einstein, I think I've taken hits!"

"Too Tall, can you control the aircraft?"

"Affirmative."

"Climb to one five thousand, turn to heading zero four zero."

"Roger, head zero four zero and one five thousand."

The two big Skyraiders quickly climbed through the clouds followed by strings of AA fire. Bud didn't know whether or not he had been hit. When they reached fifteen thousand on the new heading, they had cleared the Eastern rim of the valley.

"Too Tall, do you have any trouble lights?"

"Negative."

"Maintain heading and altitude. I'm going under you and look you over."

"Roger, Einstein. Maintain heading and altitude."

Bud slipped his Skyraider under Too Tall and pulled within twenty feet of the aircraft. He counted numerous holes in the empennage, the horizontal stabilizer and rudder.

"You have hits in you elevator and rudder. Execute another flight check of all your controls."

"Roger."

"Bud pulled clear of Too Tall and rose to fly in formation one hundred feet off his wingman's port wing.

"Einstein, no control problems."

"Roger. Check my underside for damage."

Too Tall flew under Bud's Skyraider and carefully scrutinized the undersides of the airplane.

"Einstein, two small holes in the fuselage aft of the cockpit, I can't see anything else."

"Roger, form up on me and let's get this photo run finished."

An hour and a half later, having completed the photo recon of the valley, the pilots landed at Danang. On the walk around, they saw the shrapnel holes in Too Tall's tail section and a 37mm hole that went through the flap of his right wing. There were three 23 mm hits on Bud's aircraft that had traveled completely through the fuselage about eight feet behind the cockpit. Chief Story and Pee Wee immediately mustered a crew and set about inspecting and repairing the two Skyraiders.

"Skipper, that goddamn A Shau Valley is like a hornets' nest."

"I heard about your birds, Einstein. You people are lucky the bad guys don't know how to lead. The photos you people brought back are good but inconclusive. We need some night infrared to positively identify where the guns are located. Once we know that, we can go in there and kick some ass."

"A night run through that place? Christ it's, suicide!"

"Look, Cotter, knock off the whining. We've got to get those photos. Before we can put concentrated pressure on Charlie's supply route, we've got to take out his AA guns. Now, Pee

Wee has the Air Force IR cameras ready to attach as soon as your birds are patched up. So you can figure on getting out of here around 2000 tonight. All we need is one pass between six and ten thousand. Make your run as fast as you want, they tell us that those cameras are lightening quick. HS-98 will have a SAR helo in the area in case either of you go down. He's on the guard channel, call sign Bertha. Now you and Too Tall get the hell out of here and get yourselves some chow."

"Well, that's that," said Bud as the two pilots walked out of the air ops Quonset. "Let's check the weather for tonight and then we can get a burger over at the Red Rock Saloon."

"Sounds like a plan to me."

Bud said, "Are you scared?"

"Yeah, a little."

"So am I."

They looked at one another and grinned.

That night Einstein and Too Tall ran the gauntlet of the A Shau Valley once again. The weather was their ally this night as they streaked up the valley at 300 knots and at an altitude of nine thousand feet. Tracers rose to meet them all along the choke points, once again the AA was heaviest at Dong So and on up the valley at Lam Nam. Turning east over the peak at Ko Va-A Dut, they took more AA fire. Bud decided that two runs would be better than one. He didn't want to come back here again if it could be avoided. He decided that Charlie would not expect them to turn around and make another pass. Nobody would be that stupid in a slow Skyraider. He checked his plotting board and quickly calculated the course.

"Too Tall, on the count, we will make a one eighty to one seven zero and intercept the valley at A-Dang."

"Roger, Einstein. So we're gonna do this again?"

"Affirmative, I want to make sure we get good stuff. I don't want to have to come back again."

"Roger."

The Skyraiders turned to intercept A-Dang at the Northern end of the valley. They turned south from there and flew down the valley. Contrary to what Bud had surmised, the AA fire was heavier and more accurate. The airplane jolted on two occasions. He had a flash back to the jolt he had felt that terrible night in the storm off Tern Island. His instrument panel showed all green, but the starboard wing fuel indicator began to drop off significantly. He knew that he had to be losing fuel out of the wing tank.

"Too Tall," Bud radioed as they roared past the old Special Forces Camp, "do you have any hits?"

"Negative, I don't think so."

"I'm losing gas on my starboard wing tank. Let's get up to ten thousand and head one four five to Algiers."

"Roger."

On the ground at Danang, it was discovered that Bud's Skyraider had taken several hits, one in the starboard outboard fuel tank. The hole was so large that the most of the fuel had siphoned out of the self-sealing tank.

The photos were excellent. The IR cameras revealed twenty-eight AA positions. This information was relayed to Navy Intel. The next morning at daylight a gang-bang of fast movers off the carriers, A-4 Skyhawks and A-7 Corsairs flew against these positions with napalm, white phosphorus and 500 pound HE bombs. Marine FAC's flying Cessna L-19 Birddogs followed up to survey the damage. They verified that many of the guns were out of action.

The daily grind of flying ground support and SAR missions continued through Christmas. Several days the squadron was forced to stand down because of heavy weather. Regardless of the stand downs, they flew in some very nasty weather. Their instrument flying proficiency was heavily taxed on an almost daily basis. Finding a down pilot using only grid coordinates on a map out over the jungle could be a real challenge, particularly in heavy weather and low ceilings. If the down pilot's emergency locator was working, it was a relatively simple situation to locate the pilot. Problem was, often times these bulky units did not work. The pilot's hand held radio was likewise subject to damage and failure.

Usually it was the SAR helo that would find and pinpoint a down pilot's position. These crews were the life blood of down aviators and they were unusually adept at rescuing pilots. Flying off the carriers and out of Danang, the SAR helos were armed with .50 caliber machine guns. If a pilot was injured, a crewman would be lowered to the ground to harness-up the injured aviator. Another crewman in the helo would hoist the pilot and the crewman into the helo door. This was extremely dangerous work. More often than not, a hovering helo would take fire from VC who were looking to capture the down pilot. VC-110 Skyraiders would lay down suppressing fire while the SAR helo crew retrieved the pilot. So far though, VC-110 aircraft had sustained only minor damage as a result of the small arms fire during extractions. By Christmas, VC-110 had logged a total of 67 SAR missions with no loss of aircraft or pilots.

26 December dawned gray and cloudy with scattered rain showers marching across I Corps. Reflective puddles of rainwater collected in depressions in the roads and in the craters created by incoming mortar and rocket hits. The pilots of VC-110 who had the morning Alert Watch went to chow at 0530. When they finished breakfast, they trudged to the squadron ready room Quonset. Here radiomen constantly monitored the guard channels. If a down pilot was reported, a SAR mission would immediately be activated. In the meanwhile though, the pilots sat around the ready room reading, writing letters or watching the closed circuit TV. All

was quiet this morning as the pilots watched old reruns of Sky King and Roy Rogers.

Bud was dozing with a nasty hangover when someone shook his shoulder.

"Get off your ass, son, ole Shug has finally made it to Vietnam!"

Bud jumped out of the seat and gave his friend a big bear hug. "Why you sorry piano-golf playing skater, what the hell are you doing here?"

"Son, Ah finally got orders. My request to transfer to VC-110 was finally approved. So here ah am, son!"

"Well I just will be damned! Hey everybody, this is, Shug Early, my ole bud from BP. He's our new nugget!"

The other pilots stood, shook hands and introduced themselves.

"This is one hell of a surprise," Bud said, grinning happily. "Let's go see the Skipper; he'll want to see you right away."

The friends walked through the rain across the street to Ferguson's office. Ferguson was at his desk smoking and cursing over a disheveled pile of navy correspondence. The CO stubbed his short cigarette when the two officers walked into his office.

"Well, Early, I see you finally made it. Welcome aboard."

"Thank you, sir. I'm happy to be here."

Ferguson sternly peered at his new officer, "Call me Skipper, Early. Remember that."

"Ah'll remember that, Skipper."

"Word is that you had a round-about trip out here."

"Well, Skipper, ah believe that ah was given a tour of just about every place in the Pacific. Kitty Hawk was my last stop. They didn't know what to do with me so they put me on the Checker Tail with the mail."

Ferguson lit a Camel. "Okay, look Early. After you get checked in and squared away, I want you to find Seckman and have him get you started on your qualifications and getting you checked out in the Skyraider. You won't be flying any combat missions for quite a while, maybe none at all before we get back to BP. We'll use you to relieve Burke who's my utility-ferry pilot. He's got all his quals now so he can start flying somebody's wing, any questions?"

"No, ah don't think so, skipper."

"Okay. Einstein, you show Early around and help him get checked in and squared away. And when you see Mad Dog, tell him to get his ass over here."

"Will do, skipper."

"Alright, get the hell out of my office. I've got too much shit to do to be socializing with you two clowns."

Late that afternoon, Bud and Shug walked over to the Gunfighters O Club located a few blocks from Area Sierra.

Bud said, "Want a pizza? They make a wicked pepperoni and I'll get us a pitcher of beer."

"Sounds great, son, Ah'm starved."

"The action generally doesn't start until twenty or twenty-one hundred," Bud said when he returned to their table with a cold glass pitcher of golden beer and two frost covered mugs. "Practically every night, this place fills up with a bunch of hot shot fighter and helo pilots, mostly navy and marine. They come in here and get drunk. Somebody always starts a fight and the place is total chaos. It's complete bullshit. I don't know why the Base Commander allows this crap to go on. Around twenty-three hundred, the MP's and SP's will show up and drag the drunks out and take them to sickbay for stitches or back to their rooms if they're not banged up too badly."

"Son, it sounds like a place to stay away from after dark."

"Yeah, it is. I found out about a pretty decent O Club at the Navy pier. Good food and a decent wine list. It's pretty quiet and laid back, a good place to go and get away for a night."

"Well, son, we'll have to give it try one of these nights."

"Yeah," Bud said and poured beer in the two mugs, "so how are things back at BP."

"Not much excitement with you guys gone. Hardly anything other than P-3's and C-130's use the field. Sometimes jets from Kaneohe or Hickam come in and do touch and go's. That's about it."

"Played much golf?"

"You know me son, everyday."

"How are you and Bernadette doing?"

A pall of darkness crossed Shug Early's face. "Well son, Ah didn't want to be the one to bring this up, but Ah spent a few days with Bernadette and your folks in Topeka. The visitation and funeral were really hard on Bernadette and your Mama too. Bernadette and Phyllis became real tight when her and your folks came to Hawaii."

"Yeah, I know. Phyllis told me."

"Ah can't tell you how bad Ah feel about Phyllis, and you too, son. Ah don't know what else to say."

"Thanks ole Buddy, and thanks for taking leave and flying to Kansas for the funeral."

"When Ah, heard from Bernadette that you couldn't get back in time for the funeral, Ah talked to Captain Locke and he arranged to get me ten days leave on the spot. He's a great guy."

"Yeah, he didn't have to do that. What about Phyllis's family?"

"Oh, they're great people, son. The family is devastated, as you would expect. They are really taking it hard. Mrs. Day passed out at the funeral. It was really bad."

"Jesus."

"How are you doing, son?"

"I have bad days and good days. Yesterday, Christmas was hell. I stayed drunk all day and missed Ann Margaret and the Bob Hope USO show. It's been one hell of an experience. I was talking to somebody a while back, I can't remember who it was, but I told that person that I never realized it was possible to feel such pain. I guess that pretty much sums it up."

A tear rolled across his cheek and he wiped it with the back of his hand.

"I'll tell you this, after Phyllis I'll never get close to another woman." Bud took the mug and drank half the beer out of it. "That's damn good beer," he said.

That night the bad guys celebrated Shug Early's arrival by dropping mortar rounds and half a dozen rockets into Danang. Experiencing his first time under fire, Shug Early crouched wide-eyed in the bunker next to Bud.

"Damn, son, ole Shug maybe should have stayed in Hawaii."

Bud laughed at his friend. "Don't worry. It's a million to one shot that one of those rounds will hit this bunker."

"Somehow that doesn't make me feel a whole lot better, son."

29 December was another rainy day in I Corps. Bud and Shug were sitting in the ready room. Bud was watching the TV show Star Trek on the TV and Shug was working on his Squadron Qualification course. A pudgy second class

radioman known as 'Puddin' trudged into the Quonset, looked around, and walked over to Bud

"Mr. Cotter, here's a message for you. It came in about half an hour ago. Somebody delivered it to the radio shack by mistake."

"Thanks, Puddin." Bud opened the envelope: *Lieutenant Cotter. Please call me at 4106. Dr. Margo Whitefield.*

Bud wondered what Margo Whitefield could possibly want to talk to him about. He went to the front of the ready room where a local base telephone was located on a desk.

"Trauma center," a male voice said.

"This is Lieutenant Cotter. Doctor Whitefield sent a request for me to call her."

"One moment, sir." After a minute and a half Margo picked up the receiver.

"Hello, Bud. How are you?"

"I'm fine, staying busy with flight ops, and you?"

"Busy here at the hospital, too busy at times."

"What can I do for you, Doctor?"

She hesitated for a long moment. Bud curiously waited for her to speak. "Bud, I have a rather unusual request. I hope very much that you won't think me presumptuous, but you see; the hospital staff is putting on a New Years Eve celebration in a private room at the Navy Pier Officers Club. And I was wondering, well, I really don't want to go alone. So I was wondering if possibly you would consider accompanying me."

He was more than a little taken aback. All of a sudden out of the blue Margo Whitefield wants him to be her date at a New Year's party. Immediately he understood why she was calling. She felt as though she had to make a showing at the party and that she could trust him to take her. Escorting

Margo Whitefield to a party is not something he wanted to do. The death of Phyllis Day weighed heavily on his soul and contact with another woman, no matter how innocent, seemed like outright disloyalty. Margo Whitefield meant absolutely nothing to him, and going to a boring party with a bunch of medical people wasn't his idea of how to spend New Year's Eve. He didn't want to refuse her outright, so he decided to stall.

"Doctor, before I can commit, I have to check the duty roster to make sure I'm not in the duty section that day. Can I call you back?"

"Of course Bud, and please call me Margo, there's no need to be formal."

"Alright, Margo, I'll let you know something today."

Bud hung up the phone and sauntered back to his seat next to Shug.

"Everything okay, son?"

"I've been invited to go to a New Year's Eve party."

"Who invited you?"

"A lady doctor I happened to meet a few weeks ago. I don't want to go. I made up an excuse about checking to see if I have the duty that night. I said that I'd let her know something later today."

Shug looked at the clock on the wall. "Why don't you want to go, is she a dog?"

"No, she's nice looking and all that. I just don't want to go out with her or anybody for that matter. I'm going nuts thinking about Phyllis all the time."

"Ah think you should go, son. Sitting around on New Years is going to make you feel bad, just like Christmas did. Going to the party might help get you mind off of things for a few hours."

"Maybe you're right. I don't know. I need to think about it."

At a quarter before fifteen hundred that afternoon, hesitantly, Bud called Margo. "I don't have the duty section that night. What time do you want me to pick you up?"

"Oh, Bud, thank you so much. I hope this is not putting you out."

"Not at all," he lied. "I'm glad to do it."

"This is so good of you, Bud! See you at my quarters, around eight thirty?"

"Eight thirty. Okay, goodbye."

He justified his decision by telling himself that if nothing else, being on good terms with a doctor at the hospital may be of some benefit in the future. If someone in the squadron needed special medical care, he was certain that Doctor Whitefield would agree to do it if he asked.

The New Year's celebration seemed to be socially successful for Margo. She introduced Bud to her associates, mostly naval medical personnel who were friendly and made him feel comfortable by not being condescending. As Bud had anticipated with some trepidation, there was a lot of medical talk, most of which Bud did not understand. At midnight the crowd of celebrants sang Auld Langsyne and toasted with bubbly champagne. Because everyone else kissed their partner, Bud hesitantly kissed Margo. It was a kiss without emotion, like kissing his sister. Nevertheless, a wave of guilt swept over him.

"Happy new year, Margo," he said, with a melancholy smile

Margo smiled affably, "Why thank you, Bud, happy New Year. You surprised me. I wasn't expecting you to kiss me."

He flushed, a little embarrassed. "I thought that since everybody else kissed each other to celebrate, that well, I should kiss you. I didn't want you to be embarrassed. I hope you're not offended."

"No, I'm not offended. Thank you. I sincerely appreciate your thinking of my feelings that way." She gave a little nervous laugh. "Now everyone will really be talking."

He cast a wondering look. "What do you mean everyone will really be talking?"

She laughed self-consciously, "Let's dance and I'll tell you."

He didn't want to dance, but he couldn't think of a legitimate way to refuse. The song was, *Twilight Time*. He held her nearly at arm's length.

"The day after we sat together and had dinner," she said, "the nosy busy bodies around the hospital were gossiping that a man finally conquered the "Ice Doctor."

He was astounded. "You know they call you the Ice Doctor?"

"Of course," she chortled, "along with other names like, "The Virgin Doctor," "Doctor Untouchable," "Mother Mary Margo. These things trickle back to me. I know what people are saying. My nurses are my intelligence sources. It seems that within the confines of this base, as huge as it is, there are very few secrets."

"Holy Jesus," he said, still amazed. "The day after we had dinner, the skipper called me in and told me that you and I were the talk of Danang. They even gave our squadron an award at the Gunfighters Club."

"You received an award?" She laughed heartily.

"Not me personally, the award was for the squadron."

"What is your squadron being recognized for?"

"It's some ridiculous vulgar thing a bunch of drunken fighter pilots came up with."

"That just shows you how outlandish things can get around here."

"Aren't you offended by all this gossip?"

"Oh, I was at first, very much so in fact. But after a few days, I began to realize that there were some benefits hidden in all this gossip mongering."

"How can you find benefit in vile gossip?"

She appeared to be a little embarrassed. "Well, evidently people think that you and I are involved in a romantic relationship, so for the most part the wolves have been leaving me alone."

"Okay, I see your point, but the gossip is at your expense. I really hate this loose talk."

"Is it embarrassing for you because people think we are involved?"

"No, that's not it at all. I despise the thought that the both of us are caught up in this whirlwind of bullshit." He gave her an apologetic look, "sorry about my language."

Margo laughed softly. "It's okay. I think your remark is quite appropriate to the situation. Really though, I don't mind it so much anymore. Truthfully, I'm glad that I had dinner with you that night. I almost didn't you know."

"Yeah, I remember."

Margo laughed softly. "Now that you have escorted me to this party, God knows what kind of stories will be concocted." They shared a mutual look of understanding and laughed.

Margo and Bud left the party around two o'clock and drove across the base to Margo's quarters. He got out of the jeep, opened the door for her and walked her to the door.

"Bud, thank you for everything: and thank you for being such a gentleman."

"It was a pleasant evening, Margo. It helped me keep my mind off some very troubling things."

Margo looked at him with compassionate eyes. "I'm glad, Bud. I know that you were uncomfortable tonight, and I want to thank you again for doing this for me. I have my own issues as you have seen. I am grateful to you, Bud."

"Okay, Margo. Glad to do it."

She smiled self-consciously. "Well goodnight Bud. Happy New Year and be careful when you're out there flying."

"Thanks, happy New Year to you, Margo." She watched him walk to the jeep and drive off. It had started to rain, and by the time Bud pulled up in front of his Quonset, the rain had become a deluge.

Chapter 20

TET & Khe Sanh

The Tet Offensive (Tet Mau Than) or
Tong Cong Kich/Tong Khoi Ngia.

On 30 January 1968, combined forces of the National Front for the Liberation of South Vietnam (or Viet Cong) and the People's Army of Vietnam (PAVN) initiated coordinated offensive combat operations in all areas of South Vietnam.

These operations are referred to in the West as the Tet Offensive because they were timed to begin during the early morning hours of 31 January, Tết Nguyên Đán the lunar New Year holiday. For reasons that are unknown, a wave of attacks began on the preceding morning in the I and II Corps Tactical Zones. This early attack did not, however, cause undue alarm or lead to widespread allied defensive measures. When the main NLF-PAVN operation began the next morning, the offensive was country-wide in scope and well-coordinated, with more than 80,000 communist troops striking more than 100 towns and cities, including 36 of 44 provincial capitals, five of the six autonomous cities, 72 of 245 district towns, and the national capital of Saigon. The offensive was the largest military operation yet conducted by either side up to that point in the war.

The initial attacks stunned allied forces and took them by surprise, but most were quickly contained and beaten back, inflicting massive casualties on the NLF. The exceptions were the fighting that erupted in the old imperial capital of Huế, where intense fighting was taking place, and the continuing struggle around the U.S. combat base at Khe Sanh. Although the offensive was a military disaster for communist forces, it had a profound effect on the American administration and shocked the American public, which had been led to believe by its political and military leaders that the communists were, due to previous defeats, incapable of launching such a massive effort.

Commander Jack Ferguson stood in front of his officers and men on the morning after the TET offensive had begun. The situation was becoming much clearer and Naval Intelligence provided a relatively accurate assessment of the attack.

"I want you all to know, that the VC and the NVA have taken advantage of the TET cease fire and have staged a coordinated attack across all of South Vietnam. Every major city and military installation in the country has been hit. The American Embassy in Saigon has been overrun by suicide squads. Khe Sanh is standing-by to be overrun. We have been pretty lucky here. The Marines have cleared the areas around Danang, Marble Mountain and up at Phu Bai. Intel reports that they've been getting kills in good numbers. Most of their trouble now is in the city of Hue where the enemy has occupied the area south of the Perfume River. Our job is now two fold. We will continue to provide interdicting fire for SAR missions. In addition to that, and in coordination with other Navy, Marine and Air Force air groups, we will provide fire support for Khe Sanh. Beginning now, we will keep one division of SAR Alert aircraft on standby twenty-four seven. All other aircraft will fly interdiction missions in support of Khe Sanh up in the Balong Valley. Beginning today, we will stand port and starboard watches. Division officers and chiefs need to get the new watch bill to the XO no later than 1800 today. A daily schedule will be issued which will specify the times each section or division will fly in support of Khe Sanh. You ground support guys are critical to this operation. You are being asked to work your tails off twelve hours a day and more if necessary. I am confident that every man in the squadron will give one hundred percent and then some. People, this is one hell of a serious situation. Until the enemy is defeated and brought under control, our job will be to keep constant pressure on their forces. I know that each of you will do your damnedest to do whatever it takes. Are there any questions? ....Nobody? ……Okay then, Division Officers take over."

The next several days brought about a frenzy of combat sorties for the pilots of VC-110. Khe Sanh and its surrounding fire bases were under almost constant attack by the VC and NVA forces. The Marines were calling for air support incessantly. Supply aircraft attempting to get into the base came under withering small arms and 23 mm AA fire. On the ground, an unlucky rocket or mortar round, nobody knows for sure which, fell on a VR-22, C-130 that was loading wounded for evacuation. Eight wounded Marines were killed along with the five man crew of the C-130. For all practical purposes, Khe Sanh was besieged. Enemy troops would attack the base with mortar and mobile artillery fire; then quickly retreat to bunkers and caves before fighter and attack aircraft could arrive.

Bud and Too Tall, now flying in the Chicken Wing Division, made 42 sorties in 11 days. They strafed with 20 mm, dropped napalm, white phosphorus and 500 pound HE bombs on targets identified by frantic Marines calling for air support. It was a gruesome business. The aircraft took many hits from small arms fire. Once Chicken Wing had taken two 37 mm hits in his empennage that cut his elevator-trim cable. He landed his Skyraider at Danang without incident, but it could have been much worse. Other pilots took hits of varying degrees, but the tough Skyraider always got them home.

Bud Cotter climbed out of his Skyraider following his third sortie of the day. Black bands of sweat covered his flight suit. He was tired, thirsty and distraught. On the third run of the day, they had napalmed a small village southwest of Khe Sanh that Marine Recon reported to be a VC base camp. The village and all its inhabitants were incinerated. The fact that the populace of the village was sympathetic to the VC did little to temper his feeling of remorse. Undoubtedly there had been innocent children in that village who had died in the fiery holocaust.

Bud was getting out of the shower when Low Rider walked into his room.

"Einstein, the skipper called. He wants to see us over in his office."

"What about?"

"He didn't say. I'll meet you over there."

"Okay, I'll be over as soon as I get dressed."

Ferguson sat at his desk wreathed in cigarette smoke reading debrief reports. Bud walked into his office and fell into a chair next to Low Rider. Ferguson dashed his cigarette and took a long swig from a green Coke bottle.

"As if we don't have enough goddamn trouble around here, I've been ordered to provide a crew to fly a C-46 up to Khe Sanh and evacuate 32 wounded Marines. From what I'm told, the closest available C-130 is over at Cubi Point but it's down with a blown turbine in number three engine. This morning a CH-46 tried to evacuate some wounded and the gooks shot his ass down less than a click from the base. Everybody on board was wasted. The word from Colonel Lownds is that his wounded Marines need immediate hospital care or we are going to lose them. We've got to do whatever it takes to get those guys out of there and back here to the hospital."

Sonny Miles said, "Skipper, who the hell is checked out in a C-46?"

"Nobody except pilots in that Air Force Wing over on the north ramp," Ferguson replied, "and the skipper over there is up to his ass in support sorties. He said he'd like to help us out, but he just doesn't have enough pilots. Now we need at least one pilot who is tail wheel and multiengine qualified. That's me, you Sonny, Boats Davidson, Mad Dog, Seckman and Einstein. I can't pull the division leaders out of the lineup, too much going down here in I Corps, so Einstein I need you to take this one."

Bud looked at Ferguson with an incredulous expression. "But, Skipper, I don't know what a C-46 is. How am I supposed to fly this thing without some kind of a check-out?"

"You get in the goddamn thing, find the checklist and figure it out. Hell, it's an airplane isn't it? Naval aviators are supposed to be flexible and adaptable. Now look, I don't have time to argue about this. So here's what I want you to do. Get yourself a crew together. You'll have to use Early as your co-pilot because I can't spare anybody else. Get Pee Wee to be your crew chief, he's familiar with old navy version of the forty-six, the R-5D. Pick out a couple of guys to ride in the back to help load the stretchers after you get up there. Two corpsmen are standing by to ride with you. They will take care of the Marines when you get them loaded."

"Is this something that we are going to do today?"

"Hell, yes, Cotter, those Marines are dying up there! You've got at least four and a half hours of daylight left."

"Jesus Christ, Skipper," Bud said in an exasperated tone, wagging his head. "Okay, where is this thing?"

"A tug is pulling it over here as we speak. It is supposed to be topped off and ready to go. Have Pee Wee check everything out before you fly it, and Cotter, good luck, Lad."

Bud looked at his commanding officer and shook his head, "I'm damn sure going to need one hell of a lot of luck."

Bud fell into a flurry of quick action. He recruited his plane captain JJ and another plane captain named Winston.

"Okay guys," Bud said, "the airplane is out on spot three. I want you guys to help Pee Wee give that bird a thorough going over, but before you do, I want you to stop by the armory and check out a belt fed weapon and get plenty of ammo. Got it guys?"

"Okay, Mister Cotter, we'll take care of it." They scurried out of the air ops Quonset.

Bud found Shug and told him what they were going to do.

Shug stared at him with an amazed half grin. "You're shittin' me, right, son?"

"Ole buddy I wish I were. Get your helmet and gear and let's go."

"You do know that I don't have any multi-engine time, don't you? If something happens to you, we're screwed."

"You can handle it if you have too. Hopefully it won't come to that. Grab your stuff; we don't have a lot of time."

"Son, this sounds like a guaranteed Purple Heart deal."

"Yeah, no shit."

The old Air Force C-46 looked tired, worn and abused. Bud's first glimpse of the airplane was a bit of a shock. This thing was much larger than anything he had ever flown. Pee Wee and the plane captains were on top of a wing visually checking the fuel the tanks and oil reservoirs.

"How's it going guys," Bud shouted.

"So far, so good Mister Cotter," JJ yelled.

Bud and Shug climbed into the airplane through the big cargo door on the left side of the aircraft. Thirty-two stretcher racks were mounted to the bulkheads of the cargo cabin leaving a narrow aisle down the middle of the aircraft.

In the cockpit, Bud looked around with disgust. The deck was cluttered with dried chicken bones, empty beer cans, candy bar wrappers, nuts and bolts and an assortment of unidentifiable junk.

"Jesus Christ," Bud said to Shug, "look at this shit. Help me get this garbage picked up."

They policed the cockpit and stuffed the garbage into an empty gray canvas sack they found in the cargo area. Bud picked up the checklist, found the preflight section and gave it to Shug.

"Okay, lad, the only way I see that we can do this without killing ourselves is to follow this checklist verbatim. You read off the checklist items and I'll find whatever is supposed to be checked."

The two pilots methodically began to follow the checklist, item by item. A few minutes later, Pee Wee arrived in the cockpit.

"Those two corpsmen are here, Mister Cotter."

"Okay, get them briefed. And Chief, make sure everybody is wearing a flak jacket."

"Okay, Mr. Cotter. You guys need any help with that checklist?"

"We're okay right now. Did everything outside check out?"

"She's full on fuel, oil and hydraulic fluids. There are a couple of minor leaks but nothing major. We can't check anything else until you get the engines started."

"Okay, I'll give you a call when we're ready. Did Cummings get a start cart over here?"

"Yes, sir, the cable is already connected. Just need to start it up whenever you're ready to fire up number one."

It took Bud and Shug ten minutes to get through the pre-start checklist. Pee Wee was summoned to the cockpit. He put the jump seat in place and sat between the pilots. Proceeding through the checklist, they started the number one engine. It coughed and sputtered as huge clouds of bluish white smoke blew out of the exhaust stacks. Suddenly the engine caught and rumbled into life. Number two engine belched fire and started almost immediately, quickly settling down into a deep rumbling idle.

Checklist completed with everyone aboard and all hatches secured, Shug talked to ground control. They were cleared to a run-up area where each engine was checked and re-checked until Bud and Pee Wee were satisfied that everything was working properly. Taxiing onto the runway, Bud was nervously rehearsing the lift off speeds that he had read out of a battered flight manual that Shug had found in a slot on the bulkhead behind the co-pilot's seat.

They taxied onto the runway and lined up on the centerline.

"Tail wheel locked?" Bud said.

"Affirmative," Shug replied into the mike of his headset.

"Twenty degrees flaps?"

"Roger."

"Fuel pumps on?"

"Affirmative."

"Okay, let's go."

Engines roaring, the old airplane picked up speed as it headed down the runway. The tail came up at sixty-five knots and they ran on the main wheels until at ninety knots, Bud eased back on the control yoke and they lifted off the runway and transitioned into a shallow climb. When the airspeed indicated 100 knots, Bud said, "Wheels up."

"Wheels up," came the instant reply from Shug.

"Flaps up in ten degree increments."

Shug brought the flaps up one detent at a time. When the flaps were cleaned up he said, "Flaps up."

"Okay, Pee Wee," Bud said, "let's set the rpm and manifold pressures for climb out."

Pee Wee adjusted each engine to the prescribed settings.

Bud rolled in elevator trim to raise the nose into a climb speed of 140 knots. He could relax a little now and he felt much more comfortable about handling the airplane. "Pee Wee," Bud said, "what about the cowl flaps and oil cooler flaps?"

"If I remember right," Pee Wee replied, "these old Curtis-Wright R-2600 engines have a tendency to run high cylinder head temperatures. It's probably best to leave everything full open in this heat. We can always adjust at higher altitudes if we have to."

"Okay," said Bud, "that's what we'll do."

They climbed to eight thousand feet and leveled the airplane. Bud set up a cruising speed of 170 knots as they pushed through patchy gray clouds.

They passed directly over the A Shau Valley above the cloud deck and turned to a direct heading that would intercept Highway 9 east of Khe Sanh. As the crew settled down for the flight, Shug switched the number two radio to Khe Sanh tower frequency. They monitored the radio traffic from fast mover A-4 Skyhawks off the carrier Kitty Hawk. The little jets were pounding the perimeters around Khe Sanh with bombs, napalm and 20 mm fire.

"Sounds like it's busy up there," Shug said, "I hope they have everything under control when we get there."

"If they don't, we'll orbit the area until they do. We've got plenty of gas. I'm not real anxious to get killed today."

"Yeah, son, you've got that right!"

Bud looked at his watch. Darkness was a little over two hours away. If all went well, they would be on the ground back at Danang before dark. He was surprised how well the C-46 handled and responded. At first, it had felt very heavy on the controls, but as the airspeed increased above 100 knots, things became much easier. He decided that keeping the speed up on the approach would give him better handling ability. Once they touched down, he was certain that the ground speed would bleed off quickly particularly in a combat landing with full position flaps and a three point touchdown.

"Matterhorn, Magpie six six zero inbound, fifteen miles," Shug radioed.

"Magpie, no other reported traffic in the area, you are cleared to land runway two seven. No incoming at this time. Wind 340 at 10. Altimeter two niner niner zero."

"Roger, cleared to land on two seven, thank you."

Ten miles out they could see the runway through the haze. Bud began to gradually slow the airplane to 140 knots. He talked to the crew on the aircraft IC.

"Okay guys, everybody hear me?"

"Affirmative."

"We will be on the ground in about five minutes. Remember the plan, everybody out of the airplane and get the wounded aboard as quickly as you can. I will keep the engines running at idle. If we start getting incoming fire get back in the airplane. We will get the hell out of as fast as possible. Questions?"

"No, sir."

They made a high combat approach. The airplane dropped quickly with the power reduced and flaps at forty degrees. They crossed the runway threshold at fifty-five feet. Bud planned to make the landing as short as possible.

"Quick recheck," Bud said to Shug and Pee Wee. "Wheels down?"

"Down and locked, green lights."

"Fuel pumps on?"

"Affirmative."

"Props set?"

"Affirmative."

"Tail Wheel?"

"Locked".

"I don't like not having somebody flying top cover for us," Bud said, "where the hell are the fighters?"

"This is a shitty deal all the way around," said Shug.

Bud felt a flash of uncertainty as he began to flare the airplane into a three point landing. At the last second he decided to execute a wheel landing on the main wheels. He didn't know what the beast was going to do when they touched down. Forward on the yoke, 100 knots and the old bird settled toward the runway. He reduced the throttles gradually and the main wheels touched down in a shriek of rubber and puffs of smoke. He wanted to make the first turn off. He gently forced the tail to settle and he began to tap the brakes. The airplane slowed so quickly that he had to add power to taxi off the runway.

"Magpie, right turn on Alpha and follow the truck."

"Where's the truck?" Bud said to Shug.

"I think it may be that track vehicle coming down the taxiway."

A track vehicle bristling with quad .50 caliber machine guns rumbled down the taxiway. A Marine in the vehicle held a radio to his face. "Magpie, follow me."

They followed the vehicle to a wide parking area. The burnt remains of a Navy C-130 were piled in a heap just off the steel Marsden matting.

"Jesus, son, look at that."

"I see it. Listen, when I get this thing turned around, how about you and Pee Wee going aft and make sure they get the stretchers loaded as quickly as possible."

"Got it," Shug said.

OD green field ambulances sitting on a red clay road were lined in single file just off the matting. A Marine on the ground with a hand held radio directed Bud to the parking area. Using left brake and right engine, he rotated the airplane in a half circle so that he was lined up for a quick exit.

"Okay," Bud said into the IC, "let's go!"

JJ and Winston had both cargo doors opened. The ambulances started forward and a group of Marines appeared out of a bunker and ran up to the airplane to help load the wounded. The men worked frantically while Bud sat in the cockpit anxiously looking around. Six minutes after the loading began, Shug rushed into the cockpit.

"Son, we've got more stretchers than we have racks. How about putting the last eight in the main aisle?"

"Okay, tell them to hurry up!"

The last few stretchers were unceremoniously carried into the airplane and placed on the deck in the center aisle leaving only a narrow walkway for the crew to maneuver inside the cargo hold.

"All loaded," Pee Wee said on the IC, "everybody is on board. Doors securing. Let's get the hell out of here!"

Shug came stumbling into the cockpit and fell into his seat.

"Okay," Bud said, "I want flaps at twenty as we taxi out. I'm going straight to the runway and make an intersection departure on Alpha. Call the tower and tell them what we're going to do."

Shug radioed the tower.

The control tower was a trailer fitted with a wide glassed-in booth surrounded by armored barriers that reached to the bottom of the windows.

"Roger," came the reply, "wind three one zero at twelve. Altimeter two niner niner zero."

Using brakes and engine power, Bud taxied straight out onto the runway at taxiway Alpha. He got the airplane lined up in the center of the runway.

"Tail wheel locked, twenty degrees of flaps?" Bud said.

"Affirmative, son. Let's rock and roll outta here!"

Bud brought up the power and the airplane began to roll. Off to their left, a tower of dirt and black smoke appeared, and then another and another in quick succession, each explosion coming nearer to the old airplane.

"Holy shit," Shug shouted, "that's incoming!"

More explosions threw clods of dirt high into the air as the old airplane lumbered slowly down the runway. It seemed as though the tail was never going to come up. Bud took a quick glance at the airspeed indicator; it read fifty-five. He realized that the now heavily loaded aircraft would need a lot more speed to start flying. Everything was at full power, nothing to do but sit and wait for the speed to come up. "So much for a low transition takeoff," Bud thought. It seemed like hours before the tail began to fly. Clods of dirt fell onto the airplane; the incoming rounds were getting close! Marines on the ground peered at the old transport struggling to get airborne. A Staff Sergeant sitting in a bunker with other marines said, "Those poor bastards are in a world of shit."

Now rounds were hitting on both sides of the runway, the airplane was being straddled. At ninety knots, Bud pulled back on yoke. The struggling airplane lifted off the runway, flew for a few seconds and settled back onto the main wheels. More rounds exploded all around them hurling big clods of dirt and pieces of shrapnel onto the airplane. Bud was racked with indecision. They were rapidly approaching the point where he could not stop the airplane without running off the end of the runway. More dirt and shrapnel slammed into the bulbous flying machine as it ran for its life. Then mercifully at 110 knots, the airplane rose from the runway and wallowed into the air; almost instantly they passed the end of the runway.

"Damn it!" Bud shouted in a voice of immense relief, "Wheels up!"

"Coming up," Shug replied. "Son, I thought this thing was never going to fly."

"We're not climbing very fast," Bud said a little frantically holding the throttles at maximum power. He talked into the IC: "Pee Wee, get up here!"

The little chief threaded his way past the stretchers and into the cockpit. He tapped Bud's shoulder.

"Chief, does this thing have water injection?"

"Yes sir, but I don't know if it works." Pee Wee replied. He flipped up the covers on two obscure switches located on the back of the center console and moved them to the ON position. Almost immediately the manifold pressure jumped on each engine.

"It's working on both engines," Pee Wee shouted.

"Okay, yeah, this is a lot better," Bud said.

Airspeed up to 160 knots, he turned to the left and set up a climb. Suddenly over the IC came a frenetic call from JJ. "We're taking hits back here, rounds coming through the starboard bulkhead!"

Bud immediately rolled the airplane into a steep sixty degree left bank and lowered the nose to pickup more speed. He headed directly for Danang. They were fast approaching the

A Shau Valley and they were still below the cloud deck at four thousand feet. Muffled thuds! 37 mm rounds exploded near the right engine and wing making black puffs of smoke. White hot shrapnel flew in all directions and a big piece of cowling broke away from number two engine and disappeared across the wing.

Bud rolled the airplane level onto a heading of 050. Nothing to do but set up the climb and try to get above the cloud deck. At that moment, a rocket whizzed by spewing flame fifty feet in front of the airplane.

“Holy Jesus, did you see that!” Shug shouted.

“Hell yes, I saw it!”

Gradually, after agonizing minutes, they penetrated the clouds and broke out on top at 6,000 feet. The airplane felt sloppy and heavy on the controls. Even at one hundred and seventy knots the controls were arduous and slow to react.

“Okay, Pee Wee,” Bud shouted, “what about number two with the cowling that’s missing?”

“It’s running okay right now,” Pee Wee said as he switched off the water injection. “With half the cowling missing and no baffles on that side, we’ll have to keep an eye on the cylinder head and oil temperatures.”

“Okay, let’s try and set the power to cruise. We’re heavy as hell.” Pee Wee adjusted the manifold pressures and propeller rpm on both engines. At 175 knots, the battered overloaded airplane held altitude.

Bud said, “I think we’ll be okay. Pee Wee, how about going aft and check the damage in the cargo area.”

Minutes later Pee Wee called on the IC. “We’ve got about a dozen holes in the deck plates and port bulkhead, Mr. Cotter. Two of the wounded that are on the deck were hit. The corpsmen are working with them now.”

"Thanks, Pee Wee."

Bud breathed a deep sigh of relief. "Well, lad, we made it out of there by the skin of our teeth. It's damn lucky we didn't get shot down!"

"I thought we were goners when all that stuff starting hitting around us. And then when that goddamn rocket went by us, well I was praying hard. What a hell of a way to make a living."

"And you left a cushy job in Hawaii to come to Vietnam."

Shug grinned, "Yeah I did. I don't know what the hell got into me." They laughed and savored the liberation one feels after escaping a very perilous predicament.

Thirty miles northwest of Danang, the number two engine started to trail a thin stream of whitish-gray smoke. "Look at that," Shug shouted, "we've got smoke coming out of number two."

"Unbelievable, this is all we need!" Bud snapped. He depressed the mike button, "Pee Wee, I need you up here on the double!"

When Pee Wee arrived, Bud said, "Number two is smoking." Pee Wee peered out the window and watched the smoke for a few seconds. He turned and looked at the engine instruments. "The cylinder head temperatures are a little high, but not enough to do this." He looked at the smoke trail again. "I'd say we probably dropped a valve in one of the cylinders, probably busted the piston. We'll know in a few minutes."

"Is there anything we can do about it?"

"Short of securing the engine there's nothing we can do," Pee Wee said, "if it is a dropped valve, the cylinder head will come apart and blow off."

"What then?" Bud said a little frantically. "There's no way this airplane is going to maintain altitude with that engine out."

Pee Wee shook his head and puckered his lips in thought. "Well, I've seen a couple of engines that blew a cylinder head clean off and the engine kept running. Problem is, once the cylinder head goes, it usually means that oil will start pumping out of the engine."

Seconds later the engine caught fire and began trailing a plume of flames. Pee Wee yelled, "I'm securing the fuel flow to the engine! If it continues to burn we'll have to try the CO2!"

Bud looked at the DME, nineteen miles to Danang. Starved of fuel, the engine shut down but the trail of flames continued.

"Try to feather the prop," Bud shouted. He had the left engine up to full power with the water injection engaged. The airplane maintained altitude for half a minute and then began to lose altitude.

"It's no good," Pee Wee shouted. We can't feather."

"We're in big trouble," Bud shouted to Shug, "with the load we've got, this thing is not going maintain altitude on one engine. Get Danang on the radio. Tell him we're declaring an emergency. Tell him we need crash crews to be out on the field standing-by."

Shug radioed the tower.

"Fire's out," Pee Wee said in a relieved voice, "must have severed a fuel line when that jug blew apart."

"Magpie," Danang tower radioed, "you are cleared for emergency landing, any runway at your discretion. Crash crews are standing-by."

"Tell him we'll make a straight-in on one seven right."

Shug relayed the information.

Bud talked over the IC so that everybody could hear him, "The fire is out. Now here's the plan. We've got enough altitude to make the field, so I'm going straight in. You guys in the back make sure that all stretchers are secured, especially the ones on the deck. When Pee Wee gives you word, everybody strap-in just in case. We'll let you know if anything changes."

Two miles from the end of the runway they were descending through three thousand feet. "Okay," Bud said, "at one mile I want to bring in ten degrees of flaps and put the wheels down. Once we are over the runway, we'll bring the flaps to full deflection."

"Got it," Shug answered.

A minute later, Bud said, "Okay, one mile."

Shug moved the flap handle to the first detent. The flaps did not move. "What the hell," Shug said and tried the handle again. He put it in the second detent and still the flaps didn't move.

"Pee Wee, get up here," Bud shouted, the little crew chief appeared almost instantly.

"No flaps," Shug said.

Pee Wee glanced at the hydraulic pressure gauges. "The B hydraulic system is gone. Must have been hit by the flak we took and all the fluid blew out. We won't have flaps or landing gear!"

"Jesus Christ," Bud shouted, "can't we crank the wheels down?"

Pee Wee looked ahead at the rapidly approaching runway. "Can't do it, we don't have time."

"Son of a bitch!" Bud shouted. He called over the IC, "Stand-by for a wheels up landing. All hands get strapped in on the double!"

Shug called the tower and advised them of this new crisis. The airplane passed the runway threshold one hundred feet above the ground.

"When I give you the word," Bud said to Shug very calmly, "shut off the mags, the master switches and the fuel feed."

"Roger".

Because of the quartering tail wind and no flaps, they were going touch down at a ground speed of around 120 knots. Bud eased the throttle back very carefully. As the old transport settled toward the ground, Bud shouted, "Okay, secure the engine."

He used the rudder to keep the nose straight down the center. The airplane landed flat onto the runway in a great shower of sparks and screeching metal. Blades of the left prop dug in and caused the airplane to pivot slightly. The crippled machine slid off the runway onto the grass and headed toward a steel radar structure. Incapable of steering the aircraft, Bud and Shug were now spectators. As the radar structure came closer, it became obvious that some part of the airplane was going to strike the steel object. Quite calmly Bud remarked, "Well, this is not good." The right wing and engine took the brunt of the impact. Part of the engine sheared off. Due to this one-sided impact, the aircraft rotated nearly ninety degrees and continued forward throwing up a deluge of grass and mud. Seconds later, the pilot's side of the nose struck a squat cinder block building painted in orange and white squares. The side window and a large portion of the left windshield exploded in a shower of flying pieces.

Chapter 21

Unexplained Metamorphous

The Trauma Center in the naval hospital at Danang was suddenly filled with wounded from the crash of the C-46. In order to balance the unexpected patient load, a number of the Khe Sanh Marines were air lifted to the Hospital Ship Comfort docked at the Navy Piers. The crew of the C-46 was taken to the Danang hospital. Shug Early and Pee Wee had very luckily sustained only superficial cuts from pieces of flying plexi-glass. Having been securely strapped in their seats, JJ and Winston had suffered no injuries. Two Marines had died due additional wounds they received from 23 mm rounds as the old transport climbed out of Khe Sanh.

Bud Cotter was unconscious and in critical condition with serious head injuries. A piece of flying plexi-glass the size of a dinner plate had hit him squarely in the forehead. His helmet had absorbed much of the force, but shards of plastic were imbedded in his forehead and cranium.

"Doctor Whitefield," a Navy nurse said as Margo was suturing a shrapnel wound on a Marine's leg.

Without looking up from her task, Margo said, "Yes, what is it?"

"The pilot of that crashed transport aircraft is in trauma cube four. Doctor Trudell is with him now. When we checked his dog tags, he is identified as Lieutenant Toland Cotter, USN. We think he might be the officer who was with you at the New Year's Eve Party. We thought you would want to know."

Snipping excess thread off the last suture with scissors, Margo replied. "I'm sure it's not him. The name of the officer I was with is Bud Cotter, and he doesn't fly transport aircraft, he flies those big noisy propeller planes that carry bombs under the wings. Thanks for thinking of me. It was sweet of you to let me know."

Fifteen minutes later, Margo was sitting at a nurse's station writing in a medical file. Shug Early and Pee Wee walked up to the desk. Both men had numerous small bandages and Band-aids covering wounds on their foreheads and faces.

"Excuse me, ma'am," Shug said.

Margo looked up, "Yes, what is it?"

"Sorry to bother you, but we're trying to get some information on our buddy who was hurt in the plane crash about an hour ago."

"What's his name?"

"Lieutenant jay gee Bud, I mean Toland Cotter. He's in navy squadron VC-110."

The color drained from Margo's face. She stared at the men for a moment. "Was he the pilot of that transport that crashed?"

"Yes, Ma'am."

"Oh my, God. Wait here and I'll have someone take care of you."

"Thank you, Ma'am."

Margo ran down the long hall and through two double doors into the trauma ward area. She corralled a corpsman and asked him to take care of the men at the nurse station. Several treatment cubicles were crowded with doctors and nurses. Margo hurried to cubicle four where navy Doctor Mark Trudell and a nurse were working. Through the mask of dried blood, Margo instantly recognized Bud's face. Trudell looked up, he was wearing surgical green and his face was masked. "Hello, Margo, I could use a hand here if you're not tied up."

"I'll scrub and be right back."

Scrubbed and dressed in a fresh green smock, mask and gloves, she rushed back to the table.

"What have you got here, Mark?"

"Well, right now he has several pieces of plastic windshield embedded in this face, forehead and scalp. Lot of hemorrhaging to deal with, I'm concerned that one or more pieces of this material may have punctured the skull. We won't know until we get some pictures. Right now we need to extract as much of this material as we can, isolate the hemorrhaging and get the X-rays done."

Doctors Whitefield and Trudell spent the next hour removing pieces of windshield and suturing wounds. The nurse shaved some of Bud's hair so that a large flap of his scalp could be sutured.

The x-rays indicated that one small piece of the windshield had penetrated the skull and was embedded in the bone. Surgery would have to be scheduled. Margo immediately called the Comfort and asked for the neurosurgeon, Captain John Forte. Doctor Forte consented to come to the hospital and perform the delicate surgery which lasted nearly two hours.

Listed as critical, Bud Cotter was placed in the intensive care unit where he was connected to a series of monitors that displayed and recorded his critical bodily functions. Margo sat with him until one-thirty in the morning. Through all of this, Margo was in a state so unlike herself. Never had she been so unsettled over a patient. She knew the odds for his survival and it frightened her. She understood all the complications that were possible with a head injury of this magnitude. He had been in a coma-like state since the crash, not a good sign.

Exhausted from a twenty hour day, Margo left explicit instructions for the staff to call her if there was any change in Bud's condition. Wearily, she walked to her quarters, sat down on the couch and cried. She didn't understand why she was weeping. She hadn't wept in years. She was confused and completely out of sorts. The plane crash and injury of Bud Cotter had somehow penetrated the protective wall of her austere professionalism. She decided that she needed a good night's sleep. That would rest her mind so that she could think clearly. She showered, fell into her bed and slept until six-thirty. When she awoke, she immediately called the nurses desk in the intensive care unit. The charge nurse told her that there had been no change during the night.

Bud Cotter opened his eyes and squinted at the bright light above him. He was not aware of his whereabouts. He remembered nothing of the crash. He thought that he must be dreaming and closed his eyes. A few minutes later a nurse came into his cubicle and began to record his vital signs. She was shocked when he said, "Could you tell me where I am?"

"You are in the hospital here at Danang," she said. "You've been injured and you have been unconscious for almost a day. How do you feel, Lieutenant?"

"I don't know," he said, "I don't feel anything. I'd like to go to sleep now, I'm very tired." He closed his eyes and drifted back into unconsciousness.

When the nurse called her about Bud, Margo hurried to Intensive Care. She was simultaneously disappointed and happy. This was a good sign. She lifted his eyelids and examined his eyes. He was in a comatose state again. In this condition, there existed a high probability that he would drift into and out of consciousness at various times. He was heavily sedated to keep him quiet and calm. His brain was swollen and needed time to correct itself. The fracture of his skull in the forehead had created a bruise on his brain. This would take time to resolve itself.

Bud Cotter remained in a torpid state for another two days. Suddenly he awoke. He realized that he was in the hospital, but he couldn't understand why. He felt great, except that the light hurt his eyes. He decided that he would get up and see what this was all about. Try as he may, he could not sit up. He could barely move his arms. He said in a weak voice, “What is going on?” A nurse in the next cubicle heard him. She walked in and saw that he was awake.

“How are you feeling, Lieutenant?”

“I feel fine, but I can’t get up. I can barely move.”

“Yes, I understand. It’s because of the medication. You have a very bad head injury and you have to lie still. Let me call Doctor Whitefield.”

Margo rushed into the cubicle. A flood of reserved happiness swept through her. Leaning over him, she softly said, “Hello, Bud.”

He looked at her for a long agonizing moment, “Hello, Margo.”

Tears filled her eyes and trickled across her cheek. He remembered her name! Maybe, just maybe he was going to be okay!

“Why are you crying, Margo?”

“Oh, Bud,” she said. “I’m just so happy that you are awake. It’s been a very long three days and we didn’t know how long you were going to remain comatose.” She took his hand and held it between her hands.

“I’ve been fine,” he said. “I was away for awhile but now I’m back.”

Margo didn’t know what to say. She decided that he had been dreaming, and because he was sedated he was possibly confused.

“I’m glad that you are back with us now, Bud.”

“I’d really like some coffee,” he said and closed his eyes.

During the next several days, the sedative was decreased incrementally until Bud was no longer in a state of sedation. He was sitting up with the hospital bed raised and he had begun to eat soft foods. He drank lots of fluids, mostly iced water and coffee and he often complained of a headache.

One week after the crash, Bud was moved from the ICU to an open ward. His buddies from the squadron dropped by to see him and Shug was a faithful daily visitor. Even Jack Ferguson, Sonny Miles and Mad Dog had taken time out of their busy schedules to make a couple of visits.

Whenever her workload allowed, Margo spent her free time with Bud. She sat with him until he went to sleep in the evenings and usually she was there for him when he awoke. Her days were long and arduous, but caring for Bud made her happy and gave her a new sense of accomplishment, yet she remained confused, unable to grasp what was occurring within her. She didn't understand what had happened to bring about this startling change in her emotions, and to some extent, her personality. When she was with Bud Cotter, she was no longer the austere professional Doctor Margo Whitefield. What had happened? What was going on?

Ten days after the crash, Bud could stand, and despite wobbly legs he went to the head on his own. He hated bedpans and those things you had to pee into. The IV had been removed and now he was finally free to move around the room. Margo went to the Base Exchange and bought slippers for him. He graduated from that humiliating hospital gown to short summer pajamas. Life was looking better all the time and he looked forward to the day that he could return to work.

On a sunny afternoon in March Bud was sitting outside the hospital on a covered veranda watching the aircraft takeoff and land. The veranda provided a perfect view of the runways. He was most interested in the VC-110 aircraft as they roared and rumbled aloft laden with bombs, rockets and napalm. Bud was puffing on a fat cigar and sipping iced tea from a tall glass. Margo appeared and sat in the chair next to him.

"How are you feeling, Bud?"

"I had a headache again. The nurse gave me something. It seems to be getting better."

"You know that you're going to have headaches off and on for some time."

"Yeah, I know. Everybody has told me that a million times."

They sat in silence for a while until Bud said, "Margo, I want to thank you for all that you are doing for me. I know that it's difficult for you. You have an awful lot going on to be spending so much of your time with me. I don't deserve all this special treatment."

"Oh, I think you do deserve it, Bud, and well, you see, I want to do it."

"But why, Margo? I don't understand."

She looked shyly away for a moment. "I don't know, because you're my friend, and I care about you, and it makes me happy."

"Can I tell you something?"

"Of course, you can tell me anything."

"After Phyllis was killed, I swore that I would never again allow myself to get emotionally close to another woman. The agony of losing someone is something I never want to experience again. The few times that you and I were together, as innocent as those times were made me feel very guilty, like I am being disloyal to Phyllis."

"I'm sorry, Bud. Why didn't you tell me how you felt?"

"I couldn't do that, Margo. It wasn't your fault and I didn't want you to feel regretful because of me. Being so busy flying 6 or 8 hours day in and day out was good therapy for me. It kept my mind off a lot of things, especially how much I missed Phyllis. Sometimes I thought about you, but the guilt was too much and I tried to keep you out of my mind. I wanted us to be friends, but I was afraid and very guilty. When I woke up after the crash, I don't know why, but things seemed much different. I saw your face and heard your voice and I was glad, really glad, and I didn't feel quite so guilty anymore."

Tiny tears began to stream across her cheeks and she wiped them with her fingers. "I don't know what to think about you, Bud Cotter," she sniffled. "You make me absolutely crazy. I am doing things and feeling things that I've never experienced before. I've learned what it means to genuinely care about someone outside my family, and a man for God's sake. Even as far back as high school, I have smothered my feelings and never allowed any male to get close to me. I didn't want to be close to anyone. I didn't want to be involved. I didn't trust any male outside of my family, and besides, I was too wrapped up in my studies and my career. I've been getting along very well all these years and I felt satisfied with my life the way it was, a Doctor of Medicine, a professional. I was helping my patients and our troops without attachment or emotion. Then out of nowhere you came along with your polite manners, your thoughtfulness, that seductive southern charm, your unconscious dashing demeanor. You had a jolting effect on me, something so foreign that I am frightened, bewildered and all out of sorts. I can't put into words how badly I panicked when I learned that you were injured in that plane crash. I never panic, over anything, that's one of my rare strong points, but for whatever reason, I panicked over you because I feared that I may never see you alive again. You are changing my whole life, Bud Cotter, and I truly didn't believe that anyone on this earth was capable of doing that."

“Margo, I haven’t done anything except crash an airplane and get my brains scrambled.”

“Oh, yes you have. Because of you, I have changed as a person, and in a good way.”

“Margo, what you’re saying makes me feel good inside, but I think you give me too much credit, I really do.”

She gazed at him with a sad melancholy smile. “Like it or not, Bud Cotter, you have become my closest friend and confidant. I’ve come to trust you completely. Until you came into my life, it was utterly impossible for me to befriend or trust any man.”

“There are lots of good men in this world, Margo. There are lots of good and decent men right here on this base. Not everyone is a sex crazed maniac.”

She took a Kleenex out of her white coat and wiped the tears off her cheeks. “I’m going to tell you something, Bud, something that no one outside my family knows about.” She hesitated, trying to regain her composure. “See what you’ve done to me Bud Cotter! I’ve not cried in years. Now it seems that I cry at any little thing that concerns you and me.” She daubed her eyes with the Kleenex and looked at him with melancholy eyes.

“What did you want to tell me, Margo?”

Visibly, she took a deep breath as though she were bolstering her courage. “When I was fourteen, I was raped by two drunken migrant workers. One held me down while the other one raped me. When they were finished with me, they walked away laughing. It was the most horrible, disgusting and painful thing that I could ever have imagined.”

“Jesus Christ, Margo!” He was astounded and didn’t know what to say.

“Of course the sheriff picked them up right away,” she said as she sniffled and wiped her nose. “The next day, when I was discharged from the hospital, my dad had to take me down to the county lock-up to identify them."

"I hope the bastards got the gas chamber," Bud said.

"No, they didn't. They never went to trial. They just disappeared."

"You mean they escaped from jail?"

Margo stared at him, her pretty face drawn by lines of sadness. "No, Bud, they didn't escape. They just disappeared. You have to understand. I grew up in a very conservative farming and ranching community in Montana. Justice, if you can call it that, is sometimes administered without a trial to make an example of criminals. When the two Mexicans disappeared, the word spread very quickly throughout the Mexican and Indian populations that raping a white girl in Montana is an automatic death sentence."

"Jesus, Margo, I feel so badly for you. I don't know what to say."

"I've never told anyone until now. Maybe you'll realize how much I've come to truly trust you, Bud Cotter." He took her hand and stood, and he gently held her as she quietly wept. He was moved and monumentally sympathetic for her. They stood there while two divisions of heavily laden VC-110 Skyraiders roared away from the field.

Shug Early and Too Tall walked out onto the veranda. "Son, we've been all over this place looking for you. Hi, Doctor Margo."

"Hi, guys," she said, wiping her eyes.

"You people would have to show up now," Bud said with an irritated tone as he and Margo shared a look of mutual acquiescence.

Shug and Too Tall dropped into chairs. "I've got big news, son. Real big news: the first thing is that the skipper is turning me loose to fly combat sorties. I've been working my tail off flying with Popcorn. I've flown his wing on a couple of SAR runs." He smiled proudly and stuck out his chest. "I am now officially Too Tall's wingman. I'm finally going to get some trigger time, son!"

"Outstanding, Lad, that's great! Too Tall, think you're you ready for this?"

"Ask me tomorrow after we fly our first run together."

"Shute," Shug spat, "I'll be the best wingman you ever had, son."

"That's true, since I've never had a wingman before." They all laughed.

"Well, congratulations to you both," said Bud.

"Thanks, son, now I've got more news." Shug said, "and well, maybe I should have told you this first. You have been recommended to get the Navy Cross. And you and I have been recommended for a DFC and a Purple Heart. Pee Wee is up for a Purple Heart and a Bronze Star. JJ, Winston and those two corpsmen are being recommended for a Bronze star. "

"What! What for? You've got to be kidding me, Lad. Who's goddamn asinine idea is this?"

Shug shrugged, "I don't know, the Skipper's I guess."

"The Skipper! I don't believe it! He would never do that. I just can't believe this!" A sharp fierce pain shot through his head. He stood motionless and held the bandage tightly with both hands.

Margo grasped him, "Bud what is it? What's the matter?"

"I'm okay. Just give me a minute."

Margo drew an examination light out of a pocket. "Let me see your eyes," she said, lifting his chin and focusing the light into each of his eyes as she quickly examined him. “Go and sit down.”

“Do we need to leave,” Shug said to Margo.

“No, it’s alright,“ Margo said, “as long as Bud doesn’t get upset he’ll be fine.”

“You heard the doctor didn’t you, son?”

“Yeah, I heard her. How am I supposed to stay calm when I hear crap like that? This is unbelievable, unbelievable!”

“There’s one more thing,” Shug said hesitantly, “on second thought, maybe I’d better wait and tell you another time.”

“Tell me now,” Bud said in an aggravated tone, “I’d prefer to have my bad news in one dose.”

“Well, Son, the Skipper has orders not to let you fly unless he gets written approval from COMNAVAIRPAC.”

“Why is that? What the hell is going on now?”

“Well, scuttlebutt has it that CINCPAC found out about the crash and ordered you grounded until further notice.”

“Why would this get all the way up to CINCPAC? He doesn’t get involved in minor stuff like this.”

“I don’t know. Maybe he found out when the award recommendations got to his level.”

“What did the Skipper say when he heard that news?”

“Oh, well son, you know how the Skipper is. He hit the overhead. He said he has a war to run and doesn’t have time to baby-sit his number one goddamn Prima-Donna, meaning you.”

Bud ran his tongue across his bottom lip in thought. “I can’t believe this, or maybe I can at that. This smells like something my old man would pull, but there’s no way he could have known about the crash.”

Uncharacteristically flushing, Shug said, "Well, son, you see.........I."

Bud flared, "God damn it! You told Bernadette, didn't you?"

"Well, son, what was I supposed to do? You know that Bernadette and me are tight. With that big hole in your head, well, I thought your folks ought to know."

"Jesus Christ, Early, for once I wish you'd stay out of my goddamn business!"

"Now look, son. I was just trying to do the right thing."

Following a long pause, Bud said, "Christ, I can just hear it now. Daddy will be putting on a full court press to have me shipped out to some flunky staff job again."

Margo was astonished. "Bud, does your father have that kind of influence?"

"Margo, my daddy knows practically every big shot in the world, civilian and military. He can get practically anything he wants. I'll tell you about it later. I'm going to get in touch with the Skipper and see what the hell is going on."

"Cotter, what the hell do you expect me to do," Ferguson snarled, "I can get away with a lot of stuff, but I can't directly buck COMNAVAIRPAC. He gets his orders straight from CINCPAC. You may as well get used to the idea that your ass is grounded until further notice." Ferguson lit a Camel. They were sitting at a table on the hospital veranda. "And I don't want to hear any of your whining about getting the Cross and a DFC. Yeah, I heard you had some kind goddamn fit when Early told you about it. You have been recommended and if it's approved you will accept the award. There's no room for further discussion on that point. Now that we've got that straight, I'll tell you something else. As soon as you get your medical okay to return to the squadron, I'm assigning you as my Air Ops Officer."

Bud was flabbergasted, “Air Operations Officer! Skipper, I’m only a jay gee.”

“It doesn’t make any difference if you’re a goddamn ensign. I’ll assign my officers as I see fit. Besides, you made O-3 on the latest AlNav, congratulations.”

“I did? I didn’t think I had enough time as jay gee. Wow.”

“I must have over done your last fitness report. Besides, they’re bringing some of you smart young punks up pretty quickly. With this war going on, we need the best we’ve got to fill in the critical gaps that are created because of the war.” This comment was about as close as Ferguson could come in paying a compliment.

“Thanks, Skipper. I have to tell you, it’s a real privilege to serve under your command.”

“Cotter, that suck-ass stuff doesn’t work on me, so knock it off. Mara got orders to VA-19, so Dusty McCall will run Air Ops until you get released. Dusty’s rotating back to the world for retirement pretty soon.”

“Good for him, he’s a great guy too.”

“Yeah, well, hurry up and get your ass back to work. We’ve got a squadron to run.”

When Ferguson had gone, Margo came out and sat with Bud.

“What did he say, Bud?”

“He said that I’m grounded until further notice, and when I get back to the squadron he’s assigning me as Air Operations Officer.”

“Is that good or bad?”

“It’s good, I suppose. It makes me a department head. The problem is; he’s jumping me over several guys who are senior to me.”

“Is that going to be a problem for you?”

"I don't think so, but you never know. There have been some transfers and Dusty McCall is retiring soon. Since I can't fly for now, Jack is training me in Mara's position to minimize the impact the transfers will have on the squadron."

"I think this is wonderful, Bud. I'm really happy for you."

Bud looked down at his hands and he shifted in his chair. Hesitantly, he said, "Margo, when you told me about the rape, it really made me sick. I don't believe that I have ever felt such sympathy and sadness for a person. Every time I think of it, I get this sick feeling. I just wanted you to know that."

"Thank you, Bud. I sensed how you felt when you held me. It's amazing how a simple act of touching another human being can be so therapeutic and communicate such emotion, it was a completely new experience for me."

He smiled sadly, "I'm glad it helped."

Four weeks after the crash of the C-46 at Danang, Lieutenant Bud Cotter was released to return to squadron duty. Three weeks later, during a dress inspection held on the grounds outside Navy headquarters, Bud, Shug Early, Pee Wee and the crew of the C-46 received service awards from Admiral US Grant Sharp. Bud was awarded the Navy Cross, the Navy DFC and a Purple Heart. Bud perceived no exceptional valor in the Khe Sanh sortie. In his view, the Khe Sanh mission, although non-typical for pilots and crew trained in attack aircraft, was in itself a relatively routine extraction of wounded personnel. The fact that the aircraft sustained hits from hostile fire only demonstrated the day to day hazards all air crews face while operating in a combat zone.

Chapter 22

Operations Officer

Bud spent the next several weeks training with Dusty McCall whom he would be relieving as Air Operations Officer. The job required not only administrative work but considerable short and long term planning as well. Bud led a small staff of officers and enlisted personnel and basically managed the day to day air operations of the squadron.

Sitting at his desk sorting through personal mail, Bud glanced at a letter from June Chandler. He had not heard from her since he saw her last in Hawaii. He ripped open the envelope with a long blade letter opener.

April 23, 1968

Dear Bud,

I have waited nearly six months to write to you. I want to offer my sincerest sympathy to you after the tragic loss of Phyllis Day. All of us here at the hotel in Honolulu as well as your family in Nashville were profoundly shocked. Now we have received the dreadful news that you were nearly killed in a plane crash there in Vietnam. I hope this letter finds you in an improved state of health. I pray for you every day.

I am in Honolulu at the Wai Momi which is finally completed. I have been working with our personnel staff to recruit and hire the best of the best hotel staff. Your father wants this hotel to receive a five star rating. Doing so requires not only a marvelous facility but also a facility staffed by true professionals. I anticipate being here indefinitely. As an adjunct to my teaching degree, I have enrolled at the University of Hawaii and am studying hotel and restaurant management. It is a marvelous new and interesting field.

Please take care of yourself and if you have time, it would wonderful to hear from you. My address is 204 Kalakaua St. Honolulu, HI.

Love, June

Putting June Chandler's letter aside, he opened a newsy three page letter from his mother. Bernadette has been invited to perform with the Royal Philharmonic Orchestra Christmas concert. She will be performing portions of Handel's Messiah and Vivaldi's Concerto in G Major. His father is now working full time on the Nixon campaign and has delegated the management of Cotter Communications to his Vice President of Operations, Russ Blair. Mr. Cotter and John Mitchell, Nixon's campaign manager, are flying all over the country setting up radio and TV campaign ads. Norman's direct involvement in the Nixon campaign was becoming considerably more involved than he had anticipated.

The phone on Bud's desk jangled as he was lighting a H. Upman. He had developed a taste for the H.Upman Churchill's that Sonny Miles smoked.

"VC-110 Operations, Lieutenant Cotter Speaking."

"Hello Bud, this is Margo."

"Margo! What a nice surprise! How have you been?"

"Oh, I'm fine and very busy here at the hospital."

"Same here. Well, tell me, what's going on? What can I do for you, Margo?"

"Well, I'm calling for two reasons: First of all, I want to apologize for not staying in touch. It's just that, well, I've been so busy, and a little out of out of sorts at times."

"You don't owe me any apology, Margo. I understand completely. I'm also guilty of not calling. Learning this new job has been much more time consuming and hectic that I thought it would be."

"The second thing is: I'd like to buy dinner tonight, if you can get away."

"I should be buying you dinner after all you've done for me."

"Bud, please. I really want to do this. It's, well, it's kind of important to me."

Bud hesitated. He had no idea what Margo's agenda may be. He decided to accept her invitation. A good dinner with some decent wine would be a welcomed change over chow hall and the Gunfighter O club gut bombs. "Okay, Margo, where and what time?"

Her voice brightened. "Could you meet me outside my quarters at nineteen hundred?"

"Okay. Do I need to make a reservation?"

"No, I'll take care of it."

"Okay, Margo. I'll see you then. If anything changes in operations that will hold me up, I'll let you know."

Bud wore starched summer whites. Margo wore a sleeveless emerald summer dress cut just above the knee and matching heels. She was quite seductive and drew considerable attention when they had entered the club. Once the couple was seated in a comfortable semi-circular booth, Bud busied himself with a leather-bound wine list.

"Do you have a wine preference," he asked. The large selection of Bordeaux's immediately caught his eye.

"I'm thinking of having the veal tonight," she said, "a Pinot Noir or something on that order would be good."

"This is a great selection of French wines," he remarked enthusiastically. "They have a Moueix Merlot. It's a very good Merlot from the Bordeaux region. And here's a really good Brouilly too, it would be perfect with veal. Want to give it a try?"

"Sure, sounds great."

Bud flagged the wine steward and directed him to bring a bottle of the wine.

"In the past, I paid very little attention to the aircraft flying in and out of Danang," Margo said, "but since you and I have become friends, I've noticed that your squadron is flying at all hours."

"Yeah, it's been pretty intense lately. The squadron began flying twenty four-hour RESCAP several weeks ago. As a matter of fact," he recalled, "it was just a couple of days after I got out of the hospital."

"What does RESCAP mean?"

"Rescue Combat Air Patrol, basically the same thing as search and rescue missions."

"I see. How's your new job going?"

"It is an absolute mad house most of the time. I never realized how much went on behind the scenes in squadron operations."

"What exactly do you do, Bud?"

Bud related a condensed version of his job responsibilities. Margo listened with interest. She surmised that Bud was being groomed for a future command job.

The wine steward returned and presented Bud with a bottle of 1959 Chateau de La Chaize Brouilly. Bud studied the label. "Fine," he nodded. "Listen," he said to the steward, "This wine should be slightly chilled. Say, oh, around 65 degrees. Can you take care of it?"

The steward's eyebrows went to maximum elevation, "Of course, sir," the steward made a curt bow and hurried off.

Margo regarded Bud with a surprised grin, "My, my, sixty-five degrees. Aren't you the connoisseur? You even impressed the wine steward."

He grinned self-consciously, “My parents have an excellent wine cellar. Growing up, I learned a few things about wine.”

“A regular Lord Fauntroy,” she grinned.

“That’s about it,” he admitted. “When I was growing up, I didn’t understand that we were really well off. I thought the way we lived was normal.”

“Isn’t it funny how kids perceive what is normal,” she said. “I grew up riding a quarter-horse. I didn’t learn to ride a bicycle until I went to college. I killed my first elk when I was nine. We ate beef, venison, duck, goose and trout. I thought everyone lived the way we did.”

“You killed an elk when you were nine years old!”

“Yes,” she laughed, emerald eyes twinkling. “A big bull elk had come down from the high meadow and was in mother’s vegetable garden. It was during the rut and the bull wasn’t at all afraid of us. Mother sent me into the house to get the rifle. When I brought it her, she told me to shoot the bull in the head. So I did. We put a chain around a hind leg and dragged the bull out of the garden with the tractor. Then we dressed him on the hoist at the barn.”

“You knew how to use a big caliber rifle?”

“Well, sure. Mother keeps a .35 Remington in the kitchen for wolves and rogue grizzlies. I used it many times as a kid. Daddy and my older brothers taught me to shoot when I was small. Santa Claus brought me a .22 Winchester when I was seven. On my twelfth birthday, Mother and daddy gave me a Model 700 BDL Remington 30.06. I still have my guns at home. I used to hunt with my brothers a lot, and sometimes I’d take my horse and ride up into the mountains alone and look for an old silverback grizzly that was killing our calves.”

He had an amazed grin on his face. “You’re really are something, you know that?”

She blushed. "It's how I was brought up. It seems perfectly normal to me."

"Did you ever get the grizzly?"

"No, mother did. She caught him in the blueberries one day. When she tried to chase him away, he charged her, so she killed him."

"Jesus! Your mother must be quite a lady."

"Oh, she is. Trust me, she is."

A waiter appeared to receive the dinner order. They ordered veal Marsala. Bud drank iced water from a long stemmed goblet and said, "How are things going at the hospital?"

"Very busy and very intense at times: the number of combat casualties has increased dramatically since TET."

"Tell me again, when does your contract expire?"

"In March of sixty-nine. Why do you ask?" She sipped water, leaving a trace of lipstick on the rim of the goblet.

"Just curious. What are you planning to do when you leave here?"

"I plan to spend the summer at home in Montana. I'm not sure after that. I've been toying with the idea of going back to school and specialize in pediatrics."

"Really, well I'm sure you'll make a fine pediatrician."

"I love children so much. Nothing breaks my heart more than a sick or abused child. They are so vulnerable and innocent."

"Yes, they are."

The veal was exquisite. They ate heartily and drank two bottles of the Brouilly. Heady from the wine, the couple talked about themselves, about their backgrounds and their families. Too stuffed to consider desert, they had coffee and decided to take a walk along the wharves where the ships were tied up.

A gentle breeze fanned the harbor from seaward making the evening less sticky than usual. They stopped to watch a trio of hooting tugs nudge a giant freighter into its berth. Bud lighted a cigar and they perched themselves on a pair of heavy mushroom shaped dock cleats. The couple sat there for hours, watching the ships and talking.

Margo began to paint a portrait of her life before him. Bud listened, absorbed in her tale. She was a child of the Big Sky country, and as Bud had suspected, had been a tomboy as a girl. She was the third child in a family of five children, having two older brothers, a younger brother and a sister. Her eldest brother, Clyde had been killed in 1958 when a tractor rolled over on him. The family's one hundred forty thousand acres were the inheritance from family land grants of the 1880's. Her parents, two brothers and a staff of twenty-five ranch hands managed a sizable cattle operation and a Sportsman's lodge that catered to big game hunters, water fowlers and trout fishermen. Her younger sister lived at home and was a freshman at a local college. After high school, Margo entered Montana State University at Great Falls. When she had earned her degree with high marks, she was accepted to Baylor medical school. Her study and her work became a fiery obsession with her. After receiving her degree in medicine, she came to Vietnam to serve her country. As Margo explained, the Whitefield's raised their children in a home environment where God, family and country were the primary values in a person's life.

It was near 0230 when it began to rain. Bud left Margo standing inside a covered rope locker while he went to get the jeep. Margo felt exhausted and utterly emptied as if a demon had been exorcised from inside her. Much of the pain and wretchedness pent-up inside her tortured soul for so long was being released. She had let herself go completely and unabashedly professed her story to Bud Cotter. Margo had seemed unwilling, perhaps incapable of stopping until she eventually became aware of the rain. Bud had been wholly engrossed in her parable. His view of her had shifted now that he understood what an all-encompassing desolation and humiliation she continued to suffer because of her violent rape as an innocent child of fourteen.

Bud drove to Margo's quarters through increasingly heavy rains. He stopped the jeep and reached under his seat and brought out a neatly folded rain slicker.

"Here," he said, handing the slicker to Margo, "better put this on. You'll be drowned before you get to the door."

Margo accepted the rain slicker and began to unfold it. "Bud, I can't tell you how much tonight has done for me," she said, staring into his eyes. "I could have babbled on until daylight."

"Margo, your strength and conviction are admirable."

"I'm afraid I'm not so strong," she said, fumbling with the rain slicker. "After the rape, I've isolated myself. I never even went to my high school proms. I have avoided any kind of personal relationship with men. It has been my way of protecting myself and trying to deal with all this emotional baggage that I can't seem to overcome. But I'm sure you have already figured that out."

"What I have figured out is that you have suffered a grave misfortune and have found the courage and strength to put your life back in order."

"When can I see you again?"

The unexpected question startled him, "Well, uh, I don't know. It depends. We're committed to maintaining round the clock CAP for the troops in the A Shau Valley. I'll just have to call you and let you know when I can get away."

"I'll be available anytime you call," she said adamantly as she tied the strings of the hood under her chin. "You have the number here at my quarters don't you?"

"Yes."

"And my office number?"

"Yes, I have it."

"I don't care if it's three o'clock in the morning. Please promise me that you'll call."

"I'll call you, Margo. If you're sure that's what you want. But it won't be at 0300."

"Yes, that's what I want. Well, goodnight, Bud, and thank you." She threw open the flimsy jeep door and stepped into the pouring rain. Feeling heavily sympathetic for her, Bud watched the tormented young woman scurry awkwardly through the rain in high heels.

An hour later Bud had showered and was lying on his bed in skivvies, listening to the rain, and trying unsuccessfully to read a chapter of *Pickwick Papers*. He found himself being distracted by thoughts of Margo Whitefield and the mess her life had been and still is to some extent. Since the night they met at the O Club, he suspected she was disturbed in some way, but tonight he became startlingly aware of the depth to her inner distress. He now understood that her mistrust of men stemmed from the emotional trauma created by the violent rape. Margo's zealous distrust of men was nothing less than a case study in paranoia. It then occurred to him that Margo's anxiety with men was really not much different than the anxiety he felt about women since the death of Phyllis.

Lying in his bed listening to the rain beating on the tin roof of his hooch, it was now crystal clear to him that he and Margo shared a mutual trepidation, a very real apprehension regarding close personal interaction with the opposite sex. They were perfectly safe for each other. Margo had recognized it immediately and now at last, Bud understood.

Chapter 23

Operations in the A Shau Valley

June 1968

Cloaked in low rolling gray cloud, I Corps was under the influence of a trough of low pressure spawned from the warm waters of the Gulf of India. The atrocious weather, low scud ceilings, poor visibility and heavy rain showers had continued incessantly over the past six days. Haggard weather forecasters at Danang predicted the weather would remain marginal for the next several days because the system had become stationary. Night operations at VC-110 were at a standstill. Daylight operations were drastically curtailed and limited to hit and miss patrols into the A Shau Valley whenever there was a brief break in the ceiling and low visibility.

The Communist technique in the A Shau Valley was to preposition supplies, then move in quickly with troops at the appointed time to marry up with the supplies and launch an attack. Clearly, as the Marines observed the increase in prepositioning of supplies in forward areas, the need to preempt a Communist attack was becoming paramount. The enemy's jungle logistics system therefore would have to be destroyed before it could be used."

The 3rd Marine Division was responsible for defending Quang Tri Province. An element of the division, Task Force Hotel, operated out of Vandegrift Combat Base in western Quang Tri. Major Gen. Luther H. Rinehart, a veteran of World War II and Korea, and a Medal of Honor recipient for his actions at Chosin Reservoir in 1950, commanded the division. He had taken charge in May 1968, and immediately set out to improve the unit's combat effectiveness.

"We have something like two dozen battalions up there all tied down to fixed positions, and the situation doesn't demand it," he said. "The way to get it done was to get out of these fixed positions and get mobile, to go and destroy the enemy on our terms. Not sit there and absorb the shot and shell and frequent penetrations that the NVA and Vietcong were able to mount."

The 9th Marines, commanded by Colonel Robert H. "M-1" Pippen, was the division's swing regiment, the one most easily redeployed to meet any contingency. Pippen noted that the enemy's first requirement was to move all the things of war: all of their logistics forward from the sanctuaries of North Vietnam, just across the DMZ, or from Laos. "We must do everything we can to find that stuff, wherever it exists, and obviously destroy it. And if we miss any of it, we must attempt by vigorous patrolling, radio intercept, signal intelligence, recon team inserts, and whatever else, to find out when any troops were moving in."

Bad weather, normally the curse of soldiers and airmen, became the ally of the NVA and VC troops holed up across the border in Laos. During the days of rain, wind and fog in the A Shau Valley, General Giap had his supply caravans and troops on the move. Tons of guns, ammunition and food were infiltrated into the A Shau Valley, carried across muddy jungle trails on the backs of men, mules and elephants. Antiaircraft gun emplacements were set up and cleverly camouflaged with netting and cuttings from local natural growth. Depleted supply caches could now be resupplied without the ceaseless interference from American marines and aircraft. New Soviet built field pieces were laboriously hauled up mountainsides and arranged strategically within range of Marine fire and combat bases.

At midnight on 25 June amidst torrential rains, Giap's artillery, mortars and rockets were loosed on the Marine positions. During prearranged interludes in the barrage, sappers hit the wire surrounding the Marine defenses. Exploding Clamore mines killed many of the enemy while the Marines saturating fifty-caliber machine gun fire slaughtered their comrades caught in the eerie glow of flares. But

Giap's concentrated artillery and mortar fire was taking its toll on the Marines. That night, over two hundred rounds of heavy caliber explosives fell inside the Marine perimeters. Sixty-eight marines were wounded, and four were killed. An hour before dawn the artillery fire lifted. Giap's fourth, sixth and tenth NVA regiments attacked the Marines in a three prong pincer movement. The Marines fought desperately, laying down effective fields of artillery, mortar and machine gun fire. The valley was crisscrossed with green and yellow tracer bullets. Very quickly the Marine fire disrupted the pincer movement scattering the NVA units into a retreat that quickly transformed into a rout. But the NVA officers reorganized, opening their second assault with another series of coordinated artillery and mortar barrages. The battle raged throughout the morning hours. By 1100 the situation had become a stalemate with both sides continuing to exchange artillery and mortar fire across the rain soaked valley.

Colonel M-1 Pippen desperately needed air support in order to evacuate his wounded Marines. He was convinced that he could break the back of the NVA siege with just a single hour of concentrated air cover. Pippen had been vainly calling for air support throughout the night and morning. VC-110 was on stand-by waiting for a break in the weather. Ferguson, Sonny and Bud had formulated a plan to relieve the Marines. A dozen Skyraiders and their pilots were ready to deploy in an instant when the weather opened up. Ten other aircraft and pilots would be held in reserve ready to go as soon as the first wave exited the area. Using this shuttle system, the squadron would maintain a ready strike of aircraft at all times until the Marine casualties were secured and the NVA threat neutralized.

That afternoon at 1400, succumbing to the desperate pleas of M-1 Pippen for air support, Jack Ferguson and Sonny Miles departed Danang in an attempt to reconnoiter the situation. Low black wisps of vapor hung from a heavy swirling overcast. It was raining hard, blowing in sheets. Visibility was one and a half miles at best. In the A Shau Valley, a thirty-knot wind funneled between the mountain ridges. The wind provided a bone-piercing chill for rain drenched soldiers of both sides and made aircraft operations in the cloud shrouded mountain areas extremely dangerous. Flying as low as fifty feet radar indicated altitude Ferguson and Miles could not establish visual contact with the marines. The marines reported hearing the Wright engines overhead several times, but could not obtain a visual contact on the Skyraiders. Ferguson and Miles returned to Danang frustrated and disgusted.

"Goddamn this weather!" Ferguson tossed his flight gear into a heap in a corner of his office. "We never saw that abandoned airfield. Our navigation was good too. The jarheads said they could hear our engines." He lit a Camel and slumped into his chair. His sunken black-rimmed eyes blinked rapidly in thought. His flight suit was wet and mottled, and raindrops were beaded on his short hair. Sonny's condition mirrored that of Ferguson.

"Its suicide to send pilots out in this shit," said Sonny, peeling the cellophane off an H. Upman. "We didn't see the deck from the time we raised the gear until we broke out at one hundred feet on the ILS. With all those ridges on both sides of the A Shau flying up there is suicide."

"You can't do the impossible," said Bud, handing out icy brown bottles of Schlitz beer from the refrigerator in Ferguson's office. "Colonel Pippen radioed that incoming fire lifted around 1500."

Ferguson said, "What's the weather prog for tomorrow?"

"Same as today, they think the break may come on Thursday," said Bud.

"Thursday!" Ferguson nearly choked. "Goddamn, that's two days from now! Pippen and his marines can't hold out that long!"

“What the hell can we do?” Sonny said.

“Nothing, not a goddamn thing,” Ferguson spat.

“I have 12 birds gassed up and loaded with ordnance,” said Bud, prying the top off a beer, “and I have 12 pilots standing by in the ready room port and starboard. The minute there’s a break in the weather, we’ll have three divisions flying in twenty minutes or less.”

“You know, the most acute problem is getting Pippen’s wounded out,” Ferguson pronounced, “There’s no way to get rescue birds into that old airfield without top cover.”

Sonny peered at Bud through billowy clouds of cigar smoke. “Sounds a lot like the setup you had up at Khe Sanh in that old forty-six, Einstein.”

“Yeah, kind of,” Bud agreed. “The word is they have about eighty wounded. It’ll take a couple Hercs to get that many people out.”

“Well, it’s a mute point, “Ferguson said. “Cotter, I talked to Colonel Kidd this morning. He has three Marine Hercs on ready stand-by.”

Ferguson guzzled beer and set the bottle on top of a pile of official papers and lit another Camel. “Whenever we get our birds out of here,” Ferguson said, “Kidd’s Hercs will be a few minutes behind us. They’ll orbit south of the airstrip until the marines give them word that we have the incoming suppressed.”

“Nothing to do but sit and wait and hope for a break in this weather,” said Sonny. “It’s hell that we can’t do something to get those guys out of there.”

Ferguson finished his beer and pitched the empty beer bottle into a metal wastebasket making a terrible racket. “The hell with this,” he said and gathered up his cigarettes and lighter. “We’ve done all we can do for now. I’m going to take a shower and get some chow. You guys want to meet somewhere?"

Sonny looked at Bud, "Einstein, do you know of any place besides the damn Gunfighter club and that hole Red Dog Saloon?"

Bud pursed his lips and thought for a moment. "This is Tuesday isn't it?"

"Yeah."

"Tuesday is seafood night at the Chief's Club. Why don't we go over there?"

"Meet you guys at the Chief's Club in one hour," Ferguson said, grabbing his blue and gold VC-110 baseball cap.

Margo Whitefield sat on her couch in a white terry cloth bathrobe brushing and drying her hair. She peered idly at a small black and white TV. Armed Forces television was running the comedy program, *Laugh-In*. Several times during her day at the hospital, she found herself distracted by thoughts of last night's therapeutic talk with Bud Cotter. Margo hoped he would call tonight. She glanced at the clock. It was quarter to eight.

Her phone rang at eight-thirty. "Doctor Whitefield speaking."

"This is Bud Cotter, Margo."

"Oh, hello Bud, where are you?"

"I just finished having dinner with Jack and Sonny at the Chief's Club. Do you want to have a beer?"

"I'll be ready in ten minutes."

They returned to the Navy Pier O Club took a small secluded booth in the bar area. After some small talk, Margo fell into a depressing recount of her desolation during the lonely days and nights after the two Mexicans had raped her. When her dialogue was finished she fell silent, fighting back tears. Bud related his ordeal after the death of Phyllis Day. He described the agonizing weeks and months and the endless nights spent in his room alone and deeply depressed.

Hanging onto the desperately bizarre trust they held for one another, the couple unabashedly poured out their wrenching inner pain and unhappiness, admitting to feelings neither of them would have shared with anyone else. Their discussions were horribly morbid, yet out of these tragic narratives they derived a sense of regeneration, the closing of wounds that had painfully festered for so long. They talked until the bar closed at midnight and then for another hour on the covered patio outside.

The unrelenting rain had tapered to a light drizzle when Bud stopped the jeep in front of Margo's quarters.

"I'm glad that I brought my umbrella tonight," she said. "I still have your poncho. Do you want me to run in and get it?"

"No, you can keep it. I never use it. I just run like hell and get wet when it rains."

She smiled sweetly. "Well, you know where it is if you change your mind." She fumbled with the umbrella until she had it ready to open. "Bud, I cannot truly express to you how precious our talks are to me." Her eyes glowed with emotion and sincerity. "I'm beginning to feel as if I have known you forever."

"Yeah, I know what you mean, Margo."

"I feel like I'm doing most of the talking though. I have so many things I want to tell you. Will there ever be enough time?"

"We have lots of time, until next March."

"Oh, God, I hadn't thought of that! Tell me that won't be the end!"

"Well," he hesitated, thinking, "we'll have to write, and call when there's a chance. Besides, we may have run out of things to talk about by then. It's a long time until March."

"If it were a hundred years, I would still have things to talk about."

"Well, let's not worry about March until we have to."

"Whenever we're together, I don't want our conversations to end. I guess I'm being selfish."

"I suspect it's because having someone to talk to for a change is such a good feeling."

"God, you don't know what a wonderful feeling it really is, Bud Cotter."

"Oh, I don't know. I think maybe I do," he said with a grin.

"Will you call me tonight?"

"Tell you what, Margo, let's make it easy. I'll call you every day until you tell me to stop, how's that?"

Margo gazed at him with tender eyes, "you are too good to be true, Bud Cotter. It's as though you're a genie out of a lamp. Sometimes I wonder if you're really real."

He chuckled. "I'm real. I'm just plain old Bud Cotter with a lot of my own problems and hang-ups. I'll tell you this, Margo, having you as a friend has allowed me to change my perspective about a lot of things, and in a positive way."

"It makes me feel good to hear you say that, Bud. I'm glad you don't feel as though our conversations are one sided."

Bud smiled at her. "I don't think that at all. I can let my guard down when I talk to you. I can spend time with you and not feel too guilty about it. I think it's because you know and I know neither of us wants anything other than a trusting personal friendship. We're safe for each other. We can be friends without having strings attached as you say."

“That’s it exactly. I feel safe when I’m with you. I can open up to you and not feel threatened or vulnerable.”

“What made you think that I’m not really a wolf in sheep’s clothing?” He said with a snide grin.

Margo smiled smugly. “Because Phyllis would never have loved you so much if you were like that.”

Margo’s remark stunned him like a thunderbolt. He stared at her and didn’t know what to say. It was as though Margo had opened the door to his soul and looked inside of him for her answer. Margo knew what she had done. She saw it in his face and it deepened her trust in him even more. She opened the jeep door. “Goodnight, Bud.”

Danang July 1968

Sweaty and tired, still wearing flight coveralls, Bud sat at his desk after a three hour training flight with a new pilot, Lieutenant Shelby Dowda, call sign Cowboy. Dowda had been transferred to VC-110 from VA-115 which was deployed aboard the carrier Bon Homme Richard. Cowboy was an experienced Skyraider pilot and he needed only the required NATOPS check ride in the airplane. Flying the two seat AD-5 Skyraider, they had been south to Chu Lai and Plekieu, up to Phu Bai and south again to Tan Son Hut running touch and go landings and making instrument approaches in the scuddy monsoon weather.

Following a considerable amount of begging and whining by Bud, Ferguson had reluctantly asked for and had received permission from COMNAVIRPAC allowing Bud to fly non combat training missions as a utility and NATOPS check pilot. Ferguson’s line of reasoning argued that there would be no harm in Cotter flying non combat as combination flight instructor, examiner and ferry pilot. Following a two week period, COMNAVAIRPAC issued an addendum approving Bud to fly training and ferry missions.

Sorting through his personal mail, Bud glanced at another letter from June Chandler. She had begun writing weekly, sometimes more often. June sent cards for every occasion, and cards expressing her unwavering love for him. Bud did not write back, but this lack of response seemed not to affect her devotion in writing to him. Putting June's letter aside, he opened a three page letter from his mother.

The next morning was dark, gray and gloomy as were so many mornings before. The rain stopped, and was replaced by a warm, viscid all prevailing fog. Bud and Shug Early finished breakfast and walked to flight ops to look over the latest weather and radio messages. Based on information gleaned from the weather prog charts, the two officers determined that I Corps was in for another day of rain, fog and low ceilings. The latest skeds in the radio shack brought some optimism to an otherwise depressing morning. Colonel M-1 Pippen reported only sporadic fire and no additional casualties during the night.

The break came around 1130. Unexpectedly, the fog began to lift and dazzling bright spots began to appear in the dismal overcast. By noon the clouds were an opaque glare and glimpses of blue sky were becoming more and more prevalent through the thick overcast. Ferguson was dressed in flight gear and in the ready room at 1215. He would lead the first flight out to the old French airstrip code named Alpha One Nine.

The marines were reporting breaking weather up in the A Shau Valley. The top priority was to get the C-130s and marine C-46 helos into the abandoned French airstrip. While the C-130 aircraft were on the ground loading the wounded, the Skyraiders would be busy interdicting the AA and artillery positions with continuous suppressing fire. Sonny Miles would stand-by with two sections of Skyraiders ready to relieve the first flight when Ferguson gave the call. The CH-46's bringing in troops and supplies had to have top cover when the Hercs flew out. It would be a dicey operation at best. Everything had to go off efficiently and quickly.

Bud, Shug, Cowboy and Sonny watched as the twelve Skyraiders climbed out of Danang at 1231. Fifteen minutes later three big marine C-130 transports lifted off heading for a rendezvous point a few miles south of Alpha One Nine.

Ferguson led three divisions above the broken overcast and on up to ten thousand feet. Arriving over Alpha One Nine, the Skyraiders dispersed into six sections, each section having a pre-assigned target coverage area. When the Skyraiders passed below the broken ceiling at 1900 feet, they immediately came under enemy fire. The aircraft jinked and dodged in an attempt to foil the 37mm, ZSU-23mm and 14mm enemy guns. Following the offensive attack plan developed by Ferguson, Miles, Mad Dog and Bud, the pilots first order of business was to eliminate as many of the AA positions as possible. Fourteen enemy gun positions were located and taken out by the Skyraiders in the first twenty minutes of combat. Using their 20mm cannon and dropping CBU (cluster bomb units) and napalm, the Skyraiders neutralized a large portion of the immediate threat to themselves. Their success, however, did not come without a price. The ground fire damaged three Skyraiders. Ensign "Dead Eye" Harding made an emergency landing at Alpha One Nine when his oil pressure dropped off following hits in the engine area of his A1-H. Two other aircraft, LTJG "Uncle Ben" Rice and Ensign "Brush" Fuller scurried back to Danang with heavy damage due to AA hits. Unable to lower his wheels, Brush Fuller skidded his big Skyraider down the runway at Danang. Fortunately the airplane did not burn and Brush was not injured.

With the AA positions under control, the Skyraiders received target orientation from the Marine FACs and went after the NVA artillery and mortar positions. Flying low and zigzagging radically in their tiny L-19 Birddogs, Peeper One and Peeper Two fired WP rockets into the enemy positions that they located. The billowing white smoke from an exploded WP smoke rocket immediately brought the fury of nearby Skyraiders onto the enemy weapons. Within the hour of the arrival of VC-110, the surviving enemy gun positions were ordered to shut down by the local NVA fire control commander. This was judged as necessary to save the remaining weapons from certain annihilation. With VC-110 Skyraiders swarming overhead, three C-130s and five C-46 helos touched down at Alpha One Nine at 1428 local time. Supplies and ammo were unloaded and the aircraft were airborne by 1455 carrying 84 wounded Marines and eight members of a thoroughly traumatized CBS news team.

Sonny Miles and his flight of eight Skyraiders relieved Ferguson's four divisions at 1445. By 1530 the sky had closed up and heavy rain showers once again saturated the A Shau Valley. Thoroughly frustrated, Sonny and his two divisions returned to Danang without having fired a shot.

Bud slouched at his desk, half-heartedly trying to write a letter to his mother. He twisted around in his chair and peered outside at the rain. It was pouring big silvery drops straight down. A small river of water was rushing along the curbing of the street outside. Beyond the street, out on the tarmac stood a long line of black four blade propellers aligned in twin revetments. Pee Wee's crews were working on the damaged Skyraiders from the morning sortie. The maintenance crews had rigged heavy tarps over the engines and cockpit areas of the aircraft. Bud was thinking that it was a good thing the weather had lifted long enough to get the wounded Marines out of Alpha One Nine. The latest weather prognosis predicted heavy rain showers over the next twenty-four to thirty six hours.

He turned back to his desk and tapped the end of a black Government Issue ballpoint on the yellow writing pad in front of him. His thoughts wandered from what he should write to his mother, to thoughts of how to get Harding's shot up A-1H out of Alpha One Nine, to thoughts of the previous night's narrative by Margo Whitefield describing her personal cataclysms of the past. The phone rang as his brain twirled through this olla podrida of thoughts. "Operations, Lieutenant Cotter speaking."

It was Jack Ferguson. "Cotter, get over here on the double."

"Okay, be right there, Skipper."

Bud trotted through the rain to the Quonset hut next door. Ferguson's office door stood open and Bud walked in unannounced. Sonny Miles, wearing flight gear was slouched in a chair puffing a H. Upman. He picked a cigar from a pocket and tossed it to Bud.

"Thanks," Bud said, catching the cigar and dropping into a stuffed chair.

Ferguson dashed a Camel and peered grumpily at his young Operations Officer. "Cotter, the decision has been made to pull the Marines out of the A Shau as soon as the weather breaks. What about the aircraft Dead Eye left on the ground up there?"

"I don't have a status on it yet Skipper. Pee Wee is talking to the maintenance people up there, but the few guys they have are helo mechs. They're doing the best they can to give us a good description of the damage. Pee Wee thinks they may be able to tell us something definitive by tomorrow. Dead Eye says the engine didn't seize up, but the oil pressure gauge indicated less than 10 psi, and there was oil all over the cowling and along the belly of the airplane."

"Sounds like he may have taken a round in the oil cooler or maybe cut an oil line," Ferguson speculated. "I don't want to scuttle that bird if there's any way to get it out of there."

"As soon as the weather breaks," Bud said fumbling for his lighter, "we'll salvage the bird one way or another."

"That's not our big problem though," Ferguson declared watching Bud light the H. Upman Churchill. "I've been ordered deploy four divisions out to the Coral Sea on Yankee Station."

"Four divisions!" Bud blurted blowing a cloud of blue smoke. "Christ, Skipper, that's practically the whole squadron!"

"Well, no shit, Cotter," Ferguson barked cynically, "the admiral needs our A1-H's and pilots to help with something big going on up North. I don't know the details. All the admiral would tell me is that several carriers are involved and they are short of close support birds to fly RESCAP for the fighter drivers."

"When does all this happen?"

"Tomorrow at 1400. I'm putting Sonny in command of the Coral Sea detachment. Mad Dog will be his number two. I'll stay here and do what I can to keep our A Shau commitment running on some kind of schedule." He tamped a Camel out of the pack and lit it. "Now this is what I need, Cotter. You and your people have to work out an op plan for this temporary deployment, and I need it done tonight. Once you have the logistics worked out, I want to review your plan. I'll be briefing the admiral on this at 0800 tomorrow. This is confidential until I have briefed the admiral so make sure your planning people know that."

"Okay, Skipper." Bud paused in thought. "Sonny, I'll need the names of the pilots you want to take on deployment."

"I already have them written down for you, Einstein." Sonny fished in his flight suit pocket, produced a piece of folded paper and handed it to Bud.

"Thanks." Bud stuffed Sonny's list into a pocket. "How many maintenance guys should we plan to deploy, Skipper?"

"Just the plane captains. VA-295 will take care of our maintenance aboard Coral Sea."

"Anything else I need to know about?" Bud said, looking back and forth between his CO and XO.

"You're acting XO while Sonny is aboard Coral Sea."

Bud's face instantly brightened. "Does that mean I get to fly as division leader while Sonny is at sea?"

Sonny broke into guffaws and Ferguson exploded. "God-damn it Cotter! I know damn well you said that just to piss me off! Get the hell out of here and get busy!"

At 2030 that evening Bud, Shug and Cowboy took the newly developed op plan to Ferguson's Quonset. Cigarette in hand, wearing only pajama bottoms, the Commanding Officer came out of his bedroom to review the plan. A nude Vietnamese girl of perhaps twenty was sitting up in Ferguson's bed holding a sheet over herself blinking at the three officers. When the Skipper finished reviewing the op plan, he handed the folder to Bud.

"Well done, Lads. Cotter, have the op plan folder on my desk at 0700." He turned around, walked into his bedroom and shut the door.

"Looks like the Skipper has a new live-in Mamasan," Shug remarked as the trio walked out into the rain. "What happened to the other one?"

"Jack caught her stealing and kicked her ass out," said Bud.

"Man, having a Mamasan sure is tempting," Cowboy said, "what I wouldn't give for some young gook Poontang tonight."

Shug said, "Dog Patch is only a mile or so away, son."

Cowboy grinned. "Don't tempt me."

The Marine evacuation from the A Shau Valley began two days later. The nasty tropical weather system moved up into North Vietnam and Mainland China. I Corps enjoyed a period of hot dry weather and sparkling clear visibility.

Sonny and the four divisions were aboard the Coral Sea flying RESCAP for fighter strikes in North Vietnam, a most demanding and hazardous affair. Jack Ferguson with his six remaining operational A1-H's was flying ground support sorties for the Marine evacuation in the A Shau Valley. The aircraft stranded at Alpha One Nine was unable to fly out and could not be repaired on site. The big Wright engine had sustained damage to its main oil tank and two cylinder heads. Following a great deal of cajoling with an Army Colonel at Dong Ha, Bud arranged to have the Skyraider airlifted out by a giant Sikorski Sky Crane.

Early on the morning of 24 May 1968, Bud finished briefing the pilots for the regular morning sweep up into the A Shau Valley. He sat on the steps in front of the flight ops Quonset drinking coffee, enviously watching the Skyraiders taxiing out. This morning Ferguson would be leading six A1-H's. Harding's Skyraider was being repaired and expected to be back in service the following day.

The marines were gone from the A Shau having left behind nothing except piles of smoldering trash and debris. The marines removed anything that may possibly be useful to the resourceful VC and NVA, the rest was burned.

Since the marine pullout the A Shau Valley had once again become a no man's land but remained untenable for Giap's supply caravans. The ever-present marine FAC pilots called in the Skyraiders at the first sign of enemy movement. Troops and supplies holed up in caves or hiding under the jungle canopy were no troops and supplies at all. When they could move, it was in the blackest of night. Even then, there was danger of being caught by the infrared night lenses that turned darkness to daylight for the American pilots.

Jack Ferguson had six Skyraiders dispersed in three sections. The airplanes were spread evenly across the breadth of the A Shau Valley. The idea was to cover as much geography as possible with each sweep of the Valley. On their first swing this morning, the Skyraiders passed one mile into Laos before turning back into Vietnam. The enemy was nowhere to be seen. Peeper One, Two and Three were also surveying the valley in their L-19's, and except for initial radio checks, the FAC's had been silent.

Chapter 24

Disaster in the A Shau Valley

First Lieutenant Cletus R. Johnson, USMC of Picayune, Mississippi, call sign Peeper Two steered his Cessna L-19 Bird-dog two thousand feet above the Rao Loa River. Two thousand was low, but he knew the bad guys wouldn't shoot at a FAC and give away their position. They knew if that happened, all hell would come down on them very quickly in the form of a fiery death from the dreaded American "Dragons of Death," the Skyraiders.

Lieutenant Johnson was flying his aircraft with one hand and eating chocolate covered doughnuts with the other. He brought along doughnuts every morning when he was flying. He used to bring a thermos of coffee to go with his doughnuts. But the coffee went straight through him and he was always landing on roads and in fields to piss, and that had gotten him in trouble more than once. One time, a village chief came out to trade his oldest daughter, a girl of fifteen whom the chief guaranteed to be virgin for a ride in Cletus's Birddog. Cletus told the chief that he couldn't accept the offer of his daughter, but as a gesture of good will Cletus did agree to take the chief for a ride over his village and rice paddies. Cletus thought that would be the end of it, but to the chief, a man of high ethics, a deal was a deal. Cletus R. didn't have time to argue with the chief, so in order to avoid a nasty confrontation Cletus put the daughter in the back seat of the Birddog and took off. He landed at a nearby village and put the girl out.

The worse thing, though, had been the time he was chased by a bad bull water buffalo that was hell bent on stomping his guts out. The snorting bull pawed the ground and kept Cletus R. treed like an opossum. Eventually a little girl who was maybe six years old came along looking for her father's buffalo. She stopped to stare at the silly man sitting in the tree. Cletus R. dropped a pack of Juicy Fruit gum to the little girl. Gleefully, she tore open the wrapper and proceeded to cram two sticks of the sweetish gum into her tiny mouth. The little girl then turned on the enormous bull scolding him in rapid Vietnamese. She spanked his hindquarter with a bamboo reed and guided the now docile bull toward home. Since that time, Cletus had brought along a canteen of water to replace the coffee.

Lieutenant Cletus R. Johnson was an old hand at FAC work. He'd been doing this crazy shit in Vietnam for nearly a year. He was probably as skilled at this kind of thing as anyone could be. He knew what to look for out in the jungle and on the ridgelines: a reflection, a change in color, shapes that didn't fit, a muddy spot in a creek or river, new tracks on a road or trail. Lieutenant Johnson could see things no one except another experienced FAC would recognize. He considered it a challenge to outwit the bad guys. He likened it to playing hide and seek as a kid. Charley was really good at camouflage and stealth too. He knew how to use the terrain to the best advantage making himself and his equipment practically invisible to the eye. But not to Cletus R. Johnson's eye. He could pick up a camo net a mile away, even on a cloudy day. It was the difference in the tone and texture of the colors. "Hell, a blind man ought to see that," he would say to a baffled new FAC pilot who had just arrived in country.

The Rao Loa river sluggishly wound its way through the A Shau Valley. The VC routinely used this snaky concourse to move men, ammo and supplies into the A Shau Valley. Cletus R. Johnson knew the river well, and he knew Charley didn't move on the river during daylight. But Lieutenant Johnson wasn't looking for bad guys on the river. He was searching for a place where Charlie may have made a night crossing. If he could locate a fresh river crossing, it would help him find Charlie's daylight bivouac area.

Cletus R. was approaching that portion of the Rao Loa where the river begins a westerly turn toward Laos. He crammed the last doughnut into his mouth, opened the window and tossed the empty bag into the slipstream. His cheeks bulged like a chipmunk's as he slowly chewed the pastry. Below, the river began its westerly turn. Cletus R. brought in left rudder and aileron to follow the river's course. That was when something caught his eye. "Something's not right along the east bank," he thought. He rolled the airplane almost knife edge into a very tight turn. Yep, there it was. He rolled out to the right and came around in another tight turn. A make shift pontoon bridge floated on big drop tanks cast off of American aircraft. It was tied parallel to the river's bank and camouflaged with netting and tree branches. No doubt about it, Charles had crossed here, and it had to have been during the night.

Cletus R. had patrolled the river the previous afternoon. He knew for certain that this makeshift bridge wasn't there yesterday. The bad guys must have floated the bridge out of Laos during the night. It was obvious the enemy had crossed the river to the east. Cletus R. pointed the nose of the Bird-dog in a line to follow a generally easterly track and climbed to four thousand feet. The terrain here was relatively flat and dense with vegetation. The jungle canopy was thick, broken occasionally by a meadow of elephant grass. Three miles from the river Cletus found what he was searching for, twin tracks in a marshy area that disappeared into the forest. Suddenly two streams of tracers floated up from the trees very close off his starboard side. It looked like 14mm stuff. Cletus R. broke left into a climbing turn and swallowed hard. No doubt an inexperienced and nervous NVA gun crew opened fire on him and was quickly shut down by their officers. It had been a fatal mistake. Cletus reached five thousand and executed a wide sweeping one eighty, observing and marking the spot where the AA fire had risen from on the sectored map. Even from his position over a mile away, Cletus R. could see areas of tramped grass where vehicles had driven into the forest. The tracks didn't come out into the thin woods on the other side. Cletus R. knew the convoy had stopped and was bivouacked for the day. It was obvious to him that they were headed for the north-south road a couple of miles east of the woods. When darkness fell, the convoy would be on the road headed south at best speed. Cletus R. turned south as if he was leaving the area and fingered the UHF transmit button on the control stick.

"Raider Leader, Peeper Two."

"Big Dog with you, Peeper Two," Ferguson replied.

"Big Dog, I've got a wagon train under the canopy, armed and dangerous, grid, India-one four six six."

"Roger, Peeper Two, inbound on you. Spot us some Whiskey Papa."

Cowboy was flying Ferguson's wing this morning. The two aircraft turned toward the target area. Ferguson transmitted to Cowboy.

"Cowboy, put your nape (napalm) on Peeper Two's smoke."

"Roger."

"Peeper Two, copy that?"

"Roger on the nape, Big Dog."

Lieutenant Cletus R. Johnson turned around and headed toward the enemy bivouac area. He throttled back on the 180 hp Lycoming and began an approach on the target area from five thousand feet. He was one mile out when he fired two WP rockets into the spot from where the AA fire had risen. Cletus knew what was coming. He pushed the throttle full forward, rolled the little Bird-dog knife edge into a one eighty just as the jungle erupted with gunfire. The enemy was firing everything from AK-47's to 37mm AA weapons. No use trying to hide now, the Skyraiders would be on them any second. Cletus R. Johnson's Bird-dog began to absorb rounds from the storm of fire. He heard tinks and thunks, and felt sickening bumps and jolts. Suddenly there came a flat slapping noise and warm humid air filled the cockpit. Cletus jerked his head around to see that one of the rear seat windows had been partially blown out. Jinking, turning and twisting, Cletus R. raced away at full throttle. The Lycoming was running smoothly and the airframe was intact. It remained to be seen, however, whether or not the airplane and Cletus R. would survive this tempest of flying steel.

The two Skyraiders roared down out of 10,000 feet. Peeper Two's WP rocket smoke was clearly visible three miles out in front of them, white clouds surging vertically out of the verdant jungle foliage. Also visible were myriad strings of tracers rising and arcing out of the trees, floating into the cloud flecked sky. The Skyraider pilots could not see the tiny green Bird-dog scurrying away, but they knew those tracers were chasing him. They knew too, that the now desperate enemy would hurl a veritable wall of flying steel into the air in a desperate attempt to protect themselves.

Cowboy radioed, "Going in."

"Roger, I'll be on your four and high with CBU."

Cowboy was relaxed as he came back on the throttle and pushed the prop control into low pitch. Flying at 160 knots for maximum accuracy, he pitched down and began firing the six M-3, 20mm cannons. He watched the rounds going in and wondered if he was hitting anything other than trees and bushes. His fire was immediately answered by white-hot demons of AA fire that seemed to rise from nowhere and everywhere. He felt his Skyraider jolt, and it jolted again, on the third jolt the control stick was nearly jerked out of his hand. He knew the airplane was hit, how badly he couldn't tell. Cowboy shoved the throttle against the stop, toggled the big tanks of napalm and executed a hard turn to the left. The napalm exploded in an enormous boiling orange-black fireball that quickly rose hundreds of feet into the air. Out of this hellish inferno splashed long fingers of flaming death that incinerated everything in their path. Cowboy climbed away at full power scanning his instruments for signs of trouble. Everything was in the green. He experimented with the flight controls, sluggish on aileron, everything else seemed okay. "What the hell were those big jolts," he thought, taking a quick glance around. Two feet inboard from the right wing tip was a gaping hole the size of a football. Part of the right aileron was shot away and shreds of aluminum panels flapped haphazardly in the slipstream. Inboard of that, Cowboy observed a peppering of small holes, out of each hole streamed a misty plume of 115/145 Avgas siphoned by the negative pressure above the wing.

"Big Dog, I'm hit, losing gas on my starboard side."

There was no answer. Cowboy wondered if his UHF antenna had been shot off. He banked to the left, climbing through eight thousand. Off to the left at his eight, he could see the smoke and burning jungle where his napalm had exploded. Abruptly out of the burning target area there appeared a tremendous flash, a secondary explosion producing two half mile wide pulsating concussion rings. Cowboy guessed it must have been stores of ammo going off. He couldn't imagine anyone surviving such a holocaust for a half mile in any direction.

Cowboy switched to VHF and tried the radio again. "Big Dog, do you have a copy?" No response.

"Cowboy, Peeper Two."

The VHF radio was working. He felt relieved. "Talk to me Peeper Two."

"Big Dog took a hit over the target. He flamed and went in."

Stunned silence, "Did you see a chute?"

"Negative."

"I'm heading over there. Peeper Two, can you go to guard and call in SAR and RESCAP?"

"Already done, the Cavalry's inbound."

"Cowboy, Ziffle. Four birds inbound on you for RESCAP."

"Roger Ziffle. Caution heavy Alpha Alpha in the area."

Cowboy streaked toward the burning target area. He kept glancing nervously at the gasoline being sucked out of his right wing. He had 800 pounds in his left wing cell. He thought that he could make it back to Danang if he didn't loiter much longer. As the realization of what had happened to Ferguson fully seized him, Cowboy's hands began to tremble badly, he was sweating, a knot formed in pit of his stomach. His mind raced through the possibilities for Jack Ferguson, none of them good. Over the burning area at four thousand, Cowboy saw two dozen tumbled and burning vehicles scattered like a child's toys. A deep crater and downed trees formed a charred circle two hundred yards in diameter. It had to have been an ammo explosion to make a mess like that. Between the nape burst and the ammo explosion, all of the AA gunners must have been killed. Cowboy began to make a widening circle about the target area looking for Ferguson's Skyraider. He found it on the third pass, a hundred yards from the river. The airplane was broken just behind the cockpit. The left wing, canted backwards at a sharp angle was partially burned. A trail of broken trees and foliage led to the Skyraiders final resting place on the jungle plain. The canopy was open and the cockpit was empty. Cowboy continued to widen the circle, hoping vainly to see a chute caught in the trees.

"Cowboy, this is Ziffle. I'm high on your six. I've got visual on the crash site. Have you found a chute?"

"Negative."

"Okay, Cowboy. I've got it," Ziffle transmitted, "Bertha (a Navy HH-3 helo) inbound. Get your bird home before you run out of gas. Skeeter will fly your wing."

The search for Jack Ferguson continued until the aircraft were low on fuel. Flying wing on the Navy HH-3 helo, they returned to Danang in loose formation. Cowboy, escorted by LTJG Jasper Sweeney, call sign Skeeter, landed at Danang without incident and briefed Bud on the disaster.

Lieutenant Cletus R. Johnson also made it back to Danang, but his L-19 was so badly damaged that it had to be surveyed. Miraculously, Cletus R. himself had gone unscathed. He attributed this great fortune to a good luck lock of his girl friend's pubic hair that he kept in his wallet for just such an emergency.

Bud Cotter called Commander Air Group Danang. They put him straight through to Captain Mick O'Reagan.

"Okay, Cotter. I have the picture," the CAG said, "You will assume command until Miles gets back. TF-77 can't release him at this time, not with the situation we've got up North."

"Yes, sir."

"How many operational aircraft do you have?"

"A total of five, Captain, I have four A1-H's and one AD-5 we use for training, but it's CAP and RESCAP capable."

"I want you to maintain CAP and RESCAP in the A Shau Valley. We have to keep as much pressure on that area as possible."

"Yes, sir."

"Don't hesitate to call on me or Commander Gray if anything unusual happens or if Jack Ferguson happens to show up."

"Yes, sir."

"All right. That's it, Cotter. Good Luck."

"Thank you, sir."

Immediately after Ziffle, Dead Eye and Eight Ball landed, their Skyraiders were serviced, refueled and rearmed. Bud met the pilots in the ready room. He and Shug Early had worked out a search plan. Each pilot would scour a five-mile square grid sector in the area surrounding the crash site. A radius of five miles from the center of the crash site would be meticulously searched. Bud would lead the search.

The five Skyraiders with Peeper One and Peeper Three and the Navy HH-3 SAR helo searched until the gray afternoon dimmed into darkness forcing them to give up the search for the day. There had been no sign of Jack Ferguson or his parachute, and no emergency beeper signals had been received, and no one had picked up any voice transmissions on any of the guard channels. Each pilot carried a hand held two way radio in his flight suit. In addition to the emergency frequency, Ferguson could talk to any search aircraft on 122.75, the assigned VHF frequency for VC-110 plane-to-plane or plane to ground communication.

Tired, sweaty and dejected, Bud and his pilots trudged into the ready room Quonset and dumped their gear. Eight Ball and Shug went to the reefer and began passing out ice-cold bottles of Schlitz.

"I'm having a real difficult time believing the skipper went in with his bird." Bud said. "If he did, it was because he couldn't make an egress from the airplane."

"Peeper Two told me he had a good visual on the skipper, "Shug said, flipping the pages of the debrief log. "The FAC says the skipper's bird flamed just as he released the CBU. The skipper was at about three thousand when he took the hits. The FAC says the Skipper's bird went in almost flat. That makes me wonder if maybe he was still trying to fly it."

"Or," said Bud, "he had it trimmed for a bailout. When did you talk to the FAC pilot?"

"He came over and helped me debrief shortly after you guys left," Shug said. "He was pretty sure about what he saw. "Those guys don't miss much, you know. Although he did say that the skipper's bird was obscured behind Cowboy's nape burst for several seconds."

"Personally," said Bud, "I think the skipper bailed out and is either injured or hiding or maybe both. We have to make that assumption. I want to be saddled up and out of here at first light in the morning," said Bud, rising from his chair and tossing the empty brown bottle into a trashcan. "Lads, I'm going to take a shower. I'll be in my office catching up on paperwork. Who's duty officer tonight?"

"I've got it, skipper," Harding answered.

Being called skipper startled Bud to his shoes. A shiver raced down his spine.

Bud said, "I want to make sure the watch section calls us if anything at all comes in over the SAR circuit."

"Aye, aye, skipper. I'll see to it."

"Listen fellas," Bud said a little embarrassed, "I appreciate your support and all, but considering the circumstances, well, it really isn't necessary to address me as skipper."

"Until we find Big Dog or Low Rider comes back, you're the skipper, Padna. That's just the way it is." The others nodded solemnly.

"All right then, well, thanks, I appreciate it. See you guys at 0530."

Bud went to his hooch, showered and changed into jungle fatigues. It had begun to rain when he walked to his office. Bud hoped the weather would be above minimums in the morning so they could get an early start. He sat at his desk, lit a cigar and began to wade through the stack of drudging NATOPS reports, log sheets and a full basket of boring Navy correspondence. He worked for nearly two hours until he had cleaned up the backlog. Bud sat back in his chair and thought about Jack Ferguson. The picture was glum enough. No parachute, no emergency beeper signals, no VHF or UHF transmission on the guard channel, no smoke flares, nothing. Bud thought, "Surely Jack would have managed to get off some kind of signal if he was physically able, particularly with the Skyraiders and the HH-3 flying all afternoon."

He picked up the phone to make his daily phone call to Margo. He told her what had happened without going into detail. After a solemn silence she said, "Can you come over? We really do need to talk. I have beer and Cokes in the refrigerator."

He hesitated, curious and a little confused. Margo had never invited him into her quarters. "Okay. I'll be there in twenty minutes. Do you want me to pick up a pizza or anything?"

"Nothing for me, thanks. Bring something for yourself if you want."

Margo's greeting at the door was somber and reticent. She motioned Bud to sit on the couch. "Do you want a beer?"

"Yeah, thanks."

"So, you spent the afternoon in the A Shau Valley looking for Jack Ferguson," she called from the kitchenette.

"Yeah, so far there's no sign of him."

"I'm really sorry this has happened to Jack, Bud." Margo handed him an icy cold can of beer and sat on the couch next to him. She was wearing jeans and a blue and gold VC-110 pull over jersey that Bud had given her, and she was barefoot. Her toenails were painted bright red, and like everything else about her, Margo's feet were shapely and pretty too.

"And we've been so lucky up until now. When Jakes and Harding were shot down, we got them out so quickly that they made it to happy hour at the O Club, and now this, and the skipper of all people!"

"You knew it was inevitable that someone would go down. You've said it to me many times."

"Yeah, I know. It doesn't make it any easier though."

"No it doesn't."

His focus began to expand beyond Margo and the couch. Bud was startled to see an eight by eleven photograph of himself sitting in his Skyraider. Margo had the photograph mounted in a tasteful frame and set on a table in her living room. Next to the photograph of him, was a wide framed photograph of a group of people he assumed to be her family.

"Margo, where did you get that photo of me?"

"Oh," she said, appearing a bit flustered, "a few weeks ago, I asked Shug Early to shoot a few pictures of you with my camera. That one developed so nicely that I decided to have it enlarged and frame it."

"Oh, yeah, I remember now. He climbed up on the wing one morning and took some shots. I thought he was doing it for our cruise book. Who are the people in that other picture?"

"That's my family. It was taken two summers ago during a family picnic on our ranch."

"Nice looking family."

"Thanks. I love them dearly."

"Do you think I could have a picture of you sometime?"

She smiled brightly. "Yes. As a matter of fact, I've got one for you." Margo jumped up and went into her bedroom. A few moments later she came out and sat on the couch. She handed him a beautifully framed eight by eleven studio portrait of herself.

"Wow, this is a beautiful picture of you, Margo. Are you sure you want to give it to me?"

"I had it done for you at the Exchange. Someone on staff told me about the portrait studio over there."

"You had this done for me?"

"Yes," she tittered happily. "I even put on some makeup so that I didn't look quite so plain."

"You have no idea how beautiful you really are," he said.

"No," she shyly replied.

"And you say that I'm naïve."

"It's sweet of you to say that, Bud."

"This is really a great surprise, Margo. I'll put it on my desk. That's where I seem to spend most of my time now days."

She gave him a sincere flattered smile. "It makes me very happy to hear you say that."

Bud drank beer and glanced around, "You have a nice place here."

"This is my shell where I can be alone and hide from the wicked world when I'm not working or spending time with you."

"It's too bad you feel that you have to hide yourself."

Her face became long and melancholy. "Everyone hides in their own way, I think. Where do you hide?"

Bud appeared perplexed. "I don't know," he said truthfully, "I've never thought about it."

"In the eight and one half months I've been here, except for my cleaning lady, you are the first person I've invited inside my quarters."

"Oh, really? Well, thank you, Margo. I'm flattered."

"I hope being here is not uncomfortable for you."

"No, of course not. I'm sure the busy bodies will spot my Jeep outside. People are really going to talk now that you've invited me in."

She made an unconcerned shrug. "I've reached a point where I really don't care what people say or think about us. Do you?"

He grinned. "Not in the least."

Margo sipped Coke and changed the direction of the conversation. "Bud, maybe it's none of my business, but I'm having a very difficult time dealing with the fact that you're suddenly flying again. I thought you weren't supposed to fly combat sorties."

He regarded her with a shadow of smugness. "Margo, flying RESCAP in the A Shau Valley isn't exactly like going downtown into that deluge of flak and SAMs."

"Well, I'm sorry, but I'm very concerned about you, and legitimately so. Seven aircraft have crashed or have been shot down in the A Shau Valley during the past six months."

"I know that, Margo, but the Commander Air Group has put me in command of the squadron. That changes everything."

She gave him a thoroughly cynical look. "You want to fly those missions, Bud Cotter. You've got experienced pilots who can lead a RESCAP don't you?"

Bud stared at her for a long moment. "Margo," he said in a gentle but firm tone, "I have no intention of delegating my responsibility to one of the other officers. Besides, Jack Ferguson is not only my skipper, he's my friend and I intend to do everything humanly possible to find him."

"You know, I amaze myself sometimes," Margo said reflectively. "Never in a million years would I have dreamed that I would worry about a man outside of my family, and now just look at me."

"I can remember Phyllis telling me the same thing once."

A flash of resentfulness bolted through Margo at Bud's mention of his dead fiancée. It made her angry. Her face flushed and she cast him a stiff annoyed look.

"Did I say something wrong?"

Her expression wavered and slowly relaxed. "No, you didn't really say anything wrong. Maybe I'm being overly sensitive."

"About what?"

"About you, damn it!" Her face glowed and she looked away at the blank TV screen.

"I don't understand. Why are you suddenly being sensitive about me, Margo?"

"Do you want to fight? I think I do!" She whirled to face him.

"No. I didn't come over here to fight with you, Margo."

"Just why are you here?"

He gave her an amazed half smile. "What kind of question is that? I'm here because you asked me to come over."

"That's the <u>only</u> reason?"

"Yes, that's the only reason." He calmly replied.

"Any male I've ever known," she sneered, "would come over here with the idea in the back of his head that he was going to try and get me into the bedroom."

"That's one hell of a thing to say, Margo. What's the matter with you all of a sudden?"

"Please answer the question!" She flared angrily.

"Come on, Margo. If you really believed that I wouldn't be here."

"Can't you answer a simple question?"

Bud stared at her. "Okay, Margo, I'll answer your question. I didn't come over here to try and get you into the bedroom. Not because I'm some kind of moralistic goodie two shoes, but because I made a commitment to be your friend. Besides that, I would never do anything to dishonor you. And there's something else too, I have an old fashioned fetish about mutual love and commitment. In my mind, those are the things that truly define the term making love. If I want to get laid just for the sake of having sex, all I have to do is go outside the gate to Dog Patch and get myself a Mamasan like a lot of these other guys do. And while I'm on my soapbox, I'll tell you something else, Margo, which you probably won't believe. I was a twenty four year old virgin until Phyllis and I fell in love."

Margo glared at him as she absorbed his words. "You're either a very clever liar or you are that one in a million that every woman dreams about and prays for, which is it?"

"I'm no one in a million, Margo," he replied peevishly, "and I damn sure don't have to lie to you about anything. I don't need this shit, Margo. I've got too much on my mind to be sitting here putting up with this." He picked up his overseas cap placed it on his head and stood.

"Bud Cotter don't you dare walk out on me!" Then suddenly, she became contrite. "I'm sorry, Bud. I'm sorry. Please don't leave."

He hesitated and stared at her for a long while. He dropped back onto the cushion. "All right, Margo, tell me what's really bothering you."

Flustered, practically beside herself, she said, "I've been so scared since you told me that you're flying again. It frightens me very much. It scares me to death. Tonight when you called and told me what had happened, I experienced the most dreadful feeling, a premonition of something terrible that I can't explain."

"Margo, we spent several hours up there this afternoon flying very slow and very low. Not a shot was fired. Intel tells us that Charley has moved back across the border into Laos."

Her eyes narrowed, "Don't suggest; don't even hint to me that I shouldn't worry about you. I worry about you enough as it is. This makes it a thousand times worse!"

"Jesus, Margo. Sometimes the things you say are like an echo of Phyllis."

"Phyllis worried about you because she loved you so much."

"I understand that, but I don't understand why you feel that you have to worry about me."

Her eyes gleamed with alertness. "Because you are my best friend and confidant and because I've become so damn emotionally dependent on you for support. Please don't press me on this subject."

He drank beer and regarded her. He spoke calmly and purposely. "I think I understand, Margo."

"Oh, you do?"

"You and I have been lonely and hurt for a long time. We've been afraid to get close to anyone. Now all of a sudden, we have someone who takes the loneliness away, someone to share our troubles and our thoughts with. When two people share those kinds of things, it's very easy to become emotionally attached to the other person."

"Attached, what is that supposed to mean?" Margo began to cry.

He handed her a tissue from the box on the table. “I think the problem is that we have become so dependent on one another’s support that we’re afraid of losing it.”

“Oh, God, Bud,” she groaned miserably, “you don’t know how dependent on you I have become, and it’s only been, what, six months? That’s one of the things about us that scares me so much.”

“What else scares you about us?”

She dried her eyes and blinked at him, “I don’t know,” she said dodging an answer, “just stuff.”

“What stuff?”

“Stop it! You’re pressuring me.”

“Okay, Margo. Sorry.”

She looked at him plaintively. Her mouth quivered, and she once again began to softly shed tears. “It scares me that I feel so possessive of you,” she confessed. “I want to be with you all the time. I feel warm and safe when I’m with you. My stupid hang-ups disappear when we’re together. I can be myself and completely uninhibited when I’m with you. You always treat me as an equal and not like some cheap sex object. You’re such a gentleman that it’s disgusting. I’m not used to being treated with unselfish respect and thoughtfulness. I’ve never met a man like you, Bud, and that’s the truth. Oh, and by the way,” she sniffed and gave a little laugh. “I believed you when you said that you were a twenty four year old virgin.”

Bud didn’t know what to say. He couldn’t decide whether he should be pleased or concerned with her sudden openness.

Margo dried her eyes and glanced uncertainly at him. “Have I embarrassed you?”

"No. Well, a little maybe," he said with an awkward grin. "You give me too much credit, Margo, I'm no different than anybody else."

"Bud Cotter, you are so incredibly naïve sometimes, especially about yourself."

"Maybe we are both a little naïve about ourselves."

"Maybe so," she said, "That's not necessarily a bad thing is it?"

"I don't know, probably not."

He hesitated and looked at her, "Sometimes, all the time in fact, I feel as though I'm being unfaithful to Phyllis because I spend time with you."

Margo pursed her lips and daubed at her eyes. "Maybe I have no right to say this, and I don't mean it in a negative way, but you've got to let go of Phyllis, Bud."

His face flushed and he blinked at her, "I can't do that."

"Do you think she would want you torturing yourself like you do?"

"No, of course she wouldn't, but you have to understand, Margo, Phyllis is still a part of me."

Margo touched his cheek with gentle fingertips compelling him to look at her, "Of course she is. She will always be a part of you, Bud. The love that the two of you shared will remain in your heart forever, but you have to let go of the guilt and stop unfairly tormenting yourself."

"I know you're right," he said miserably, "but it's a feeling that I can't just make go away."

"I think Phyllis was very fortunate in one respect," Margo said in a melancholy tone, "she died wearing your engagement ring knowing how much she was loved."

"She was buried with that ring on her finger. I insisted."

"I'm glad you insisted. It was the right thing to do."

"Yeah, I thought so."

The couple silently considered one another. Bud took her hand and held it. "We committed to always be up front and honest with each other. Well, I've got a confession to make, Margo. I've begun to enjoy our times together more than I should."

"Our times together have become the happiest moments of my life," she said. "Want to know a secret?" She grinned shyly.

"Sure."

"This may sound really banal to you, but every time my phone rings, I practically race to answer it, hoping that it's you calling."

He said with an embarrassed grin, "I must ask my yeoman half a dozen times a day if there are any messages from Doctor Whitefield."

"Do you really?" She said, happily surprised.

"Yeah," he grinned. "I think he's beginning to get suspicious."

They fell silent. Bud drank beer and gazed at the pictures on the table.

"What are you thinking?" Margo said to him.

"You don't really want to know what I'm thinking, Margo."

"Yes I do, very much."

"You don't understand, Margo, let's drop it."

"I want to know," she said softly yet forcefully.

He looked into her clear wondering eyes. Gathering all the courage he could muster, he said, "I'm thinking that we are talking like two people who have fallen in love and are afraid to admit it."

She was jolted to her very soul. Suddenly it was as though a dam had burst inside her heart. Overwhelmed, she lost her breath as an intense flare of joy and fear gripped her. "Oh, Bud," she breathed, "Oh, Bud, I'm so scared."

"So am I."

Their eyes met in mutual search. He gently drew her to himself and kissed her. He was literally overcome with dazed surprise and joy when Margo surrendered herself and returned his kiss. Every second of their embrace brought about wild, wonderful, exhilarating emotions. They kissed with deepening ardor, their minds and bodies flooding in fiery rhapsodies. Breathless, their lips parted, but mutually they were unwilling to release the embrace. Margo gazed lovingly into his eyes and whispered, "That kiss was for Phyllis, wasn't it?"

"No, it was for you. I love you, Margo."

She held onto him and whispered, "I love you, so very much. I feel so happy and scared all at once. I won't sleep tonight."

"Neither will I." He was thrilled, dizzy, guilty, and very unnerved. He stood and took her other hand. She rose to meet him and he pulled her close and kissed her again feeling the delicious passion of their first kiss intensify. When finally they stopped, he said, "I've got to go, Margo."

"I know you do. Please be careful tomorrow. I'll be praying for you and your pilots."

He quickly kissed her again. "I love you, Margo, and I'll be careful." Carrying the portrait she had given him, he walked quickly to the Jeep. She watched as he drove off. Her head swirled through a mélange of intense, tempestuous emotions. Tonight changed everything. Margo finally accepted the reality that she had been trying to avoid for months, she was in love with Bud Cotter, and now she knew, he was in love with her. She was frightened, confused, hesitant, and incredibly happy.

Chapter 25

Jungle Odyssey

Early August 1968

Jack Ferguson dared not move from his position under the dense foliage fifty yards from the river. Early that morning, he had squirmed into a maze of tangled roots and enormous elephant ear size leaves. His egress from the burning Skyraider at the last possible second had scared him badly. The chute deployed less than one hundred feet above the treetops. Luckily he drifted into the river narrowly avoiding being snagged by tree branches. Splashing down in chest deep water, he quickly freed himself from chute harness and scrambled up the muddy riverbank. He buried his chute under hundreds of thick tentacle-like roots which emerged from the trunk of a gigantic odd-looking tree.

Just after his chute deployed, he heard a huge explosion. Seconds later, two powerful pressure waves pulsed past him whipping the tree tops as would the winds from a thunder-storm. It was the force of these pressure waves that had blown him clear of the trees and into the river. He wasn't sure what had happened and assumed it was ammo burning off after Cowboy's nape drop. What Jack Ferguson heard was in fact the massed explosion of two-dozen supply trucks heavily laden with 14mm, 23mm and 37mm antiaircraft ammunition.

Secured inside his burrow of heavy foliage, Ferguson heard the Skyraiders and a SAR helo orbiting the area searching for him, but because the NV's were all around him he couldn't move or signal to his would be rescuers. Ferguson could hear Vietnamese voices off and on throughout the day. Once he had seen two men walking near his hiding place. Their weapons were slung across their shoulders and they moved slowly. One of the men was bleeding from his nose and ears and leaned heavily on his buddy for support. Each time a Skyraider or the SAR helo flew near the area, the men huddled against a tree and looked skyward with obvious fear. Once the aircraft moved away, the men would resume their slogging trek to the northwest. Based on the constantly changing direction of sounds and voices, Ferguson deduced that the NV's who had survived the morning holocaust were moving in a generally northwestward direction. Nevertheless, he was afraid to activate his beeper. He knew the bad guys had direction finding equipment and they knew the UHF and VHF guard frequencies. In order to minimize the potential of being discovered by radio homing devices, Ferguson decided he would transmit intermittently and only when he was in a good position to be picked up.

Lounging in his cramped root bound burrow, Ferguson spent the day alternately dozing, swatting insects and formulating an escape plan. He felt confident that his hiding place was secure. After dark, he planned to move in an easterly direction toward the road he had located on the area map he kept in a zippered pocket of his flight suit. Ferguson reasoned the road should be an easy place for a helo to pick him up. Once he found the road, he could locate a suitable hiding spot within sprinting distance of the road. Christ, he wished he were in better shape. Smoking three packs of mules (non filter Camels) a day had really kicked his ass getting out of the river and into the woods. He thought his lungs were going to blow out. And now he was dying for a smoke. The pack of Camels in his flight suit pocket was damp. "You weak cunt," he thought, chiding himself, "out here in the goddamn boondocks with bad guys everywhere and you're worrying about a cigarette!" Ferguson resolved at that moment to quit smoking, from now on, the hell with cigarettes.

Darkness comes early under the multiple canopies of trees. Ferguson had not heard voices for several hours, but he had heard the Skyraiders searching for him until after dark. He wondered where the bad guys had gone. He suspected that they had a base camp somewhere close by, probably across the river in Laos. He looked at his watch as the last vestiges of light reached the floor of the forest. It was 1928 hours, still early, and Ferguson needed to piss something fierce. He stood slowly. His legs were stiff and cramped. His right knee was swollen and sore as hell where he had banged it getting out of the airplane. Once he had relieved himself against a tree, he limped around in circles until his atrophied muscles loosened up.

He spent the next two hours becoming accustomed to the night jungle sounds and adapting his eyes to the darkness. He checked his survival gear and rechecked his compass with a red night vision penlight. He ate a chocolate bar from his survival kit and immediately felt better as the sugars were absorbed into his blood stream. At 2200 he decided to move out. He walked very slowly and deliberately. Even though it was cloudy, his eyes adapted to the darkness well enough to allow him to avoid walking into trees and large objects. Ferguson calculated he should reach the road somewhere around 0100.

Walking through the jungle at night is an eerie experience, particularly so for the unaccustomed. Every sound is magnified, every leaf that brushes you has the cold touch of a snake, every rustle of an animal sounds like a tiger rushing at you. The fragrance of the jungle ranges from the delightful sweetness of flowers to the putrid nauseating stench of rotting flesh. Jack Ferguson found himself making painfully slow progress. The undergrowth was impassable in places forcing him to make wide detours. He slogged through a smelly swamp where at one ghastly point he thought he was mired in quick sand. It was not quick sand at all, but rather knee deep, boot-sucking black muck. His hands and face itched and burned from scratches and scrapes administered by the sharp and thorny talons of the jungle. Mosquitoes sucked his blood and left itchy welts. The screeches, howls and screams of monkeys and birds kept his nerves in shards. His mind was tortured by fearful thoughts of cobras, bamboo vipers, krait, tigers, pungi sticks, trip wires and little black clad men flourishing AK-47s. Several times he stopped, not to rest but to try and gather his nerves. This was a thousand times worse than he had imagined it would be. He was badly frightened. Jack Ferguson had always been smug about the fact that nothing rattled him in a tight spot. That was before tonight. Jesus, what he wouldn't give for a cigarette. He fished in his pocket and withdrew the pack of Camels. He tamped the pack on his hand and fingered two of the cigarettes in the darkness, they were damp, but they would probably smoke later on. A cigarette would help settle his jittery nerves. Besides, he wasn't that out of shape.

Half an hour later, he began to notice a new and different odor. Faint at first it became potent and pungent as he slowly made his way through vines and dense foliage. The acrid smell began to combine with odors of burned leaves and something like charred meat. He walked another two hundred feet and the foliage became much less dense. It had been displaced in an odd unnatural manner like a wind from a vicious storm had whipped about the trees and plants. The jungle was changing, but he wasn't sure why. He was tiptoeing clumsily through a complex tangle of massive tree roots when his right hand brushed against something very different. Ferguson froze with fright. He was touching something cold, clammy and pliant. It didn't move, and Ferguson didn't dare move his hand. His mind was spinning through a hideous catalogue of possibilities, all too terrible to ponder. He thought of the red pen light in the breast pocket of his flight coverall. If he could get to it with his left hand, maybe he could see what he was touching. Slowly, very slowly, moving his left hand one inch at a time, he located the penlight. Ever so gently, he pointed the pen light toward his right hand. He hesitated, almost too afraid to flick on the light. Ferguson gritted his teeth as his thumb flicked the switch of the pen light. What he saw in the pale red light made him gasp in horror! A human body was partially suspended in thick vines. The eyes were wide, fixed and staring. The slack jaw hung open. Ferguson's entire body convulsed as he jerked his hand away and let go a deep involuntary groan. He tripped on a big tree root and fell sideways. Another body cushioned his fall. The corpse moaned as Ferguson's weight pushed the air out of its inert diaphragm. He shined the light at the sound, a grotesque grinning face and bulging eyes glared at him. He rolled away from the corpse, gasping with pure fright. Ferguson staggered erect and stumbled forward a few feet. His right knee gave way and he collapsed to the ground once more blustering and blowing. He dragged himself ahead and sat against a tree trunk.

It took twenty minutes to get himself calmed down. He couldn't get the frightful picture of those horrible faces out of his head. He waited until the trembling subsided enough for him to take out the pack of cigarettes. He clanked open the Zippo and cupped shaking hands around it to hide the flame. It lighted on the first try. He kept it filled with 115/145 octane Avgas instead of lighter fluid. The damp Camel burned precariously but Ferguson drew deeply and filled his lungs with delicious nerve-soothing smoke.

He finished the cigarette and chain lit another. Feeling much better now, he was able to think more coherently. He realized that the bodies were dead VC, no doubt killed either when Cowboy's nape exploded or in the huge secondary detonation. Although he had only fleeting glimpses of the dead VC, he didn't think they were burned. Possibly they had been suffocated when the nape went off and sucked the oxygen into its all-consuming inferno.

When Ferguson finished a third cigarette, he stiffly pulled himself erect. His right knee was giving him hell. He rubbed it lightly. It was tender and painful. Ferguson flicked on the penlight and began to look around. He returned to the bodies.

They showed no signs of having been burned. He examined them carefully and rifled through their pockets. The soldier suspended in the vines had a banana clip of ammo, a map and some papers in his pocket. Ferguson took the papers and put it into a zipper pocket of his flight suit. Maybe the stuff would be useful to navy intelligence. He put the clip of ammo in another zipper pocket. If it looked like he was going to be captured, he would have to get rid of the stuff. Ferguson knew the bad guys would make things especially difficult if they found North Vietnamese papers and maps on him. He shined the pen light around looking for the AK-47. The weapon had to be close by. He found it immediately. He was practically standing on it. Holding the pen light in his mouth, Ferguson partially opened the bolt and saw that the weapon was loaded. He adjusted the strap and slung the weapon over his shoulder, took out his compass, got his bearings and started walking east.

He walked less than twenty feet when he froze in his tracks. Jack Ferguson thought that he heard a groan. He stood perfectly still. Yes! There it was again! Ferguson carefully removed the AK-47 from his shoulder and clicked off the safety. Another moan, very close, he flicked on the penlight and began to search in the direction of the sound. A moment later he found a VC soldier lying on his back. The soldier was young, maybe fifteen years old. Next to the soldier was an AK-47. Ferguson held onto a thick vine and kicked the rifle away with his good leg. The soldier's eyes were partially open. There was caked black blood under his nose and a dried blood stream around his mouth and chin and across his throat. He mumbled weakly in Vietnamese and gestured for help. The soldier could not know that he was reaching out to the enemy.

Ferguson re-shouldered the AK-47 and thought about what he should do with the young NV soldier. He decided that he would have to kill him. This was war. It was the right thing to do. If the tables were turned, this kid would kill him and not bat an eye, but how to do it. Jack Ferguson had never killed a man at close quarters. He thought of his .38 Smith & Wesson in his shoulder holster, but he didn't want to draw attention to the sound of a gunshot. Ferguson took out his K-Bar sheath knife. He would kill the boy with a blade into the heart. Ferguson held the pen light in his mouth and stood over the young soldier straddling him. He bent and pushed the soldier's extended arm away. Ferguson ripped open the boy's black shirt and felt his chest for the tip of the breast-bone. He would ram the K-Bar upwards at an angle under the rib cage and into the heart. It would be quick and silent. He had once seen this killing technique demonstrated in a hand-to-hand combat class. Ferguson brought the K-Bar to the boy's chest next to the place where his thumb had located the tip of the breastbone. The boy's eyes opened wide with terror as he felt the point of the knife. Realizing what was happening, the boy opened his mouth to scream. Ferguson cupped his hand over the soldier's face. He gritted his teeth, hesitated; and then steeled himself again. Shit! He couldn't kill this kid. He pulled the knife away and returned it to the sheath. The soldier was so frightened that he became wracked with involuntarily sobs and vomited. Ferguson dragged the NV by the arms and propped him against a tree. He took out a damp Camel, lit it and put it in the boy's mouth. The terror in the soldier's eyes lessened. He took a draw from the cigarette and pulled it from his mouth with a listless hand. The boy whispered something in Vietnamese. If the boy lived, Ferguson hoped that he would remember the American's mercy if ever the tables were turned.

Four and one half hours after he had begun his trek toward the east, Ferguson limped out of the thick jungle. He found himself in an area where the trees seemed to be aligned in deliberate patterns. The going was much easier here and Ferguson hobbled along pondering the arrangement of the trees. The landscape seemed vaguely familiar, somehow like a place he had once seen, but of course that was impossible, he had never been here. A few minutes later the answer came to him. "Of course, this is a rubber plantation!" He decided the plantation was probably owned by Goodyear or Michelin and had been abandoned because of the war. The relative openness of the rubber trees was much less terrifying than the tangled ghostly horrors of the forest. Ferguson surmised he must be nearing the road and began referring to the compass more often. He walked on until the rubber trees thinned and suddenly ended on his right. He peered out across a large open expanse of rice paddy. This was not good. It meant there was a village nearby and up in this part of the A Shau, one had to assume that many of the villagers would be VC or sympathetic to their cause. Ferguson checked the compass and looked at the map once again. No way he could he have missed the road. He had been walking a base line of due east for over five hours. Ferguson flashed the penlight onto the face of his watch, 0340.

He decided to rest a while and smoke a cigarette. He sat down and lay the weapon on the ground and put his back against a rubber tree. He lit a cigarette and began to think about home and his folks. They were getting old. He wished he had spent more time with them when he had the chance. When this deployment was over and the squadron was back in Hawaii, he was going to take leave and go home for a month. He and his dad could play golf and do some fishing, and he would take the folks down to Corpus Christi Beach for a few days. His dad loved the golf courses and the seafood. His mother liked to walk on the beach and shop.

By and by his thoughts drifted to his ex-wife, Colleen. She was a real sweetheart. After all this time, they still wrote to each other. There was no animosity between them like with most divorced couples. Colleen just couldn't hack Navy life. She was the kind of woman who needed a full time husband who came home every night, not one that was here today and gone for a year tomorrow. He remembered the day Colleen left him on Guam and flew home to live with her family in

Cape Girardeau, Missouri. He was sure she would be back, but after all this time she's still living with her folks.

His daydream was broken by the startling sound of a trumpeting elephant. Ferguson dashed the cigarette and lay flat on the ground, listening. In a few minutes he heard distant muffled voices. He moved the AK-47 out in front of himself and lay still. The sounds drew closer. No mistaking it now, he clearly heard elephants grunting and snorting and Vietnamese voices gabbling. "It must be a supply caravan headed south," he thought. "What an opportunity to catch Charley out in the open." Ferguson took out his hand held radio and switched it on. A tiny red indicator told him the unit was working.

"Mayday, mayday, mayday," said in a low tone. He waited, the radio hissed with static. "Mayday, mayday, mayday, down pilot calling Mayday." The radio hissed with static. Ferguson transmitted a mayday several more times and got no response. He changed frequencies and listened. Nothing. He shut off the radio and carefully slipped it into the web pouch. He lay low in the grass and listened to the caravan parading by in the distance. Ferguson estimated at the closest point, the caravan must be about three hundred yards away. He wondered how many bad guys he could kill with two clips of ammo. He would have the advantage of complete surprise. He could certainly break up the caravan and cause one hell of a panic. Putting those fanciful thoughts behind him, he waited until he no longer heard sounds of people or animals. Ferguson stood and staggered slowly in the direction where the supply caravan had passed nearest to him. Five minutes later he found the road.

Dawn broke slowly in the A Shau Valley. Gray 1200 foot ceilings rolled slowly from Northwest to the Southeast. A misty gluey drizzle adhered to everything. The air was thick, wet and stuffy. Jack Ferguson huddled under a lush palm-like bush twenty yards from the road. His bush was one of maybe a hundred like it scattered along both sides of the road. It wasn't such a bad bush, it concealed him totally, but allowed sufficient space to see the road, and best of all, it was dry under the dense fronds. He smoked a Camel and waited for 0700 to arrive. That was the time he had decided to activate his locator beeper for a period of fifteen minutes. His plan was to turn it off for ten minutes and then activate it again. Next time he would vary the length of time he would have the unit on and then off again.

Chapter 26

From Hell to Heaven's Gate

It was 0714 when the word came in from an Air Force FAC flying a Cessna O-2. He had picked up a locator beeper signal on the guard frequency in the A Shau Valley. The FAC was passing over the valley near A Loi headed for Danang. He was above the overcast at six thousand, but before he could get a fix on his DF, the locator beeper signal went off the air.

"It's got to be the skipper!" Bud exclaimed excitedly, "There's no other down pilots reported in the area. Let's get up there, Lads!"

Ferguson had heard the engine noises of the Air Force FAC flying above him. He left the beeper on longer than ten minutes and was about to call on his hand held when he heard the trucks coming. He couldn't see the trucks from his hiding place, but they were approaching from the north. Ferguson surmised the trucks had been moving all night and were taking advantage of the low ceiling to make it further south before stopping to bivouac for the day. He waited as the vehicles rumbled slowly closer. When the lead truck came into his view, he could see that it was new or very nearly so. It was built of heavy thick steel and rode on big wide knobby tires. The truck was painted olive drab and splotched brown and black. Set against nearly any background it would be practically invisible. Ferguson guessed it was Russian built. When the back of the truck came into his view, Ferguson saw quad barrel ZSU-23mm antiaircraft guns. A three-man gun crew was sitting on the sideboards of the truck smoking and talking, evidently feeling secure from air attack under the low overcast. The next five or six trucks were filled with wooden boxes and crates covered with duck canvas. The next truck was equipped with a quad 23mm like the first truck. Ferguson counted twenty-five trucks in the convoy, four of them carried an antiaircraft weapons platform and a crew to operate it.

When the trucks were out of earshot, Ferguson switched on his beeper and took out the radio.

"Mayday, mayday, mayday, down pilot calling mayday."

"Down pilot, this is Raider 102, copy?"

Ferguson was flooded with delicious relief. "Raider 102, read you clear."

"Is that you, Big Dog?"

"Roger. Do you copy my beeper signal?"

"Affirmative, verify DPC (down pilot code)."

"Papa Tango one one zero."

Verification of the DPC was standard procedure. It assured the rescue pilots that the down airman signal was legitimate and not a ruse by the enemy to set a trap for the rescue aircraft.

"Big Dog are you injured?"

"Bunged up knee, nothing serious. Get me the hell out of here."

"SAR helo is inbound, report your ceiling."

"Estimate one thousand AGL (above ground level)."

"Do you have an LZ for the helo?"

"Affirmative. Advise Victor Charley convoy Dixie bound, three clicks, heavy two three mike mike."

"Roger on Victor Charlie."

A minute later the SAR helo pilot called Ferguson, "Big Dog, Riding Hood inbound on you, maintain position until advised, copy?"

"Roger, Riding Hood, maintain position."

The big navy HH-3 SAR helo pilot was cruising just above the clouds following an indicator that pointed directly to Ferguson. When the helo crew had pin pointed the exact location of the beeper, he began a slow let down through the overcast.

“Big Dog, advise obstacles.”

“Negative obstacles on the road. Estimate ceiling at one thousand AGL.”

”Roger, Big Dog, maintain position.”

Ferguson needed to see better, he wriggled his way out of the thick fronds and stood erect. He was horrified to see two trucks north bound on the road less than a mile away.

“Riding Hood, inbound bandits. Dixie me, repeat, Dixie me.”

“Roger, Big Dog, standing-by for RESCAP interdiction.”

Ferguson rushed back to the bush and threw the AK-47 off safe. The trucks were coming hard, making black diesel exhaust smoke. Now he could see both trucks were quad ZSU 23mm units. The vehicles stopped one hundred yards south of Ferguson’s position. The gun crews listened to the helo engine and the thumping rotors. One of men in the lead truck was directing the gunners with a long wooden pointer. Both quad mounts fired several bursts into the clouds, each burst aimed very deliberately. Ferguson admitted to himself that these guys were good. They were firing rounds into sectors at different elevations based on the sounds coming from the helo’s engine and rotors. Ferguson was instantly on the hand held, “Riding Hood, you are under fire, repeat under fire.”

The NVA gun director had evidently guessed correctly.

“Riding Hood is hit! Riding Hood is hit!”

Ferguson despaired. He thought the helo was probably going to crash. To make things worse, the bad guys now knew they had a down pilot in the area. His mind raced through strategies to avoid capture. In a lightning estimate, he concluded that his options were poor at best.

The sounds from the SAR helo quickly faded. Ferguson hoped the crew would make back to Danang. The trucks began to move very slowly. The vehicles passed directly in front of his bush and moved on another fifty yards. Suddenly each truck turned off the road and parked next to the trees. Ferguson threw his radio to his face, "Einstein, two Victor Charlie Alpha Alpha units either side of expressway. Yankee me, repeat Yankee me."

"Roger, Big Dog, advise you take cover, repeat, take cover."

"Roger." Ferguson lay flat on his face under the bush. Seconds later, two Skyraiders popped out of the clouds north of his position.

Flying in trail formation, Bud and Cowboy saw the two trucks at about the same time the gun crews saw them. The gunners of one truck panicked, jumped off the vehicle and began running. Better disciplined, the gunners of the other truck swung their guns to bear. The Skyraiders initiated fire before the gun crew could bring the guns to bear. Two walls of dirt, chunks of other debris exploded in two columns as the six M-3 20mm cannon of each Skyraider walked into the trucks. The trucks physically jumped from the ground disappearing in horrific clouds of disintegrating steel, dirt and human body parts. In two blinks of an eye it was over. The enemy vehicles were smoldering junk. The gun crews and drivers had been instantly killed.

Bud and Cowboy roared past five hundred feet above the road. The panicky gunners who had jumped rose from the ground and began to run toward the mangled smoldering trucks. Ferguson, with the vague and foolish intention of taking the two NV gunners prisoner, rose from the bush, tripped and fell. The NV gunners saw him. One of them drew a small semi-automatic pistol and began firing wildly at

Ferguson. Adrenalin galloping, Ferguson rolled onto his stomach, took quick aim and killed the pistol-wielding gunner with a single burst of the AK-47. The other gunner froze and threw his hands into the air. Ferguson stumbled erect. His knee was killing him. He held the AK-47 on the terrified soldier who shook with a lethal fear. Bud and Cowboy were strafing in the distance. They must have located the convoy and were working it over, a risky business at so low an altitude.

He watched as the two Skyraiders pulled up into the clouds in steep climbing turns.

"Big Dog, copy?" Bud radioed.

"Affirmative."

"Bad guys Yankee bound. Inside the trees, two clicks. Deploy smoke at your pick up position, copy?"

"Affirmative," Ferguson radioed. "I've got a prisoner."

"Say again."

"Bigdog has a prisoner." Watching the prisoner carefully, Ferguson pulled a smoke flare from a zipped pouch of his gear. He jerked the cap off and threw it toward the road, immediately thick green smoke began to billow almost straight up.

"Einstein, smoke deployed."

"Roger, stand by for pick up."

His heart pounding with fear and excitement, Ferguson looked for the advancing NV troops and waited for a helo to come out of the overcast. Now three Skyraiders appeared out of the clouds north of him. They raced by barely below the base of the clouds and began strafing the forest on either side of the road. The trailing Skyraider let go cans of CBU. A hundred softball size bombs scattered and began air bursting creating loud booming reverberations in the distance. Hearing the radial engine of another aircraft to the north, Ferguson spun around. He was appalled to see a Skyraider with wheels and flaps down about to land on the road. For an instant, Ferguson thought the aircraft had been hit and was making a forced landing, but just before the aircraft touched down on the road Ferguson heard Bud on the radio, "Bigdog, I'm going to stop close to your smoke. I need you to get aboard as quickly as you can."

Ferguson shouted, "The crazy bastard!" He prodded the prisoner along ahead of himself and began limping toward the road as fast as his injured leg would allow. Touching down Bud steered the big Douglas around a wide sweeping curve in the road and stopped the aircraft abaft the smoke. He saw Ferguson limping badly, carrying a weapon. The VC prisoner stumbled along in front of him with hands in the air. When Ferguson reached the aircraft he was in a full adrenaline rush. He jerked open the hatch to the lower cargo compartment and roughly thrust the horrified prisoner inside; and then he dragged himself aboard. Bud had the airplane rolling when he saw Ferguson climb through the hatch. The road was relatively straight for a good distance along the rice paddies. Bud felt confident he had enough room for a short field departure and climb out before they would get to the trees at the far side of the paddies.

Exhausted, Ferguson fell against the rear bulkhead. The petrified NV soldier sat on the deck with his back against the forward bulkhead and drew his knees in front of himself. Ferguson was gasping for air. His lungs were on fire. His heart pounded wildly. His knee felt as though it had a knife stuck through it. He drew his .38 revolver and pointed it at the prisoner who stared at him with terrified eyes.

The roaring Skyraider struggled to free itself from the muck of the road. Its tires seemed glued into the ruts made by the heavy trucks and the trees were coming up very quickly. With the airspeed indicating a hair's breath above stall speed, Bud brought the stick back and jerked the airplane into the air. Immediately it settled back to the road, but he was able to keep the tail flying with a bit of forward pressure. This served to eliminate the drag of the tail wheel in the mud but also created the possibility that the aircraft could quickly nose over before Bud could make the correction. Bud glanced at the airspeed indicator. It seemed to be stuck on 90 knots. The tires of the main gear cut through the quagmire flinging clouds of mud and water over the underside of the wings, into the wheel wells and into the slipstream of the enormous four-blade prop. The approaching trees seemed to tower above the struggling Skyraider. Bud was half a second from aborting the takeoff when the wheels broke free. Back on the stick, climbing at a dangerously steep angle the roaring machine hovered and shuddered on the razor edge of a stall. Bud raised the wheels just as the tires went through the treetops sending leaves and branches cascading to the ground. He felt the jar of the landing gear nesting into the wheel wells. Bud pushed the nose down to pick up speed. He had intended to stay well clear of the village on the far side of the rice paddies, but now that wasn't possible. Climbing faster now, indicating 120 knots Bud simultaneously retracted the flaps and brought in left rudder and aileron. Turning short of the village, but much closer than he wanted to be, he began climbing southeast and set course for Danang.

Seconds from entering the base of the clouds and feeling aglow with the euphoria of having escaped a perilous predicament, Bud prepared himself for the transition to instrument flying. Abruptly he felt a series of rapid metallic thunks and thuds and he felt the airplane shudder. His right arm was suddenly and brutally thrown away from the control stick and the back of his legs felt as if a sledgehammer had hit them. Something slammed into his chest and knocked the breath out of him. The moment Bud's Skyraider entered the clouds, an alert quad ZSU-23mm gunner managed to get off a snap burst, a portion of which went into the cockpit of the aircraft. The big rounds exploded in the armor plate under Bud's seat sending chunks of the floor plate into his legs and right arm and chest. Other rounds exploded behind Ferguson's seat, a half dollar size piece of metal ricocheted off a bulkhead and grazed the back of the skipper's head. He grabbed the back of his head, withdrawing his hand there was blood on his fingers. The prisoner, miraculously unscathed, fainted from sheer fright.

Bud grabbed the stick with his left hand. Struggling to breathe, he was terrified to see bright red blood gushing from the right sleeve of his flight suit. Instinctively he knew a vein or an artery was severed. His legs were burning as if they were on fire. The initial numbness in his right arm quickly transformed to excruciating pain and now he couldn't move it.

"Cowboy," he groaned on the radio through gritted teeth. "I'm hit. I'm bleeding. I can't use my right arm."

Cowboy saw Bud's Skyraider break out of the clouds vacillating erratically as Bud struggled with the aircraft. "Can you use your left hand?"

"I'll have to do everything with my left hand. I'm bleeding like hell. I've got to get this thing on the ground."

"Okay, Padna," Cowboy radioed. "I'm out here at your nine. We'll get you on the ground, no sweat."

Flying the Skyraider was an agonizing horror for Bud. Nausea became acute; he kept thinking that he was going to puke. His breathing came in short desperate gasps. Each breath brought with it a sharp frightful pain. Never in his life had he experienced such fierce pain. He wanted to scream out, but his chest couldn't bear the pain of screaming. He had to force himself to fly the airplane. He wasn't sure if he could get the beast of an airplane on the ground in one piece. His blood was spouting into his lap on onto the floor of the cockpit. It scared him fiercely to see his blood gushing out of his body. He was terrified of bleeding to death. He thought of tying something around his arm to try and slow the bleeding. He looked around the cockpit. On the side panel to his left was the coiled wire that provided power to a map light. He let go of the stick and grasped it with his knees. The pain was wrenching. He jerked the wire loose and clumsily tied it around the bicep of his right arm as tightly as he could manage using his teeth to hold one end of the wire.

"How are you doing over there, Padna?"

"I think I'm going to pass out," he gasped.

"Negative. You're not going to pass out! You are not going to pass out! Fly the airplane, Padna! Stay with me, we'll be on the ground in a few minutes. Don't lose it, Padna, you're okay, you're going to be okay."

"I can't fly an approach," Bud said feebly.

"Danang is visual, Padna. I'm on your wing. I'll navigate for you. You'll be okay, you'll be fine."

The fire-like pain in his legs was horrible. Bud looked at the blood pulsing out of his arm, the makeshift tourniquet had slowed the bleeding, but it was not nearly enough.

"Navy Raider 104, Danang tower, you are cleared for emergency landing, any runway. Navy Raider 106, you are cleared for a low pass with Raider 104."

"Roger, tower. Advise on the emergency vehicles."

"Navy Raider 106, emergency vehicles are standing-by on the taxi way at mid field. MP's are standing by to handle the prisoner."

"Roger, thanks."

The Skyraiders broke through scattered clouds at twenty-five hundred feet. The parallel runways were two miles in front of them. Bud gurgled from deep inside and spit bright red blood. Horrific pain shrieked through his body. His head fell forward, his helmet resting against the instrument panel, the Skyraider began to waver and lose altitude.

"Level it up, Padna," Cowboy radioed. There was no answer. "Talk to me Padna!" Cowboy snapped. Bud's aircraft dropped away toward the trees, left wing low. "Come on, Padna. Level it up! Get the nose up! Pull up! Pull up!"

The left wing rolled even further. Nose down the Skyraider rapidly picked up speed and raced toward the jungle now less than a thousand feet away. Cowboy screamed desperately on the radio. Struggling frantically to breathe, Bud raised his head and saw glimpses of green and brown earth through the windscreen. He tugged on the stick. The nose of the Skyraider began to rise, left wing low into a skidding climbing left turn.

"Talk to me, Padna. You've got to talk to me!" Cowboy frantically transmitted.

Bud transmitted weakly, "Oh, Jesus, I'm bleeding like hell."

"You're okay, you're gonna be okay, Padna. Now listen to me. Turn right. Get your left wing up and turn right. Can you see runway one seven right at your three?"

"Yeah."

"Okay, Padna, put the nose of the airplane on the runway. Put the nose on the runway."

The Skyraider gradually swung to the right until it was more or less aligned with the runway.

"Come back on the power and pitch up a little. You need to get you airspeed down to one twenty. One twenty. Copy me, Padna?"

Bud gingerly grasped the control stick with his legs. The burning pain in his legs was fierce. He came back on the throttle and watched the manifold pressure drop. He took the stick in his hand and instinctively raised the nose to slow the aircraft. The airspeed wavered, and then fell off to 115 knots. That would have to do.

"Put your gear down, Padna. Do you hear me? Put your gear down."

Cowboy was immensely relieved to see the muddy wheels drop out of their wells and lock into position.

The tower crew and the emergency crash crews listened spellbound to the radio exchanges between Cowboy and Bud. The word had spread around Danang like a wildfire. Practically every radio on the field was listening to the drama unfold. A Navy corpsman responding to the emergency stopped at Margo's office door and told her what was happening. She bolted out of the building and jumped into someone's jeep. She drove madly toward the taxiway falling in behind a network news van that was racing toward the taxiway. Other camera crews were already out on the grass filming the approach and recording the emergency radio transmissions between the pilots and the tower. Margo pulled up next to one of the waiting ambulances and jumped out of the jeep. The corpsmen and the crash crew were listening to the radio, waiting for the Skyraiders to land.

"Okay, Padna, you're looking good," Cowboy radioed, "now deploy your flaps. Give me full position down flaps"

Bud held the stick with his legs. The pain was appalling. He let go of the stick moved the flap switch and quickly grabbed the stick again. The nose of the Skyraider came up as the flaps deployed. Bud held the stick with his legs again, pulled the throttle back a little and shoved the prop control into full low pitch.

"How are you doing over there, Padna?"

"I don't know___I don't know if I can land this thing." His voice was barely above a whisper.

"Sure you can, you're doing great, Padna, just fine. Got your prop into low pitch?"

"Yeah."

"Tail wheel locked?"

"I don't know. Yeah it's locked"

The two Skyraiders crossed the threshold of the runway side by side. Bud was rapidly going into shock and he was desperately fighting it.

"You're at ninety knots. Start your flare, Padna."

Bud obediently drew back on the stick. The aircraft floated momentarily than began to gradually settle. The big Skyraider continued flying another five hundred feet slightly nose up, and then began to quickly settle.

"Back on the stick! Back on the stick!" Cowboy shouted.

Shrieking pain shot through his body as he hauled back on the stick. It was too late to fully recover the sink rate and the big Skyraider dropped in hard and bounced back into the air. The jolt very nearly made him pass out. Bud shoved the stick forward and spit blood onto the instrument panel. The airplane leveled and began to settle again. Bud intuitively held it off with back pressure on the stick, but all sense of height and speed had deserted him. It seemed as though he was floating, but he couldn't be sure. He hauled the stick all the way back. The Skyraider quit flying and dropped three feet to the runway shuddering fearfully, but it remained on the ground. Bud had the presence of mind to shut off the engine. He tried to push the toe brakes, unimaginable pain bolted through his legs and shot through every nerve ending in his body. He moaned in agony and surrendered to his torment, no longer able to operate the machine. The Skyraider coasted, its big four-blade propeller becoming motionless. The airplane freewheeled to a stop near the four thousand foot marker of the runway.

The terrible pain began to seem more bearable somehow. He was in deep trauma. It was too difficult to try and think about anything at the moment. Bud closed his eyes, and when he did, a most wonderful calm came over him, but his pleasant rest was momentary, interrupted by excited voices and jostling all around him. He opened his eyes. A young corpsman frantically cut the electrical cord away and began wrapping a rubber tube around Bud's bleeding arm. Once that was done, the corpsman unzipped Bud's flight suit and cut open his skivvy shirt. The corpsman stuffed a thick battle dressing against the gaping wound on his chest. Bud wanted to tell him not to worry, it would be okay, but it was too much effort to speak. Two men of the crash crew removed the shoulder harness and lap belt and carefully hoisted him out of the airplane. More men lifted him off the wing and gently lay him on a litter. Camera operators scurried everywhere, jockeying to record Bud Cotter's bloody agony for the morning news in the states.

Margo ran to him as they lay him on the litter. When she saw how terribly he was injured, she panicked. She had seen innumerable combat casualties during her tenure at Danang and she knew immediately that Bud was in very serious trouble. The upper portion of his flight suit was soaked black with blood. His complexion was gray; his eyes were becoming glassy. Margo began wiping Bud's face with an antiseptic soaked cloth that one of the corpsman had given her. He tried to raise his left hand and touch her face. She took his hand, kissed it and held it against her face.

A big HH-3 helo was landing nearby. Two corpsmen scurried to Bud, picked up the litter and hurried to the waiting helo. Margo ran alongside holding his left hand. Her white medical waistcoat was splotched with Bud Cotter's blood. As the corpsmen hoisted Bud into the open cargo door, Margo climbed up the steps into the personnel door of the helo. Two corpsmen and a Navy Chaplain also climbed into the helo. Cameramen were crowding around the open door taping the frenetic drama inside the helo. Bud could see Margo talking to the corpsmen. One of the corpsman cut away the right sleeve of Bud's flight suit, located the spouting blood vessel and clamped it with a hemostat. Bud's eyes followed Margo as she went forward to the cockpit to speak with the pilots. He wanted to tell her that everything was okay.

A corpsman took out Bud's dog tags. The dog tags and a Miraculous medal June Chandler had given him were covered with blood. The corpsman wiped a dog tag with gauze to locate Bud's blood type. In another moment, Margo was kneeling beside him. She was no longer unnerved rather she was working quickly and efficiently. She straightened Bud's left arm and taped a green board to it. Margo put a large needle into the vein of his left arm and taped it while a corpsman hung a small glass bottle of blood plasma from the overhead. The corpsman and Margo cut away part of Bud's flight suit with heavy offset scissors. Margo removed the battle dressing from Bud's chest. A thin, jagged, half dollar size piece of metal protruded from a gaping wound in Bud's chest. She examined the wound and despaired at bloody bubbles emitting from the wound with each shallow breath he took. Bud heard Margo say to the corpsman, "it's penetrated into the chest cavity. We'll have to get it surgically." The corpsman placed a clean battle dressing over the wound as the helo was floating off the ground. Margo tenderly wiped Bud's blood-caked face and throat with a cloth. He tried to smile at her. She bent down and kissed him.

The Chaplain kneeled next to Margo. He wore a narrow purple scapular; a big crucifix attached to a chain hung around his neck. He made the sign of the cross and began to pray. During his prayer, the Chaplain opened a small bottle of oil and anointed the dying pilot. When he finished the prayer, he noticed Bud trying to speak to him. He put his ear next Bud's lips. "Father, I'm not afraid, I want to speak to the doctor." The Chaplain looked at him and nodded. He bent low and spoke into Bud's ear. "God is here with you, son. All your sins are forgiven you." He raised himself and made a sweeping sign of the cross over Bud. He turned to Margo and shouted loudly over the noise of the helo, "he wants to speak to you, Doctor."

Margo wiped her eyes with the back of a hand and put her ear next to Bud's lips. It required all his strength to speak. "God is with me, Margo. I love you." His strength spent, he could speak no more.

"Oh, Bud. I love you! I love you," she shouted. Margo held his face in her hands and kissed him. She knew he was dying. The color in his eyes began to fade, and there was no longer awareness in them, his stare was no longer of the living. Margo wept as she caressed his face. The priest knew that death had come. He had seen this many times here in Vietnam, far too many times. He made the sign of the cross over the dying pilot, raised his eyes to heaven and continued to pray.

Margo's face gradually faded away. There was no longer the sound of engines and rotor; there was only the purest of calm. Incredibly, Bud Cotter found himself watching over the scene inside the helo. Margo was frantically ripping the battle dressing from his chest. A corpsman handed her a large metal syringe tipped with a very long needle. Bud watched Margo carefully insert the needle deep into his chest. How odd it was that he didn't feel the needle. He felt wonderful. Never before had he enjoyed such tranquility and well being. He wanted to speak to Margo. He wanted to tell her not to worry, everything was just glorious, and the scene inside the helo paled into marvelous soft white light.

Overwhelming serenity and exultation filled the spirit of Bud Cotter. All pain had vanished, there was no struggle to breathe, no fighting to live. The universe was soft, glowing, immaculate and beautified. Never could he have imagined such phenomenal peace and exhilaration. It was at this moment that Phyllis Day came to him. Aglow with profound happiness and serenity, she radiated a luminous splendor far beyond his wildest earthly human comprehension. Instinctively, Bud understood that Phyllis was a divine specter. She took his hand. The loving touch of this spectacular seraph brought him incredible joy. Hand in hand, Phyllis spoke to him, but she made no sound. Her words came not to his ears, but as thought to his sentient spiritual being. Now he was beginning to understand, death was not the end, but a marvelous new beginning! Phyllis showed him a distant gloriously scintillating place. "Therein is the paradise that God has promised humanity."

Bud said, "This place where we are is not heaven?"

"We are in an indeterminate state between physical life and the spiritual life of heaven."

"Will I stay here with you?"

Phyllis radiated understanding. "God is All Things and God is Love. Those who know God know Love. God and Love are one and the same. Our love prevails through eternity; therefore, through me, God reveals His Will to you." Phyllis began to instruct him, and his spirit was filled with the most intense love and understanding. And when she had finished, Phyllis kissed him, and he was filled with the most indescribable joy. Then she was gone, and the deepest blackness shrouded the spiritual being of Bud Cotter.

NASHVILLE

Late August 1968

Norman Cotter spent a busy morning reviewing the state of Cotter Communications with his executive managers. It was Norman's first meeting with his staff since February. Throughout the Presidential campaign, Norman had entrusted the operation of the company to Russ Blair, Vice

President of Operations at Cotter Communications. The presidential campaign was both mentally and physically draining.

Working with John Mitchell, Bob Haldeman and their staffs, Norman had been the key element in putting together the most successful media campaign in history. Both Mitchell and Richard Nixon were difficult to work with and to manage. Haldeman usually took Norman's advice well and didn't get involved in the business of television and radio ads. Mitchell tended to be overbearing and tried to micro-manage. The situation peaked in March when Norman took Mitchell into a private room to clear the air. It was a clash of two very forceful personalities. When the meeting was finished, they had an understanding. Norman would manage the campaign ads, media spots and arrange the time and place of Nixon's televised press conferences.

Nixon's paranoia of the media made things even more difficult. Norman insisted there be no televised debate. Nixon had been perceived to stumble and lack confidence during the televised 1960 debate with Kennedy. Nixon's ardent paranoia and distaste for reporters had been another obstacle. More than once, Norman heard Nixon remark, "They are out to get me." If Nixon didn't like a question, he tended to become cynical and even hostile with members of the press. Determined not to allow Nixon and his staff to repeat the mistakes of the 1960 campaign, Norman delicately guided Richard Nixon through a well rehearsed and orchestrated media campaign.

Norman was able to convince Mitchell and Haldeman that it was in everyone's best interests to select the time and place where Nixon would speak publicly and the speech would be well rehearsed. In the end, Norman was convinced these strategies would accomplish two things: It would guarantee Nixon's nomination at the Republican National Convention, and secondly, on November 2nd, it would bring about the defeat of Democrat Hubert Humphrey.

The campaign planning was a strenuous endeavor and would not fully conclude until Nixon had won the election in November. Norman was home during a two week lull while the Nixon's vacationed in Palm Beach.

Now he looked forward to getting back to his first love, the Cotter Communications Company. Russ and the staff had done a good job of keeping things in order. But to Norman, keeping things in order was only part of the equation for success. He knew that the company needed the force of his personality and the drive of his leadership in order to grow and prosper.

It felt good to be back in the studio. Norman sat back in his chair and sipped fresh brewed coffee his sister and secretary, Harriet had brought in. He was in his element here. This was his place to think and to create. Norman often said, "Business is like a game of chess." He delighted in the competition of other stations. Nothing brought more satisfaction than outfoxing his competitors, staying one jump ahead of them with innovative ideas and new technology.

It was eleven thirty when, Eddie Fleming, one of the control room engineers knocked on the door. Eddie's normally passive face was twisted and anxious. "Mr. Cotter, turn on your monitor. There's something you should see."

Norman pushed a switch hidden in a panel of his desk. A 25-inch color monitor began to warm up. "What is it Eddie?"

"We think it may be Bud, Mr. Cotter. We just recorded a Consolidated News release from Danang in South Vietnam. It's about twelve hours old. Jerry is patching it through to your monitor."

Word spread through the studio like wild fire. Harriet rushed into Norman's office as the flickering monitor settled into a clear picture. The tape was unedited and had no audio. It showed two men lifting a pilot out of a big propeller aircraft garnished with guns, bombs and rockets. The limp pilot was handed down to another crew who placed him on a litter. The camera zoomed a close up of the bleeding pilot's face. It could be Bud, but because there was so much blood on his face, they couldn't be sure. Blood trickled from on corner of the pilot's mouth; his flight suit was sodden with blood. A woman, apparently a doctor, knelt next to him and wiped the pilot's face with a cloth. When the woman had cleaned his face, there was no mistaking the pilot was Bud Cotter.

"Oh, no! Oh, no, no, no!" Harriet wailed.

Norman sat motionless, saying nothing. The employees were silent, bewildered by what they saw. The woman was holding Bud's hand talking to him. The camera operator had positioned himself to clearly record the scene. Everyone in the room wondered who the woman doctor was. In the background a big helicopter landed. Two corpsmen picked up the litter and rushed towards the helo. The woman ran alongside holding Bud's hand. She bounded up steps into the helicopter. Moments later the camera arrived at the wide cargo door of the helicopter and began to record the activity inside. The woman doctor and a corpsman were putting an IV into Bud's arm. Another corpsman cut away the right sleeve of Bud's flight suit. People were all around him, fighting to save his life. The camera backed away from the helicopter as it lifted into the air and swiftly headed away. The tape ended.

The scene in Norman Cotter's office was one of shock and disbelief. Women were softly weeping, the men muttered among themselves. Norman shut off the monitor.

"Before we jump to any conclusions," Norman said calmly. "Let me make some phone calls. I should be able to get an answer about Bud's condition in a few hours. Usually these things appear much worse on the tapes than they are in reality." Norman believed no such thing. He said it for the benefit of the employees. He was stunned and very deeply concerned for his son's life. It wouldn't do for the employees to see how distressed he truly was. He asked everyone to leave. When he had composed himself, Norman buzzed Harriet's intercom. "Harriet, see if you can get Admiral John McCain on the phone out at CINCPAC Headquarters."

"Norman, it's six a.m. in Honolulu, do you want me to try and reach him at home or at his office?"

"Try his home first."

The Admiral's wife informed Harriet that Admiral McCain and his staff was in-route to a meeting in Saigon with General Abrams. Norman instructed his sister to try and get the Chief of Naval Operations on the phone. Ten minutes later Harriet received a call from an amateur radio operator in Nashville. He had a phone patch set up with a Navy radio operator at Dining Air Base. A navy lieutenant at Danang wanted to speak with Norman. Harriet forwarded the call. The radio operator explained that he had to switch his set from transmit to receive, so the Norman should say "over" when finished speaking.

Fearing the worst, Norman picked up the receiver, "Norman Cotter speaking, over."

"Mr. Cotter, this is Shug Early at Danang Air Base. Over."

"Hello, Shug. I assume you're calling in regard to Bud."

"Yes, sir, ah, I've been asked to brief you. Over."

"I've seen a video clip of him being taken out of his aircraft and placed into a helicopter. That's all that I know at the moment. Over."

"Sir, they took him out to the hospital ship Comfort for emergency surgery about 14 hours ago. I just got off the phone with Doctor Whitefield. She is aboard the Comfort with Bud. She told us that he is alive, but in very critical condition. A large piece of shrapnel pierced his breastbone and penetrated into a lung. It also severed part of his esophagus. A large blood vessel was severed in his right arm. Both of his legs were hit. The worse news is that he went into cardiac arrest twice. Once on the helicopter while they were on the way out to the ship and again during the surgery. Luckily they were able to revive his heart both times. He came out of surgery about three hours ago. He's in an intensive care unit. Doctor Whitefield and a pulmonary surgeon are treating him. Doctor Whitefield has arranged for nurses to be with him on a full time basis. The prognosis isn't very good I'm afraid. They're giving him a forty percent chance of recovery at this point. I'm sorry to have to tell you this Mr. Cotter. Over."

"Thank you, Shug. I appreciate you calling me. What time is it there? Over."

"It is 2130. Over"

"Shug, is Doctor Whitefield the doctor who performed the surgery? Over."

"Yes, sir, she was assisted by a pulmonary surgeon. I don't know his name, over."

"Would it be possible to have Doctor Whitefield get in touch with me? Any time will be fine. Over."

"I'm sure she will do that, Mr. Cotter. I'll see that she is notified. I'll give her your office and home numbers if that's okay. Over"

"Thank you, Shug, I appreciate everything you have done. Please don't hesitate to call me at anytime of the day or night if something changes. Over"

"I'm sorry about this, Mr. Cotter. Bud is my best friend. I'll let you know if there's a change. Good-bye, sir. Over"

An hour later Norman received a call from the CNO Chief of Staff at the Navy Department in Washington. His information was basically a reiteration of what Shug Early had said. The Chief of Staff told Norman that he would personally obtain a detailed briefing in regard to Bud's situation and get back with Norman as soon as possible.

Norman arrived home early in the afternoon. At six o'clock, Consolidated News would be running an exclusive interview with a Navy spokesman at Danang regarding the rescue. Mrs. Cotter, Bernadette and the house keeper, Katy and her husband Mose were waiting for him. The atmosphere in the house was silent and somber as a wake. At six o'clock, everyone gathered in the den to watch the network news. The network went to the Danang story following the first commercial break.

"This is Mike Rogers reporting from Danang Air Base in South Vietnam. Today we have learned of the incredibly daring rescue of a downed Navy airman in an area known as the A Shau Valley. With me is Commander Ed Gray, Navy Air Operations Officer here at Danang Air Base. Commander, can you tells us what you know about the rescue at this point."

"This morning at approximately 0740, Lieutenant Toland Cotter, acting as temporary CO of Squadron VC-110 was leading a rescue combat air patrol in the A Shau Valley. They located the down pilot, Commander John J. Ferguson. The rescue helicopter that was dispatched to pick up Commander Ferguson came under hostile fire and was damaged. The pilot of the helicopter abandoned the pickup because his aircraft was rapidly losing fuel. Lieutenant Cotter called for a second rescue helicopter. However, before the second unit could arrive on station enemy troops and vehicles were observed moving toward Commander Ferguson's position. Lieutenant Cotter directed the pilots in his division to provide interdicting fire on the advancing enemy troops and vehicles. At that time Lieutenant Cotter landed his aircraft on an unpaved road near Commander Ferguson's position and executed the extraction of the Commander. While he was climbing out of the area, Lieutenant Cotter's aircraft came under enemy antiaircraft fire. Lieutenant Cotter was severely wounded, but did manage to fly the aircraft and land safely here at Danang. That is what we know about the mission at the moment."

"Commander Gray. It has been reported locally that Commander Ferguson is Lieutenant Cotter's commanding officer. Can you verify that?"

"Yes, that's correct. Commander Ferguson is Lieutenant Cotter's CO."

"What is Commander Ferguson's condition at this time?"

"He's in good condition. The commander was treated for a knee injury sustained as he executed an egress from his own aircraft. The Commander also sustained a slight head wound aboard Lieutenant Cotter's aircraft when the aircraft was hit by enemy fire during the extraction. The Commander had survived in the jungle approximately one and a half days prior to his extraction by Lieutenant Cotter. Just prior to the extraction, Commander Ferguson captured a North Vietnamese soldier."

"And what is Lieutenant Cotter's current condition, Commander?"

"Lieutenant Cotter is aboard a hospital ship and is listed in critical condition."

"Commander is landing a heavy fighter aircraft on a road typical in rescue operations here in Vietnam?"

Gray smiled slightly, "Quite the contrary. This is a highly unusual incident."

"Assuming he survives, will Lieutenant Cotter be given special recognition for his actions?"

"Well, I can't answer that. A full debrief of the mission has to be conducted. Once a debrief has been completed, appropriate action in regard to Lieutenant Cotter's performance can then be recommended."

"Thank You, Commander Gray." The reporter turned and faced the camera. "Well there you have it, the sensational rescue of Commander John J. Ferguson and his North Vietnamese prisoner. The Commander is recovering here at Danang thanks to the raw guts, courage and extraordinary flying skills of Navy Lieutenant Toland Cotter whose own life hangs in the balance tonight. We will bring you more on this story and the condition of Lieutenant Cotter as the situation develops. This is Mike Rogers, Consolidated News, reporting from Danang Air Base in South Vietnam."

Chapter 27

Hospital Ship Comfort

0240 10 August 1968

Margo Whitefield stepped out of the shower and toweled herself dry. She was utterly exhausted and profoundly worried about Bud Cotter. She refused to leave him and had arranged for a stateroom in the women's senior officers quarters of the Comfort. She had requested and received the approval from the Comfort's Chief Surgeon to serve as visiting physician in the case of Lieutenant Cotter. She and a navy pulmonary surgeon, Doctor Owen Trent had teamed to perform the complex emergency surgery to save the young pilot's life. Her nurses at the Danang Hospital packed some clothes and personal kit items and had them delivered to the doctor's quarters aboard ship. Margo was gratified by the amiable cooperation she was experiencing on the Comfort. Certainly it didn't hurt that she knew and had worked with a great majority of the doctors and nurses who staffed the Comfort, but even so everyone went out of their way to assist and to do whatever Margo asked.

Hours after being taken out of surgery, Bud's condition had not stabilized significantly. His breathing was erratic and he was running a fever of one hundred and two. The surgery on his lung and esophagus had been difficult. Margo had removed the jagged shrapnel that had pierced his breastbone. The shrapnel had done a considerable amount of tearing and gouging to bone and tissue. The serrated razor like edge of the shrapnel had missed Bud's heart by mere fractions of an inch. Even now, Bud Cotter teetered on the edge of death. Tubes protruding from incisions in his chest carried excess fluids away. A wheezing respirator pumped oxygen into his lungs. His body systems were so weakened by the trauma and loss of blood that they could not properly function. Beeping, blinking machines monitored his heart rate and other vital signs. IV bottles hovered from a tall stand next to his bed feeding fluids and medications into his body. Two nurses were never more than a few feet from him. His condition was closely checked and recorded every fifteen minutes.

Margo opened an official navy mailgram sent by Shug Early. It was a request asking her to call Bud's father in Nashville. She knew the Cotter's must be frantic with worry. Bud had talked about his family so much that Margo felt as though she knew each of them personally. She decided to try and get a few hours sleep before telephoning the Cotters. She mentally calculated the time difference and made a mental note to call the Cotters during daylight hours in Nashville. She left a message with the nurses in Intensive Care to call her instantly if there was a change in Bud's condition.

Margo swallowed two aspirin, lay on the bed and closed her eyes. She had a headache from the tremendous stress of the surgery. She reflected how dismal her existence had been until Bud Cotter had come into her life. Very innocently, he had brought a new meaning into her being. Because of him, she was emerging from years of self-imposed isolation. When she was with Bud, Margo was totally happy, uninhibited and pure Margo. Quite unintentionally she had fallen in love with him. It was a deep mature kind of love that seemed so natural, yet so foreign to her. Bud Cotter was good to her. He respected her. He made her feel good about herself. Margo had experienced a unique abandonment when Bud had kissed her the night before. It was not simply passion, although those feelings were certainly strong. Her surrender to him went far deeper than desire. It had been a spiritual experience like nothing she had ever known, and at that moment she knew that her life would be forever changed. She didn't know how all this would work out in the end. For now it was good enough to know that she needed him, and that he needed her. She had so much love to give him. If only he could survive this crisis. God, she was desperate to have him to get through this! That night before she fell asleep, Margo did something very uncommon, something she hadn't done in years. She prayed. She asked God, she begged Him to spare the life of Bud Cotter.

VC-110 Compound

AREA SIERRA

"I'm all right, goddamn it!" Jack Ferguson swore. "You guys are treating me like a damn cripple. Knock it off!"

Cowboy released the grip on his commanding officer's arm after helping Jack Ferguson climb the three steps into the Q-hut where his office was located. Ferguson glared irritably at Cowboy and Shug Early and hobbled to his desk with a single crutch under his right arm.

"Of all the goddamn luck, I had to go and bust up my knee. This cast is a real pain in the ass. What's the latest report on Cotter?" Ferguson sat in his chair and scowled, his right leg extended stiffly in front of him. He took out a Camel and lit it.

"Same, Skipper," answered Shug. "He's in a coma. They're not giving him much of a chance. Best case, forty percent."

"I'm surprised he's alive. Christ, did you guys see the cockpit of that bird? I don't see how in hell he got us back here and on the ground in one piece. When they dragged me out of the airplane, I could see up into the cockpit. I thought for sure he must have bled to death."

Shug said, "Pee Wee says they're going to have to pull all the instruments and avionics and give the cockpit a wash down with solvent, he says the engine is okay, but they don't know about the structural damage yet."

"It wouldn't surprise me if that aircraft has to be surveyed," Ferguson said.

Cowboy poured coffee. He and handed the monogrammed mug to Ferguson. "Skipper, what're we supposed to do about these news people who keep calling over here, and they're hanging around outside the gate too."

"Oh, yeah," Ferguson said and sipped coffee, "glad you reminded me about that. The admiral wants his PR people to handle the media so he can control the information that gets out. So I want the word put out to all hands, no talking to reporters or any of those TV people. They're to refer all questions and phone calls to COMNAVAIR Danang PR Officer."

"Okay," said Shug, we'll make the announcement at noon muster and put it in the POD (Plan of the Day)."

"I also recommended to the Admiral," Ferguson said, "that VC-110 stand down until the Coral Sea detachment gets back. We're down to four operational birds. The Admiral agreed."

"How long will you be out of commission with your knee, Skipper?"

"Aw, that goddamn quack told me six weeks before the cast comes off. I told him I wanted it off in four."

"What did he say?"

"Hell, the son of a bitch laughed at me! Those goddamn medical people think they're so goddamn smart. I'll show the son of a bitch!"

The phone rang on Ferguson's desk. He picked it up with annoyed motions, "Commander Ferguson speaking."

"Jack, this is John Bennett."

"Good morning, Admiral."

"How's that bum knee of yours, Jack?"

"Stiff as hell, Admiral, they have it in a cast. Otherwise I'm fine, sir."

"Good, good. Listen, Jack, this thing with Cotter getting you out of the A Shau is turning into a damn media circus. The bastards are beating the doors down over here hollering for interviews and briefings. I'm sending Dan Wilson over there to talk to you and Lieutenant Dowda. I want you fellows to give Dan a detailed debrief so we can review it over here before we issue any further statements. Consolidated News has already run an interview with Bob Gray that I authorized. Now all the networks are clamoring for more details on this extraction. I have to control this as much as possible."

"Yes, sir, I understand."

"I'm going to run a court of inquiry, Jack. Are there any circumstances connected with the extraction that a court might dig up that could be a problem?"

"Well, sir, Cotter is restricted to non-combat flight operations on orders from COMNAVAIRPAC. I don't know if that will be a problem or not, admiral."

"Mick O'Reagan put him in command after you were shot down, Jack. I'll see that it won't be a problem."

"Well, sir, in that case I see no problem with running a court. May I ask why you're running a court, Admiral?"

"I want to be prepared for all eventualities. I've been briefed that SecNav and CNO are getting their staffs involved in this. I want to have all the facts and be one step ahead of them. Plus the way this thing is shaping up, we'll be recommending Cotter for an award whether he survives or not."

"I understand, Admiral."

"Well, that's all, Jack. Dan will be over later today. Take care of that knee. Good-bye."

"Thank You, Admiral. Goodbye, sir."

Nashville

12 August 1968

"Telephone, Mr. Cotter," Katie called from the open doorway of Norman's library.

"Thank you, Katie." Norman picked up the receiver. It was the local MARS radio operator with a phone patch from the hospital ship Comfort in Danang Harbor.

"Norman Cotter speaking. Over"

"Mr. Cotter, this is Doctor Margo Whitefield aboard the hospital ship Comfort. Over"

"Yes, Doctor, thank you for calling. Has there been any improvement in my son's condition? Over."

"I'm sorry to say that there has been no significant change. His breathing continues to be dependent on the respirator. There was some post-operative internal bleeding, but we now have that problem under control. The prognosis continues to be guarded at best. Over."

"Doctor Whitefield, Bud's mother, our daughter and I are flying to Danang. We leave Nashville early tomorrow morning. We will be billeted aboard the Comfort in flag quarters. Can we call on you once we are aboard? Over."

Margo was stunned. She nearly stammered. "Yes, of course, by all means. I look forward to meeting you and your family. Hopefully when you arrive, Bud's condition will be improved. Over"

"Yes, I hope so. Uh, Doctor, this is a bit awkward to ask, but do you happen to know if a Catholic priest has seen my son since he was wounded? Over."

"Yes, sir. The Catholic chaplain gave Bud last rites on the helicopter as we were flying out to the Comfort. Over"

"You were on the helicopter with him and witnessed it personally? Over."

"Yes, sir, I was kneeling next to Father Martin. Over"

"Are you the Doctor who was administering to Bud when they got him out of his aircraft? Over."

"Yes, sir, how did you know that? Over."

"Why you were on national television here in the states. Millions watched you caring for our son. Over."

"I was so concerned with Bud that I didn't notice news cameras. Over."

"I'm looking forward to meeting you, Doctor Whitefield. Thank you for all that you have done for Bud. We'll see you in a few days. Good-bye. Over"

"Good-bye, Mr. Cotter. Have a good trip. Over"

USS Comfort

16 August 1968

Margo walked into the Intensive Care unit at 1100 to check on Bud. She would be greeting the Cotter's later in the day. The young pilot hung on to life by a mere thread. His fever was down to one hundred, but his breathing remained dangerously erratic, shallow, irregular, controlled mostly by the gasping respirator. His face was pallid: his lips colorless. Margo greeted the nurses and examined Bud's chart. She went to his side and kissed his forehead. She gazed at him, and offered a silent prayer to God.

The Cotter's arrived aboard the Comfort in the admiral's staff helo. The Captain of the Comfort greeted the Cotter's as they stepped out onto the ship's helo pad. The Captain escorted the Cotter's through spotless, brightly lighted, pale green passageways. A marine sentry snapped to rigid attention in the passageway outside the door leading to flag quarters. Bernadette flashed a beguiling smile at the marine whose eyes never flickered. The Captain opened the door and led them inside.

"Once you folks are rested and refreshed," said the Captain cordially, "Doctor Whitefield will escort you down to the IC unit. She has graciously agreed to be your escort while you're aboard Comfort."

Two hours later, Margo was summoned to flag quarters. Bernadette opened the door.

"You must be Doctor Whitefield." Bernadette smiled, extending her hand.

"Yes, and I'll bet you're, Bernadette," Margo said sweetly, taking Bernadette's hand, "Bud has told me so much about you."

"Oh, he has?" Bernadette grinned and stepped aside enviously appraising Margo. Bernadette was flabbergasted that a woman with Margo's face and figure would be a medical doctor working on a hospital ship in Vietnam.

"He has said only good things about you," Margo said.

"I couldn't ask for a better brother. Of course, I would never tell him that, ha, ha, ha."

"I know what you mean, Bernadette. I have two brothers."

Mr. and Mrs. Cotter walked into the sitting room. Bernadette introduced her parents. They too were taken aback with Margo's beauty.

"It's so good to meet you, Doctor," Millie said, giving Margo a tiny hug. "We can't thank you enough for everything you're doing for Bud."

Norman extended his hand to Margo. "It's a pleasure to meet you, Doctor Whitefield."

"Please call me Margo," she said, taking Norman's hand, "there's no need to be formal. I feel as though I already know you. Bud has told me so much about you. I've been looking forward to meeting you."

"And we, you," said Norman.

"How's Bud doing today, Hun?"

Margo pursed her lips. "I'm afraid his condition hasn't changed significantly. His pulmonary functions continue to be erratic. He continues to have a fever which is somewhat normal following such trauma, but a fever can also be indicative of an infection. We study the results of daily lab work in an attempt to identify the first sign of an infection."

The Cotter's were horrified when they saw Bud for the first time. They had expected the worse, but even those grim expectations had not prepared them for their first glimpse of him. He looked like a cadaver. His face was sunken and absent of color. Tubes protruded from his bare chest and a line of zipper-like sutures could be seen through the transparent surgical tape. The beeping monitors, IV tubes, the shiny metal furnishings and the appalling wheezing of the respirator all combined to make the scene even more ominous. One of the nurses had pinned a happy face button onto Bud's pillow, but it offered no cushion to the terrible sight of him. Millie and Bernadette immediately broke down and began to weep. Norman, shaken to the core of his being, fought to maintain his composure. Margo turned away and stepped over to the nurse's station feeling very much out of place in the presence of the Cotter's.

The family remained with Bud for twenty minutes, holding his hand, caressing his expressionless face and weeping for him. Margo escorted the women to a head where they could compose themselves while Mr. Cotter lagged and remained with his son. When the women emerged, Margo led the family to a small conference room. Doctor Trent and Margo formally briefed them. The two doctors painted a grim and pessimistic picture. The doctors suggested that the reliability of his pulmonary and cardiac functions were their major concerns. The loss of blood plus the severe chest trauma had drastically reduced the ability of his vascular system to function normally and to fight off infection.

When the briefing concluded, Margo took the Cotter's to the wardroom for lunch. The Captain had a special table set aside for the Cotter's. All this extraordinary treatment of the Cotter's amazed Margo. Clearly these people were highly regarded in the hierarchy of the Navy. She was beginning to understand that the Cotter's were something more than just a well to do southern family. The mere fact that a civilian family was in Vietnam aboard a Navy hospital ship spoke volumes for their prominence.

The Cotter's were upset from the shock of seeing Bud, and they were tired from the long trip. To make them feel worse, their days and nights were completely reversed here on the opposite side of the globe. They returned to their quarters and slept until they were awakened several hours later.

Everyone was much refreshed and in better spirits at dinner. The ship's Captain entertained everyone with witty anecdotes of his early days in the Navy as a PT boat Skipper at Tulagi and Vella Lavella in the Solomons. Norman Cotter contributed his kamikaze story from the invasion of Okinawa.

After dinner, Margo escorted the Cotters to the open fantail where they could enjoy the evening breeze across the harbor. The broad fantail was partially covered by a neatly corded white canvas tarpaulin and furnished with tables and chairs. Mr. Cotter lighted a Don Diego and took his wife for a stroll around the decks of the ship. Margo and Bernadette leaned on the life rail and watched two destroyers steaming in line for the harbor entrance.

"After all the bitching I've done about the Vietnam War," Bernadette said, "I can't believe that I'm actually here. I was expecting to see the rockets' red glare, and bombs bursting in air, but except for all these battleships or whatever they are, there's no sign of war anywhere. I may as well be standing in Mobile Bay."

"Have you participated in anti-war demonstrations?"

"I participated in a small protest once, while I was in college. I spent seven days in jail with women so vile and disgusting that I actually couldn't keep my food down. Since then, my political disapproval is vented in conversation and in the voting booth."

"You went to jail?"

"Oh, Margo, it was horrible. The experience taught me some very valuable lessons. As badly as I hate to admit it; that was one time my archaic father was right."

"Well, I certainly agree with you about the war. We definitely do not need to be here."

Bernadette appeared surprised. "I assumed that all you military people were in agreement with being over here."

Margo shrugged. "Actually I am a civilian, but since I've been here I've learned that military personnel are in favor of winning a war and going home."

"You're a civilian!" Bernadette sputtered. "What in the world are you doing in this godforsaken place?"

"I want to do my part to help the wounded and sick GI's survive and go home. It may sound kind of banal, but that's why I'm here."

Bernadette regarded her admiringly. "Good for you, Margo. I wouldn't have the guts to do something like that."

Margo smiled, "I'd wager you have plenty of guts when you need them."

Bernadette looked sideways at Margo, "I hope I never have to find out. I'm pretty much a spoiled brat piano and fiddle player."

Margo laughed at the remark. She liked Bernadette and thought they just may become friends.

"Bud tells me that you are the first non European to win the International Chopin Piano Competition, a remarkable achievement."

"Ha, a miracle that was! Enrico Rizzi who is an absolute genius and master played much better than me. I was astonished when they announced that I had taken first place."

"What did you play?"

"Chopin's Waltz, Opus 42 in A-Flat, it's my favorite Chopin piece."

"Is it a difficult piece?"

"No, not really, but you know each time I play his work, it is as though Frédéric Chopin and I become one in spirit. It's difficult for me to clarify such a mystical unification. Most people think I'm a nut anyway, so I don't have to do very much explaining."

Margo was amused. "Bernadette, you are certainly not a nut. I suspect the music must come directly from your soul, and that is why you won that competition no doubt. I'd love to hear you play."

"Thanks for the compliment. I've got a new album coming out in October on the RCA label. I'll send you a copy."

"Why thank you, Bernadette. That is so gracious of you. I'm honored."

The women gazed silently across the harbor and Bernadette lit a cigarette.

"May I ask you a personal question?" Bernadette said, leaning against the rail and turning to face Margo.

"Sure."

"I'm curious to know why someone as beautiful as you decided to pursue medicine and come to a place like this."

Margo's face burned with blush. She gave Bernadette a wry smile. "It's kind of you to say that, Bernadette. I've wanted to be a doctor since I was a child. All in all, I'm just a simple Montana ranch girl."

"Still, I envy you your looks."

"Don't envy me, Bernadette, and why would you say that anyway? You're a beautiful girl."

"Bah! I'm a hag!" She snorted, exhaling smoke. "Max Factor is my only salvation, and look at this chest. I'd get a boob job except that I'd have no peace from daddy for the rest of my life."

Margo couldn't help but laugh. "Bernadette, you're perfect the way you are."

"Where can we go on this ship to have a gin and tonic?"

"Liquor isn't allowed on Navy ships, but we can go over to the Officer's Club. It's a short walk from here."

"Oh good, I'm getting depressed looking at all these battleships."

They sat in a booth in the bar section of the club. The place was relatively crowded with officers and Margo and Bernadette drew substantial attention as they walked in unescorted and were seated. The waiter took their cocktail order.

"This place is amazing," Bernadette remarked, looking around. "I thought everyone lived in foxholes over here."

"No, as you can see we do have a few civilized amenities. This is a place where one can come and forget there's a war going on outside."

Bernadette lit a cigarette. "My God, look at all the gorgeous men in this place. I may change my mind about the military and sign up."

Margo was amused. “The ratio of men to women around here is probably a thousand to one. If you can’t find one you like in here, there’s thousands more outside.”

“Do you suppose some of the men in here will actually fight in the war?”

Margo sadly surveyed the room. Some of these men you’re swooning over will be dead tomorrow, Bernadette.”

Bernadette was horrified. “Oh, Margo, don’t tell me that for God’s sake! But look at them, they don’t seem to have a care in the world.”

“Not a man in this club believes it will be him who will be shot down over Hanoi or Haiphong or Khe Sanh tomorrow. They think it’ll be the other guy. If they didn’t have that attitude, they’d probably go crazy.”

“Oh, my God, that is so horrible, Margo!”

“It’s the reality and the cruelty of war, Bernadette.”

Bernadette silently gazed around the room. A tiny glimmer of the veracity of war permeated into her viscera. It sickened and depressed her. She tried to ignore it.

The waiter brought their cocktails. Bernadette raised her glass to toast and Margo picked up her glass. “Friends,” Bernadette said.

Happily surprised, Margo raised her glass, “Friends.”

“You know,” said Bernadette, “before we met I envisioned you as being rather austere and strictly professional, but after we met I realized that you’re really a warm down to earth person, Margo. I like you a lot.”

Margo smiled happily. “And I like you too, Bernadette, very much. Bud talks about you all the time. I felt as if I knew you and your family before we met.”

“Have you and Bud known each other very long?”

"We met briefly last November, shortly after Phyllis was killed. I didn't see him again until New Year. I saw him again in March, when he brought those Marines out of Khe Sanh and was badly injured in the plane crash; I treated him in the hospital. Since then we have become good friends."

Bernadette was regarding Margo over the rim of the glass. She set the glass onto the table and picked up the cigarette. "May I be perfectly blunt, Margo?"

"Okay," Margo said a bit uncertainly.

"I think you're in love with my brother."

Margo could feel the blood rushing to her cheeks. She looked unflinchingly into Bernadette's eyes and said, "Yes, I am."

"I rather thought so. Mama thinks so too."

"Is it that obvious?"

"To Mama and I. Daddy on the other hand wouldn't have a clue."

"Do you or your mother object?"

"Oh, to the contrary, now that we've met you we're overjoyed about it. He needs you, Margo. Since Phyllis was killed he has cloistered himself in the Navy. Her death was totally devastating for him."

"Yes, I know," Margo said sadly. "Bud has told me all about her, and another woman named June Chandler."

"Oh my, he's told you about June Chandler?"

"Yes, he tells me that she's in love with him."

"God is she ever! Don't get me wrong, Margo. June is really a wonderful person. I love her like a sister. But she's, well, let's say, different. She works for Daddy in Honolulu. She's a workaholic and deeply religious. She doesn't go out or date anyone. It's like she can't concede to the fact that Bud dumped her way back when."

"Sooner or later she'll have to accept it."

Bernadette dashed her cigarette. "Are you and Bud serious? Or am I being too nosy?"

Margo smiled pleasantly. "No, you're not being nosy, Bernadette. Truthfully, I don't think Bud has gotten over Phyllis to the point where he is capable of becoming seriously involved."

"You mean he hasn't proposed yet," Bernadette teased.

"No, not yet," Margo grinned.

"I'm in love with one of Bud's flying buddies, Shug Early," Bernadette said with starry eyes, "we fell in love when I was in Hawaii with the parents."

"Oh, yes," Margo said gaily, "I know Shug very well. He's a wonderful guy and a really good friend to Bud."

"Tell me," Bernadette breathed blissfully. "I'll get to see him tomorrow. I can hardly wait."

"How wonderful, Bernadette. Now it's my turn to ask. Are you two serious?"

"God knows I am. I'd marry him tonight. We've been writing regularly, almost daily actually for about a year, but we really haven't talked about marriage."

A waiter appeared at the table. "Doctor Whitefield?" He was glancing from Margo to Bernadette, not sure which woman was Doctor Whitefield.

"Yes?"

"They want you back on the ship right away." He glanced at a note in his hand. "They say come to the I--C--U."

Three nurses and two doctors were huddled around Bud when Margo breathlessly rushed into the room. It was a terribly morbid scene that confronted her. The hour she had so desperately feared was at hand. Margo's throat tightened, her heart wrenched with pain and tears burst from her eyes.

When one of the nurses noticed Margo, she looked up and said, "He asked for you, Doctor Whitefield."

"What! Oh, my God!" She ran to him. The nurses stepped aside, smiling. His eyes slowly opened and he looked at her. Very weak, he whispered, "I've been away, Margo. I'm going to be better now. You and I____You and I____" He closed his eyes. Margo held his hand and wept tears of relief and joy. Margo had the nurse summon the Cotter's. When Bud heard their voices and opened his eyes for a brief moment. Margo and the staff were overjoyed by this extraordinary improvement. Late that night, Margo knelt in the ship's chapel and thanked God.

At noon the next day, Bud's condition was upgraded from critical to serious. The Captain put on special celebration dinner that evening for the Cotters. After dinner, Bernadette entertained a packed wardroom of doctors, nurses and officers. She played the ship's Baldwin baby grand and performed a piano concert of lively classical melodies, soft rock and jazz. The following day, Bud's condition was stable and Margo cautiously took him off the respirator to allow him to breathe on his own. Margo and Doctor Trent, ever suspicious of such an unexplainable improvement kept Bud in the ICU. Three days later however, Margo and Owen Trent agreed that Bud could be moved to a private room. Two days after that, the Cotter's bid farewell and departed Danang for Hawaii where Norman would meet with his hotel staff at the Wai Momi.

Chapter 28

Rest and Recuperation

Out of immediate danger, Bud faced a lengthy recuperation and strengthening period. On 22 September, orders from COMNAVAIRPAC arrived for Bud. Upon release from the Comfort, he was to report to the Naval Hospital at Bethesda, Maryland for further examination. This news was a blow to Margo and Bud. It meant an indefinite separation for them.

Margo returned to her staff position at the Naval Hospital. She rose very early each morning and drove across the base to the Comfort to review Bud's chart and spend some time with him. In the evening, when her watch was done she returned to the ship and attended to Bud, leaving him only to sleep a few hours at night.

During the early weeks of his recovery, Bud spoke infrequently. When he did speak, he could only manage whispers. The injuries to his chest and the subsequent surgical repair made speaking terribly uncomfortable for him. When he wasn't sleeping, he lay still, satisfied to gaze at Margo. She read the newspaper to him every morning and evening. Sometimes they watched TV. Other times they listened to Armed Forces radio.

One morning Bud astounded everyone including himself by sitting up on the edge of the bed. It was a very painful exercise, but he needed to be in a position other than on his back. Within two days of sitting up, he was shuffling himself to the head. Margo and the staff were delighted with this progress. Bud seemed to take it all in stride, as if he expected his progress to proceed without interruption. Although he was doing very well otherwise, his silence continued. Margo assumed he simply did not feel like talking because it was so uncomfortable for him. Often she noticed him staring blankly as though his mind was far removed from his surroundings. Margo suspected that the harrowing experience he had survived played heavily on his mind. She was satisfied to be with him. She would care for him, and get him through whatever travail lay ahead. Bud responded to her love and tenderness falling more deeply in love with Margo each day.

One muggy October morning after breakfast, Bud surprised Margo by asking her to walk him out to the fantail. Determined to make the journey himself, he refused to be carted in a wheelchair. It was slow going for him and required ten minutes to make a journey that would typically take only a three or four minutes. Bud was wholly winded by the time they reached the fantail. The couple sat in padded deck chairs under the canvas and looked out upon the harbor. The air was heavy with dissipating fog, only a mere suggestion of a morning breeze was beginning to stir the air.

"How do you feel?" Margo's face was lined with concern at his breathlessness.

He grinned with one corner of his mouth. "I feel like hammered mule shit!"

His answer was so spontaneous and unexpected that Margo had to laugh. "You are definitely getting back to normal."

He peered around the harbor while he caught his breath. It was good to be out on deck and breathing the salt air wafting in from the sea. A diminutive Filipino steward, prim in white smock and black trousers appeared with two steaming mugs of coffee on a small ornamented metal tray. Margo took the tray, thanked the steward and dismissed him.

"I requested coffee be brought up from the wardroom. I thought coffee would be nice while we sat out."

"Yeah, great, thanks," he said. It then occurred to him, "Don't you have to work today?"

"No, believe it or not, I'm off for a full two days."

His wearied face suffused with happiness. He picked up the cup with his heavily bandaged right arm and hand. The crock mug felt as though it weighed a ton.

"Careful with that hot coffee," Margo warned, she shifted to help him.

"I've got it. I'm okay." He gritted his teeth and managed to bring the cup to his lips and sip coffee. He sat it on the table very deliberately. "See," he grinned. "I can do it."

Knowingly, Margo said, "Hurt like the dickens, didn't it?"

"Yeah it did," he admitted. "I've got to start using this arm sometime."

"That's fine, but you should do it with something besides scalding coffee for goodness sakes."

Bud stared at her through dark ringed eyes. Margo thought he looked so haggard and weak. Throughout his ordeal, he had lost fifteen pounds and his features were gaunt and drawn. Happily, she knew that he was recovering and regaining his strength much more quickly than anyone, including herself could have imagined. As his physician, and being fully aware of the extent of his wounds, she knew that by all odds he should not have survived his devastating injuries. Margo regarded it as almost miraculous that Bud had endured.

"I haven't felt like talking very much," said Bud in a raspy voice. "It's getting easier now, not quite so uncomfortable. I've been meaning to ask you how things went with my family."

Margo's face brightened. "Oh, Bud, they're such wonderful people. Bernadette and I have become really good friends and your mother is the sweetest thing. She's so wonderfully southern and charming. I just love the way she calls everyone, Hun. Your dad is a little hard to know. He's so formal and proper most of the time, but he gave me a hug as they were leaving. What he said to me made me cry."

"What did he say?"

"He said, he said, I was your gift from heaven." Her lips pursed and she blinked.

"You truly are my gift from heaven," he said in a tone full of understanding.

Margo smiled sweetly, "I'm glad you think so."

Bud drank coffee and appeared pensive. "Lying around here on my back all this time, I've had a chance to do a lot of thinking, Margo. I want to ask you something, would you consider going to Bethesda with me?"

Astonished, she said, "Oh, my goodness, Bud. I can't just leave. I have a contract with the Navy."

"Well, I've been thinking about that. I'm sure your contract can be taken care of with no negative reflection on you, if you want it that is."

"God knows I want to go with you. I've been beside myself knowing I was going to be stuck here until March, but I have a contract, Bud. That is something that I do not take lightly. Besides, who do you know that can get my contract amended?"

Bud grinned weakly. "I don't know anybody, but daddy knows everybody."

Flustered, her thoughts vacillated with indecision, she said, "I don't know. I just don't know, Bud. Are you sure this is what you really want?"

"Margo, I won't leave here without you, not unless you tell me something differently." He leaned forward, wincing, and kissed her. "I love you so much that it scares me," he whispered. "I've never felt like this before, not even with Phyllis."

Margo gasped, visibly jolted. She held slim fingers to her lips. Incredulous somber eyes searched his face. "Oh, Bud. I can't believe you said that."

"When I realized that I was dying in the helo, I thought of God, and I thought about how much I loved you, Margo."

She stared at him through moistening eyes, "Oh, Bud. I've fallen so desperately in love with you. I never really understood that love could be this intense, so, so all consuming. Until now I never understood that love could be so spiritual, so unquestionable. Everything is happening so fast. It's all so crazy and mixed up. I'll do anything you want. I'll go anywhere you want, just as long as we can be together."

He gazed at her affectionately and sipped coffee. "It was inevitable that we would fall in love like this, Margo."

"Inevitable," she said reflectively. "Before I knew you, I would have never believed it possible. I often wonder if all this is really real."

He kissed her again, touching her lips as gently as the brush of a feather. "It is very real," he whispered.

He sat back in his chair and regarded her through tired shadowy eyes. "Margo, I want to tell you some things, and now is the right time, I think. Since we met and began sharing the chronicles of our lives, I've mentioned to you, several times in fact, that I was brought up in the Catholic Church and educated by nuns and priests in parochial schools. They gave me a truly wonderful education and deeply instilled into me my Catholic faith. But despite all that, I've never really been a devoutly religious person. Actually, since I left home after college and went to flight school, I've drifted away from the Church. I can't remember the last time I went to Mass."

He paused to sip coffee and gather his thoughts. "Anyway, for whatever reasons, I've always tended to be pragmatic about most things. Generally speaking, I view things in the most logical and simplistic form. A bottom line sort of mentality I guess you could say. Studying physics in college, I began to look at much of the world and the universe in terms of what could be determined or proven mathematically or scientifically. To my way of thinking, what cannot be proven mathematically or scientifically is either hypothesis or simply acceptance through blind faith. Actually I'm quite cynical about the metaphysical, suggestions of spirits, apparitions, and the supernatural, that kind of stuff. Now, having said all that, I'm going to tell you some things that will sound completely fantastic. Things that I would never have believed possible until this episode occurred."

He paused again to drink coffee. For a few moments, he gazed across the harbor appearing distant and detached. Curious and somewhat perplexed at the direction of his conversation, Margo waited patiently for him to again begin speaking. When he spoke, his words came slowly and very deliberately.

"When my heart arrested in the helo that day, the damnedest things began to happen to me. Now I know this is going to sound really off the wall, Margo, but my mind, my spirit, my soul, however you want to define it, became separated from my body. I could see and hear everything that was going on. At the same time I felt the most incredible happiness and peace. I watched you and the Chaplain kneeling next to me. I watched you scream to the corpsman when you realized my heart had stopped. I watched you insert that big needle into my heart. I wanted to tell you that everything was going to be okay. I don't know how I knew that, but I did. And then, at some point, I wasn't in the helo anymore. A spirit, what we think of as an angel came to me. The angel was Phyllis. She took me to a place so beautiful and so peaceful that I really can't describe it properly. Things that I never before understood were made perfectly clear to me. I became aware of the reality that there is a design, a purpose if you will for everything that happens. Daddy said you were sent to me by heaven. I'm sure he said it as a figure of speech, but I now believe that it is by God's Will that you and I were brought together here at Danang. I now believe that things are happening as a step toward achieving an end. I know how this must sound to you, but it's as real as you and I are sitting here. This wasn't some kind of drug-induced dream, Margo. I'm convinced of it because I had separated from my body before you or the corpsmen had given me morphine."

Margo stared at him for long moments, her pretty face shaped by wonder and curiosity. "It doesn't sound crazy at all." Margo said, "It's wonderful and mysterious and exciting. In medical school, during a parapsychology discussion, we talked about a phenomenon known as autoscopy. People who have died but were revived as you were have told of similar experiences." Her inquisitive emerald eyes searched his face.

"Tell me, what did Phyllis say to you?"

"She told me that God will reveal something, some message to me."

Margo stared at him. "Oh, Bud, that is so beautiful. Tell me what heaven is like."

He sat back and appeared thoughtful. "I wasn't in heaven, although I thought I was. Phyllis led me to comprehend that I was in a limbo, a state of transition between physical life and the spiritual life. It was a place of the purest happiness, Margo. A place where there's no worry, no fear, no regret, no pain, no doubts, no uncertainty. It's a place of perfect love and contentment. If you could gather up all of the wonderful and beautiful things of nature and combine all that splendor with the happiest most exciting feelings you have ever known, and then take away all of life's negatives, you would have some tiny idea what this transcendent state was like. I was on the doorstep to heaven, if you will."

"Did you see God?"

"No. I suppose only those who are in heaven actually see Him fully. But I now understand that we see the living God everyday in many different ways and forms. For human kind God is the ultimate abstract, the ultimate enigma, and I think, He probably always will be. Yet we see, feel and hear God every day. He is the splendor of nature and all that is good and beautiful, and God is Love. God is happiness. Those who know God know Love. God and Love are one and the same. Love is the purest form of God. God is love to all humanity. What we know as our soul is the spirit within us, and because God has no boundaries, He resides within every human being. He is mercy and He is forgiveness. Even the most wretched can turn to God, recognize Him and ask His forgiveness. I learned that the two most powerful forces in the universe are love and prayer to God. I used to be terrified of dying, but now when the time comes, I won't be afraid and you shouldn't be afraid, Margo."

Margo stared at him for a long while. "That may be the most profound thing I have ever heard. I truly do believe that God will guide you."

"I don't know how this will come about, Margo. Phyllis led me to understand that it is our individual decisions and subsequent personal deeds that allow God's purpose to be fulfilled or not fulfilled."

Margo's pretty face twisted with curiosity, "But how will you know what to do? It seems so enigmatic, so ambiguous."

"I've thought about that a lot, Margo. I've come to the conclusion that doing the right thing will come from within. I think it's a matter of following our conscience. I suspect that it is that inner voice we sometimes hear but don't always listen to. Possibly there's an angel who gives us direction, I don't know."

"I wonder if everyone has an angel."

"Maybe, I don't know, Margo. He sipped coffee and looked out across the harbor.

"What's going to happen now, Bud?"

"Well, the first thing I'll do is get in touch with daddy and see about getting your contract nullified. Then, when I'm released here, we will go to Bethesda. When that's over, I'm not sure what to do. I haven't thought things that far out. Maybe I should get out of the navy."

"What will you do, work with your father?"

"No. I don't think that Cotter Communications is part of the plan. At this point, the one thing I am absolutely sure of is that I need you, Margo. I'll not accomplish a damn thing without you." Bud hesitated, appearing nervously unsure of himself. "One thing that has been revealed to me, very clearly Margo, is that you and I together are one piece of this confusing puzzle."

"We are! Me?"

"Yes you, Margo. I was going to wait on all this," he said hesitantly, "because I'm not sure how you feel. I mean it's not something we have even discussed, and all of this is happening kind of suddenly, and I don't want to push you into anything, so______."

"Bud, what on earth are you talking about?"

He reached into his pajama pocket and took out a small felt box. He opened it and removed a brilliant 3-carat Van Cleef & Arpels diamond engagement ring. He took her unresisting left hand and slid the ring onto her pretty slim finger. "Is it too soon to ask you to marry me?"

Margo's face lighted in dazzling surprise and amazement. "Yes! I mean no! I mean, yes I want to marry you! Oh, my God! Oh, my God, Bud! Oh, Bud, this ring! It's so beautiful!" She practically threw herself on him and kissed him, a long luxurious, wet, passionate kiss.

"Jesus, Margo," Bud panted heavily when they parted. "You're going to give me a heart attack kissing me like that!"

She grinned at him, her expression brimming with wicked license. She kissed him again.

Margo sat back into her chair, breathlessly happy. "Oh, I love you, Bud Cotter. I love you so much," she said with zestful sparkling eyes. "I love this beautiful, marvelous, stunning ring. How in the world did you manage it?"

"I asked Cowboy and Shug if they would help me out. I made a little sketch and gave them some money. They flew down to Saigon and picked it up for me."

"Oh, Bud. You've made me the happiest girl on this earth! You are truly my dreams come true."

"I don't know why you think so, but I'm glad that you do."

She kissed him again. "Yes, I do think so."

"I'm getting addicted to us kissing like this," he grinned lecherously. "I'm not sure how long I can keep my hands to myself."

"You can put your hands anywhere you want to, Teddy Bear," she whispered erotically into his ear.

"I don't think my heart can stand too much of this, Margo."

She kissed his mouth and sat back in the chair, admiring the dazzling diamond. "Oh, my God, Bud. Mother is going to absolutely <u>die</u> when she meets you and sees this gorgeous ring."

"Do you think your family will like me?"

"Oh, my goodness, yes. They already know all about you. I write to mother two or three times a week." Margo gazed at him with a soft sweet smile. "You're so incredibly amazing, Teddy Bear, do you know that? No, of course you don't."

Large intimate emerald eyes scrutinized him affectionately. “When do you think we should get married?”

“Anytime is fine with me. I think women are better at making decisions about that kind of stuff. I’ll go along with whatever you say.”

She pondered for a moment. “Oh, Bud. I don’t know. I need to think about it. This is all so sudden, so unexpected,” she squirmed happily. “Oooh, our wedding day is going to be the happiest day of my life.”

“What about going back to med school, Margo?”

She blinked at him. “You said that we have a vocation to fulfill. If I’m in med school another two or three years, we won’t get very much accomplished, now will we? I want to be married to you. That became my life’s highest priority a few moments ago. If I’m supposed to go to back to med school, I will someday. In the meantime, I can practice medicine wherever we land.”

“You’re taking all this at face value. You’re giving up an awful lot, Margo.”

“I’m giving up nothing, and I’m gaining everything. I’m going to marry the most courageous, wonderful, precious man in the whole world, and together we’re going to fulfill our destiny whatever it may be.”

Margo stood and bent to kiss him. Her sweet kiss lingered and lingered.

“All right, Cotter, knock off the fooling around out here!” Jack Ferguson walked out of the port passageway scowling, appearing cross and irked. Using a single crutch, he hobbled toward the kissing couple followed by the grinning duo of Cowboy and Shug.

“Cotter, the hospital people have been telling us that you were in one hell of a bad shape. It looks to me like you’re in better shape than we are.” Ferguson’s wide mouth stretched into a rare grin. "You must be Doctor Whitefield. I'm Jack Ferguson," he extended his hand to her. Margo was hurriedly wiping lipstick off Bud's mouth and face with a Kleenex. She smiled guiltily and took Ferguson's hand.

"That's me," she said girlishly. "I'm so glad to meet you Commander Ferguson. I've heard a lot of good things about you. How's your leg?"

"Getting better, the cast is coming off in two weeks."

"It's four weeks," Cowboy corrected.

Ferguson turned on him. "No, goddamn it! It comes off in two weeks, if I have to saw the son of a bitch off myself!"

Margo laughed brightly and Bud grinned. Shug and Cowboy shook their heads like children ashamed of their parents' behavior.

"Gentlemen sit down," Margo said. "I'll go and round up a fresh carafe of coffee."

"Outstanding," Ferguson said. He sat awkwardly in a chair, laid the crutch on the deck and lit a Camel. When Margo disappeared into the passageway, Ferguson said, "Cotter, we've been over here half a dozen times to check on you, but they weren't allowing you to have visitors. We were sweating you making it there for awhile."

Bud nodded appreciatively. "Thanks, Skipper, I guess things were touch and go there for a while."

"Anyway, Cotter, I want to say thanks for getting my ass out of the A Shau that day. What you did was an extraordinarily courageous thing along with some damn good flying. I've told you people a thousand times, I won't have any Audie Murphy stunts going on in my squadron, but this one time, and this one time only," he said, looking sternly at his three officers, "I'm having to bite the bullet because the circumstances were extremely extenuating, and <u>not</u> because it was my ass in the grass either!" He swung his head heavily glaring at his officers. Bud, Shug and Cowboy exchanged half amused, half surprised glances. This was possibly the highest allocate Ferguson was capable of giving someone.

"Thanks, Skipper, you or any of the other guys would have done the same thing."

The horse face skewed into a grimace of disgust. "Cotter, don't start with that, I was just doing my job shit. The Admiral ran a full court on the mission. Based on the Court's findings, Cowboy is up for a DFC, I'm up for the DFC and a Purple Heart, and you get another Purple Heart and are being recommended for the Medal of Honor."

"What!" Bud nearly choked. Thoroughly bewildered, he stared at Ferguson. The three officers were looking at him, anticipating a reaction. When Ferguson couldn't stand it any longer he spat, "Well, goddamn, Cotter, don't you have anything to say!"

Bud looked at his boss. "Well, I don't quite know what to say."

"That's it! That's all you've got to say? Did you hear what I said, Cotter? We're talking about the goddamn Congressional Medal of Honor and all you can say is, "I don't know what to say!" Shug and Cowboy broke into hee-haws. Ferguson shot them a malicious look and turned back to Bud.

"Don't screw around with me, Cotter. The Admiral is serious about this!"

Bud laughed, holding his chest to minimize the pain. "Skipper, I appreciate it very much. I really do. And I know that you had to do the initial paperwork. But this whole thing is bullshit. You know damn well I don't deserve any Medal of Honor or any other medal for that matter. What options did I have, Skipper? Leave you out there in Indian country and let the bad guys capture you? I don't think so. We didn't have time to wait for another helo. So I did the only thing me or anybody else could have done, but it's considerate of you and the Admiral to put me up for it."

"You really don't think it was any big deal, do you, Cotter?"

"Come on, Skipper. I made a short field landing on a road in an aircraft that is rough field capable. Why is everybody making such a big deal out of that? Medal of Honor? No way in hell, Skipper."

"Cotter, sometimes you're not all that bright. Everybody knows that a Skyraider is rough field capable. What you did was land the goddamn thing in the middle of the NV Army and got your ass shot all to hell. Then you flew the airplane back to Danang with one hand while you goddamn near bled to death! Now, the Admiral thinks it's a big deal and so does CINCPAC and so do a lot of other people. So I don't want to hear anymore of your bullshit!"

Ferguson took out another Camel and lit it. "And another thing I want to know, Cotter," he said, clicking his lighter shut and blowing smoke, "How in the hell did you manage to hook up with this luscious red head doctor? She's got a rep of being absolutely the most <u>untouchable</u> damsel since the Virgin Mary. Now how the hell did you pull this off?"

Bud glanced around at his three friends with a little embarrassed grin. Everybody was struggling not to laugh. Bud shrugged. "I don't know. It just happened, but our relationship isn't at all like it appears."

"Aw, horseshit," Ferguson snorted. "Hell, I thought she had you straddled when we came through that hatch a few minutes ago!" Shug and Cowboy exploded into guffaws. Ferguson glared and puffed on the Camel.

Margo returned followed by the Filipino steward who was pushing a rolling buffet burdened with carafes of coffee and plates of pastries.

“I’m glad to see everyone is so jolly,” Margo said good-naturedly. “What did I miss?”

“You don’t want to know,” said Bud clutching his pain-streaked chest.

“I can just imagine. Amaldo has brought some refreshments for you gentlemen.”

“Outstanding,” Cowboy said appreciatively, “I’m about to starve.”

“So am I,” said Shug. “Jesus, look at this, son, cream cheese sweet rolls.”

“Enjoy guys,” she nodded to the steward, “Thank you, Amaldo.”

Bud glanced at Margo with an impish smile. “Margo, why don’t you show the Skipper your ring?"

She smiled happily and displayed her proffered hand for him. Ferguson shot Bud a look of complete surprise and took her hand into his rough bony fingers. He examined the sparkling diamond. “Isn’t it gorgeous,” said Margo, unable to suppress the bliss from her voice.

“Yes it is, especially on your hand, Doctor.” He forced a quick acid grin and released her. Ferguson cast an amazed look toward Bud. “I’ll have to hand it to you, Cotter you damn sure know how to pick a beautiful woman and the diamond to put on her. And that reminds me of something else.” The normal scowl returned. “What the hell are you doing sending my officers down to Saigon to buy jewelry for your girl?”

Bud grinned bashfully. “Well, skipper, it was a training mission. I figured they need all the flying time they can get.”

“Cotter, for once I’ll have to agree with you,” Ferguson snapped, glaring at Shug and Cowboy.

"Shute," Cowboy spat with a smirk, "I've got more time sittin' on the crapper than most of these other guys have in a Skyraider."

Ferguson snorted, billowing cigarette smoke, "That's because, Lad the vast bulk of your naval career has been spent either in the head or in your goddamn rack!"

Ferguson stubbed the cigarette and said to Margo, "We got the word yesterday that you fiancé here is being recommended for the Medal of Honor."

"The Medal of Honor!" She gawked at Bud, her face a mask of mixed astonishment and joy.

Bud said, "The Skipper sprung it on me when you went for the coffee."

"Oh, my goodness, Bud, the Congressional Medal of Honor!" She glanced at Ferguson. "Is this confirmed?"

"Well, it's been approved all the way up through CINCPAC. That pretty much assures it will get through CNO. When it hits the SecNav level, that's where it can get tangled up in politics. But in view of all the press and media attention this thing has generated, it will almost assuredly get through the approval committees in the House and Senate."

Bud said, "Media attention, what media attention?"

"Christ on a crutch, Cotter, where the hell have you been? Every network in the world was running the video of the crash crew dragging your ass out of that Skyraider. You ought to hear the fantasyland stories they've come up with. Hell, Cotter you're a bigger hero back in the world than John Wayne or Steve McQueen."

"I don't believe this," Bud said, shaking his head.

Ferguson set his coffee cup on the side table. "And another thing, Cotter. Thanks to your being laid up over here and restricted by these medical people, the Admiral ordered me to give a press conference. Now I'm in the dog house with the Admiral over that."

"What happened?" Margo asked.

"The press conference was a complete fiasco," Cowboy quickly interjected, giving Ferguson a reproachful glance. "Our Skipper went on national television and publicly humiliated one of the network reporters."

"What did you say to him, Skipper?"

Ferguson started to speak but Cowboy quickly cut him off. "The skipper said, and I quote, 'Mister, if you want to ask me a question, you're going to have to get a goddamn shower, a shave, and a haircut'."

Margo began laughing and almost spilled her coffee. Bud grasped his chest and bore the pain of laughter.

"Cowboy and I tried to warn the Admiral," said Shug shaking his head, "but he was in no mood to listen. He said the pressure was on and he wasn't about to cancel the press conference so that someone could coach the Skipper ahead of time. He said a naval officer is supposed to know what to do in all situations."

"Well, goddamn, what did they expect me to do?" The son of a bitch had a pony tail halfway to his ass with enough grease in it to lube the tracks on a tank! I'd bet the son-of-a-bitch hadn't had a shower in a month."

Bud said, "What did the Admiral say when he heard the press conference?"

"Oh, hell he blew up like a claymore mine! Told me I had displayed a total absence of tact and judgment in dealing with the press. He said it is mandatory that all hands tolerate these media civilians even though they are a bunch of left wing maggots. Then he kicked my ass out of his goddamn office!" Ferguson glowered terribly and puffed the Camel.

"This is all your fault, Cotter. Goddamn hero crap of yours gets my ass in trouble with the Admiral!"

"Sorry, Skipper."

"Now that you two are engaged," said Shug. "Have you made any wedding plans?"

Margo and Bud looked at each other and smiled, "I gave her the ring about five minutes before you guys walked up the gangway," said Bud. "We really haven't made any plans as yet."

"Don't be thinking about getting out, Cotter." Ferguson was glaring through squinted eyes, "we've got a Navy to run and a war to win, Lad."

Bud flushed, stole a glance at Margo and shrugged, "Like I said, Skipper. We aren't sure what we're going to do yet."

"You and I need to talk, Lad. It will not be acceptable for you to transfer to reserve or resign your commission."

"Skipper, I can't predict what's going to happen. They may find something wrong with my heart or lungs that will muster me out."

"Horseshit, Cotter. After what I saw you two doing a while ago, there's not a goddamn thing wrong with you."

Margo was nearly in tears, "Ah, Ha, Ha, Ha."

Ferguson flicked a roguish glance at Margo.

"Son, Ah'd say you and Margo are going to be mighty busy. We've heard scuttlebutt that they're talking about making a movie about you rescuing the Skipper."

"Yeah," Cowboy said, "We might have to start calling you, Hollywood. Maybe you and John Wayne could do a new war flick together."

"Give me a break," Bud grinned, wagging his head.

"Cotter, we need to talk before you fly out," Ferguson said rising awkwardly from his chair.

"I'll be over to see you, Skipper. When is Sonny due back with the detachment?"

"Another two weeks, and by the way, Cotter, this extended deployment is finally ending. On 15 December, we'll be turning our remaining birds over to the South Vietnamese Air Force. VC-110 will deploy back to BP for a reissue of aircraft and training."

"That's great news, Skipper. We've been here, how long? Almost fourteen months isn't it?"

"Affirmative. We really got the shaft on this deployment. The Tet offensive back in January started it. Then the major air push up north."

"Do you know what equipment the squadron will be getting?"

"Scuttlebutt has it we will get A-4's, but that's just scuttlebutt." Ferguson looked at Margo. "It's been a pleasure, Doctor. Congratulations on your engagement and well done on taking such good care of this lad."

"Thank you, Commander Ferguson."

"I'm lucky as hell having Cotter save my bacon out there in the A Shau. Well, let's go, Lads. I'm supposed to have lunch with the Admiral. Christ knows what kind of trouble I'm in now."

"Good-bye, guys," Margo sang, "thanks for stopping by."

Bud and Margo watched the trio make their way out. "That Jack Ferguson is so salty that he's actually charming," Margo softly chuckled, "I can see why you guys like him so much."

"Yeah, he's a great skipper. He likes to put on a lot of hot air and BS, but when it comes to being a tough and effective commanding officer, he is as good as they come. I'm really going to miss working with him."

"Oh, my goodness, Bud, I can't get over you being recommended for the Medal of Honor!"

He cast a cynical smile. "That will never happen, Margo. This is nothing but a knee jerk reaction to this media coverage Jack talked about. The Admiral did it to cover his butt politically. He knows it will never get through the House and Senate."

"You really think that, Bud?"

"Sure. Picking up Jack doesn't justify any Medal of Honor for Christ's sake. The SAR helo crews pick up down pilots every day, I just did it with an airplane rather than a helo."

"But you landed on a muddy road, not a runway. And Jack said you did it in the middle of the North Vietnamese Army."

"That's an exaggeration. The skipper has a tendency to overstate things sometimes. There was plenty of room on that road and it was relatively straight. I had three other Skyraiders flying top cover for me. Those guys were cutting the NV's to pieces with cluster bombs and twenty-millimeter fire. There's nothing magic about landing on a dirt road. The Skyraider is built to handle off airport short landings. We were hit by antiaircraft fire, not small arms from infantry. Forget about this Medal of Honor business, Margo. It'll blow over."

Later that day, Pee Wee and his men came traipsing up to Bud's room. Everyone was shaved and wearing clean uniforms and shined shoes. They brought a cake with a big Skyraider done in thick blue icing. Following a great deal of bashful hemming and hawing and ogling at Margo, they cut the cake and passed it around on small paper plates. They then presented Bud with a beautifully crafted model of an A1-H Skyraider made of metal from a bent Skyraider propeller blade. They each had a hand in making the model in the machine shop and the cowling was adorned with nose art that was painted onto Bud's Skyraider, the word Einstein. Bud made a choking little speech thanking them for all their dedication and hard work and he talked about how much he was going to miss serving with them.

When Pee Wee and his group had noisily filed out, Bud asked Margo to walk with him down to Main COMM on the ship. They tracked down the communications officer who obtained approval to send two radiograms. The first message went out to Mr. Cotter in Nashville. Bud asked his father to intervene on Margo's behalf to have her contract with the Navy rescinded. In a terse last sentence, he announced their engagement. The second message, sent by Margo, went out to her family in Big Timber. In a few quick sentences, she informed her family that she is leaving Vietnam, that she is engaged and that she is going to Bethesda Maryland with Bud. She wrote that she would call them as soon as she arrived on the mainland.

Later that evening Margo and Bud were sitting on the fantail enjoying the breeze and awaiting the showing of the evening movie, a new film entitled *Bonnie and Clyde*. A sailor in undress whites and carrying a clipboard came out of the hatch and surveyed the people sitting on the fantail. His focus quickly narrowed on Bud and Margo.

"Lieutenant Cotter?"

"Yes Lad."

"You have visitors on the quarter deck, sir."

"Visitors, who are they, Lad?"

The sailor glanced at the clipboard, "A Jim Baxter and a Randall Clark. They're reporters, sir."

"Reporters? What do they want?"

"The OOD didn't say, Lieutenant."

"Well, I don't want to see them. Tell the OOD to please get rid of them."

"Yes, sir, I'll tell him. Thank you, sir." The sailor glanced at Margo, turned and walked away.

Ten minutes later, the sailor returned followed by an Ensign wearing tropical whites. The ensign walked up to Bud and Margo's table.

"Lieutenant Cotter, I'm Ensign Mike Brown the JOOD."

"Okay, Mike, what can I do for you?"

"Lieutenant Allen, the OOD has asked me to brief you in regard to the reporters who want to see you. These two gentlemen insist on seeing you."

Bud and Margo exchanged glances. "Mike, as you can see, I am recovering from surgery. I don't feel up to seeing visitors. I would appreciate it if you would pass that on to the OOD."

Margo spoke up. "Ensign Brown, I am Doctor Whitefield, Lieutenant Cotter's physician. Please pass on to the OOD that Lieutenant Cotter is too weak to deal with reporters or other media personnel."

"Yes, ma'am. I'll give him the word." He nodded to Margo, "Ma'am." Ensign Brown and the Watch Petty Officer left.

Eight days later Margo and Bud were having coffee in the ship's wardroom. A third class yeoman came into the room and delivered an official sealed navy envelope to Margo.

"Teddy Bear, your dad is amazing," she said, smiling happily as she read the typed form. It was an official letter from the Navy Department releasing Margo from her two year contract. "It must be nice to have this kind of pull."

"This is the only time I've ever asked daddy to use his influence on my behalf."

"Thank you, Teddy Bear, I love you so much."

"Angel, you saved my life twice, and I'll never be able to repay you for that."

"Oh, yes, you've already more than repaid me," she smiled extending her hand to observe the dazzling engagement ring.

One week before the couple was due to depart for Bethesda Naval Hospital, a tidy sailor in starched and pressed summer whites carrying a clipboard filled with dispatches approached Bud and Margo in the ship's wardroom.

"Lieutenant Cotter?"

"Yes Lad."

"A priority action message for you, sir. Could you initial here?"

Bud scribbled his initials on the form with a weak right hand. "Thanks, Lad."

"You're welcomed, sir." The sailor shot an admiring glance at Margo as he departed. She thrilled him with a smile and a flash of green eyes. Bud unfolded the message form.

14 November 1968 2142Z

FROM: CINCPAC

TO: LT. TOLAND COTTER VC-110, DANANG DET.

DESIRE LT TOLAND COTTER USN REPORT TO THIS COMMAND IN ROUTE BETHESDA. PRIORITY ONE TRANSPORTATION AUTHORIZED.

MCCAIN

bt

"Now what the hell is this?" Bud handed the message to Margo.

"Oh, wow, Teddy Bear. What does it mean?"

"It appears as though Admiral McCain or someone on his staff wants to see me."

“Do you think it’s about rescuing, Jack?”

“No, I don’t think so, CINCPAC wouldn’t want to talk to a peon like me about that, Angel. I can’t imagine what this is all about. Well,” he said and shrugged resignedly, “it looks like we’re going to Hawaii in a few days.”

“I’ll look forward to it,” Margo smiled happily; “I’ve never been to Hawaii.”

“Cotter Communications owns a new hotel down on Waikiki. I’ll send a telegram ahead so that they know we’re coming.”

“Oh Bud, a hotel on Waikiki?”

“Yeah,” he grinned. “Daddy built the largest hotel on the beach. It’s called the Wai Momi.”

“I’ll bet it’s gorgeous.”

“Probably so, it was maybe half completed when I last saw it.”

“Are you sure that you feel up to a meeting with CINCPAC, Teddy Bear?”

“Yeah, I’ll be okay. Actually I’m feeling pretty good now.”

“Well now don’t get carried away and try to do too much. You don’t want to stress your surgery and have it start bleeding.”

“I’m saving all my strength for you,” he grinned.

Chapter 29

Hawaii

Honolulu November 1968

A bright, temperate Hawaiian day greeted Margo and Bud as they walked out of the Hickham AFB receiving area and into the early afternoon sunshine. Bud's appointment with CINCPAC was scheduled for 1000 the next morning. As their bags were being loaded into a long black limousine dispatched by the Wai Momi Hotel, two men abruptly appeared through the glass doors of the receiving area and accosted Bud and Margo.

"Lieutenant Cotter. Aren't you, Lieutenant Cotter of VC-110?"

Bud looked at the two men, estimating them to be in their early thirties. They wore wrinkled slacks and sweat stained wrinkled short sleeve shirts. Both men were unshaven and had oppressive body odor.

Margo got out of the limo and stood close to Bud.

"And you must be Doctor Whitefield," he said appraising Margo with a lusty eye.

"Who are you," said Bud suspiciously.

"I'm Jim Baxter, and this is Randall Clark. I'm with Mutual Broadcasting and Randall is with the New York Times. I'll tell you, Lieutenant, you're a hard man to get to. We just got in from Saigon. We managed to get on an Air Force C-141 coming out of Tan Son Hut yesterday. We heard you were on a NATS flight from Danang to Hickham."

Bud stared at the reporters. He had to admit these guys were damn resourceful, and persistent. Bud surmised that they were going to be a pain in the ass too.

"What do you want?" Bud said.

Randall Clark answered. "We want to do an exclusive interview on your rescue of Commander Jack Ferguson. No one has been able to get to you since you were injured. A lot of reporters and writers have been waiting a long time to talk with you, Lieutenant. We've been through hell trying to get to you first."

"You people were given briefings out at Danang. I'm under orders not to discuss the incident. You need to contact Navy PR at Danang." He motioned Margo into the car and followed her.

"Wait a minute, Lieutenant! You can't just brush us off like that," Baxter said, putting his hand on the car door. "We've busted our tail to get to you! You owe this to the American people!"

"I believe I told you gentlemen that I am under orders. I have nothing to say." Bud jerked the door away from the reporter and slammed it shut. The driver raced away from the terminal building.

The hotel manager and his staff had prepared the Presidential Suite for the couple, a grandiose six bedroom, eight bath affair encompassed by sweeping windows providing a spectacular view of Honolulu, Pearl Harbor, Waikiki and Diamond Head. The suite occupied the entire top floor of the hotel. The luxury residence was lavishly furnished with amenities including a sauna, a game room, a media TV and theater room, a well-stocked library-office, a music room dominated by a huge grand piano and a bar that was stocked with an impressive selection of wines and liquors.

Carlton Stanley, the hotel manager was a notorious stickler for detail and impeccable service. He greeted the couple and personally escorted them to the fastidiously furnished 20th floor penthouse.

Perfumed fragrance of fresh cut flower arrangements drifted throughout the suite as Stanley walked the couple out onto the wide sweeping balcony furnished with rattan tables, chairs and couches and myriad potted plants. Soft Hawaiian guitar music floated from concealed stereo speakers as the hotel manager waved a proud hand revealing the view of curving white beach pegged with towering hotels, clumps of palms and the gaudy familiar shape of Diamond Head as a distant backdrop.

"The most magnificent view on Waikiki," Stanley smiled proudly with arched eyebrows. He was stout, tallowy, deeply tanned and carefully barbered. His snow-white suit was custom tailored. The lapel of his jacket sported an orchid boutonnière.

"Oh, my, this is incredibly beautiful," Margo purred as she absorbed the view.

"I would like to congratulate you both on your engagement." Stanley nodded to Margo. "Your ring is stunning Doctor Whitefield."

They stared at Stanley. Margo's brilliant emerald eyes searched the hotel manager's face. "Thank you, Mr. Stanley. How did you know about our engagement?"

He smiled politely, feigning a bit of embarrassment. "Ah, but such good news travels quickly. I spoke with Mr. Norman Cotter earlier today. He informed me of your engagement, and please, call me Carlton."

"You have a beautiful hotel here, Carlton," said Bud. "I understand that you have been awarded a five star rating."

Stanley's eyes glowed with professional pride, a hint of hauteur leaking into his smile. "Yes. The staff and I are quite elated by the honor. Of course your family made it all possible. Working with your father is a grand pleasure, and," he nodded with a charming grin, "I look forward to working with you at sometime in the future, Bud."

"Well, Carlton. If that should come to pass, I shall look forward to working with you as well, but for the foreseeable future the Navy has first call on me."

"Of course, I understand." He smiled and nodded. "By the way, Bud, Miss Chandler sends her regards and her regrets. Due to the death of her grandfather, she has returned to Nashville to attend the funeral."

Bud nodded somberly. "Thank you, Carlton."

"I must say how much we all admire you for the rescue of your Commanding Officer, it was a most inspiring and impressive feat. Is your recovery progressing well?"

"Yes, thank you for asking."

"Fine, well, I'll leave you now. Don't hesitate to call on me for any reason and at any time. I'm at your service. The desk or the Concierge can reach me in an instant twenty four hours a day."

"There is one thing, Carlton," said Bud. "We want to avoid all contact with reporters and journalists. We've been briefed to expect media attention in regard to this rescue business. There were two reporters at Hickham whom we had to avoid. They evidently followed us from Vietnam. These people can be very clever and quite resourceful. I would appreciate it very much, Carlton if your staff could help us in this regard."

"Of course, by all means," he nodded adamantly, his face serious. "I will see to it that you are not disturbed."

"Thank you, Carlton. The reporters who followed us from Danang are Jim Baxter of Mutual Broadcasting and Randall Clark with the New York Times." Carlton made a small leather notebook appear and jotted down the names.

"Rest assured that my security staff and I will see to your privacy. Is there anything else that I might do for you?"

"No, but thank you for asking, Carlton."

"Very well, then. I'll be off. Good-bye now, and enjoy your stay." He smiled and hurried out.

Minutes later two Hawaiian bellboys wearing untucked Hawaiian shirts arrived pushing a heavy brass rolling cart with clothes bar carrying the couple's luggage and suit bags. Margo directed them to place the valises and suit bags in the sprawling master bedroom. They finished quickly and went out, refusing to be tipped. When Margo had seen the bellboys out, she took Bud's hand and the couple walked out onto the curving balcony and settled onto a cushy rattan couch.

"You look so tired, Teddy Bear. I worry about you."

"It's been a long trip," he said, rubbing his eyes. "Jet lag, I suppose."

"Jet lag for sure. I'm exhausted myself."

"I'm just glad to be off that airplane."

"It is so wonderful to be out of Vietnam. This place looks like paradise to me."

"I'll bet it does, Angel. Having you out of that stinking hole gives me much peace of mind."

After a long silence, Bud said. "How do you like the hotel?"

"Oh, Bud, this place is unreal! I can't get over that gorgeous bubbly waterfall in the main foyer, and I just love all the colorful fish and the tropical plants. It's really wonderful the way they have combined elegant formality with a casual Hawaiian atmosphere."

"This suite is designed for use by the President and heads of state. There's an equipment room next to the elevator, they can connect these telephones to anyone, anywhere in the world.".

"This hotel must have cost a fortune to build."

"Six million dollars. Daddy says it will pay for itself six to eight years."

"Wow, that's a lot of money, Teddy Bear."

"It's ours to use anytime we're in Honolulu." He leaned and kissed her. "I love you, Angel. You make me happier than I could have ever imagined."

The big green eyes were filled with love for him. "I love you," she whispered. "You are truly my gift from God."

He cast a tired smile and gently kissed her. "You are my gift from God, and I believe that together we will accomplish much." After a long moment of silence, he said, "Have you thought about when we should get married?"

"I've been thinking about Valentine Day, Teddy Bear," she smiled happily. Visions of Phyllis saying those same words, making those same plans flooded his mind. He gave Margo a wistful glance then turned his gaze to the sea.

"Is Valentine Day not a good time?"

"Valentine Day is perfect," he said forcing a smile. "Where should we be married? In Montana or Nashville?"

"Oh, my God, not Montana in February, it'll be forty below!"

"Nashville can be bitter in February too, not quite forty below, but still cold."

"I saw an ad in a magazine on the airplane about Key West. I've never been there, but I hear it is beautiful. What do you think?"

"Key West is beautiful in February, Angel. Our family owns a large complex on the Key, and between the main house and the bungalows, there's room for both families and a lot of friends. If you want, I'm sure that Mama and Bernadette would love to help arrange the wedding down there."

"Oh, would they? That would be wonderful!"

"Do you have a church preference?"

Margo appeared surprised. "Well, since you're Catholic. I assumed we would be married in a Catholic Church."

"Are you sure about that?"

"Yes, I'm sure. My family is Lutheran. When I was growing up, the closest church was about 35 miles from our house, but Mother and dad took us nearly every Sunday. Anyway, I have no qualms about being married in a Catholic Church, besides there doesn't seem to be great deal of difference between the two churches. I've come to believe that God doesn't really care what religion we are as long as we believe in Him."

Bud was nodding. "Margo, you have made a truly profound statement. During the time I was separated from my body, when I was with Phyllis, one thing was made unmistakably clear to me. God has given each human being the opportunity to believe in Him. Although God comes in many forms to many different people, if we accept Him and believe in Him, He will never abandon us. The power of praying, talking to God, and love, those are the two greatest powers in the universe second only to God. I have been brought up and educated in the Catholic Church, and therefore I believe in God as a Catholic sees God. No doubt you see God as a Lutheran sees God. He is the same God. The division of churches within Christianity and all religions for that matter is a product of man struggling to understand and interpret scriptures and the Will and the Word of God."

"You've become a regular theologian," Margo said, grinning.

"Actually my comprehension of theology is pretty simplistic. I am certainly not capable of grasping complex mysticisms on my own."

"I want us to be married in a Catholic Church," Margo said somberly. "I believe it is the right thing to do. Maybe I feel this way because it is what God wants us to do, I don't know."

"Possibly. Maybe our getting married is the thing that Phyllis was talking about. Maybe that is what God is revealing to you and me. How will your family feel about you getting married in a Catholic church?"

"Oh, that won't be a problem at all."

"Well, that being the case, we can get married in Saint Mary Star of the Sea. It is the only Catholic Church in Key West. We can be married in the church or we can have an outdoor wedding at the complex. I'm sure the priest will marry us wherever we want. Tell you what, we'll fly down to the Keys during Christmas leave and you can check it all out. If you like Key West, that's where we'll be married. If not, we can come up with a plan B."

"That sounds fabulous, Teddy Bear. I just know that I'll fall in love with the Keys. I can hardly wait."

He stood wearily. "Angel, I'm going to get out of these cruddy whites and take a shower. I've got some khaki shorts and a tee shirt somewhere in my bag I'll put on until we go out."

"A shower would be fabulous. I'm about to curdle myself."

"Why don't you go first, then?"

"No, you go ahead Teddy Bear. I want to unpack a few things and straighten up a little."

When Bud came out of the shower with a bath towel wrapped around his waist, Margo was sitting at the dressing table in an embroidered white terry cloth Wai Momi robe brushing her hair.

"I feel like a human being again," said Bud. He went to her and kissed her forehead and stroked her hair. "Your hair is so beautiful, Margo, I've never seen it let down before. You are absolutely gorgeous."

She put her hands on his waist and kissed his tummy. Hmmm, you smell good, and you taste good too." Spine tingling erotic sensations raced through his body. "Jesus, Margo," he hissed through clenched teeth.

"Get used to it, Teddy Bear. There's millions more kisses where that came from. I made us a drink. Here."

He took the glass from her and sipped, "This is great whiskey."

"It's George Dickel," she replied, casting him a sensuous glance. "I was presumptuous enough to have the boys bring our luggage in here," she said examining her sparkling engagement ring. "I intend to stay close to you, Teddy Bear, permanently."

"Being together is all that matters, Angel."

She stood, her mouth curled into a shy sumptuous smile, "My feelings exactly. Don't go away, Teddy Bear. I'll be right out."

Margo was not quite as fervent to experience her first sexual encounter as she pretended to be. Despite her outward display of eagerness, Margo harbored a poignant anxiety about having sex. The pain and humiliation of her rape as a young girl was never far from her conscious. It had become the dark obsession of her life. She wasn't sure she could go through with this, her first lovemaking experience. Even with all her knowledge and training as a physician, she harbored fearful doubts. She didn't know how she would react once they were in bed together and he touched her intimately. She wanted desperately to gratify him, but her apprehension and her lack of experience with love making troubled her terribly.

When Margo came out of the shower, she saw that Bud was fast asleep. She breathed a sigh of relief. He had folded down the bedspread and was lying on his back half covered by the top sheet. The scar on his chest appeared red and angry. Margo smiled tenderly. The trip had been exhausting for both of them. She drew the louvered window shutters, dumped her bathrobe on a chair and strangely not quite so apprehensive, she slipped under the sheets. She snuggled next to him and kissed his lips ever so gently. He stirred but did not wake. Margo lay next to him, savoring the touch of his body against hers. At this moment, she felt perfect happiness deep within her soul. She considered this day as a new beginning for Bud and herself. She loved him fiercely and she was determined to do whatever was necessary to make their lives happy and fulfilled. Margo too, was desperately tired after the long trip. She said a little prayer and thanked God for Bud Cotter. In a few minutes she drifted off, and they lay together in a slumbered peace.

Bud awoke some hours later. Margo lay next to him sleeping peacefully. Her rounded erect breasts heaved with each breath. Even in sleep without the benefits of mascara, she was incredibly beautiful. He gazed at her for a long time thinking how ironic it was that they had fallen in love. Never in his wildest dreams had he imagined being in love with a woman like Margo, but even more unbelievable was having such a storybook creature fall in love with him. Because she is a doctor, he wondered if she would think him naive in bed. With Phyllis, lovemaking had happened spontaneously. They had made love in many ways: guiding each other, learning the things that aroused and stimulated each of them most. Lovemaking had become natural, uncomplicated and wonderfully satisfying. Once in a while, usually when they were tipsy, he or Phyllis would do something differently wild and outrageous, but no matter how they had made love to each other, sex with Phyllis had always been wonderful. Beyond his happy sex life with Phyllis however, Bud had no other sexual experience with women. He decided that the best strategy with Margo may be to simply let things happen naturally. With that thought in mind, he rolled onto his side and allowed his lips to brush the nipples of her wonderfully tantalizing breasts.

Margo's thrusting breathless orgasms dramatically heightened the fervor of his lustful arousal. She climaxed quickly and did so multiple times, crying out in ecstasy as her body bowed, utterly consumed by explosions of outrageous joy. And when Bud reached the point of losing control, he grasped the mounds of her bottom whereupon she wrapped her legs around him and abandoned herself to the rhapsody of his hot surging orgasm. The heightened emotional drama of this first lovemaking encounter spurred Margo to repeated ecstatic orgasms that evening. Her fears, so intense in the beginning were forever vanished. Bud was gentle, considerate and loving, and she responded to his love with unbridled passion of her own.

They dozed for a while. Margo slept facing him with a long shapely leg across his thighs as if to hold him close to her.

"What time is it, Teddy Bear?"

"I don't know, and I don't give a damn," he groaned.

"Ah, ha, ha." She kissed his lips and glanced at the bedside clock radio. "It's nine thirty, Teddy Bear."

"AM or PM?"

"PM Are you hungry?"

"A little, I guess. What about you?"

"I'm starved. How does bacon, eggs and toast sound to you?"

He rose up on an elbow sleepily squinting at her. "Jesus, that would be wonderful, and some coffee. I'll call room service and have them bring it up. Let's eat out on the balcony. What do you say, Angel?"

"I say that I love you, you sexpot, and I'll call room service."

"In that case, I'm going to take a shower."

She smiled, tingling all over and gently caressed his genitalia. "You're just so marvelous, Teddy Bear. My God, the way you manipulate me! I think you know my body better than I do." Margo's eyes sparkled with lusty fire. He was becoming aroused as her fingers caressed and massaged him.

"I'm yours anytime you want me, Teddy Bear. You'd better go take your shower." She grinned wickedly. "I'll order the food. How do you want your eggs?"

"How the hell do you expect me to think about eggs with you doing that?"

She giggled, rolled over and picked up the telephone receiver. "How about scrambled eggs, Teddy Bear?"

"Wonderful," he breathed and sat up on the edge of the bed.

Margo pleasantly surprised him a few minutes later when she stepped into the shower with him. They washed each other pausing for long passionate kisses and embraces. Bud grasped her buttocks and lifted. She gave a little jump and he held her against the tile of the shower. She wrapped her legs around him and they made love under the shower of water.

"These eggs and bacon are fabulous," Margo said. The waiters served them on the balcony. The couple ate ravenously and enjoyed the sparkling night lights of Honolulu from their lofty perch above Waikiki.

"This is perfect," Bud agreed pouring coffee. "I could get used to living like this."

"I'll say, Teddy Bear. I've never been this happy. Being in love like this, together with you, it is the absolute pureness of joy."

“I love you, Angel.” He gazed lovingly, watching her eat. “Want to take a walk on the beach a little later?”

“Yes! How wonderful! I’ve never been on Waikiki.” She paused and frowned. “But I don’t know what I’ll wear.”

“Shorts and sandals are the uniform of the day around here.”

“I can do that.” She grinned happily.

The happy couple walked on Waikiki Beach, stopping to buy ice cream at a beachside stall. Bud led Margo into the International Market Place, stirring memories of Phyllis and he being here in another time, in another life so it seemed. They stopped in to see a show at Don Ho’s, and strolled barefoot along the beach back to the hotel. Bud opened a half bottle of chilled Moot & Chandon and poured two glasses. He took Margo in his arms and kissed her with great lusty passion.

They cuddled on the balcony couch, murmuring affectionately, gazing at the blaze of Honolulu and gulping the wonderful bubbly wine. In a few minutes Bud rose and opened another half bottle. When he had poured and was handing a goblet to Margo, a frightful thought occurred to him.

“Angel, do you take birth control?”

She flushed and tittered, “This is one heck of a time to be asking me a question like that, sexpot. You have deposited enough sperm inside me tonight to make a dozen sons, but yes, I started taking the pill on the day we were engaged. I knew when you were better neither of us would be able to keep our hands off the other.”

“I’m in love with the most beautiful, sexy, unbelievably desirable woman in the world. I still can’t believe we have fallen in love like this. I’ll never know why God has been so good to me by bringing you into my life, Angel.”

"I'm yours forever, Teddy Bear and you are mine forever. God has given us to each other. Now we have to try and understand what will be revealed to us."

"Yeah, I think about it all the time. I'm convinced our getting married is part of the plan."

"I know it's a piece of the puzzle of my life," she said with a twisted smile. "God knows what a lonely mess my life has been. I had no real idea how screwed up I was and what I was going to do with my life. Then suddenly, there you were, sitting at that table in the O Club. I shocked myself when I decided to sit with you. Any other time I would have walked away. I can tell you it raised a lot of eyebrows when I sat down with you." She smiled reflectively. "Doctor Fine Bottom, the 'Fort Knox of Tail,' walked into the Navy Pier O Club and sat with a male officer. It was all over Danang the next day"

"You know about them calling you the Fort Knox of Tail?" Bud interrupted.

Margo softly chortled, Oh, lord, yes. I heard those names and others. Well, as I was saying, I had no idea why I decided to sit with you, I couldn't believe it myself."

"Angel, you don't know how close I came to saying no when you called and invited me to the New Years Eve party. Just like you didn't understand why you sat with me in the O Club, I didn't understand why I accepted your invitation, but," he grinned happily, "now we know."

"Yes, we do."

After a pause, Margo said, "Do you think we are being wicked having this wonderful sex together?"

"No, and I'll tell you why. The day you accepted that ring from me, we fully committed our love and our lives to one another. In my view, our commitment has spiritually married us already. Standing through a ceremony with witnesses makes it legal to the law of man, but in effect, we have already made the vows of marriage with each other. I am no theologian, and a lot of people including the churches will disagree with my point of view on this, but as far as I am concerned, we are married and committed to each other forever."

"Somehow I feel as though I am being naïve. Am I?"

"No, Angel. You are not being naïve. As a matter of fact, I believe you are the most un-naïve person I have ever met."

Margo snickered at him. "I guess I should take that as a compliment."

"Yes you should."

The couple sipped champagne and silently gazed at the sea and at the blazing lights of Waikiki. After a while, Margo said, "I've got a small confession to make."

Bud looked at her curiously. "You do?"

"Yes, I do. When we arrived here at the hotel today, I was terribly apprehensive about us having sex. I wasn't sure whether or not I could go through with it. Not so much for moral reasons, but because I have never really been able to put that horrible rape behind me and because I have had no experience. As a doctor, I understand how everything is supposed to work, but tonight Teddy Bear you have erased away all those repressed feelings and fears. I love you all the more because of what you have done."

He smiled softly. "Our love for each other is what makes making love so incredibly wonderful. It is the perfect physical union of our love and commitment to one another."

They finished the champagne and Margo looked at the clock on the sitting room wall. "Do you realize that it's two thirty in the morning, Teddy Bear? You've got an appointment with CINCPAC at ten."

"Two-thirty? Boy this time change has got me all fouled up." He stood and extended a hand to her. He took her in his arms and kissed her with a hungry feverish passion and led her into the bedroom.

Admiral McCain

Admiral John S. McCain, Jr., a submariner, became Commander-in-Chief of the Pacific Command in July 1968. As such, he directed all U.S. military operations in the vast Vietnam Theater, exercising command through Commander-in-Chief of the Pacific Fleet and Commander- in-Chief of the Pacific Air Force. Additionally, he exercised command over ground and air operations in Vietnam through CONMUSMACV commanded by U.S. Army General Creighton Abrams who had relieved US Army General Westmoreland.

The Admiral's son, Lieutenant Commander John S. McCain III was a pilot assigned to Squadron VA-163 onboard the aircraft carrier USS ORISKANY CVA-34. On October 26, 1967, he launched in his A4E "Skyhawk" attack aircraft as the number three aircraft in the first division of a strike group against the Hanoi thermal Power Plant. The flight met with considerable resistance in the form of anti-aircraft fire and surface-to-air missiles as it approached the target. As McCain rolled into his dive, his aircraft was observed by his wingman to take a direct hit from anti-aircraft fire and to burst into flames. McCain was able to eject from his crippled aircraft and landed in a nearby lake in Hanoi. He was captured immediately and confined in the Hanoi prison system. During the egress from his aircraft, McCain was severely injured, having broken both arms and his right leg.

Lieutenant Cotter walked into the CINCPAC building and went directly to the Duty Officer's desk. He had been here in the past and knew the protocol. Bud presented himself to the

OOD, a youngish Lieutenant Commander whom he didn't recognize.

"Lieutenant Toland Cotter reporting for a ten hundred appointment as ordered, sir."

The tanned, smooth-face OOD regarded the young senior lieutenant for a moment. His eyes surveyed Bud's ribbons and fixed on the Navy Cross. He shifted to his log that indicated Bud's scheduled appointment.

"I see you are you just in from Danang, Lieutenant Cotter."

"Yes, sir. I arrived at Hickham yesterday at 1430."

"Are you billeted at the BOQ at Pearl?"

"No, sir, I'm staying at the Wai Momi hotel on the beach."

The commander's eyebrows rose. "Pretty pricey hotel isn't it?"

"I really don't know, Commander. You see, my father owns the hotel."

"Oh, I see. Very well, Lieutenant, the admiral will see you when he is free. Have a seat. Coffee, Lieutenant?"

"Ah, no thank you, sir."

He waited until 1040 before being summoned. During that time he endured curious glances from the duty officer, an Annapolis man on the fast track up the promotion ladder. The OOD knew the story surrounding Bud's rescue of Jack Ferguson. The paperwork recommending Bud for the Medal of Honor had passed across his desk on the way to CINCPAC's office. The commander envied this young aviator. Wearing the Navy Cross, the DFC and a Purple Heart, he was now being recommended to receive the nation's highest military honor. The commander felt pangs of shame at having successfully manipulated his own career to avoid duty in Southeast Asia. His job at CINCPAC kept him at home with his beautiful wife who was a local TV personality. The duty officer assuaged his guilt by convincing himself that his desk job at CINCPAC was just as important to the war effort as a combat assignment. The young senior Lieutenant sitting in front of him wore three full rows of ribbons topped by the blue ribbon of the Navy Cross; by comparison his own three measly ribbons were a joke. It was humiliating, but not so embarrassing so as to move him to apply for a combat assignment.

Bud knew very little about Admiral McCain except that he was a submariner and that his son had been become a prisoner of war. Therefore, Bud decided to be straightforward and speak only when asked a question.

The duty officer opened one of two navy blue double doors leading into the CINCPAC office. He announced Bud and withdrew to his desk. Mick O'Reagan, former Commander Air Group Danang, now a Rear Admiral, was CINCPAC Chief of Staff. He held a delicate china cup and saucer and sat comfortably in a wing back chair to one side of CINCPAC's sprawling desk. The room had been redecorated since the retirement of Admiral Grant Sharp. The walls were festooned with sea paintings and portraits of famous admirals, most notably, Nimitz, Halsey, Spruance, and of course the Admiral's father, Admiral John McCain.

"Hello, Cotter," O'Reagan nodded.

"Good morning, Admiral O'Regan," said Bud in a formal tone, "Congratulations on making flag, sir."

"Thanks, Cotter."

Bud stood in front of CINCPAC's desk. The admiral courteously rose and extended a hand to Bud. He was lean and wintry with piercing hard blue eyes under bushy eyebrows and a crop of steel gray hair. The narrow face supported a wide nose but otherwise sharp features, and a clear complexion. He held an expensive Punch cigar between the long thin fingers of his left hand. Bud immediately decided that the admiral was probably a tough old bird.

"Lieutenant Cotter, I'm John McCain." The grip was firm and cool. "Well done with that gutsy extraction of Jack Ferguson out in the A Shau Valley." The hand withdrew.

"Thank you, admiral."

"Have a seat, Lieutenant."

"Thank you, sir." Bud sat in the wing back chair the Admiral had indicated with a flick of his hand.

"How are you injuries, Lieutenant?"

"I'm making good progress, Admiral. Thank you for asking, sir."

"Good. I understand you are in route to Bethesda for additional evaluation."

"Yes, sir. I'm not sure exactly what they are going to do."

"Well, Lieutenant. You are young and strong. I'm confident the results will be positive."

The admiral paused, struck a match and put it to his cigar. Without preamble McCain said, "I want you, puff, puff, puff, to work for me, Lieutenant. I need a liaison officer who can interact with the new White House as well as with the field commanders in Southeast Asia. Our recently elected Commander in Chief will be taking the oath of office in January. Much of his focus will be on Southeast Asian operations that are directed by this command. Therefore I'm in need of an officer who: a. knows the President, and b. one who the President will trust, and c. is an experienced officer with combat experience in Southeast Asia. Our Chief of Naval Operations, Admiral Moorer has expressed concern over potential transitional problems with the new White House staff. He and I feel that you fit the bill as the liaison officer who can best deal with these people. You will report to me directly and dotted line to Admiral O'Reagan for admin purposes. When you are in Washington, you will report directly to Admiral Moorer. This is an extremely high profile position, Cotter. I need not tell you that if you are successful, it would mean and very rapid rise in your naval career. Now Admiral O'Reagan has made me aware that you prefer a duty assignment as an aviator. That is understandable, but having you out there dropping napalm and chasing MIGS is not in the Navy's best interest at this time. We now have an ample supply of pilots in the fleet, and more being trained every day. By accepting this assignment, you can make a far greater contribution to our success in Southeast Asia than you possibly could as a fleet aviator." The admiral paused to puff on the cigar. "Many difficult decisions have to be made in the coming year, Lieutenant. A majority of them will require approval by the White House. It is critical that CNO, CINCPAC and CINCLANT quickly establish credibility and trust with the new Commander in Chief. I believe that as liaison officer, you can help establish that trust and credibility. I'd like you to give this assignment serious consideration." The end of the big cigar disappeared between thin lips to await an answer.

Bud felt sickened. He knew that if he was going to stay in the Navy he had no choice in the matter. He glanced nervously toward O'Reagan whose face was blank. "Admiral, may I speak candidly, sir?"

The steely blue eyes narrowed over the cigar, "By all means, Lieutenant."

"With all due respect, sir, I should point out that I'm not that close to Mr. Nixon. Our relationship has been purely social and very brief. My father has Mr. Nixon's ear, Admiral, not I."

Icy penetrating eyes were fixed on him. "Mr. Nixon knows you personally and your father is one of his most intimate confidants. There's not another officer in the Navy who I would consider more qualified to handle this job, Lieutenant."

Bud blinked at CINCPAC. He understood. "In that case, Admiral, I look forward to being in your service."

McCain's face brightened for a fleeting second. "Excellent, Lieutenant. I'll request BuPers to cut your orders. I'll recommend 45 days basket leave when you are discharged from Bethesda. Your orders to that effect will be issued to you there."

"Thank you, Admiral. That is most generous of you."

"I'd say you could use a little R&R, Lieutenant." Puff, puff.

"I'm very sorry about your son, Admiral. Has there been any recent word?"

McCain pursed his lips. "A SEAL team went in and located John III and several others. Uncontrollable factors made it impossible to get them out. The NV moves prisoners from place to place, presumably to foil rescue attempts. Presently Hanoi's Enemy Proselytizing Bureau maintains several locations where American POW's are detained. The communists may attempt to use John III as a political pawn. I've been advised to expect such activity."

"I don't envy you your position, sir. It must be very difficult."

"Yes, well." McCain cleared his throat. "Now that you're working for me, I'll be expecting some pointers from you on the golf course, Lieutenant. Mick tells me that you are quite a golfer."

Bud glanced at O'Reagan and grinned wryly, "Admiral, I will be most pleased to help in any way I can, but I sometimes have a bad habit of losing my game. I blew a seven shot in the 3rd round of the Tennessee Amateur Championship round when I was in college."

"You did? Tell me about it, Lieutenant." Puff, puff, puff.

"Begging your indulgence, Admiral, I couldn't get my head out of my ass that day."

McCain burst into genuine hearty laughter. "Lieutenant, I think we're going to get along just fine."

"Yes, sir," said Bud self consciously glancing at O'Reagan who was laughing too.

"By the way Lieutenant, your Medal of Honor nomination is being withheld until after Mr. Nixon is sworn in. There is legitimate concern at CNO about lame duck vindictiveness with the current administration."

"Admiral," Bud said hesitantly, "I must respectfully submit to you, sir, I do not feel that I deserve that award. Begging the Admiral's indulgence once more, this entire Medal of Honor thing is bullshit, sir."

The cigar whipped out of McCain's mouth. Cold steel eyes seemed to drill through the impertinent young aviator. "That's not your goddamn judgment to make, Lieutenant!"

"Yes, sir," Bud answered submissively, but his eyes remained fixed on the Admiral's. A shivering quiet fell over the room until McCain broke the silence.

"Lieutenant, my PR people tell me they're getting heavy pressure from the media. There have been numerous complaints from the media because you have refused to make yourself available for interviews."

Bud hesitated. His eyes locked into McCain's stare. "That's correct, Admiral. I have been directed by COMNAVAIR Danang to refer all media requests to Navy PR."

"Good, I want you to keep it that way, Lieutenant. Continue to refer the reporters to Navy PR and let them handle it."

"Yes, sir. Thank you, admiral."

"Well, good luck at Bethesda, Lieutenant Cotter." McCain picked up his reading glasses. It was a dismissal.

"Thank you, Admiral," Bud rose from the chair and nodded to O'Reagan. "Admiral."

"Good luck, Cotter," O'Reagan answered with a half grin and slowly shaking his head at Bud.

When Bud had gone, McCain turned to his Chief of Staff. "Mick, Jack Ferguson was right about Cotter. He's not afraid to say what's on his mind and he doesn't give a damn who he says it to. I'll have to give the Lad that."

O'Reagan smirked, "John, I can count on two fingers the officers who would have the balls to walk into CINCPAC's office and say what Cotter said."

"He's going to need a pair of big balls dealing with those birds at the White House. I wouldn't want the damn job. I think Cotter is the right officer for this touchy White House liaison thing. He's clearly not an ass kisser. I'm betting he's smart enough to use his father as a resource to help him in this job. If this works out, Mick, we'll have a direct line to the President. The field commanders will cooperate with Cotter because they'll know that he's working for me personally, and more importantly, they'll know he's tight with the President. They'll want him to bring up their name around Nixon and CNO, and me too for that matter. If he goes out there wearing a Medal of Honor, it'll be icing on the cake. Coming up with Cotter for this job was a damn good call on your part, Mick."

"Thanks, Admiral. That kid has tremendous potential. It's understandable why Jack Ferguson is so high on him. It would be one hell of a loss to the Navy if we were let him get away."

"By the way, Mick, you said you could count on two fingers the officers that would have the balls to talk to me like Cotter did. Who's the other one?"

"Jack Ferguson."

McCain looked at O'Reagan and both men started laughing.

Bud kissed his fiancée as she met him at the door of their suite. "How do you like Hawaii, Angel?" Margo followed him into the bedroom. He unbuttoned his white uniform shirt and tossed it onto a chair.

"What I have seen so far is fabulous, but, what's the matter, Teddy Bear, you look upset. What happened with the admiral? I've been dying to know since you left this morning."

He took Margo in his arms and kissed her with a great deal of tenderness. "I love you, Angel." He sighed deeply when they parted. "The admiral wants me to work for him."

"He does? My goodness, Teddy Bear, CINCPAC! What will you do?" She affectionately wiped lipstick from his mouth with her fingers.

"He wants me to be one of his liaison officers, in other words, a goddamn messenger boy between himself, the Chief of Naval Operations, President Nixon and the field commanders in Nam."

"What did you say?"

"I made a couple of excuses which the Admiral just pooh-poohed. I had to accept the damn job, either that or get kicked out of the navy."

"Oh, wow, Teddy Bear. This kind of changes things for us doesn't it?"

"Maybe not. He's ordering me to take 45 days leave once I'm discharged from Bethesda. Add in the travel time, it basically means being back here to go to work in March. This is predicated on the assumption that I will be released from Bethesda before Christmas."

Her face etched with lines of anxiety. "Tell me you won't be flying in Nam."

"No, no way, not with this job. Whenever I go over there, I'll be a safe as the President."

"Well, Lover, she smiled sweetly, "in that case, I can think of worse places to live than Hawaii."

"I'm glad you feel that way, Angel. If I'm going to stay in the Navy and fulfill my eight-year active duty commitment, we have to take this job, from a purely selfish point of view, it means that I won't be flying at all. If I resign and get out, I don't know what I would do. I suppose we should come up with some kind of plan B."

"The only plan I care about is us getting married, Teddy Bear. Everything else will take care of itself." She pecked his lips with a kiss.

"Key West on Valentine's Day," he grinned. "That's the plan."

"And it's a perfect plan, Teddy Bear." Margo radiated pure happiness. Her joy was his joy. "How about lunch down on Waikiki, Angel, we can use the hotel courtesy car, and while we're out, we can stop off at Barbers Point. I'll show you around the base and maybe we can take a spin in the flying club Stearman if it's available."

"That sounds wonderful, Teddy Bear."

Margo luxuriated in the thrill of flying in the vintage biplane. A little tentative at first, she quickly forgot her initial qualms and began to absorb the delights of Oahu's tropical greenery. Flying low over colorful reefs, zooming high between dizzying mountain peaks, buzzing sugar cane and pineapple fields, Margo experienced the wonderful freedom of open cockpit flying that only a fortunate few are privileged to know. She squealed with tremulous delight as Bud performed loops, slow rolls, Immelman turns and a hair-raising split-S with the sturdy old airplane. When they landed, Margo walked around and around the airplane touching it with admiring fingers, marveling at its lines and its 1940's vintage.

"That was unbelievable, Teddy Bear. Now I understand what you mean when you say that flying is the next best thing to sex." She put her arms around his neck and hugged him, "Oh, Teddy Bear. I love you so much."

During the next several days, the couple took long drives around the island. They ate in many of the quaint out of the way places that Bud and Phyllis had once frequented together. Margo was enchanted by Oahu's tropical beauty, its quaint Polynesian culture and the diversity of the island people. Bud introduced Margo to golf at the Waialae Country Club and taught her the fundamentals of the game. It was her first experience on a golf course, and she very quickly became an enthusiastic self-proclaimed duffer.

Four days before they were scheduled to fly out to Bethesda, Bud withdrew money from his bank account and made a down payment on a house on Kahala Avenue. He and Margo found the house quite by accident while driving through the Kahala section of Honolulu one evening. The next day Bud solicited the broker to show the house. For Margo, the house was love at first sight, and she thought, a wistful dream. The house had four bedrooms: three baths, and there was a one bedroom: one bath apartment over the garage. There was a pool, a gourmet kitchen, ceiling fans, an entertainment area, a wet bar by the pool, and a small workshop for Bud. The yard was a tropical delight of bougainvillea, coconut palm and breadfruit trees. The property was being sold as part of an estate settlement complete with furnishings. Bud felt as though he was getting a bargain since he had negotiated the sale price at less than the appraised value of the house. If nothing else, it was a good financial investment. The rambling 2,850 square foot house would be their first home together.

Chapter 30

Margo vs. June Chandler

Nashville Christmas Eve 1968

Having endured two grueling weeks of medical examinations, X-rays, testing, probing, picking, needles, tubes, wires and smelly antiseptics at Bethesda Naval Hospital, Bud was pronounced fit for duty in all respects. He and Margo arrived in Nashville on a flight from Washington at three-thirty on the clear cold Christmas Eve afternoon. Mr. & Mrs. Cotter and Bernadette met them at the airport. The arrival of the engaged couple now safely back from Vietnam was a cause for great celebration. A cocktail party was planned for the evening at the Cotter home. Mrs. Cotter, Bernadette, Katy, Minnie and a new employee, Valerie, a niece from Mose's side of the family, had been busily preparing for holiday celebrations. The house had been in a flutter of excited anticipation since Bud and Margo called from Hawaii and announced that they would be spending the Christmas holidays in Nashville.

The majestic plantation house twinkled and glowed in holiday splendor. The house seemed magnetized with a fervent electricity of holiday euphoria. Even Norman was caught up in the festive atmosphere and wore a fur trimmed red Santa Claus hat to the airport. When they arrived home, Bernadette and Mrs. Cotter whisked Margo away for a tour of the house. Each room of the opulent home provided Margo with some new amazement. The elegance and old southern charm of the house and its occupants were something completely new and fascinating to her.

While the women toured the house, the men went to Mr. Cotter's library. Bud poured 15-year-old Wild Turkey whiskey for his father and himself. Father and son lounged in two leather chairs separated by a large walnut table containing smoking paraphernalia.

"So if I understand you correctly," Norman was saying, "they found nothing wrong with you that would affect your long term health."

"That's it in a nutshell. My chest wound seemed to be the greatest concern. There's some scar tissue on my right lung, and my breastbone hasn't completely healed. Other than that, they say I'm okay."

"What does Margo say?"

"She's okay with their conclusions."

"You're damn lucky to be alive."

"I know it better than anybody."

The senior Cotter opened the humidor on the table and picked out a Don Diego. "Are you going back to the squadron?"

"No, it looks like I'm done with VC-110. By the way, Jack turned over the remaining aircraft to the Vietnamese. He's already brought the squadron personnel back to Barbers Point. He wanted to get as many of the men as possible home for Christmas."

Bud hesitated and drank whiskey savoring its smoothness and warmth. "Margo and I will be going back to Hawaii after we're married. I've been railroaded into working for CINCPAC."

"CINCPAC, humph! Doing what?" Norman was toasting the end of his cigar with a lighter.

"You don't know about it?"

The senior Cotter viewed his son over the cigar. "No, I haven't talked to John McCain since we left Hawaii after our trip to see you on the Comfort."

“Did you have anything to do with the Admiral selecting me for this assignment?”

“No, why do you ask?”

“Just curious, that’s all.”

“So what is it you’re going to be doing at CINCPAC?”

“I’m going to be the liaison officer between CINCPAC, CNO, the new President and the field commanders in Nam.”

“What!” Norman snatched the big cigar out of his mouth. “Christ almighty!” Norman stared at his son. It was one of the very rare occasions when Norman Cotter was at a loss for words. Bud was amused but managed to conceal a smile.

“Admiral McCain and Admiral Moorer anticipate possibly having transitional problems with the new White House. They feel that I will have Mr. Nixon’s ear if problems arise.”

“What the hell are they thinking? You don’t know a damn thing about diplomacy at that level. You’ve had no training or experience. You won’t accomplish a damn thing except to get yourself in the middle of one hell of a lot of trouble!”

Bud pursed his lips and shrugged. "I tried to tell the Admiral that my experience with Mr. Nixon was social, and very limited at that, but it seemed to make no difference to him.”

Norman Cotter sipped whiskey and sat back in the chair. He stared into the fireplace, his eyes narrowed in thought. Bud studied his father. The wheels of genius and experience were churning away in his father’s head.

“You know,” Norman said thoughtfully after a long pause, “maybe I’m underestimating the admirals.” Norman began to nod as if he had suddenly made a revealing discovery. “John McCain and Tom Moorer had it figured out all along.” Norman pointed his cigar at Bud. “They know damn well you’ll be calling me for advice when you get in the middle of a hot issue with the White House. And they know that I’ll tell you what to do because I know how Dick Nixon thinks. Humph, and I'll tell you something else; they're using you to deal with the field commanders because they'll know you're close to the President and the White House staff. This is one hell of an opportunity for you, son. You're going to be directly involved with the most powerful and influential men in the world. You'll be privy to conversations and decisions that could potentially change the history of the world."

"Well, I'm not overjoyed with this assignment. I went into the Navy to fly. I could care less about being a messenger boy for CINCPAC and CNO."

Norman glared at his son and threw up a hand, thoroughly exasperated. "Son, sometimes you can be the most short-sighted kid I have ever seen! Any idiot can fly an airplane, and haven't you had enough of getting yourself shot up on these rescue missions of yours for Christ's sakes!"

Bud calmly sipped sour mash whiskey and set the glass on the table. "Daddy it's Christmas Eve. Let's not argue about my naval career tonight. I've got some other things I want to talk to you about."

Norman puffed clouds of smoke into the air: "Humph. Well, we can discuss this later. What is it you want to talk about?"

"I've been nominated to receive the Medal of Honor."

Norman almost choked on whiskey. "The Congressional Medal of Honor!"

"That's right. I didn't think you knew about it."

His father's mouth dropped open. He stared at his son in astonishment. "Why, why this is incredible, son, I can't believe that I haven't heard about it. Are you sure about this?"

"I'm sure. The reason you haven't heard about it is because CNO is keeping it under wraps until Mr. Nixon is sworn in. Admiral McCain told me they think Johnson and his people would try to shoot it down just to be vindictive because they are aware that I am your son."

Norman nodded thoughtfully. "Hmm, well he's probably right about that."

"Personally I think the whole Medal of Honor thing is a travesty. I told Admiral McCain so."

"Christ almighty, son!" Norman exploded, wagging his head, "You're going to have to learn to use a little tact and diplomacy. Admirals, Generals and Presidents won't tolerate disagreement with their decisions, and especially from an insolent young lieutenant."

Bud looked at his father with a piercing gleam in his eye. "All I've got to say is that if McCain or Nixon or those admirals and generals over in Nam expect me to kiss their ass, they'd better find another messenger boy." Norman stared at his son and slowly shook his head. "For God's sake, son, don't you understand the difference between diplomacy and kissing someone's ass?"

"Daddy, I don't know anything about diplomacy, and I don't want to know anything about diplomacy. The Navy trained me to be a pilot, not a diplomat. I'll be courteous and respectful and pass on the information I've been given. That's the only way I know how to operate."

After a long silence Mr. Cotter said, "What did John McCain have to say when you told him the Medal of Honor recommendation was a travesty?"

"Actually, I told him that I thought it was bullshit. Oh, he bristled up and wasn't happy about what I said. He told me that it wasn't my judgment to make."

"Well, he's right. Medals of Honor aren't handed out unless there is one hell of a good reason with a lot of documentation, credible witnesses and so forth. I can't believe that you were that tactless and undiplomatic with John McCain.

You're going to get yourself in one hell of a lot of trouble if you don't learn to use some tact. You can't talk to these powerful men like that."

Bud shrugged. "If these people don't want a straight answer, then as I said, they better find themselves another messenger boy."

Norman drank whiskey, slowly shook his head and looked at his son. "I'm very proud of you son. As much as we disagree about a lot of things, I couldn't have asked for a better son. You've brought a great deal of honor, respect and pride to this family."

"I love you, daddy, Merry Christmas."

"And I love you, son, Merry Christmas."

They sat silent for many minutes, sipping whiskey and gazing into the fire. Father and son had shared profoundly emotional words that neither of them could remember uttering since Bud was a child.

"Margo and I have decided to get married on Valentine's Day," said Bud, taking a Don Diego out of the humidor and snipping the end with the scissors cutter. "We've decided that a Key West wedding would be best for February, it'll give everyone a break from the cold weather."

"Have you met her people?"

"Not yet. We're flying up there for a visit on the 27th."

"Do you know anything about them?"

"A little. They own and operate a cattle operation and a sportsman's lodge for hunting and trout fishing. I think Margo said they own around 140,000 acres."

"That's one hell of a spread, how many kids in the family besides Margo?"

"She has a sister and three brothers. The oldest brother was killed in an accident back in the late 50's. Her other brothers and her sister live at home and help run the ranch and lodge."

"This is where, in Idaho?"

"Montana. Puff, puff, puff, puff. . . Big Timber, Montana."

"Big Timber, Montana. . . . Humph."

"I made a down payment on a house in Honolulu," said Bud squinting at the fat cigar. "It's a couple of blocks from the Waialae Country Club. It sits in a little inlet just off the reef. Four bedrooms: three bathrooms: twenty eight hundred square feet, a pretty nice place and it's all furnished. I got it for twenty thousand less than the appraised value. I think it'll be a good investment for us."

"Where'd you get the money for that?"

"Out of my bank account at the Bank of Hawaii. If you recall, you have been depositing three thousand a month in that account since I went over there in January of sixty-seven. It's added up after all this time."

"You haven't been spending it?"

"I've hardly had time to touch it, which is good now that I'm going to be married and a home owner."

"Well, real estate in Hawaii is a good investment. Short of Diamond Head erupting, you can't go wrong. Who's going to have the mortgage?"

"I'm financing it on a GI loan through the Bank of Hawaii."

"Well, good, I'm glad the two of you will have a home to call your own. After you're settled in, Millie and I will have to come out there to see the place."

"That will be great, daddy."

“What do you and Margo plan to do after the Navy?” Norman puffed the Don Diego with a calculating glance at his son.

“You know,” Bud said pensively, “we really haven’t talked about it. It’s something we need to think about, with all that’s been going on we haven’t looked that far ahead yet. I know that Margo wants to continue practicing medicine.”

“Humph--Well, it’s something you should be thinking about.” Norman drank off his whiskey and put the glass on the table.

“Do you want a refill?” Bud asked.

“No. That’ll do me until tonight.” Norman looked at his watch and stood. “Well, son, we’re having a house full this evening. I’m going to take a nap. We’ll probably be up half the night.”

Margo was beside herself with wonder and excitement. “Oh, my goodness, Teddy Bear this house is unbelievable! It’s like something from *Gone With the Wind*! Boy do we live a sheltered life in Montana. I didn’t know plantations still existed, and,” she dropped her voice to a whisper, “your parents have Negro servants. Oh, my God, Teddy Bear, and this is 1968!”

They sat on the couch in the twinkling den. “Angel, everyone who works here is very well paid. Katy and Mose are part of the family. They live here in the house. It’s not quite like the old days.”

“Wow.” She happily surveyed the room, “I never dreamed that places like this still existed.”

“Did Bernadette and Mama get you settled in your room?”

“Yes, and oh my goodness,” her eyes were wide with excitement. “That room is so beautiful. Did you know the bedroom suite was hand made in France in 1809, and it belonged to your great-great grandparents? And____.”

Smiling, Bud pulled her close and kissed her tenderly. "Welcome home to Tennessee, Angel. I love you."

"This is so much like a dream to me. I mean it's been that way since the moment you gave me this ring. Then we go to Hawaii, and of all things, you buy us a house! And now you bring me to this grand wonderful home and everyone makes me feel so much like part of the family. It's too good to be true. I pinch myself everyday to make sure I'm not dreaming. Oh, I love you so much Teddy Bear." She threw her arms around his neck and kissed him hard.

"What's going on in here?" Bernadette exclaimed. "I see you two can't be trusted alone." She wore jeans, an oversize Belmont College sweatshirt and was barefoot. "I've been dispatched by Minnie and Valerie to find you two and bring you to the kitchen table. The girls have sandwiches and coffee made for everyone. Where's daddy?"

Bud stood and took Margo's hand. "He's taking a nap. Weren't you supposed to be in London tonight?"

Bernadette frowned. "Oh, that. The Queen's itinerary changed. They asked if I could reschedule for New Years Eve."

"Did you?"

"Of course, they pay me a fortune. Shug and I are flying out on the 30th."

"Shug!"

"Yes, Shug, he's taking leave beginning next week."

"Are you two going to London alone? What about Daddy? He'll have a fit."

"He and Mama are going too," she moaned in a revolted tone. "So everything will be on the up and up." Her face brightened. "Say, why don't you two come along too?"

"We'll be in Key West making wedding arrangements."

"Ha! You'll be in Key West making whoopee!" She taunted laughingly.

Bud bolted around the couch after her. "Oh, ho, little sister, you'll pay for that!" Bernadette squealed and ran down the hall twittering and laughing, her bare feet slapping on the polished hardwood floor.

By eight o'clock in the evening the party was in full swing. Over one hundred guests packed the sparkling grand music room. Relatives, friends, politicians, employees of the company and chums of Bernadette and Bud had been invited. In a corner of the room, a beautifully decorated twenty-foot blue spruce tree stood twinkling in stately fashion. Bubbling multicolored candle-like lights illuminated the tree. Mose and Valerie tended bar while Katy and Minnie served hors d'oeuvres: grilled jumbo scallops wrapped in bacon and finger sandwiches from silver service on linen covered rolling trays.

Bud and Margo found themselves the center of attention. Margo's elegant bright red three-bow-back column evening dress sparked envious and admiring whispering among the women and not so subtle spirited glances from the men. Her dazzling engagement ring was widely admired and goggled over, particularly by the women. Bud wore a navy blue blazer, white trousers, a bright Christmas tie and a broad smile of male pride holding Margo on his arm. The happy couple moved among the guests, introducing Margo, chatting and answering eager questions about wedding plans, Bud's injuries and the couple's Vietnam experiences.

Bud's Aunt Harriet appeared out of the crowd wearing a tight fitting scarlet dress cut well above the knee and matching spike heels. She was actually quite captivating and enjoyed the undivided attention of her escort, Jud Jensen an impeccably barbered and manicured WLVX news anchor. Harriet raved over Margo's ring and began to babble on and on about the horrors of seeing Bud and Margo on the Danang video. Initially Bud was embarrassed, but his aunt quickly began to get on his nerves. Margo smiled sweetly and remained silent. Jud sensed that Harriet was making Margo and Bud uncomfortable. He subtly interrupted and led her away to chat with Norman and Millie who were talking with Mayor and Mrs. Briley near the tree.

June Chandler also mingled among the guests. Smiling and talking enthusiastically about her work at the hotel in Honolulu, she was in Nashville to spend Christmas at her parent's home. June positioned herself so as to have a clear view of Bud and Margo, making subtle glances at the couple from a safe distance. June's initial glimpse of Margo had been thoroughly jolting. Margo's reputed femme fatale was dramatically enhanced when observed in person. Gripped by searing jealously, June conceded that Margo was indeed beautifully seductive. No wonder Bud had fallen for her! Maneuvering herself through the crowd, June maintained a position where she could easily, yet inconspicuously observe Margo and Bud. June took out a cigarette and lighted it. Dick Thompson, a young studio camera operator and sound technician, whisked away June's cocktail glass to have it refreshed. Dick Thompson was entirely infatuated with June Chandler. Only once had he steeled his nerve enough to ask her out to dinner. When June graciously refused, Dick's courage deserted him and he had not asked her since. Since then, she had moved to Hawaii. Whenever she was in town, Dick found every excuse possible to be near this beautiful woman that he so ardently admired.

June casually drew from her cigarette staring at Margo through the throng of jocular, cheery guests. She peered at Bud's fiancée as though she were trying to see into Margo's soul, averting her eyes if Margo happened to glance her way. Oh, how she would love to feel Bud Cotter's arms around her once again, to taste his kisses, to delight in the gentleness of his touch. It sickened her to think of Margo and Bud tumbling naked in the throes of wild hot passion. June felt sure they were sexually involved. She perceived an unmistakable aura, a halo of fervid eroticism radiating from the sparkling couple. June seethed bitterly as she noticed their unconscious affections and their inability to keep their hands off one another. Even from her somewhat distant vantage point, June could clearly see glittering reflections of light magnified by the gorgeous 3-carat diamond. She began to wonder why she had come here tonight. Why was she subjecting herself to such invidious agony? Her fingertips caressed the heavy golden necklace Bud had given her as a Christmas gift. She would wear it to her grave.

"Here's your drink, June."

"Thanks, Dick. It's very kind of you."

"The boss puts on a great party doesn't he?"

"Yes, he does. Everyone seems to be enjoying themselves."

Dick glanced nervously at June. "Bud Cotter's fiancée is a real knockout, isn't she?"

June glared straight ahead. The comment annoyed her fiercely. "Yes she is." She turned on him. "Dick, if you don't mind. I'd like to be alone."

His face flushed. "Sure. Okay, June."

June was immediately sorry for having treated the fellow badly. "It's nothing to do with you, Dick. You're really a nice guy and I like you a lot. I just need to be alone for awhile."

"Sure, okay, I understand. I'll see you later." He ambled off into the din of people, embarrassed and feeling very discarded at his dismissal.

Eventually Margo noticed June staring, and not knowing who she was, gave her a friendly smile. June responded with a tiny smile, a nod and disappeared into the crowd. Several times as they moved through the guests, Margo caught glimpses of June staring at her. Eventually she asked Bud about the woman.

"Teddy Bear, who is that pretty woman over there, the one with the long dark hair wearing the cranberry dress?"

Bud noticed June for the first time that evening. She was chatting with one of the station engineers and his wife.

"That's June Chandler, Angel. Would you like me to introduce you?"

Margo's first thought was that June Chandler was quite beautiful and capable of being a formidable rival. "No, not now, Teddy Bear, maybe later."

Later in the evening, however, Margo and June came face to face in the hallway as Margo came out of one of the guest lavatories. The two women assessed each other like vying cats in the night.

"Hello," Margo said, severing the thickness of the moment.

"Hello."

"I'm Margo Whitefield, Bud Cotter's fiancée."

A brief acid smile, "Yes, I know. My name is June Chandler."

"Yes, I know your name as well."

June's eyebrows went up. "Oh? How did you know my name?"

"I noticed you looking our way several times tonight. I asked Bud about you."

"I see. I'm afraid I've not been so subtle."

"Why were you attempting to be subtle? I've been looking forward to meeting you. Bud has told me so much about you."

"Has he?" June hesitated a moment, "Doctor, why don't we talk alone and get to know one another better?"

"Okay, I'd like that. Did you have somewhere in mind?"

June motioned to the far end of the hallway with a nod of her head. "We can talk in Mrs. Cotter's conservatory, through the French doors at end of the hall. Shall we meet there in, let's say, ten minutes?"

Margo whispered to Bud that she was going to meet privately with June Chandler in the conservatory.

June was waiting when Margo walked into glass sunroom filled with plants, flowers and garden furniture. A burbling fountain trickled into a large basin at the feet of Saint Francis of Assisi. The women considered one another across a heavy white glass-top table.

"May I smoke?" June said.

Margo pursed her lips and raised her eyebrows, "Of course, if you wish."

"I hope you won't lecture me about the health risks of smoking."

"Miss Chandler, if you prefer to smoke it is none of my business."

"Thank you for not pontificating to me." June paused and adjusted a large crystal ashtray. "So, here we are, meeting at last," said June. She lit the cigarette and turned away from Margo to exhale. She picked up her cocktail glass and sipped.

"Yes, here we are Miss Chandler. Bud has told me so much about you. I understand you are living in Hawaii now."

"Yes. I work at the Wai Momi hotel which is owned by Cotter Communications, and please, call me June, Doctor."

"Okay, June. Please call me Margo."

"I will, then." June wasted no time going on the offensive. "Your engagement ring is magnificent, Margo. I must tell you, I desperately wish it were on my hand."

The remark startled Margo. Their eyes probed the other. For all her grit, Margo suddenly felt jealously intimidated by this odd young woman.

"I treasure this ring as I treasure the man who gave it to me."

"I'm in love with him too," said June spontaneously.

"Yes, so he tells me."

"Oh, has he? The man is candid to the core. Another reason to love him all the more, I believe I always will be in love with him. You cannot imagine how painful it is for me to see him with you."

Margo sat up straight with her head held high, her eyes combatively shiny. She stared at June Chandler and remained silent.

June drew on the cigarette. "How much has he told you about our relationship?"

"Everything I assume. He did neglect to mention how beautiful you are."

June discounted the compliment with a hitch of her shoulder. "It's kind of you to say that, but then you must look like a goddess to him."

"He's not so shallow as to fall in love with me because of my appearance."

"No, of course he's not." June grasped the cocktail glass and tipped it to her lips. Her dark eyes focused, never wavering from Margo's. She set the glass on an ornate alabaster coaster. "He's not the same Bud Cotter I once knew," said June reflectively. "The Navy, the war, the death of Phyllis Day, all these things have combined to change him strikingly."

"Oh, really? Tell me how he has changed."

June looked away, puffed the cigarette and dashed it in the ashtray. Her eyes returned to Margo's. "He's become hardened where once he was gentle and innocent. His eyes once were soft and affectionate, now there is the cold darkness of death and the horror of war in his eyes. He used to be naive and carefree, now he moves with incisiveness and confidence. He radiates the courage and strength of a cavalier, and now tonight, sadly for me, I see another change in him. His every movement, his very demeanor signals ferocious devotion and love for you."

"I must say, June, you are quite perceptive, and I regret to see, quite passionate about him."

June grinned wryly. "Yes, I am quite passionate about him, and the changes I perceive in him make him even more desirable."

Margo leaned forward, her emerald eyes blazed with the warning of a viper about to strike, "I want you to stay away from him."

June waggled her head regretfully. "I am no threat to you, Margo. Your love for each other has defeated me, as did the love he shared with Phyllis Day."

"Then why do you continue to pursue this futile course? It is perplexing to me, and to many other people."

June cast Margo a sharp glance. "I'm not interested in what other people perceive. Opinions and perceptions are utterly irrelevant. I will answer your question by saying that I cannot simply switch off my feelings and emotions. My love for him courses far too deep."

Margo sipped her cocktail and stared. She was gripped by the full realization that June Chandler was recklessly and irrationally obsessed with Bud. June Chandler frightened Margo. Such a woman might well be completely unpredictable and an ominous threat to her relationship with Bud. Margo felt as though June Chandler somehow had the upper hand here. June's assertion that she was no threat as a rival to Margo did nothing to relieve the jealous anxiety Margo was feeling.

"June, I want assurances from you that you'll not interfere in our life together."

"You don't understand, Margo," June said in an indulgent tone. "I would never interfere." Then, with a look of resolute forewarning she said, "But if you ever let him down, I'll be there for him."

"I could never hurt him," Margo said with stout conviction. "I love him with all that's in me. He is a part of my soul and I his."

"Yes, I can see that. What you share with him glows like a halo when you are together. You have something quite unique and intense."

"Yes, we do, June. I believe it is a gift from God."

June studied Margo with skeptical curiosity. "From God you say. Do you pray often?"

"Mostly when someone I love is in trouble. However, through all this travail with Bud's injuries, I have begun to pray on a daily basis. I admit that I'm not a devoutly religious person nor am I Catholic, not yet anyway, but God seems to tolerate me nevertheless."

"Are you considering becoming a Catholic?"

"Possibly, I don't know yet. It's not something I have discussed with Bud."

"And you believe your relationship with Bud came from God?" .

Margo drew a mouthful of martini from the glass and regarded June Chandler. "What I am about to say will no doubt sound completely bizarre to you, but I'll tell you anyway. Whether you choose to believe it or not is your own affair. On the day Bud was so badly wounded, he went into full cardiac arrest on two occasions: once in the helicopter, and once during emergency surgery aboard the Comfort. I was treating him and performing the surgery. He could only be resuscitated by injections into his heart muscle and by the use of shock paddles."

"Oh my God!" June was appalled. "I had no idea it was that serious!"

"Weeks later, when he was strong enough to speak, he told me that during the time his heart had stopped, his spirit, his soul if you will, left his body and ascended into a state of limbo, a reality that exists somewhere between human biological life and the spiritual existence. He was directed by the spirit of Phyllis Day. He experienced the circumstance of life after death and he was given a glimpse of what we think of as heaven. During this transcendent period of time, many things were revealed to him. Part of the revelation made him aware that he and I had been brought together to achieve a purpose that we don't yet understand. The experience was quite profound for Bud. It has changed him and in turn, it has changed me."

Margo's narrative left June stunned. She sat blinking at Margo, attempting to grasp the significance of the doctor‘s words. The two women speechlessly contemplated one another for interminable moments. It was June who broke the ashen silence.

"I wasn't going to come here tonight. I knew how much it would hurt to see you and Bud together. I guess it was female curiosity that got the best me, and against my better judgment I came anyway. My first glimpse of you with him consumed me with the vilest jealously. I hated you because you are so beautiful, and so happy; and because you have him." She stopped and took a heavy gulp of rum. "I'm beginning to understand why I came here tonight. It was to have this talk with you. Through you, I believe God may be answering questions I've been asking for a very long time." June stood. "I'm going now, Margo." Her face was drawn in melancholy lines. "I'm no less tormented and no less jealous I'm afraid, although I can no longer hate you, Margo. I'm going home now, and I'll sit in my room and have a good cry. I'll forge ahead and trust that I'll be guided each day. Good-bye, Margo. Be good to him."

"Good-bye, June."

Margo stood as June walked towards the door. Bud entered the room, his face a mask of concern. June went to him and kissed him tenderly. She turned and looked at Margo whose face was burning with jealous hostility and said, "Don't begrudge me a last kiss, Margo. It has to last a lifetime." Then she said to Bud, "God has been good to you, Bud Cotter. You are very lucky to have her. I wish both of you all the happiness possible, Merry Christmas, and good-bye."

He watched June walk out, and then he turned to Margo. "What the hell has been going on in here?" He could taste June Chandler's lipstick and wiped it from his mouth with the back of his hand. Margo ran to him. She threw her arms around him. "Oh, Bud, I love you. I love you so very desperately! Hold me. Hold me close!"

Chapter 31

BIG TIMBER, MONTANA

28 December 1968

Billy Whitefield, second son of John and Margaret Whitefield, and two years Margo's senior, helped Bud unload the couple's baggage from a 1940 vintage twin engine Lockheed 12. The aircraft had been the Cotter Communications company aircraft since 1948. A modern Lockheed Jetstar had replaced the classic aircraft in 1965.

Billy was 29 years old, tall, slim, sinewy and rustically good looking. He was quiet, and when he did have something to say, he spoke in deliberate, sober tones. The two young men piled the baggage into the back of a long wood-grain Ford station wagon embellished advertisements on the front doors which read: "W BAR Fork Ranch & Lodge".

During the twenty minute drive to the Whitefield ranch, the trio sat on the front seat of the station wagon. Margo sat in the middle and fired rapid questions at her brother whose answers were grunts, nods or simple yes and no's. The deep snow blanketing the Crazy Mountains, the rolling prairie and the tall forest evergreens was freshly pure and sparkling in the frigid afternoon sunlight. Peering around at the wintry whiteness, Margo shivered and remarked: "Now I remember why I left this place. Billy, turn on the heater. It's freezing in this car! I can see my breath for goodness sake!"

Billy obediently operated the heat controls. He was wearing faded jeans, a green chamois shirt, a fleece lined denim jacket and a stained, well-worn Resistol western hat. Billy was not a bit chilled. Margo and Bud on the other hand, shuddered in heavy winter coats and huddled against one another for warmth.

The Whitefield's two-story home sat on a wooded valley floor facing south. The house over-looked a broad valley and a mile wide lake, not yet frozen, which ambled through the valley below. Behind the house, the land began a gradual rise to the Crazy Mountains through vast forests of fir, aspen and pine. Two hundred yards east of the house, an icy roaring river fell heavily over boulders worn smooth over eons of time. The river began its winding journey somewhere high in the mountains, ending its long tumultuous odyssey as it slowed, running sluggishly into the valley lake dotted with beaver houses. A long hunting lodge constructed of heavy sorrel-color logs occupied an area east of the house. A cluster of corrals, barns and outbuildings beyond the lodge appeared squat, bleak and barren against the backdrop of white snow.

The Whitefield home was bright, cozy and homespun western. Mrs. Whitefield, slighter than her daughter, was a sturdy and buxom woman of forty-seven. Her reddish-blonde hair was done in a tall beehive arrangement enhancing a clear blanched complexion, emerald green eyes, perfect teeth and pretty features. Shedding tears of joy, Mrs. Whitefield ran to the door and embraced her daughter.

"Oh, Honey, it's so good to have you home! It's been so long." She hugged her daughter and then held her at arms length, "My goodness, you look so good and what a nice tan you've got!"

"It's wonderful to be home, mother. I've missed you all so much." Margo turned to Bud and beamed. "Mother, I want you to meet Bud."

"Bud, my goodness aren't you nice looking. It's so good to finally get to meet you," she gave him a brief hug. "Margo has told us so much about you in her letters. We felt so terribly bad when we saw you on the news. Are you feeling better now?"

"Yes, ma'am, I'm fine, thanks to Margo." he said, grinning bashfully. "I've been looking forward to meeting you too, Mrs. Whitefield. Thank you for inviting me."

Margo removed wool gloves and wriggled her left hand.

"Margo, oh my goodness!" Mrs. Whitefield grasped Margo's left hand, "Oh, my goodness, look at this! Why, it's magnificent! Oh, my Lord! Bring it here under this light." She dragged her happily grinning daughter to a lamp set on an end table next to a couch.

"Oh, my Lord, I can't get over this! Billy, did you see you sister's ring?"

"Um," Billy grunted. He closed the heavy front door, took off his hat and jacket and hung them on a peg. A girl of perhaps 19 bounded down the stairs. She wore jeans, a red check flannel shirt and fur lined deerskin house shoes. Her strawberry blond hair was pulled into a thick ponytail.

"Phyllis," Mrs. Whitefield cried, "come look at Margo's ring! Oh my Lord, Margo, I just can't get over this!"

Phyllis eyed Bud with a suspicious sidewise appraisal. She admired Margo's ring and gave her sister a warm hug. "Your ring is gorgeous, Margo. I've been dying for you to get home," Phyllis said excitedly, "I've got so many things to tell you."

Margo smiled happily. "And I've got so much to tell you too." She radiated happiness toward Bud and said to her sister, "Phyllis, this is Bud. Bud this is my baby sister Phyllis."

"Hi, Phyllis," Bud smiled and put out his hand. She took his hand for a brief second, appraising him with the eye of a horse trader. "Hello," she said coolly. "It's nice to meet you."

"Come into the dining room and sit down," Mrs. Whitefield said enthusiastically. "I've made a pot of fresh coffee. Billy, make those dogs stop barking." Her son went to the front door and opened it. He stared at two big collies until the dogs stopped barking and sat. Billy held the door and allowed the dogs to rush into the house. They went immediately to investigate Bud. He rubbed under the dog's chins and scratched behind their ears while they sniffed him. Billy closed the heavy front door and snapped his fingers, instantly both animals went to lie on a long oval rug in front of a wide stone fireplace. A plump, glossy black cat came down the stairway meowing and disappeared into the kitchen. Margo came out of the kitchen carrying a large clear-glass coffee pot.

"I see you've met Molly and Bo," she said to Bud.

"Yeah, they're beautiful animals."

"They usually won't go to a stranger," Mrs. Whitefield remarked as Bud held the chair for her. "Why thank you, Bud, you're such a gentleman."

"Isn't he though," Margo sang with cheerful pride while Bud held her chair. Phyllis rushed to seat herself and avoided looking at Bud which amused him. The cat came out of the kitchen and walked around under the table meowing, rubbing around everyone's legs.

Mrs. Whitefield said, "Phyllis, does Webster have food in his bowl?"

"Yes, mother. I fed him when I came home from class." Phyllis shoved the cat with a foot and said, "Webster, go lay down." Indignant, Webster threw his tail into the air and ambled into the next room where the dogs were lying on the rug. He rubbed himself against Bo and then leaned against Molly purring. When both dogs completely ignored him, Webster curled up on the rug between the big collies and immediately fell asleep.

Everyone sat around the table and drank coffee while Mrs. Whitefield and Phyllis eagerly quizzed Margo about the wedding plans. When Margo brought out the pictures of Hawaii and the Kahala Street house, her mother and sister became even more excited and animated. Bud and Billy drank coffee in silence and shared the evening newspaper.

Twenty minutes later, Mr. Whitefield and the youngest Whitefield son, Buck, who was 18, walked into the house through the breezeway door. Bud stood and the dogs rose to greet them, tails beating rapidly. Margo ran to her father and hugged him tightly. When she had hugged her brother Buck, Margo turned to introduce Bud.

"Dad, Buck, I want you to meet Bud. Bud this is my dad and this is my brother Buck."

Bud shook hands with both men. Mr. Whitefield's hand was rough and coarse with a granite hard grip. Buck's hand was likewise rough but his grip was gentle, almost submissive. Mr. Whitefield matched Bud's height of six feet. He possessed a red leathery face cured by years of sun and wind. He had a wide nose, coal black hair and dark clear eyes. It would be easy to mistake him as Paiute or Shoshone.

"Glad to meet you, son," Mr. Whitefield said, looking Bud in the eye. "You and Margo have a good trip up from Nashville?"

"Yes, sir, we had to climb over a little weather coming across Nebraska and Wyoming, but after that it was clear."

"Margo says you land planes on aircraft carriers," Buck said enthusiastically. He was tall and lanky with a smooth, almost pretty face and dark, perpetually smiling eyes. His coal black hair, inherited from his father, was trimmed short under a worn red Purina Feeds baseball cap.

Bud smiled self-consciously. "Well, yeah. I've done it a few times, Buck."

"Margo says you're the best pilot in the Navy."

Bud laughed heartily and glanced at his beaming fiancée. "No, I'm afraid not, Buck. I think Margo may be a little bit prejudiced."

"I surely am prejudiced," Margo sang sweetly, and slipped an arm around Bud's waist, "but you're still the best pilot in the Navy, Jack Ferguson said so too, and you know Jack doesn't hand out compliments"

Bud grinned bashfully and shook his head.

Mrs. Whitefield kissed her husband and commanded, "Buck, you and your father get washed up. Supper is ready to go on the table. Billy, make Bo and Molly behave. I don't want them begging at the table."

Billy stopped reading the paper, placed his mug on the table and snapped. The dogs went to lie on the rug in front of the family room fireplace. Webster, curled into a black furry ball, didn't stir when the big dogs lay down on either side of him.

The standing rib roast was delightful, served with red new potatoes, corn on the cob, green beans, hot rolls and dressed eggs. The Whitefield's were obviously hard working people of sturdy stock who were used to eating as heartily as they worked.

Finished beautifully in natural spruce, the family room was dominated by the wide stone fireplace. An elegant old key-wound clock chimed seven o'clock as the men walked into the room. Two mule deer heads hovered above the heavy mantel and held the largest antlers Bud had ever seen. Centered underneath the trophy heads Bud recognized a rare, very old .30/.40 caliber Kraig lever action rifle.

"Those are the largest mule deer antlers I have ever seen," Bud said.

"Both of those deer were killed up on the west ridge above the falls." Mr. Whitefield remarked. "They both made the

Boone and Crockett record book, one in fifty-five and the other one in sixty-one. Good advertising for us. Several of the big name sportsman's magazines have done articles on several of the trophy animals taken on the ranch over the years."

Admiring the trophy heads Bud said, "Who killed the deer?"

"Billy killed the one there on the left and Margo killed the on the right."

"Margo killed that deer?" Bud was astonished.

"Yep," Mr. Whitefield said with unconcealed pride, "that girl is one hell of a fine shot. Always has been. She's just a natural hunter, quite a fisherman too."

"I'll be damned," Bud said slowly wagging his head.

Buck threw several big split logs onto the andirons and then stoked the coals underneath with a heavy poker. Mr. Whitefield dropped into his accustomed easy chair near the fireplace and lit a hand rolled cigarette. Billy took out a curved pipe, loaded it with tobacco and put a lighter to the bowl.

Mr. Whitefield said to Bud, "Have a smoke?"

"I may have a cigar later, sir. Thanks."

"Your wounds about healed up now?"

"Yes sir. Margo and the navy doctors at Bethesda Hospital say everything is okay now."

"Margo says you two will be stationed in Hawaii. Are you going to be flying those same fighters?"

"No sir, the way things look, I'm not going to be doing much flying. I'll be working as a liaison officer for Admiral John McCain. He's the Commander In Chief Pacific."

"What does a liaison officer do?"

"Well, sir, the way I understand it, I'll be spending time running between the White House, Hawaii, and Vietnam."

"The White House, huh? I don't trust that shifty eyed son of a bitch Nixon," Mr. Whitefield said and flicked ashes into a heavy glass ashtray, "but if he can get us out of Vietnam like he said he would, that'd be a good thing for the country. Stop all this damn foolishness that's going on at some of the colleges and in the big cities."

"The sooner we're out of Vietnam the better," said Bud. "I believe the problem of getting out of Southeast Asia is going to be more of a political problem than a tactical one. Mr. Nixon has his hands full with this one I'm afraid." Mr. Whitefield peered at Bud as though the young man had said something profound. "Yep, I'd say you're probably right about that." He changed the subject. "Margo says you bought a house over there in Hawaii."

"Yes, sir, I made a down payment on the place and applied for a GI loan. We'll close on it after we're married. Margo brought some pictures of the house if you'd like to see them."

"I'll look at them later. Plan to be there awhile, do you?"

"It's hard to say, Mr. Whitefield. Duty assignments are typically twenty-four to thirty-six months. My tenure at CINCPAC is kind of uncertain though, it's totally dependent on how long the Admiral wants me on his staff."

Mr. Whitefield threw the spent cigarette into the fire. He took out cigarette papers and tobacco and expertly rolled another smoke using one hand. Bud was astonished at the man's dexterity.

"That's amazing how you do that with one hand," said Bud.

"Something I learned from my granddaddy. In his day, they rolled a smoke with one hand. It's kind of a lost art nowadays."

"Wouldn't it be easier to buy packaged cigarettes and smoke them?" Mr. Whitefield shook his head. "Those damn factory made smokes ain't no count."

Bud took out a Don Diego, cut the end, toasted it, and lighted the cigar. Mr. Whitefield eyed him with interest. "You smoke cigars much?"

"Maybe four or five a week, I never inhale the smoke. It makes me sick as a dog."

Whitefield grunted, amused. "Probably just as well, smoking ain't the healthiest thing."

"I read in the paper that some doctors think that smoking causes cancer," Buck interjected.

"They can't prove it," Mr. Whitefield snappily replied. "Hell we've had cattle and horses die of cancer and they damn sure didn't smoke. A client killed a big bull elk one time, up on the east range. When we opened him up to gut him, we found a tumor on his rib cage big as a football."

"Maybe there are different kinds of cancer," Buck said.

"Maybe so, maybe not," Mr. Whitefield said and twisted to look at his son. "If you'd go to college like Margo did, you could be a doctor like your sister and figure out how to cure cancer in people, and animals too for that matter."

"You know I don't want to go to college, Pop. I want to be a rancher."

Mr. Whitefield peered at Bud and slowly wagged his head, "I can't get Billy or Buck to go to college, nothin' but ranchin' and huntin' in their blood."

"I think it's great that they want to follow you, Mr. Whitefield."

"Yep, I'm right proud of 'em all right," he said and puffed his cigarette, "but ranchin' is gettin' more and more modern. They already know as much as I do about cattle and ranchin', but they'll need to know more about business and animal husbandry as time goes on. The state college teaches those things, and I was hopin' to have a vet in the family someday, but it doesn't look like that's going to happen."

"Any chance that Phyllis may go to veterinary school?"

"That's a funny thing," Whitefield said, "she's talked about it and she's taking several pre-med courses at the Junior College, but she changes her mind every so often and says she wants to do something else. So her mother and I don't know what she's going to."

"Most freshman students change their mind a lot," Bud said, "usually by the end of their second year they will settle into a major."

"Yeah, I expect you're right."

"If I joined the Navy, could I fly like you do?" Buck asked grinning hopefully. "We have a Piper Super Cub here on the ranch that I fly all the time. We use it to check on cattle and to spot elk, deer, goats and bear for our clients."

Bud motioned at Buck with the cigar. A gesture that was a mirror image of the way Mr. Cotter gesticulated with his cigar. "I'll tell you, Buck, it's great that you can fly, but if you want to fly in the Navy, you have to go to college first."

"Why is that?" Buck said, surprised and disappointed.

"Well, because every naval officer has the potential of becoming an admiral someday. That means you need to have a good education."

Buck blurted, "Margo says that you're the smartest person she's ever met."

Bud broke into a spontaneous laughter. "I'm no smarter than you are, Buck, probably not as smart."

John Whitefield said, "I hear your dad has a good deal of political influence down in Tennessee."

"Yes, sir. He's made some valuable political allies over the years."

"Republican?"

"Yes, sir, but he has many friends and associates who are Democrats."

Buck spoke up. "Margo says your family runs a plantation down there in Tennessee. She says you've got darkies working there just like in the olden times."

Bud grinned at the young Whitefield. "Well, Buck, it's nothing like the old times. The Negroes who work on Cotter Plantation are paid very well. My several times great grandfather, Jacob Cotter settled there in 1757. In the old days, Cotter Plantation covered more than one hundred thousand acres and owned over five hundred slaves. It and Andrew Jackson's Hermitage plantation were the two largest in Tennessee. Over the years, parcels of the land have been sold off, now there are only about ten thousand acres left."

Buck said, "What happened to the slaves after the Civil War?"

"Some families moved away to the city, but most of the Cotter Negroes stayed on the plantation and lived there until they died. There's a cemetery on the plantation where the Cotter Negroes are buried. The Cotter slaves were well treated and cared for. A house was built for each family. All the kids had to go to school. A lot of them went on to college and became teachers and doctors. Over the years, the Cotter Negroes have gradually died out and their descendents have moved away. There are only two of the original Cotter Plantation Negroes still living on the farm, and they are part of our family. The other Negroes who work on the farm live close by but not all of them are direct descendants of the old Cotter slave families."

"The W Bar Fork was one hundred and ninety thousand acres when my great granddad got a government land grant back in 1888," Mr. Whitefield said. "The government bought fifty thousand acres to be a part of the Gallatin National Forest. We have about one hundred and forty thousand acres now. That's plenty, especially when tax time comes around. We never worked any darkies, always have a few Indian and Mexican hands though."

The women appeared from the kitchen and sat down. Phyllis turned on the 25 inch console TV. The picture was slightly snowy despite a tall outside antenna. The TV could receive two channels, one from Bozeman and the other from Billings. Phyllis kept the volume low and began giggling at the Red Skelton show.

Glowing happily, Margo sat on Bud's lap. She put her arms around his neck and kissed him. His face flared.

"Teddy Bear, have dad and the boys been giving you a hard time?"

"No, not at all," he answered glancing around self-consciously.

"We're talking about ranches and plantations," said Mr. Whitefield.

Bud said, "Margo, your dad told me that you killed that Boone and Crockett mule deer there on the right. You never told me that you killed a record deer."

Margo grinned prettily, "I killed him when I was in college, before I went to med school. I'd been getting glimpses of him for a couple of years. I knew he was big, but I never dreamed he was a record deer."

"That is really something," Bud said, beaming at Margo.

"I'll tell you what's really something," Margo said with a great deal of pride, "Dad, did Bud tell you he's been recommended for the Congressional Medal of Honor?"

"Why, no." Mr. Whitefield straightened in his chair. He eyed Bud with a degree of curious surprise and admiration.

"The whole thing is political, Mr. Whitefield," Bud said quickly in a tone of disgust. "This Medal of Honor thing is ridiculous. If anyone deserves a medal, it's Jack Ferguson. Not only did he survive in the jungle and avoid being captured, he actually captured a North Vietnamese soldier."

"Oh, stop it, Teddy Bear. Everyone except you thinks you deserve it." Margo grinned and pecked his nose embarrassing him again.

A telephone rang in the next room; Phyllis jumped up to answer it. She returned a few moments later, "Bud, it's for you." Margo and Bud exchanged an anxious-curious glance as he rose from the chair. The caller was Norman Cotter. He instructed Bud to tell the Whitefield's that the company aircraft was available for their use to fly them to Key West for the wedding. He then began asking Bud a lot of detailed questions about the Kahala Avenue house. He hung up after complaining about having to be in London on New Year's Eve.

"Who was that Teddy Bear?" Margo said. She put a throw pillow on the floor in front of Bud's chair and snuggled between his legs.

"That was daddy," Bud said, laying his hands affectionately on her shoulders. He turned to Mr. Whitefield. "My daddy wants to know if it would okay with you if his company aircraft comes to Big Timber to take your family to Key West for the wedding."

Mr. Whitefield squinted and blinked at Bud as if he were in very poor light. Mrs. Whitefield screeched with excitement. "Oh, my lord, that would be wonderful, wouldn't it John!"

"Now wait just a damn minute, Margaret!" Whitefield's face twisted into a fierce scowl. "We can't afford something like that, why it'll cost a damn fortune!"

"Mr. Whitefield," Bud said quickly. "I'm sorry, sir. I didn't make myself clear. The use of the aircraft won't cost you anything. My daddy is sending his company aircraft."

Mr. Whitefield said a bit sharply, "Tell your daddy that we're much obliged, but we can take the airlines to the wedding."

"Let me put it another way, Mr. Whitefield," said Bud. "Because Margo and I are going to married in February, Daddy considers all of you as family. He wants to do this as a way of helping to bring our families together."

"John Whitefield," Mrs. Whitefield scolded, "we are going to accept Mr. Cotter's invitation. Sometimes you can be so tacky and tactless."

Mr. Whitefield stared at his wife for long moment. "Well," Mr. Whitefield said hesitantly, "since Bud says it's a family matter, well, that's different. I suppose it'll be okay."

Mrs. Whitefield frowned at Margo, "How do we know what to wear down there? We've never been to Florida. None of us have ever seen the ocean. Is it hot there? We're not used to a lot of hot weather."

"Don't worry, mother," said Margo, "You and Phyllis and I can go shopping in Bozeman while I'm home."

"The weather in Key West in February is very nice," Bud said, "it won't be very hot at all. Mostly in the low 80's."

"Oh, thank goodness it won't be too warm there," Mrs. Whitefield, gasped. "This is just too much, going to Key West, Florida. And Lord—I've got to lose some weight too. Oh my goodness, John, why have you let me get so fat!"

"Mother, stop it," Margo fussed. "You look great, doesn't she, Bud?" Bud nodded with a sincere smile.

"Margaret," her husband chimed in, "you look better now than you did when I married you."

Mrs. Whitefield's eyes twinkled as she reveled in the compliments, "Oh, John stop it, you're just saying that."

"I think I'm going to be sick," Buck groaned.

"You're going to be a lot more than sick if you don't get those horses fed and bedded down," his father threatened.

Making a terrible moan, Buck slowly rose from his chair.

Margo laughed happily, "Welcome to the family, Teddy Bear."

Chapter 32

Till Death Do Us Part

Key West February 1969

The Cotter Complex, located on a secluded peninsula of Key West had never seen such tingling excitement and activity as the wedding of Doctor Marguerite Whitefield and Lieutenant Toland Cotter brought about. The complex consisted of a sprawling main villa: five individual four bedroom guest houses, a long pier and a seaplane and yacht anchorage. Overlooking the Gulf of Mexico, the complex sat amid brick walks, floral hedges and picturesque gardens. Huge white mangrove, key lime, gumbo-limbo and coconut palm trees shaded the houses and grounds. Bougainvillea in combination with varieties of palm and massive flower beds of colorful impatiens and begonias were scattered about carefully barbered lawns.

Henry Flagler had built the 10-acre complex in 1920. After the great hurricane of 1935 destroyed most of the "overseas railway" that connected the Keys with South Florida, the only means of getting to the Keys was by water, and because of the effects of the great depression, the complex became nearly worthless. Even the US Navy had pulled out of Key West after the 1935 hurricane. Between 1935 and 1940, the property changed hands three times. In January of 1940, Norman Cotter's father, Toland J. Cotter purchased the Flagler complex for $12,000.00 as a speculative investment. Now it was 1969 and the complex was worth millions, and the sprawling property had become not only a family heirloom and vacation spot, but also a convenient place for Cotter Communications to entertain clients and political friends.

At 0730 on the day before the wedding, Jack Ferguson and Cowboy arrived at the bachelor guesthouse where Bud and his life-long friend, Doctor Caldwell Kreer had been pigeon-holed. Bud and Margo were seeing very little of each other during these final days of preparation. Bud desperately longed to hold her in his arms. These last two days seemed like an eternity to him. Margo and her sister Phyllis shared a suite of bedrooms in the main house with Bernadette. The Whitefield's occupied a room in the main house while relatives from Montana occupied two of the five bungalows.

The main house was a hornet's nest of frenzied feverish activities as the preparations went forth in a panic-like atmosphere. Margo, Millie Cotter, Bernadette, Mrs. Whitefield, Phyllis Whitefield and a harried wedding director, John Pierre DeLuce each took their turn directing the hysteria from a large secretary in the library. A veritable command center, the secretary held a multiplex telephone system equipped with an array of lighted buzzing buttons, a speaker and a facsimile machine, and to add to the pandemonium, there was a blaring two-way intercom system networked to all parts of the complex through which frantic multidirectional summons were made.

"Cotter," Ferguson bellowed irritably, limping into the house while Bud, squinty eyed from sleep, held the screen door and grinned, "we've been living on NATS gut bombs since we left Pearl yesterday. I think my goddamn colon has a hydraulic lock. We need some real chow and coffee. And don't be expecting any goddamn wedding presents. We didn't have time to screw around with that."

Bud embraced a grinning Cowboy around the neck. "Having you guys and Shug make it for the wedding is the best gift you could have given us." He grabbed Ferguson and gave him a stout hug. "Thanks for coming, Skipper. It really means a lot to us."

"All right, all right, Cotter. Knock it off!" Ferguson hobbled to a stuffed chair, fell stiff-legged into it and lit a Camel.

"We ran into Early at Alameda. He's flying civilian from Frisco. Did he make it yet?"

"Shug called last night. He was spending the night in Miami with his aunt and uncle. He's going to rent a car and drive down. He'll be here sometime this morning. That leg still giving you trouble, Skipper? I thought the cast would be off by now. How long has it been?"

Ferguson billowed cigarette smoke. "Aw, those goddamn dumb-asses back in Hawaii decided they didn't like the way it was healing. So they went in there and took out half of my goddamn knee cap."

"They took some small fragments of floating cartilage from behind his knee cap," Cowboy said. "The skipper makes it sound like his whole knee cap is gone."

"How long is this cast going to be on?"

"Another five weeks," Cowboy quickly answered before Ferguson could respond.

"Until I say it comes off," Ferguson snarled turning on Cowboy. "What about some chow, Cotter?"

"Come on out to the kitchen," Bud said. "There's fresh coffee on the stove. I'll call and have breakfast brought over."

"Where do we put our gear?" Ferguson said, rising awkwardly with jerky agitated motions, refusing to be helped by Bud.

"Just pick an empty bedroom and throw your stuff in it." Bud picked up a telephone receiver and began dialing. Caldwell staggered out of his room hung-over, yawning, wearing khaki shorts, no shirt and scratching his hairy chest.

"Hey you guys," Bud said, "this is my blood brother from Nashville, Doctor Caldwell Kreer. Cowboy introduced himself, "Good to meet you Doc," they shook hands.

Caldwell offered his hand to Ferguson, "Caldwell Kreer."

A bony hand reached out to Caldwell. "Jack Ferguson, Doctor."

"Glad to meet you, Jack."

Bud hung up the phone and walked past the trio. "Come along, Lads, the coffee should be ready. Breakfast will be here in a few minutes."

They dined on eggs, sausage, bacon, biscuits, grits and jams. The four men also managed to gulf down two sweating pitchers of freshly squeezed orange juice. First to finish, Ferguson pushed his empty plate away and lit a cigarette.

"Cotter, what's the word on your assignment at CINCPAC?"

Bud shrugged and mumbled through a mouth full of biscuit. "I don't know." He gulped orange juice and swallowed. "The admiral didn't say, and I wasn't given a chance to ask."

"What are you going to do about staying qualed and getting your flight skins?"

"I don't know, Skipper. I'm going to need the flight pay now that we bought the house."

"Well, goddamn, Cotter, you didn't have to go and buy the Taj Mahal. Tell Mick that I'll approve you coming out to BP and flying with us."

"Hey, that's great, Skipper. Thanks."

"Yeah, well. As of yesterday, we have eight new birds on the field. Sonny's out there trying to get everybody qualed in the two D's. Pee Wee and Chief Story have their hands full. We're bringing in some new maintenance personnel because we now have a combination of jets and recips. The chief's have the ADR's going to ADJ school and the new ADJ's going to ADR School in Memphis. We sent our pilots who don't have jet time to Miramar to train with VT-8. It's going to be a long while before we can even think about beginning carquals."

"Any idea what the squadron assignment may be when you're operational?"

"Same as before: training for another WestPac."

"If Nixon can get us out of Nam within a year," Cowboy observed, "maybe we won't have to worry about another WestPac."

"Yeah, but there's trouble brewing in the Middle East. Those goddamn ragheads are threatening another war with the Heebs," Ferguson said exhaling smoke. "We could get sucked into that Charlie Foxtrot if Israel can't handle it alone. By the way, I heard from Mick O'Reagan that they've been studying a Middle East problem at War College."

Cowboy grunted, "Well, that probably means something's imminent in the Med and the Mid East."

Bud said, "Hell, that won't be anything new, those people have been fighting in the Mid East for the past five thousand years."

"What about all this anti-war squawking, Cotter," said Ferguson changing subjects, "How's it going to affect our new Commander in Chief? Does your old man think he be intimidated by all this anti-war hype?"

Bud shook his head. "I don't believe so. Daddy says Nixon is pretty strong willed. He thinks Nixon won't allow his decision making to be influenced by a bunch of loud mouth college students, pinkos, pacifists and hippies."

"Those loud mouths had a lot to do with forcing Johnson out of the picture," Caldwell interjected.

"The way I see it, Doc," said Ferguson, "the media is out of control, it has definitely gone pinko. A President and his staff have to know how to control the media and not allow them to control him. Johnson and his people never did understand that."

"Well, I'll tell you what," Cowboy said. "I voted for Johnson in sixty-four. I thought Goldwater was too much of a right-winger, but I've had to change my opinion. Lyndon Johnson definitely was not a crisis leader. He tried to carry on with Kennedy's Indochina policy and got us into the jam we're in now. He didn't know how to sell the idea that bailing out South Vietnam is the right thing to do."

Caldwell said, "Do you think it's the right thing to do?"

"I don't know, Doc," Cowboy replied thoughtfully. "You can make a pretty good case either way. Philosophically and morally it's probably the right thing to do. We basically did the same thing in Korea. Strategically, I'm not sure it's really necessary. The way I see it, if we had secured North Vietnam back in sixty-five, this thing would have been over four years ago and that would have been the end of it."

"Johnson got a lot of bad advice from his people," Ferguson said. "They were afraid of what the Chinks and those Red Russian bastards might do. If Ike or Goldwater had been in office at the time, we would have taken North Vietnam in short order. There's no way the Reds would have gone to all out war over a chicken-shit country like Nam. Oh sure, there would have been a lot of official bitching and snarling and saber rattling, but that would have been the end of it."

"Yes, but how do you know that?" said Caldwell. "It's one mighty huge gamble."

"Hell, Khrushchev backed down in Cuba didn't he? Mao backed off on Formosa after we showed him our war face, and again in Korea after we spanked their Red asses all the way back across the Yalu into Manchuria. I agree with Cowboy, Johnson should have bombed hell out of North Vietnam, cut off their supplies and landed the 3rd Marines. It would have been over in a month."

"How did we get off on this subject," said Bud, "the hell with world politics this early in the morning."

Cowboy rose to get the coffee pot off the stove. Through the kitchen window he saw two navy patrol boats cruising in the lagoon.

"Hey, look at this" he said, "there's two PBR's out here."

Caldwell rose and looked over Cowboy's shoulder.

"Yeah, they've been out there for the past couple of days, they're checking out any boats that come around."

"What are they doing? Trying to catch drug smugglers?"

"No. They're part of a Navy and Marine Corps security task group assigned to protect the President. They're working with the Secret Service."

"The President?"

"Yeah, the President and First Lady are coming to the wedding."

"Are you kidding me?" Cowboy said in a tone of unqualified amazement. "The president is really coming to the wedding?"

"That's what I'm told."

Cowboy turned and peered at Bud with an expression of bewilderment. "Damn, man. How the hell do you rate this? Holy, Jesus!"

Bud shrugged and said, "My parents invited them. I didn't have anything to do with it."

"But Christ, the President?" Wagging his head, Cowboy retrieved the coffee pot and poured for everyone.

"I'll make sure you get to meet them," Bud said, chortling at Cowboy's awe and amazement.

"I'd rather meet some foxy chick," Cowboy replied with a crafty grin.

The next afternoon when Margo began her bridal procession down the brick aisle of the formal garden, over five hundred smiling guests stood on either side of her. Stony-face Secret Service men wearing over size aviator sunglasses and dark suits stood about the grounds suspiciously surveying the guests. President and Mrs. Nixon occupied chairs in the front row next to the Cotters. Air Force One had landed at the Naval Air Station on Boca Chica Key at 1300. Half an hour before the wedding was scheduled to begin, the Nixon's made the quick hop by helicopter to the grounds of the Cotter complex

Father Harry Cleveland, a witty good-humored Franciscan with a cheery flushed face would conduct the marriage ceremony. Father Harry was pastor of Key West's only Catholic Parrish, Saint Mary Star Of The Sea. He had received permission from the Diocese to conduct an outdoor Nuptial Mass. The Key West Chamber Orchestra performed the musical pieces that Margo and Bernadette partnered to select: Pachelbel's Canon in D-major, Handel's Fireworks (Allegro) and Bach's Ave Maria. The wedding party consisted of Phyllis Whitefield as Maid of Honor. Bernadette and three of Margo's cousins who had made the journey from Montana served as the Bride's Maids. Caldwell Kreer stood as Best Man for Bud. Ferguson, Cowboy, Shug and the Whitefield brothers served the dual function of Groomsmen and ushers. Margo's gown had been custom refitted for the wedding. It was the wedding dress in which her grandmother and her mother had been married. Modestly cut, the gown made the dazzling bride appear even more exciting and seductive.

Bud beamed proudly as Margo, on the arm of her father, paraded along the flower strewn garden walk to the elevated gazebo where the Mass would be celebrated. His own formal Mess white uniform created an impressive sight. Bedecked with sword and garnished with combat medals, the handsome groom epitomized the vision of a dashing naval warrior. The admiring eyes of the wedding guests, especially those of an invidious June Chandler, fell upon Bud as he stood waiting for his bride to appear. No one could forget the network videos of him bloody and limp, being lifted out of the cockpit of the big Skyraider at Danang.

The Mass and ceremony concluded when Bud lustily kissed his wife to the applause and bravos of the guests. When the photographers finished with the photographs, the wedding party moved to the central garden. The Valentine's Day weather was perfect. A cloud flecked sky shone bright, azure and sunny. The fragrant air, a balmy 80 degrees, stirred the palms and tree tops with gentle breezes from the sea. One hundred fifty round tables, each surrounded by chairs, were draped in white lacy linens and topped by colorful and fragrant floral centerpieces. Three buffets staffed by a covey of chefs and servers filled the guests plates with delightful and delectable meats, seafood and gourmet vegetables. Three open bars offered a grandiose variety of refreshments for the wedding guests.

The President and First Lady sat at the long head table with the smiling bride and groom and their happy parents. The President, rising at a prompt from the wedding director, John Pierre DeLuce, picked up a microphone that had been strategically positioned in front of him. The applause was spontaneous and enthusiastic when the President stood. The famous jowls framed a happy smile as Mr. Nixon waited until the applause subsided.

"It is a grand pleasure, and I must say, a real honor for the First Lady and I to be here with all of you today. This is indeed a day to celebrate and one that we will remember as each future Valentine's Day comes around. What we are celebrating here I believe, goes beyond the wonderful love and devotion that Margo and Bud so clearly share with each other. We are also celebrating the union of two courageous

American patriots who have unselfishly risked their lives in the service of their country." Someone shouted, "here, here," and the guests began to applaud, and then stood interrupting the smiling President who joined in the applause for the blushing couple. When the applause dwindled, the President continued: "This is not a time to talk of politics, and I promise that I'm not going to bore you too much." A brief ripple of laughter arose and quickly subsided. "I see that the members of our distinguished press corps are here with us this afternoon. Now fellas, I want you to be sure and get what I say correct this time." Another surge of good natured laughter. The President chuckled and waved graciously to the small assembly of handpicked reporters who had been allowed access to the reception.

The President swept a hand toward the Whitefields and the Cotters. "I want to point out to all of America these two marvelous American families, the Whitefields and the Cotters. They are shining examples of what grass roots America, what I call the silent majority is all about. These two deeply patriotic families and millions more families like them are silently supporting our great nation. From these wonderful families come Doctor Marguerite Whitefield Cotter, a daughter who gave up the opportunity of private medical practice to help our men and women in Vietnam, and Lieutenant Toland Martin Cotter, a naval officer twice bloodied in war while courageously saving his fellow servicemen. We all know that our military presence in Southeast Asia is the most unpopular of any armed conflict in which the United States has engaged. I have committed to end America's participation in this conflict with honor. I've made it clear, however, that it is our judgment that a unilateral withdrawal from Southeast Asia is not in the best interests of our country, nor in the best interests of our allies. Therefore, we continue to have a difficult task ahead of us in Southeast Asia. Until a positive peace accord with Hanoi can be reached, the support of patriotic American families like the Whitefield's and the Cotters will continue to be a vital element in convincing the leaders in Hanoi that the US is firm in its commitments to its allies. Those Americans who insist upon public displays of irresponsible behavior are in fact the minority in America. Here, in front of me today is the soul of America."

Nixon swept an arm over the wedding guests. "Each of you, individually, makes America strong with your willingness to do the right thing for America and your refusal to be influenced by subversive, disruptive and radical conduct. I commend you for your patriotism and your dedication to the core values that makes us the greatest nation in the world."

The guests broke into a standing ovation for the President. When the applause began to ebb, the President lifted a stemmed goblet of bubbling champagne from the table. "Now, I would like to offer a toast, to Bud and Margo Cotter. May your years together be filled with love, happiness, good health and prosperity. I want to render our sincerest gratitude, and I say this for all Americans: thank you, Margo and Bud for your unselfish service, and thank you for the hard personal sacrifices you have made for this great nation of ours. Here's to a wonderful couple and to their new life together." The President lifted his glass. There was a mass clinking of tapping goblets after which there arose great cheers and applause.

When the clamor subsided, the President remained at the microphone. "Now, I have one other thing to say, and then I'll sit down. On March 12th, I am going to experience a great personal honor as your President. On that day, I will have the grand pleasure of presenting to Lieutenant Toland Martin Cotter our nation's highest military allocate, the Congressional Medal of Honor." A single start of astonishment rose from the guests; widespread bravoes and applause mushroomed across the wide garden. Bud squinted and shyly grinned. Margo put her hands on his cheeks and looked into his eyes, "Oh, Teddy Bear, oh my God, the Congressional

Medal of Honor! It's really going to happen!" The President grinned, sipped champagne, and whispered something into Mrs. Nixon's ear that made her laugh. Norman Cotter, bursting with pride, hugged his wife and accepted congratulations from those sitting near him.

When the crowd had calmed, the President continued. "Additionally, I will be awarding to Commander Jack Ferguson and Lieutenant Irving Dowda, the two officers sitting over here, our nation's second highest award for valor, the Navy Cross." The crowd erupted once more. Cowboy and Ferguson looked at one another and grinned. "And last but certainly not least," the President grinned jovially, "Doctor Marguerite Whitefield Cotter will be presented with the Vietnam Cross of Gallantry with Palm, and the Navy Commendation Medal."

When the laudations of the guests finally subsided, the President concluded his talk: "All of us here today share in the rare privilege of being among four of America's most courageous compatriots. I hope that you young people, you teenagers and college students who are watching this on TV will use this opportunity to allow these inspiring Americans become a role model for your life. Well, I've said enough." Nixon turned toward the bride and groom, "Margo and Bud, thank you, and God bless you." The President thrust his arms into the famous Nixon victory pose, "Let's give our bride and groom a big cheer for all America!"

A second marvelous surprise for the wedding guests came with the opening of the curtain on the wide portable stage. Promptly at seven o'clock, the Benny Goodman Orchestra opened with the ever-popular Goodman tune, Don't Be That Way. Benny Goodman, the undisputed King of Swing, led his orchestra into an evening of first class entertainment and dance music.

At 8:00 o'clock, the orchestra paused and played, Hail to the Chief as the President and First Lady climbed the steps into the Admiral's staff helicopter. The First Couple paused at the door of the helicopter, smiling and waving to the cheering wedding guests. Minutes later, the big machine rose into the air and whisked the President and First Lady away to the Naval Air Station where Air Force One awaited them.

The liquor and champagne flowed as the grand wedding celebration coursed on into the night. Margo and Bud, euphorically happy, gulped champagne, kissed often, danced occasionally and enthusiastically mingled with the wedding guests. Never releasing the clasp of their hands, they seemed incapable of separating and moved everywhere as one.

Around nine thirty the newlyweds disappeared into the main house to change out of their wedding finery into casual and more comfortable attire. Laughing and giggling, giddy from slurping champagne, they bounded up the stairs to the second floor of the house. Inside the bedroom, Bud hurriedly closed the door and locked it. Kissing, caressing, blistering with desire, they eagerly undressed each other and fell naked onto the bed in a frenzy of fervid nuptial passion.

Chapter 33

Unlikely Couple

June Chandler and Bud's Aunt Harriet sat at a table in the far corner of the garden. During the past few years, the two women had become devoted friends and confidants. Harriet knew of June's feelings for her nephew and she was enormously sympathetic. Yet Harriet judged June's fierce emotional attachment to Bud to be bizarre and frivolously immature. Harriet learned early on that June was not amenable to the idea of meeting other men. June's impassioned reaction to that suggestion curbed all notions of match making on Harriet's part. Three champagne bottles sat on their table, two were empty and the third was half full. Both women were pleasantly tipsy. They chirped and tittered girlishly, commenting on each male who happened by.

Out of the lively crowd of wedding celebrants, Ferguson and Cowboy appeared. Cowboy, eager to meet June Chandler had been keeping an eye on her since he first noticed her at the rehearsal dinner. He knew that June and Harriet had been sitting alone during the evening drinking a lot of champagne. As reinforcement for his own meager courage, Cowboy persuaded Jack Ferguson to accompany him. Both men were quite gallant in their dress whites. June and Harriet regarded the two officers as they approached the table.

"Hello, ladies," Ferguson said with a wide smile. "I'm Jack Ferguson, and this is Shelby Dowda, but everybody calls him Cowboy. We were wondering if possibly we might join you."

"Yes, we know who you are. Sit down, gentlemen," Harriet said pleasantly. "This is my friend, June Chandler. She works for Bud Cotter's father. I'm Harriet Pugh. Norman Cotter's much younger baby sister."

Cowboy and Ferguson exchanged an amused glance as they sat down.

Experiencing a mutual yet unconscious nervous impulse, June and Harriet immediately brought out cigarettes. Ferguson clanked open his old Zippo and lighted each woman's cigarette, and then lit a Camel for himself.

"Well, gentlemen," Harriet said, opening the conversation. "How long have you been back from Vietnam?"

"We arrived in Hawaii in early December." Ferguson said, "We wanted to get as many of the men home for Christmas as possible."

"I noticed you limping, Commander Ferguson," said June, "have you injured your leg?"

Ferguson made a small self-conscious grin. "Yeah, I banged up my knee a few months ago. When we got back to Hawaii the bone people decided it wasn't healing properly, so they operated on it and took out some small pieces of cartilage."

Harriet exhaled a thin stream of cigarette smoke and said, "How did you injure your knee, Commander?"

"I bumped it getting out of an airplane, and please call me Jack."

"I'd say you must have given it quite a bump to do all that damage," Harriet said.

Ferguson made a crooked grin. "Actually, I didn't feel it at the time. It was much later before I realized the knee was injured."

"So," said Cowboy, "did you come down from Nashville together?"

June nodded. "Yes, we arrived day before yesterday. I flew in from Hawaii to attend the wedding. We'll be flying out tomorrow afternoon."

Cowboy said, "Tomorrow, huh? That's too bad."

June started with a curious-amazed expression. “What did you say?”

“I said it’s too bad you have to leave tomorrow.”

“That’s what I thought you said. Why would you say that?”

“Well, the skipper and I are going to be around Key West for a few days. We’re planning to take in the sights around here. Maybe take a day trip out to the Tortugas and see Fort Jefferson. We were thinking, it would be a lot of fun to have nice ladies such as the two of you to accompany us.”

“What makes you think we would want to do that?” June said a bit huffily.

“We didn’t know until we asked,” Cowboy grinned and shrugged. “It seemed like a good idea. But since you’re leaving, it’s kind of a mute point isn’t it?”

“Yes, it is.”

Harriet perked up. “June, we can always get our tickets changed.”

June shot Harriet a thoroughly murderous look. “I have commitments in Nashville. I have to leave tomorrow,” she firmly stated, “you can stay if you want to, Harriet.”

The two officers exchanged an uncomfortable glance. Ferguson stood. “Harriet, do you think you could endure a dance with a crippled sailor?”

“It would be my pleasure, Commander. Oh—Ha, Ha. I mean, Jack.” She dashed the cigarette. Ferguson extended a hand to her. When they were gone, Cowboy said to June, “Would you care to dance?”

June gave him a cold petulant glance. “No, I don’t care to dance, thank you.”

“I noticed you during the rehearsal dinner yesterday.”

“Oh, you did? Why did you happen to notice me?”

"I picked the prettiest face in the group," he said, probing curiously and cautiously.

She turned on him. "Look, Cowboy, not to be rude, but I may as well tell you now, there is someone else."

"Okay. I understand. I just wanted to dance at the wedding of two of my best friends. I was hoping you would humor me."

June stared at Cowboy for a long moment. "Okay, I'll dance one dance with you."

She was like a mannequin, and she held him practically at arm's length. Cowboy couldn't believe a woman could be so rigid and unfeeling. He was glad when the tune finished. They walked to one of the bars. Cowboy had rum and Sprite mixed for June and he took a beer.

"Feel like walking out on the pier?"

"I suppose it would be okay." The sight of Bud and Margo coming happily out of the house wearing casual summer clothes distracted her. She had to concede that they were indeed a handsome couple. When the newlyweds stopped on the porch steps and kissed lovingly, a horrible searing sword of bitterness pierced June Chandler's heart. Great tears rushed to her eyes. She forced them back and turned away, unable to endure the sight.

June and Cowboy stood at the end of the Cotter's yacht pier looking out across waters glittering in the light of a three quarter moon.

"It's really pretty here," said Cowboy.

"Yes it is."

"Is this your first time in Key West?"

"Yes."

"Mine too."

June brought out a cigarette and lighter. Cowboy took the

lighter from her and lit the cigarette.

“Thank you.”

“Tell me about the lucky guy you’re in love with. Why isn’t he here with you?”

She snapped her head around and glowered at him, unbecomingly snorting smoke through her nostrils. “My personal affairs are really none of your business.”

“Okay. Sorry.”

“I’m afraid that I won’t be very good company, Cowboy,” she said in a more subdued tone. “Don’t you have someone to be true to?”

“I used to. We broke up about a year and a half ago. I went to Nam after that. There really hasn’t been a chance to meet anyone.”

“Well, I’m sure a guy like you won’t have any trouble meeting someone.”

“A guy like me is at a big disadvantage when it comes to meeting women.”

June puckered her eyebrows curiously. “Really? Why is that?”

“Being a Naval Aviator nowadays isn’t exactly conducive to attracting women.”

“Oh, you’re talking about the war being so unpopular.”

“That’s it.”

“I’d think Hawaii would be an easy place to meet people, war or no war.”

“Not really. Hawaii can be a pretty lonesome place.”

After a long silence, June said, “We should probably go back. I feel rather awkward being out here alone with you.”

He regarded her with a resigned half smile. "You go ahead. I think I'll stay out here a while. It's quiet and peaceful. Kind of reminds me of a place out in the Pacific called Majuro." He drank beer and leaned against the wooden rail, staring at a long motor yacht anchored to a buoy in the bay.

June stared at him, a little taken aback by his indifference.

"Okay, well, it was nice meeting you, Cowboy."

"My pleasure, June, have a good trip home tomorrow."

"Thank you, I will, and by the way, congratulations on your Navy Cross."

"Thanks." He nodded and returned his gaze to the sea.

June hesitated for a brief moment and walked away.

June Chandler returned to the reception to find Harriet and Jack Ferguson sitting among Bud, Margo, the Cotters, and the Whitefields. Having no desire to endure further heartache by seeing Bud and Margo together,

June had her drink refreshed and walked around the complex until she found an old fashion slatted swing next to the seawall. She sat in the swing and gently moved it back and forth with her feet. Thoughts of Bud and Margo kept returning, torturing her soul until tears ran freely across her face. As she sat there, June reminisced about her lonely life. Tonight things were eminently different than before. Bud and Margo were now unconditionally married. June had been clinging to a secret hope that somehow the marriage would not really happen, that some modifying circumstance would arise and nullify the marriage. Her secret hope now dashed, June tasted the searing pain of having lost her one true love. She choked down her bile as the bitter mood reached the depths of her dismalness. All prospect of having Bud Cotter for herself was now gone. For nearly three years, the uncertainty of having a future with Bud Cotter had plagued her like a migraine. Tonight her pain and frustration had reached an intolerable peak. Something had to change. She felt as though she could no longer bear the serrated agony of loneliness and heartache. Even her faith in God seemed to waiver. After all the prayer, all the Masses, all the abstinence, had God forsaken her? What had she done to deserve this? Where should she go? What should she do? The convent? No, that would only be a temporary escape. In her heart June conceded the convent was truly not her vocation. She could stay in Hawaii permanently, but no, that was no good either. Like the convent, she perceived Hawaii would be only a temporary escape. She dropped her head into her hands and wept.

Margo and Bud Cotter were whisked away in a sleek limousine at ten thirty on that balmy Key West evening. A few minutes later the enraptured couple boarded the cruise ship, Savannah scheduled to sail at midnight. During the next two weeks, the newlyweds would cruise the Caribbean, romping and frolicking on some of the most beautiful and exotic islands on earth. When the Savannah was at sea the impassioned couple, famished by an incessant erotic hunger for one another, would see very little of the ship. Two weeks hence, they would depart the Savannah in San Juan and fly to Nashville for a few days and then on to Honolulu and their new home. The deed to the Kahala Street house had been their wedding gift from Norman and Millie Cotter.

The coral-shell crunched under Cowboy's dress white shoes as he walked toward the garden from the pier. It was well after eleven. The band was packing and loading their instruments into waiting buses. Following the departure of the bride and groom, the guests had thinned considerably. Small knots of celebrants lingered here and there talking, laughing, and enjoying the last cocktails of the evening. Despite the celebration and fine weather, Cowboy was feeling despondent and gloomy. He'd been thoroughly jilted by a very pretty woman, but that was nothing new. It happened often with these modernistic women of the 60s, many of whom viewed Naval Aviators as ruthless, napalm wielding killers of women and children.

Standing alone out on the pier, his thoughts drifted across the vast seas to Vietnam. His mind returned him to the oppressive suffocating heat of the lowlands, a place where his nostrils were perpetually filled with the hideous ever present stench of jungle united with the foul oily fumes of diesels and jet exhaust. He could hear the incessant thumping of helos, the rattle of .50 caliber Brownings, the thumping of M-3 twenty-millimeter cannon, the metallic chugging of M-60s, the popping of M-16s and the desperate scream of pinned Marines pleading for air support on the radio. Once again he was gripped by the dreadful nauseating fear of looking into the flashing muzzles of NV guns. Even as they desperately tried to kill him, Cowboy could not help but feel a twinge of sympathy for the enemy at that instant before he incinerated them into ash with a hellish explosion of boiling fire. His tortured mind presented him a sea of Indo-Chinese faces killed by his hand. Like a Technicolor film, the nightmare pictured for him the last terrible seconds of their lives, the hopeless horror-filled disbelief as canisters of napalm tumbled toward them from the wings of his roaring Skyraider. All these things were memories he struggled to blot out but somehow could not. These terrible moments of recounting left him downcast and emotionally drained. What he needed was a good stiff slug of whiskey.

Cowboy went to the last open bar and asked for a double of Jack Daniel. The bartender grinned and handed him a freshly opened fifth of Black Label Jack Daniel and a glass.

“Go ahead and take the bottle, Navy,” the bartender said. “It’s paid for, and we’ll be closing in a couple of minutes.”

“Thanks.” Cowboy grinned happily. He decided to find a quiet place to sit near the water. He ambled around, and by and by came upon June Chandler sitting in the swing of the East garden. She was sobbing and sniveling and didn’t notice him until he sat down next to her. June looked at him in the shadowed light, teary eyed and astonished. He handed her a couple of dry paper napkins from his pocket.

"What are you doing? For God's sake, I must look gruesome," she said dabbing at her eyes with the napkins.

"You don't look too bad, very pretty actually. Have a drink?" He lifted the bottle toward her.

"No! Please go away and leave me alone."

"Look, sister, I feel like shit myself and I don't want to drink alone."

"I really don't care how you feel. Please go away and find someone else to annoy."

Cowboy gulped a slug of whiskey and looked at her. "You've got your heartaches and I've got mine. I don't have anyone to talk to. So I intend to drink my bad memories away, at least for tonight. That is unless I puke or pass out first. In that case, I'll forget about my troubles anyway."

"Well, please go somewhere else to drown your sorrows. I want to be alone."

"Don't you hate being alone? I do. I think it really sucks."

"Will you please leave me alone?"

"I promise that I will sit here and not bother you. I won't even look at you. I need a place to sit where I won't ruin these whites."

She looked at him, ardently annoyed by his brash presumption. "Oh, for God's sake, I'll leave then." She stood and began to gather her things. He grabbed her wrist and pulled her back into the swing. "Sit down, goddamn it. Stop being such a snotty bitch!"

Incredulous, her mouth dropped open. She glared at him. "Of all the nerve, who do you think you are!" She slapped him hard. Some of the whiskey spilled out of his glass and onto the ground. His cheek began to puff up. She looked at him with a mixture of anger and sympathy.

"Damn it, you've got quite a right hand there," he said, working his jaw.

"Oh, I didn't mean to hurt you," she said.

"You did mean to hurt me, and you did, shit!" He held a hand to his stinging cheek.

"I'm really sorry, Cowboy. I, I don't know what to say."

"Don't say anything. Just sit here and keep me company while I drown my troubles."

Caught in a crisscross of conflicting emotions, June sat back and made a deep resigned sigh. "Well . . . a few minutes maybe. It's been a long day. I'm tired and I have to pack tonight." She took out a cigarette, lit it and picked up her drink. They silently stared across the water. When the cigarette was half smoked, June said, "What are you trying to erase with that bottle of whiskey?"

Cowboy took a big swallow. "After you left me totally rejected out on the pier, I started thinking about Vietnam. It really gets me down when I start thinking about it."

"I didn't reject you. I told you that I'm in love with someone else."

He looked at her with a sidewise glance. "I don't think he's in love with you."

Tears instantly flooded her eyes. She threw the cigarette away and began to wipe at her eyes, sobbing.

"Sorry," he said apologetically.

Her bottom lip trembling, she shook her head and struggled to check the tears with the sodden napkins. "You don't need to apologize," she sniffled. "You're right. He doesn't love me. I'm such a fool for trying to hang on."

"I know how you feel. I've been there a few times myself. Makes you feel like shit, and completely worthless."

"It sure does," she said as she wept.

"So what are you going to do about this guy?"

"I can't do anything about him. He's married now, and he's very much in love with his wife." She began to weep profusely. Cowboy looked away and drank whiskey.

After a while, when she was better, he said, "Would it make you feel better to talk about it?"

"No, it would make me feel worse." She lifted her glass, drank off the rum and fumbled for a cigarette.

"You smoke too much," Cowboy said, watching her.

She took the first draw of the Salem. "Maybe I do, but it's none of your business."

"No, it's not, but you do smoke too much."

She regarded him with an annoyed half smile. "You really do have a lot of nerve talking to me the way you have tonight."

He held up the bottle of whiskey and grinned, "Courage in a bottle, try some?"

June hesitated, curiously searching his face. She picked up her empty glass and handed it to him. He poured smooth aged sour mash into the glass and handed it back to her. She exhaled smoke and sipped tentatively.

Her face twisted into a fierce grimace. "Oh, my word, how can you drink this stuff? It's terrible!"

"You have to get past the first couple of shots, after that, it starts to get real good."

"Why were you thinking about Vietnam tonight?"

"I don't know. Sometimes it just gets into my head and I can't get it out. Tonight happened to be one of those nights."

"It's really terrible over there, isn't it?"

"Yeah, it's pretty bad, but then we had it easy compared to the grunts."

"What is it that bothers you most about Vietnam?"

Cowboy sipped Jack Daniel and stared into the night, "All the killing. All the waste of humanity."

"Do you feel guilty about killing the Vietnamese?"

"No, I don't feel guilty. Killing bad guys is my job, but killing leaves me cold. War is a dirty lousy business."

"Why don't you get out of the Navy and do something else?"

He looked at June as though she had said something foolish. "The Navy is my life. I gave up a career in major league baseball to come into the Navy and fly. I knew that sooner or later I'd end up in Nam. Killing bad guys go with the territory, but that doesn't mean I have to like it."

"You were a baseball player?"

"Yeah, I played ball at Texas. The Saint Louis Cardinals tried to recruit me, but I wanted to fly."

"There seems to be something very powerful that draws men to become Navy pilots. Every one of you guys that I have met is intensely dedicated to the Navy and to flying. Why is that?"

Cowboy took a drink. "I don't know. I guess it's because you have to be a little crazy to begin with. Naval aviation is a lot different than anything else. A relatively high percentage of the cadets who begin flight training are bilged long before graduation. Using a Texas analogy for Naval Aviators: We're a lot like rodeo bull riders. You've got to be thoroughly nuts to want to ride bulls or to fly off aircraft carriers."

“I wholeheartedly agree with that,” she said with a trite grin. “You guys fit that mold perfectly too.” June sipped the whiskey and grimaced, “God this stuff is awful.”

“If you promise not to run away, I’ll go and to find a bottle of rum and some Sprite for you.”

“No, that’s okay. I’ll suffer through this. I’ve got to go anyway.”

“Thanks for staying around and talking with me. It’s really nice having someone besides another male to talk to.”

“Well, I still haven’t forgotten that you called me a snotty bitch. No one has ever talked to me like that in my entire life.”

“No one has ever slapped the shit out of me like you did either.”

She tried not to laugh, but couldn’t hold back. “You deserved it,” she chortled.

“Yeah,” he grinned at her. “I suppose I did. I wouldn’t have the nerve to talk to you like that if I was sober.”

“Really?”

“Well, not unless I was really mad about something.”

“Why did you break up with your girl friend?”

“She wanted to get married and I wasn’t ready. At the time, I was in the middle of flight training at Pensacola. One day when I was out flying, she packed up her stuff and went home to Big Spring, that’s in Texas.”

“Why didn’t you want to get married?”

“I was in the middle of flight school. They were bilging guys right and left. I wanted to be sure that I was going to graduate. I also knew that I after I graduated, I’d be going to Nam sooner or later. I didn’t want to get married and then leave her alone.”

"She did the right thing, leaving you I mean."

Cowboy sat up and gave June a startled look. "What's that supposed to mean?"

"You couldn't have really and truly loved her. If you had, you'd have married her regardless of the circumstances. I'm sure she realized it and that's why she left."

He sipped slowly, thinking about what June had said. "You know, maybe you're right. I thought that I loved her, maybe I really didn't."

"Of course you didn't. You liked having her around for sex and to do your laundry, but you couldn't have been in love with her. If you were, you'd have gone to Big Spring, Texas and brought her back."

"How do you know that I didn't try?"

"Because she would have come back with you if you had of gone after her."

Cowboy appeared thoughtful. "I never thought of it like that."

"Sometimes it takes a woman to explain these things." She emptied her whiskey and cringed. Cowboy picked up the bottle and reached for her glass.

"A couple of more sips and you'll be loving this stuff," he said as he poured.

"I hope I'm not going to get sick," she chuckled skeptically. "I have to admit that having this bizarre talk with you is making me feel much better. I think I'm getting a little drunk too."

"Good," he said with a hint of smugness, "because I'm going to kiss you."

Their glances met. "No you're not," she said emphatically. "I'll slap you silly if you try."

Cowboy gave her a self-satisfied grin. "I believe you will, but you know and I know that I'm going to kiss you tonight, and you know damn well that you're going to like it."

"Why, you are the most egotistical, vain, rude, disgusting_____."

Quick as a cat, his hand curved behind her head and he kissed her. Her body went rigid. He sat back and beamed. Her expression was a kaleidoscope of emotions. She gritted her teeth and set her jaw. "You bastard! How dare you take liberties with me!" She slapped his face much harder than she had the first time. Ignoring the stinging, numbing pain, he kissed her again, but this time things were different. She stiffened for a moment, and then, astonishing herself as well as Cowboy, she began to surrender herself to wild and wonderful emotions she had deliberately repressed for years. Slowly, hesitantly, her arms went around his neck. Cowboy embraced her shoulders and pulled her close. The kiss deepened, as did desire. They separated, panting breathlessly, looking into each other's eyes.

"Oh my, God, no!" She jumped up. Her glass tumbled into the grass spilling whiskey. June stood with her back to him. Her mind fluttered with exciting joyful panic. She stared at the sea, disbelieving her own self. Cowboy stood behind her and put his hands on her shoulders. He pressed gently, encouraging her to turn to him. June shook her head. "Don't," she whispered. But her voice held no conviction. He embraced her with strong arms, crushing her body against his. Her mouth opened and tongues met in desperate excited probing. Their ardor ran rampant: his hands ran up and down her back and onto her hips. When their lips broke free, she hissed, "This is insane. Stop it! Stop it!"

"I don't want to stop." His hand went to her breast. He gently caressed it and began to kiss her neck and ear. "Do you really want me to stop," he whispered into her ear as his lips brushed across her neck.

"No, oh, God, no—but we have to stop—we must!" She pushed his hand away and twisted herself free from his grasp. "I've allowed myself to get completely out of control," she panted. "This is outrageous. I've had far too much to drink."

"The liquor makes it easy to do and say what your heart is really feeling."

"Damn you, Cowboy! My life was just fine until you showed up tonight! I hate you for doing this to me!"

"Your life is as miserable and lonesome as mine you beautiful liar." He pulled her to himself and kissed her again; she collapsed in his arms. Their passion intensified until neither of them could bear it any longer. He released her and began to undo the buttons of her blouse as he kissed her face and neck. For a moment she didn't resist.

"Oh, my, God! Oh, my, God!" She groaned and pulled herself away from him. "Stop it! We've got to stop this! Please, no more! I can't stand this any longer!" She quickly buttoned her blouse. "We've got to stop this. Sit down and pour me a drink for God's sake! We've got to talk. I need a cigarette!"

"I don't think I can sit down," he said, quite sincerely.

"Oh, my God!" She began to laugh hysterically when she realized what he was talking about.

They sat on the swing, sipped whiskey and June smoked. Cowboy had an arm hooked around her shoulders across the back of the swing.

"Now that I can think a little clearly," she breathed, looking at him. "You have to understand that I won't go to bed with you. I can't go to bed with you. This is all a very big mistake. It's not your fault, Cowboy, it's all my fault."

He appeared puzzled, "But why not?" We both want to."

"Wanting to and doing so are two very different things. My word, I've just met you. I don't know anything about you. You don't know anything about me. I don't do this sort of thing. I don't know what is happening to me tonight. I've been looped plenty of times in the past, but I have never allowed myself to get out of control like this, and I've never allowed anyone to touch me like you did a while ago. I think it must be because I'm tipsy and because you look so damn good in that white uniform and you caught me when I was really down and feeling sorry for myself." She drew deeply on the cigarette, tossed it away and took a sip of liquor. "You know, you're right about this whiskey," she said and smiled, "this stuff is getting better all the time."

He grinned. "Yeah it has a way of doing that." He kissed her tenderly. She tasted of tobacco and whiskey. It didn't matter. She was the most beautiful woman he had ever been with. His mind and body tingled with magnetism toward her and a longing to win the heart of this woman.

June blinked at him and touched his cheek. "You're so wonderfully sweet, Cowboy."

"Did you say that you live in Hawaii?

"Yes. I work for Mr. Cotter at the Wai Momi Hotel. You can call me sometime if you want to."

"Is that a promise?"

"I said you can call me, but you must understand up front. I can't . . . I won't sleep with you."

"I don't understand, June. We're both adults. Is there something wrong with me or what?"

She threw her head back and laughed beautifully. "Not hardly you pretty sailor. Look, sweetie, this is how it is. I am very Catholic, very straight laced about sex, and I'm not on any kind of birth control. I am still a virgin, and I intend to remain a virgin until my wedding day. You may think it prudish and old fashioned, but that's how it has to be with me."

He slowly shook his head, "Damn if this doesn't beat all. Here I am with the most beautiful and exciting woman I have ever known and she's a virgin, and intends to stay a virgin." He slowly wagged his head. "Why me?"

She tittered girlishly. "If you want this cherry gorgeous sailor boy, you're going to have to marry me first." Her eyes suddenly lighted. She threw a hand over her mouth and flushed with embarrassment, "Oh, my, God! How absolutely obscene! I can't believe I said that! Don't let me have any more of that evil stuff!"

He lifted the bottle and grinned. "Not only is this stuff courage in a bottle, it doubles as a truth serum. It's hard to hold back your real feelings when you've drinking this stuff. Would you please call me Shelby?"

"If that's what you want, of course I will. The way I feel at the moment, I would do anything for you."

"Anything?" His eyebrows shot up.

"Except go to bed with you." She smiled sweetly waving a finger.

He gulped whiskey and stared at her. He put his hand on her cheek and kissed her. "I'm falling in love with you, June," he whispered. "I want you to stay here in Key West as long as you can."

"Oh, Shelby, don't say that. Please don't say that. I'm frightened. I'm confused. Can't you understand? This is not supposed to happen. Not to me. It can't! It just can't! Things just got out of control tonight. I'm drunk. I don't know how I really feel about you. I don't know how I feel about anything at the moment. I need time to think. Stop staring at me! You're making me crazy!"

"I don't want you to leave tomorrow. If there's any chance for us, it'll all be lost if you leave."

"Oh, God, this is so crazy. I need some time to think! I've got to get myself together. I'm so out of sorts now. I don't know. Take me to breakfast in the morning. Let's see how we feel then."

"What time is your flight tomorrow?"

"Oh, I'm not sure. Three, I think. I'm all fuzzy from this liquor you keep feeding me."

"If you leave, I'll be on that plane with you."

"What! No you won't. Don't be ridiculous. Stop looking at me like that!"

He leaned forward and kissed her. "How am I supposed to look at an angel?"

"Darling, listen. I'm very drunk and very vulnerable at the moment. What's more, you are terribly gorgeous and sexy in that uniform. I'd like very much for you to walk me home and kiss me goodnight. If you are truly Prince Charming and I Cinderella, tomorrow will take care of itself."

"Damn it!" Cowboy took a deep swig from the bottle.

June smiled sweetly and patted his cheek. "Take me home and kiss me goodnight. I'll be ready for breakfast at ten."

Chapter 34

CINCPAC Assignment

Honolulu March 1969

"How was my Teddy Bear's first day working for CINCPAC?" Margo ran out onto the drive, threw her arms around Bud's neck and kissed him. A snug fitting yellow sundress broadcast Margo's potent feminine sexuality like a beam of sunlight.

Bud gave her a wry grin. "I didn't see the admiral, Angel. The Flag Lieutenant showed me around and helped me get squared away. They put me in a two room office two doors from CINCPAC. I have a big window and a TV and a WAVE yeoman. The Flag Lieutenant says having the office next door to Deputy CINCPAC is a big deal."

"Wow, Teddy Bear. Aren't you the young executive staff officer?"

"Yeah," he hissed through gritted teeth. "I'm a horny young executive staff officer. I've been thinking about you all day, Angel. Coming home and seeing you in that dress is the final straw. Come on, let's go to our room."

"Now?"

"Now." He took her hand and led her inside the house toward the bedroom.

"Ooh, Teddy Bear, I love your overactive libido."

"So do I."

"Ah, ha, ha."

An hour later they were showered and sitting on the lanai next to the pool drinking iced sun tea Margo had brewed in a big glass jar out on the lanai.

"Oh, Teddy Bear, I still can't believe this fabulous home is really ours. It's going to take awhile for it to all sink in."

"I still can't believe that I'm really married to you, Angel, and us living in a place like this. It's incredible."

"What would you like for dinner," she said with a sensual smirk.

"I think I'd like to eat at the Y."

She screeched with glee. "You're so terrible! Ha, ha, ha."

"Let's try out the gas grill," said Bud. "What did you get at the commissary today that we can cook out?"

"Ah, let's see. I have pork chops, hamburger, chicken and shrimp."

"Let's try something easy like hamburgers, what do you think?"

"Perfect," she said, and jumped up happily. "I'll go patty the hamburger. Why don't you open a bottle of wine? I think I'd like a glass of that wonderful Chateau Montelena Merlot we bought in California."

"Okay, Angel."

A few minutes later, as Bud fiddled with the charcoal grill, the phone rang.

"Would you get that, Teddy Bear," Margo shouted from the kitchen. "My hands are messy with hamburger."

Bud picked up the lanai extension phone. It was Jack Ferguson. He wanted to come over and see the house. Bud knew Ferguson well enough to know that he didn't give a damn about seeing the house: something else was on his mind. Bud invited him for dinner and hung up.

"Doctor, you have a beautiful place here," Ferguson said, after Margo had toured him through the house.

"Thanks, Jack, we love it as you can imagine. It's going to take a while to get used to it. And you're supposed to call me, Margo, remember?" They walked out onto the terrace where Bud was cooking the hamburgers over the flaming, smoking grill.

"Cotter," Ferguson said, prying the cap off a cold sweating bottle of beer Margo had given him, "I'll have to hand it to you. The two of you have one hell of a layout here."

"Thanks, Skipper. Yeah, it still hasn't really sunk in yet."

"How'd the honeymoon go?"

Bud gave him a smug male grin. "Jesus, it was something else."

Ferguson lit a Camel and sat down in a cushioned slatted chair. "How'd it go over at CINCPAC today?"

"They gave me an office. I didn't really talk to anyone except the Flag Lieutenant and the girl who is assigned to be my yeoman."

"Well, once you get squared away over there. I want you to come out and fly with us whenever you can get away. We'll get you checked out in the Skyhawk."

Bud's face lighted happily. "Hey, thanks, Skipper, that's great! It'll be great to finally get some time in a jet. Maybe it won't be so bad being stuck on this staff duty if I can get some stick time once in a while."

"One of the hazards of a naval career, Lad. Staff duty goes with the territory. It happens to everybody sooner or later."

"It's hard for me to do too much bitching; being stuck at CINCPAC keeps me at home with Margo."

"Yeah, I know what you mean," Ferguson said with a knowing smirk.

The phone jangled loudly. Bud shouted, "I'll get it."

The CINCPAC Duty Officer was on the phone. The duty officer informed Bud that Admiral Mick O'Reagan and his wife would be stopping by at 1930. The admiral had urgent business to discuss.

Ferguson fidgeted and lit a Camel. "This is mighty goddamn strange, Cotter, a flag officer coming to visit an O-3 at his home. What do you suppose this is all about?"

"I have no idea, Skipper."

"Well, look, Cotter. There's scuttlebutt floating around CAG that some squadron realignments are in the works. It could affect us at one ten but then it could be any of the squadrons. How about asking around CINCPAC tomorrow and see what you can find out."

"Okay, skipper. I'll check around."

The admiral and his wife arrived at 1935. Margo, having no prior experience entertaining wives of high ranking officers was understandably nervous. Earlier, Ferguson, tactless and salty had put things into perspective for her. "Doctor, don't sweat it. She's accustomed to having her ass kissed by the wives of officers junior to her husband. But what you should do is treat her like an equal. She'll respect you for it, especially since you are a medical doctor. Trust me on this one, Doctor."

Margo led Mrs. O'Reagan on a tour of the house and yard while the men retired to the lanai. Attractive but not overly striking, Mrs. O'Reagan was forty-five, thin and deeply tanned. She had clear brown eyes, a rounded face surrounded by coal black hair flecked here and there with freckles of gray. She wore bright red lipstick; a showy red flowered blouse; white shorts; sandals and large gold hoop earrings. She seemed friendly enough, and Margo felt guardedly comfortable with her.

"Glad to have you boys back in Hawaii," O'Reagan said. "Congratulations on your Medal of Honor Cotter. And to you Jack on your Navy Cross."

"Thanks, Admiral. We appreciate it," Ferguson replied.

"Nice place you've got here, Cotter."

"Thank you, sir. It is a wedding gift from my parents. I think we're really going to enjoy it."

"Sorry we missed you at the office today, Cotter. CINCPAC and I were tied up in intelligence briefings most of the day." O'Reagan shifted in his seat and accepted a beer from Bud. "Thanks, Cotter." O'Reagan swizzled ice cold beer and set the bottle onto a coaster. "Bud, I hate to tear you away from your new bride so soon, but something has come up. CINCPAC feels strongly that you are the officer to handle this assignment and it has to be right away. Based on the briefings we received today, CINCPAC is considering making recommendations to CNO that will have to go straight to the White House for a decision. But before he makes those recommendations, he insists that he must have positive eyewitness verification of his intelligence information. Our intelligence from the field is sometimes skewed, sometimes over-stated and sometimes under-stated." The admiral paused to swig beer. "Here's the plan, Cotter. Be at Hickham flight ops tomorrow morning at 0400 for transportation to Clark. You'll get your orders at Hickham. There will be an F-4 waiting for you at Clark. He will take you over to Tan Son Hut. People will meet you there. Any questions?"

Head spinning, Bud looked at O'Reagan. "No, sir. I'm sure that I'll think of a hundred later."

"I understand. Everything you need to know will be included with your orders. You have unlimited authority in the execution of your orders. They know you're coming and they know you are representing CINCPAC. You won't have any trouble in that regard. The main thing is to get the information and get back here ASAP."

"Yes, sir."

"Jack, I'm glad you're here tonight, saves us both sometime tomorrow. Effective 10 April we're relieving you at VC-110 and giving the squadron to Miles."

Ferguson and Bud glanced at each other. "Yes, sir," Ferguson said in a tone of surprised uncertainty, "may I ask why I'm being relieved, Admiral?"

"You'll be receiving orders within the next few days to report aboard Kitty Hawk. You'll be training in all departments: deck, air, gunnery, engineering and so forth. This will begin your qualification for sea command. The way this war is going, you'll probably have a carrier in eighteen months, if you can stay out of trouble that is," the admiral chuckled. "Congratulations."

Ferguson's face lighted into a rare happy smile. "Thank you, Admiral, this is great news."

"You deserve it, Jack. Pulling off an extended combat deployment and not losing a single pilot is an outstanding achievement." O'Reagan made a sly grin. "Jack, are you sure your pilots were out flying combat and not in the Gunfighters Club all day?"

Ferguson's long face broke into a bashful grin, "Maybe if they'd been at the club, they wouldn't have bent up so many airplanes, Admiral."

"Oh, and by the way, Jack," O'Reagan said with a foxy smile, "CINCPAC sends his congratulations on you boys inheriting the I Corps Poontang Award out at Danang."

"Jesus H Mother of God," Ferguson said in a disgusted tone, snapping a fierce glare at Bud. "Now CINCPAC has heard about it. Cotter, this goddamn poontang thing is going to haunt me for the rest of my naval career!"

"Sorry, Skipper."

Bud went to get three cold beers. When he returned, O'Reagan was quizzing Ferguson about the VC-110 Danang deployment. He seemed particularly interested in the training methods they had employed when preparing the squadron for the combat flight operations. Ten minutes later the women appeared.

"Oh, Mick," Mrs. O'Reagan happily exclaimed, "I just love their home. Margo's given me some great ideas for redecorating."

The admiral cut his eyes at Bud and Ferguson. "Margie, didn't we just redecorate a few months ago?"

"Oh, Honey, it's been forever. Before you went to Viet Nam last year. Anyway," she smiled, "Margo is going to help me pick out the paint and wallpaper, so you won't have to suffer through that again. See what it's like when you've been married for over twenty years," Mrs. O'Reagan said. She bent and kissed her husband. "But you're still just too wonderful, darling."

"Whew, thanks, Doctor Cotter," the admiral jested, "You saved me."

"Admiral, please call me Margo. I can't get Jack to do it, maybe your example would coax him a little."

O'Reagan smiled and chuckled. "Okay, Margo. You heard that didn't you, Jack?"

"Yes, sir," Ferguson answered bashfully.

O'Reagan drank off his beer and rose. "We have to be going, folks. Thanks for the beer, Bud. Doctor, I mean, Margo. I'm afraid we have to take him away from you for a few days. He should be back to you in a week or less."

Margo's face dropped, "Oh, honey, when?"

"0400 tomorrow morning."

"I'll call you tomorrow, Margo," Margie O'Reagan said sympathetically. "Maybe we can have lunch. I know that feeling so very well. You would think that after twenty-two years of being a Navy wife, a woman would get used to her husband leaving, but you don't."

"Thanks, Margie," Margo smiled ruefully, "it's so thoughtfully sweet of you."

Margie twittered. "Just because you're the Admiral's wife doesn't mean you have to be a haughty old bitch."

Margo threw her head back, "Ah, ha, ha, ha." Mrs. O'Reagan was all right.

Chapter 35

Fragile Love

Honolulu April 1969

"This is quite an office you have here," Cowboy said as he took in the Waikiki ocean view from June Chandler's 2nd floor office in the Wai Momi hotel. A large vase containing a dozen roses garnished with Baby's Breath sat on her desk.

"Yes, it is nice isn't it? Although I do become envious watching our guests enjoying themselves so much."

"All work and no play?"

"Something like that."

"Well, maybe we can do something about that today."

"I want to thank you for the beautiful roses," she smiled warmly. "You really shouldn't have."

"I'm glad you like them. It's something I wanted to do."

Cowboy drove to a small café off Nimitz Highway that overlooked the cruise ship harbor. They were seated at a window table next to the pier.

"Would you care for a glass of wine with your lunch?"

"Yes, please. A glass of pinot blanc if they have it."

Cowboy ordered the wine and a glass of beer for himself. "I'm glad that you agreed to have lunch with me, June. I was beginning to think that you were avoiding me when you didn't return my calls."

"I have been avoiding you. I'm sorry to be so blunt."

He stared at her for a moment. "But why, June? When we left Key West, you told me to call you when I got back to Hawaii."

"I know," she said avoiding his eyes. "Shelby, you need to understand that I'm not sure about things, about us. I mean that night at the wedding and the next two days in Key West, well, it left me so confused. I was on a horrid rebound. And besides that, you called me a bitch and then got me drunk. How awful. I won't forget that, mister."

He couldn't stop himself from laughing. "I did do that, and I'm sorry about calling you a bitch."

"Aren't you sorry for getting me drunk too? I had a wicked hangover the next morning."

He smiled guiltily. "I remember, and I'm sorry about the hangover too. But I had to get you drunk. I didn't know how else to break the ice with you. I was desperate."

"Well, you did break the ice in more ways than one. You've shaken me out of that idiotic trance I was in over Bud Cotter."

"I'm glad it didn't work out."

She snapped an annoyed glance at him. "Shelby Dowda, what a nasty thing to say! I don't appreciate it one bit!"

"Now don't get upset, June. You miss my point. Maybe I'm being selfish, but if it had of worked out between you two, I wouldn't be here right now."

She regarded him humorlessly until slowly, her expression began to soften. "Well, it is still a nasty thing to say. In a way, I should be flattered, I guess. I don't know. It seems I am always confused when I'm with you."

"There's nothing to be confused about," he said. "I've told you a least a hundred times that I am in love with you. I don't know how much clearer I can make it."

"Oh my, God, Shelby, do you have to be so direct? You hardly know me. It's not that simple, Shelby. A relationship is a serious matter, a very serious matter."

"Yes, I know it is. Our relationship is the most important thing in my personal life. I love you and I need you in my life, and I know what's in my heart. Nothing else matters."

Flustered, she shook her head and took out a cigarette. Cowboy picked up a book of matches from the table and lit it for her.

"Thank you." She drew deeply and turned her head away from him to exhale.

The waiter brought their drinks and they ordered lunch. Changing the direction of the conversation, June said, "Is your base near here?"

"As the crow flies it is about fifteen miles. But the highway to get out there goes all the way around Pearl Harbor. So it's about a thirty five mile drive."

"You know," she said. "I really haven't seen anything of this island other than the airport and the strip along Waikiki."

"Oh, really, well, after lunch we can take a ride and do some sightseeing. How does that sound?"

"It sounds nice actually. I'll call my secretary and tell her I'll be out for the afternoon."

The couple drove around the island, stopping whenever they came upon something that interested them. As the sun was setting, Cowboy parked the car next to the Beach on Waia-mea Bay. Huge twenty-foot breakers thundered across the reef and onto the narrow beach.

"This is really beautiful," June said. "I can't get over the size of those waves."

"They are big alright," Cowboy replied. "Surfers come from all over the world to ride these monsters."

"Wow. It's a wonder they don't drown."

"Some do."

She laid her head back on the seat and watched a magnificent sunset behind distant billowy vertical clouds. "You know, Shelby. This is the first time I have really let my hair down and just relaxed in a very long time. Thank you for today."

"You are very welcome, June." He turned and kissed her. "Being with you makes me happier than I've ever been."

Big brown eyes searched his face and she touched his cheek. "We have to take this slowly, Shelby. I need time."

"Sure, June. I understand."

"Do you?"

"Yes, I do understand. And I won't push you: that I sincerely promise."

"You're so sweet." She kissed him very tenderly. "I'd like a picture of you if you have one, for my desk at work."

His face brightened. "Okay, sure. Can I have one of you?"

"Of course."

He took her in his arms and kissed her passionately. "I do love you, June."

"I think you are going to be good for me," she whispered. "I need someone strong."

"I'll always be here for you."

She touched his face. "But I'm scared, Shelby. It frightens me to have fallen in love with you so quickly. That's the reason I have been avoiding you."

"But why, June, what is it about me that scares you?"

"It's not you."

"Then what is it?"

"It's many things, I guess. I don't know. I just need time, Shelby, lots of time to sort through everything."

"I understand."

He pulled her close and kissed her again. When they parted, he said softly, "Would you like to take a walk on the beach?"

"Yes, I'd like that.

The couple walked along the beach for an hour taking in the magnificent surf and the waning sun. They held each other's hand, and they stopped and kissed often. Cowboy desperately hoped this was the beginning of something wonderful, and maybe even something permanent. June for her part wasn't so sure. She had fallen in love with Cowboy, but on the other hand she worried that her sudden change of heart had come about because she was so deeply distressed by the marriage of Bud Cotter and Margo Whitefield. She needed time to sort it all out. Time, she was convinced, was her most valuable ally.

"You know what?" June said as they approached the car in the twilight. "No what?"

"I think I would like to go somewhere for seafood. Can we do that pretty sailor boy?"

"Absolutely."

Chapter 36

Born Again Hard -The Crucible

Bud Cotter opened his closet and fished around the shelves inside. He tossed his personal pistol and holster onto the bed. His K-Bar knife and a well worn OD green flight bag followed the weapons. He began stuffing the bag with his faded old jungle cammies, khakis, skivvies and socks. The thought of returning to Vietnam was dreadful. Margo came into the bedroom misty-eyed.

"Teddy Bear, I'm going to be a wreck until you get back. Why are they sending you back to Vietnam for God's sake? My God in heaven, haven't you given enough of yourself in that dreadful country?"

He tried to appear nonchalant. "I don't know anything other than I'm supposed to get some Intel information for CINCPAC and bring it back. I assume there will be some kind of briefing. By whom I have no idea."

"At Tan Son Hut?"

"I think so. The admiral says everything I need to know about the assignment will be given to me at Hickham."

"Hopefully you won't be at Danang. God, it makes me shiver just to think about that place, even though it is where we met and fell in love."

"Yeah," he said with a melancholy smile, "that's a place neither of us will ever forget."

Margo drew his custom combat Colt .45 from its stained, worn leather shoulder holster and expertly released the full clip from the handle. She pulled the slide back and checked the chamber. It was empty. She snapped the clip back into the grip and holstered the weapon.

"Once you're on the ground over there, Teddy Bear please make sure you wear your pistol all the time."

"I will." He stuffed the last couple pairs of socks into the bag. "Let's go for a swim in the pool."

Her face brightened. "Oh, let's do. I'll get my suit on."

"You don't need a suit. No one can see you, except me," he said with a sly grin.

Her bottom lip curled between her teeth and she gave him a sexy sensuous look. "You are so wicked, Teddy Bear."

At 0350 the next morning, Bud morosely watched Margo drive away in their new Mustang convertible. The night air was warm and still on the sidewalk in front of Hickham Air Ops. Bud picked up his bag and walked into the building.

Lieutenant Cotter?" An Air Force Captain in light blue short sleeve shirt, and dark blue pants extended his hand.

"That's me," Bud took the officer's hand.

"I'm Al Dolby. We're all set, Lieutenant. I'll need to see your ID if you don't mind."

"Sure." Bud opened his wallet and presented his ID and Top Secret card.

Dolby examined the cards. "Okay, thanks, Cotter." He handed Bud a sealed 9X12 inch manila envelope labeled TOP SECRET in bold red letters. "We have flight gear for you in the air crew area. Take your bag?"

"Ah, no thanks, it's not heavy."

Bud followed the Captain through a series of gleaming hallways to the aircrew area. The place was deserted except for one man who was putting on a flight suit resembling something an astronaut would wear.

Captain Dolby walked over to the man. "Major Chambers, this is your passenger, Lieutenant Cotter."

The major straightened and extended his hand. "Joe Chambers. Glad to meet you, Cotter."

"My pleasure, Major."

"Done much high altitude flying?"

"Not much above 20,000."

"Well, you're in for a new experience tonight. We'll be cruising at 81,000. You'll get a whole new perspective of the world."

Bud blurted, "Jesus Christ, 81,000 feet!"

Chambers laughed. "That's it. You'll ride in the RSO seat."

"What's an RSO?"

"Reconnaissance Systems Officer. He operates all of the electronic gear and helps navigate."

"What kind of an airplane is this?"

"Oh, no one told you?" The Major appeared amazed. "We're flying the SR-71."

Bud searched his memory. "I don't believe I've heard of it."

The Major chuckled. "Not many people have, Cotter. Its existence is known in intelligence circles, but we keep it under tight security for obvious reasons. Well, your gear is in that locker. Sergeant Puckett will help you get suited up. He should be right back. We have to be out of here before daylight. I'll brief you on the systems prior to departure."

Bud followed Sergeant Puckett's instructions and clumsily got into the pressure suit. "I'll load your bag in the aircraft, Lieutenant. If you will go through that red door, Major Chambers will go over the aircraft systems and pre-flight with you."

"Okay. Thanks."

Puckett took Bud's bag and disappeared through another door.

The briefing amazed Bud. They would be flying the SR-71 Blackbird at a speed of mach 2.9. According to Chambers, this was a relatively conservative speed for the Blackbird. They would refuel once from an airborne tanker at a rendezvous point over the Mariana's somewhere near Guam.

The SR-71 was 101 feet 8 inches long with a wingspan of 55 feet 7 inches. Two Pratt & Whitney J-58 axial-flow turbojet engines with afterburner powered the aircraft. The engines each produce 40,000 pounds of thrust. The SR-71 can reach altitudes higher than 85,000 feet and cruise at speeds in excess of mach 3.2 (approximately 2330 knots). The aircraft weighed 60,000 pounds empty and 140,000 pounds when fully fueled. Chambers proudly explained that the SR-71 was constructed with a titanium alloy. The black paint consisted of a pigmentation containing minute iron balls. These acted to dissipate electro-magnetically generated energy effectively lowering the possibility of the aircraft being painted by radar. The fuel is a high kerosene base and is ignited by a catalyst, tetraethyl borane. The fuel tanks must be pressurized with nitrogen to prevent an inadvertent vapor ignition. "A lugubrious and hazardous state of affairs," thought Bud.

By the time Chambers had briefed Bud on the operation of the life support, communications and ejection systems, Bud's brain was thoroughly dazzled. His first glimpse of the Blackbird left him in awe. Inside the closed hangar the needle nose seemed to emerge from wide engines and tall vertical fins like the tip of a dart. Inside the RSO cockpit was a mind boggling array of radars, screens and instruments. A duo of efficient Air Force technicians helped Bud get his enclosed helmet secured and the pressure suit connected and tested. Once more, Bud was briefed on the operation of the communications, life support and egress systems. In the front seat, Chambers was rapidly running through a checklist with technicians standing on the hangar floor via plug-in intercom. Checklist completed, the hangars doors opened and a yellow tug sporting four massive tires began to pull the SR-71 out into the early morning darkness.

Three hours and forty-seven minutes later they touched down at Clark Air Force Base, Philippines in dank tepid blackness. An Air Force Lieutenant Colonel waited at the bottom of the ladder as Bud climbed out of the aircraft. Ground crews were connecting a tug to the Blackbird. Standing orders for Blackbirds dictated securing the aircraft into a hangar as quickly as possible.

"Lieutenant Cotter, I'm Lieutenant Colonel Mark Johnson." Bud saluted and the two men shook hands. "We have an F-4 standing-by to take you over to Tan Son Hut, Lieutenant. Would you care for some breakfast first?"

"That would be great, thank you, sir."

"How was your trip in the Blackbird?"

Bud grinned, shaking his head with wonder. "Colonel, it was unbelievable. This is one experience that I'll never forget."

"You get to do it again on the return trip you know."

"No, I didn't know that."

"Evidently they want you back in one big hurry, Lieutenant."

"I was instructed not to open these orders until I arrived here. I'll look them over after breakfast and find out what this is all about."

Bud read the top secret packet while sitting through a head call after breakfast. The orders were simple and straightforward. He was to meet with Navy intelligence, SEAL and CIA personnel at Tan Son Hut. The Boss of Seal Team Bravo One One would pick him up at Tan Son Hut. The SEAL team Boss would serve as a combination adviser and escort for Bud. Bud's mission was to verify the existence of heavy North Vietnamese troop and supply activity taking place across the border inside Cambodia. Once he had verified the information presented him at the briefing, he is to return to Hawaii.

The young Air Force F-4 Phantom pilot coached Bud through a fairly decent landing on the big runway at Tan Son Hut airfield near Saigon. It was 0640 local time when Bud climbed out of the rear cockpit feeling fresh and exhilarated. The first lieutenant had allowed Bud to fly the Phantom from Clark AFB to Tan Son Hut. Unlike Navy Phantoms, the Air Force versions had a full set of flight controls in the rear cockpit. After some initial fumbling, Bud acquired the feel of the big fighter and handled the airplane commendably well through to the landing at Tan Son Hut. The tower had been briefed to give this particular F-4 top priority. Ground control directed the Phantom to an area where several camouflage Navy helos were spotted on the ramp.

LTJG Clyde Eaton, the Boss, more commonly referred to as the Honcho of Seal Team Bravo One One, stood six feet tall and was 180 pounds of solid muscle. He was deeply tanned and the sleeves of his faded jungle fatigues were rolled above his elbows. The leather of his jungle boots was worn white.

"Lieutenant Cotter, I'm Lieutenant jaygee Clyde Eaton." His grip was hard as steel. His eyes were deep blue and without humor. "I've been assigned to you while you're in country. We need to get you out of those khakis and into some fatigues with no insignias."

Bud nodded. "Okay, where can I change?"

"In this hooch over here, had chow yet?" They began walking across the tarmac.

"Yeah, I had breakfast at Clark a couple of hours ago."

"The word is you're getting the MOH (Medal of Honor)."

Bud glanced at the SEAL, vaguely annoyed. It was obvious they knew all about him. “Yeah, it’s political horseshit though. I don’t deserve it.”

“One of our guys was awarded the MOH last October. He thought it was horseshit too.”

Bud nodded and didn’t comment.

“Got a weapon, Cotter?”

“I have my .45 and a couple of spare clips in my bag.”

“Colt Government?”

“Yeah, it’s a customized combat model.”

“Nice weapon, lot of knock down power.”

“Yeah, that’s why I like it.”

“Ever killed a man with it?”

Bud smirked, “No, but I’m hell on rats and beer cans.”

Eaton grunted with good humor. “After you get changed, we’ll go get a cup of coffee and maybe a roll if you want one. You’re scheduled for a briefing at 0800.”

Bud sat at a table with three other officers in a hot stuffy Quonset style hooch with screen windows. The senior officer was CO of Naval Intelligence, Saigon: a Captain named Peters. The other two officers were Navy Seals’, LTJG Eaton and his boss, Lieutenant Commander Mike Allison, CO of SEAL Detachment Bravo One One. A SOG (Studies and Observation Group) civilian from the CIA conducted the briefing. These men treated Bud with an unusual amount of wariness and respect, making him somewhat self-conscious. He understood clearly that this kid gloves treatment was a result of him being a direct report to CINCPAC. Even the CIA man, Butler was walking softly with this young Medal of Honor officer who was a member of the CINCPAC inner circle and a personal acquaintance of the new President.

"Glad to have you with us Lieutenant Cotter," Butler began. He was thin, hairy and bullet-headed. He had tiny ears that projected straight out from his head and coal black haircut in a tight flattop. He stood in front of a large detailed pull down map of Vietnam, Laos and Cambodia. "As you are aware, Lieutenant, Navy Intelligence and SOG are recommending to CINCPAC direct interdiction of NV supply and staging areas inside Cambodia. The sophistication and complexity of NV facilities inside Cambodian territory has increased dramatically and creates a severe threat to our operations in the southern Corps areas. There are three areas of particular concern to us." Using a small pointer, Butler turned to the map. "The first two areas are known to us as the Parrot's Beak—-located here, and the Angel's Wing—-here. As you can see, these are oddly shaped stretches of Cambodian territory that extend deep into Vietnam about 50 miles northwest of Saigon. The third area is called the Fishhook, located—here. It's also northwest of Saigon. Since all three areas are close to Saigon, as well as to the northern sections of the Mekong Delta and War Zones C and D, they are ideal sanctuaries for regional communist forces. In addition to these three areas, Navy SEAL, Marine Force Recon and Army Special Forces personnel have been monitoring supply traffic along the Sihanouk Trail. This trail is a secondary communist supply route that originates in Cambodia's main seaport city of Sihanoulville. It stretches northeastward and ends at several staging areas located in the Parrot's Beak, Angel's Wing, and Fishhook sectors. Two days ago, a Recon patrol consisting of SEAL Team Charlie located a very large bunker and supply complex under construction in the dense jungle around Snoul, located—here, just north of the Fish-hook. SEAL Recon surveillance has confirmed that each of these Cambodian areas are feeding troops and supplies into the Saigon area as well as zones C and D by way of the Truong Son Corridor—here. This is a secondary supply route inside South Vietnam beginning—here—and ending about—

here. As you can see, it parallels the, quote, Ho Chi Minh trail."

Butler paused and tamped a pack of Lucky Strikes on the table. He opened the pack and offered cigarettes around. Everyone declined. Butler lit a Lucky and continued. "Now, these numbered manila envelopes in front of me contain a series of photos taken by SEAL Recon teams and Army Special Forces Recon teams. Envelope number one contains photos of the Parrot's Beak. Number two contains photos of the Angel's Wing; the third envelope contains photos of the Fishhook area. The photographs clearly indicate base camps and supply caches the NV's have set up and amassed. If you would care to look through the photographs, Lieutenant, I think you'll agree there is more than sufficient evidence to support our recommendations to CINCPAC."

Bud opened the envelope marked 'Fishhook' and began to methodically examine the black and white and color photographs. Each picture revealed detailed evidence of weapons, ammunition and food supplies. Bud was shocked to see truck convoys, tanks, 37 mm antiaircraft batteries and scores of heavy and light field guns lined up in precise military order under the jungle canopy. Most surprising was a machine shop, apparently deep in the jungle, complete with electrical generators to run lathes and milling machines that were turning out what appeared to be mortar tubes. Another photo showed women making "Ho Chi Minh sandals", constructed from scraps of truck tires. These sandals were made on heavy duty sewing machines inside a well-stocked jungle hooch. There was even an open front bicycle factory hidden under a canopy of netting in the forest shade. Most appalling of all was a photograph of a jungle operating room set up in a swamp. Such resourcefulness and innovation jarred Bud to his shoes. It dawned on him that people with such will and conviction were a formidable adversary indeed. The pictures of the Parrot's Beak and Angel's Wing showed similar manufacturing and supply installations.

Bud looked at Captain Peters. "This is a disaster, Captain. We've got to stop the bastards or lose this war."

"Exactly, Lieutenant. We hope CINCPAC, CNO and the White House think so too."

The SEAL CO, Allison spoke up. "Lieutenant, do you think these photographs are sufficient supporting evidence for CINCPAC to make recommendations to CNO?"

"Yes, sir, that is, once I have reported to the Admiral that I have physically sighted the evidence."

"What do you mean by physically sighting the evidence, Lieutenant Cotter? Aren't the photographs enough evidence for you?"

"I seem to be between the proverbial rock and a hard spot here, Commander. My orders are quite specific, stating that I must personally verify what these photographs are showing is factual, and in no way exaggerated or replicated. Based on those orders, I cannot accept the pictures at face value and neither will the Admiral. Somehow, I'm going to have to see it for myself."

"What! Oh, hell no," Captain Peters bellowed. "We can't afford to have anything happen to you, Lieutenant. God Almighty! You, a Medal of Honor winner and a CINCPAC staff officer out in Indian country! Holy shit, Lieutenant Cotter, no way!"

The Captain's remarks drew a low level of amused laughter from the others. Bud said, "Is there an alternative, Captain Peters?" I don't know how to go about this without actually sighting the evidence myself."

The Captain paused, pensive and uncomfortable. He glanced at the other men present. "Do you gentlemen have any suggestions? I'm open for ideas." They shook their heads. "Very well, then. This is what I'm going to do, Lieutenant. I'll shoot a message out to CINCPAC explaining that based on your interpretation of orders, you insist on going into Oklahoma Territory (code word for Cambodia) for verification of the photographic evidence. Additionally, I'll inform CINCPAC that physical verification is going to be extremely hazardous, and therefore inadvisable for you to personally carry out. Is that a fair statement, Lieutenant?"

"Yes, sir."

"Very well, I should have an answer shortly." The Captain picked up his garrison cap and hurried out.

Peters returned an hour later with a teletype message flapping in his hand. Bud and the others were sitting around a picnic table in the shade drinking Coca Colas and talking about baseball. The Captain silently handed the CINCPAC reply to Bud.

FROM: CINCPAC

TO: CO SPNAVOPS SAIGON

LIEUTENANT COTTER TO ACT AT DISCRETION.

MCCAIN bt

"It's up to you Lieutenant," said Peters. "Although I already know what your answer is going to be."

Bud looked at Peters and glanced around at the others. "Captain, I don't see where I have any choice in the matter. I've got to see some of those installations."

"Very well, this makes it a whole new ball game." He looked at Allison. "Mike, this has to be your baby. You guys will have to coordinate an insertion into whatever areas the Lieutenant selects. I'm damn sure not qualified to tell you how to do your business out there, but for Christ's sake do whatever it takes to keep Lieutenant Cotter in one piece and out of Indian hands."

Allison nodded. "I understand, Captain."

"Very well," Peters smiled and extended a hand to Bud. "Good luck, Lieutenant Cotter. I'll see you back here in a few days."

"Thank you, sir."

Half an hour later, Bud, Allison and Eaton were riding inside a Navy UH-1B Huey gunship helo heading northwest out of Tan Son Hut. The crew chief, sporting helmet and flak jacket, squatted next to the open door casually holding onto an M-60 machine gun. He ignored the three passengers and diligently surveyed the earth below for signs of VC as the Huey raced along barely above the treetops.

Genuinely nervous, Bud tried to appear relaxed and nonchalant. He suspected the two SEALs sensed his apprehension but they said nothing and appeared to be dozing in the web seat. He didn't know what to expect of this mission. The gnawing anxiety he felt was fear of the unknown. He was going into the jungles of Cambodia to observe bad guys first hand. Bud knew if he were captured in Cambodia, the Navy and the US Government would deny all knowledge of him regardless of whose son he was or who he knew. Coupled with that was the intimidation factor of being in company with the toughest, most capable, most lethal men the world had ever seen. Bud knew that he didn't pack the gear to become a SEAL. These were the most extraordinary of men, both physically and mentally. His presence here would be a burden to them and make their job much more difficult and dangerous. Bud resolved himself to do all that he could to minimize the impact of his presence with the SEAL's. He suspected the coming days were going to be one hell of a challenge for him.

Twenty-five minutes later, the Huey touched down at a Special Forces camp near Tay Ninh located a few miles north of the Parrot's Beak. Carrying his bag, Bud followed Allison and Eaton across the PSP helo pad and into one of five large OD buildings fitted with canvas tops. Inside the hooch was hot, humid and smelled like a combination locker room and hot canvas. Two SEALs stripped to the waist wearing only OD green cutoff shorts and Ho Chi Minh sandals manned radios, telephones and an ancient clacking radio teletype machine. Bud noted several electrical outlets inside the hot stuffy hooch, but there was not one fan to be seen.

The duo greeted the two SEAL officers and curiously regarded Bud as he followed them. Allison walked through an open door and into another room. He seated himself behind an old French Army field desk and shuffled through several messages. Eaton and Bud sat on OD green director chairs. When Allison had scanned the messages, he sat back in the chair and peered at Bud.

"Cotter, I think the best way to handle this is to put you on Eaton's Bravo team. We'll give you a crash course in procedure, communications, stealth and so forth. I'm thinking today and tonight we'll get you familiarized and acclimated. It won't be easy. Any screw up out there; a move at the wrong time: slap a bug, cough, sneeze, fart, not just yourself, but the whole team could get wasted. You're going to have to think about every move you make in advance. Your brain has to be constantly in high gear, but your body has to be in slow motion."

Bud nodded grimly. "I understand."

"Okay, good. The first area Team Bravo One One will take you into is the Parrots Beak. That area is always active so you should get a good feel for what the zipper heads are doing there. When you think you've seen enough, it's your call, the team will call for extraction. Next recon will be an insertion into the Angels Wing. The last area will be the Fish Hook. Does that sound like what you have in mind?"

"Yes, sir, exactly."

"Good. Lesson one, Cotter. Out here we don't recognize rank. Everyone, enlisted and commissioned freely fraternizes and calls each other by their given name or nickname. Charles has good ears, and he'd love to polish off an officer, especially a SEAL."

"Okay, I've got it," Bud said.

"All right, Clyde, he's all yours." Allison rose from the chair and grinned. "Welcome aboard, Cotter, and good luck. Don't hesitate to give me shout if there's anything you need or that I can do for you."

"Thanks. I'll remember that."

The first twenty-four hours with the SEALs were, for Bud Cotter, a veritable nightmare of discomfort, pain and misery. It was also a period of stimulating enlightenment and endless wonderment. LT(jg) Clyde Eaton was a patient and methodical tutor and instructor. Very early on, Bud developed a great deal of respect for this quiet, intelligent and highly skilled SEAL officer. Following a long, hot, tiring day of training, Bud spent his first night back in Vietnam not sleeping on a bed or cot, but rather squatting, kneeling and lying on his belly in deep jungle, nervously gripping a stubby Remington 870 shotgun loaded with flechette and 00 buckshot. He carried a 35mm Leica camera in a pouch on his web belt, a canteen and two other weapons: his .45 Colt and his issue K-Bar knife.

As part of Bud's crash training, Seal Team Bravo One One set an ambush along a well used foot trail inside the Parrots Beak. Here a sluggish waterway provided a nautical highway perfect for smuggling men and supplies into the Parrots Beak. The ambush served a twofold purpose. It would develop Bud's ability to withstand and deal with unaccustomed fear and discomfort. Secondly it would help Bud to adjust his body and his mind to operating as a team member in the dark jungle environment. In the event that the VC appeared during the night, Eaton's instructions to Bud were quite specific. Bud was to lie flat on the deck until the firing was over and someone speaking English told him to get up. "If you only hear gook noises when the shooting stops," Eaton grinned and shrugged, "well, you've got two choices. You can unlimber that 870 and probably get yourself a couple of zipper heads before you get killed, or you can let the gooks capture you and take your chances up north in the Hanoi Hilton."

Bud grinned and said, "Both of those options really suck, Lad."

Eaton chuckled. "Yeah, I know. Ain't war hell?"

Visually, Bud appeared no different than the other members of the SEAL team. He was dressed in jungle camo fatigues and wore a camo bush hat. His face, neck, hands and exposed arms were covered by black and green face paint. All vestiges of perfumed deodorant and bath soap had been expunged from his body. Eaton's thoroughness amazed Bud. The SEAL had Bud remove his dog tags so if he were captured in Cambodia, the government would deny all knowledge of his being there. Bud was filthy, sweaty and covered with grime and dirt. His day and evening meals consisted of prudent amounts of fish, rice and vegetables. Such a diet was typical for the population in Southeast Asia. This diet also lent itself to modifying his body and fecal odor so that it blended with that of the local populace and surroundings.

He spent the night with gritted teeth, enduring irritating mosquito and insect bites. Gnats flew up his nose in into his ears. Spiders, one the size of a Moon Pie, paraded across his body. Once in a while, even though his pants were bloused in his boots, one of those nasty biting, stinging black ants would somehow get inside a pant leg and bite him. The bite or sting, Bud wasn't sure which, would leave a nasty painful welt. He wondered how long his resolve could withstand the incessant stinging pain and near to screaming itching. So far he hadn't seen a snake, and he certainly wasn't looking forward to that first encounter. He knew the place was crawling with cobra, krait, bamboo viper, python and Christ knows what else. Bud's mind waged a constant battle with his lifelong natural instincts. Several times he had checked himself from sneezing or coughing. Even the natural act of clearing his throat or wiping away sweat had to be repressed.

Forcing himself to bear those painful ant stings seemed the greatest challenge to his will and determination. Bud had sworn himself to one thing. He would die right here before he would move to scratch or to squash one of the torturous insects. He would not cave and humiliate himself in the presence of the three SEALs who monitored him very closely and, he was sure, fully expected him to throw in the towel at any moment. Occasionally his thoughts would turn to Margo and he would think about how much he missed her. "Jesus, Angel, if you could see me now," he thought, smiling to himself in the blackness.

By 0200 his terror of the jungle darkness, sounds and smells had vanished. He was almost totally consumed by his physical discomfort. All of the distressing thoughts of an encounter with the bad guys had now transformed into a desperate hope that the VC would show up. At least if there were an ambush, he would be relieved from this torture either by a swift death or the chance to scratch and rub if he survived. His mind began to rollick through fantasies of cool showers and hours, even days of uninterrupted ecstatic scratching.

An hour before dawn, the Honcho decided that the VC was not going to use the trail or the canal this night. He signaled the team to secure the ambush. Quietly, like phantom shadows, the team began to stealthily move parallel to the canal avoiding animal or human trails. Bud followed the Honcho who was following a few yards behind the point man. The Honcho carried a Smith & Wesson Model 76 9mm sub machine gun. On his hip, the Honcho wore another Smith &

Wesson weapon, the Model 39 automatic pistol, more commonly known as a Hush Puppy. The Hush Puppy had a highly specialized silencer incorporated into the barrel making its discharge almost inaudible.

The point man, referred to as Monster by the others, wielded a modified M-16, wore a Hush Puppy on his hip and was the RTO or team radio operator. Monster was a twenty-year-old second class boatswain's mate and a hulking fierce-looking young man. Monster very much reminded Bud of his old VC-110 nemesis, Mad Dog. Jesus, those days seemed like an eternity ago. The fourth member of the team was a quick and wiry twenty one year old second class gunner's mate known as Mouse. Mouse carried an M3A1 .45 caliber "grease gun" and wore a Hush Puppy on his hip. A spotting scope and tripod sheathed in a reinforced web carrier was slung across his back.

When the Honcho signaled the team to move out, Bud could hardly stand erect. His joints were painfully stiff from a day of unaccustomed exercise and a night of maintaining uncomfortable positions. Once standing, he allowed himself the luxurious relief of a few subtle scratches on the worst of his itchy places. He tried to be subtle about it until he noticed that the SEALs scratched themselves or rubbed a sore spot. After that, he didn't feel quite so much like such a weak-kneed tulip.

Moving along the canal inside thick forest, the team slowly made its way through a soggy area that smelled of rotten eggs, and then began climbing a hill densely covered by palm and banana. Half way up the hill, the Honcho dispatched Mouse to check the apogee for VC. A few minutes later, Mouse abruptly appeared like a specter from the darkness startling Bud badly. Mouse used hand signals to indicate that the hill was secure. The team then carefully moved to the apex and quickly set up an observation post using the spotting scope that Mouse carried on his back. By this time, Bud was convinced that his strength was thoroughly spent. Every cell of his body tormented him. He yearned desperately for a shower and sleep. The aching in his bones, the misery of the insect bites: the pureness of exhaustion he felt were like nothing he had ever endured. This was like a dream, a very bad dream. He fervently hoped that the team was going to rest and sleep here on top of the hill but no, Mouse signaled that Bud should low crawl to where he had set up the spotting scope. The dim, gray first light of dawn was beginning to appear in the eastern sky. Bud seriously doubted that he could crawl the ten feet to the spotting scope. More than anything, he wanted to groan in his agony and tell the Honcho to call in the extraction helo but somehow, some way, he found himself at the scope.

Through the small valley below the hill, the canal they had been following widened and merged with three larger canals combining to form a small river. As Bud panned the powerful light gathering spotting scope, the four canals and river appeared as silver spidery ribbons, disappearing into the jungle in varied directions. The Honcho slowly moved himself to a position next to Bud. He whispered into Bud's ear and pointed with a grimy painted finger to the valley below.

"Watch the canal at your two," he whispered. "Cambodia is about half a click upstream. Charlie uses these canals like highways. It's an efficient way of getting more zipper heads and supplies into the Saigon and Mekong Delta areas. If we're lucky, Charlie will run a convoy for us this morning."

Bud nodded, took out his camera and, using an adapter, connected it the powerful spotting scope. He watched for fifteen minutes, struggling not to doze off. Abruptly a tiny movement in the canal caught his eye. He blinked and squinted through tired eyes. A moment later a long low boat with a rounded roof arching across its center beam moved into view.

A lone coxswain stood on the stern of the boat steering it with a long handle attached to a rudder. Now fully awake and alert Bud scanned the boat more thoroughly. A man was squatted on the deck near the bow and the squatter was holding a weapon across his arms. The faint sound of a putt putt engine drifted through the morning midst. Bud turned his head toward the Honcho and whispered. "There's a guy with a rifle squatting in the bow of that boat." The Honcho nodded and said, "Charles." He indicated with a head motion for Bud to photograph the boat. Ten minutes later, Bud had photographed seventeen boats that had come out of Cambodia. The boats were now in South Vietnamese waters. Using hand signals, the Honcho signaled Monster to call in a flight of fast movers to interdict the NV boats. Ten minutes later two Navy A-7 Corsairs came screeching out of the morning scud clouds and began firing rockets and 20mm rounds into the boats. A few minutes later, two Air Force F-100 Super Saber fighters joined the Corsairs and rolled in on the boats with cannon and rocket fire. Bud enthusiastically watched and photographed the fighters making repeated strafing runs on the boats. Tall spumes of water rose high above the distant foliage as the rockets and 20 mm rounds cut the boats to shreds.

Bud felt the Honcho's hand on his back. They were securing the OP and moving out. Bud painfully crawled out of the way so that Mouse could disassemble and pack away the camera and the scope. The Honcho signaled Monster to take the point once again.

In the bright morning light, they low crawled fifty yards along the edge of an open grassy area. Bud despaired after they had negotiated the grassy area and the Honcho signaled the team to stand and move out. Bud had convinced himself that the open grassy area was the pickup point for the extraction helo. He wondered how many miles it was back to the camp. He was positive that his weak aching legs and feet couldn't carry him another hundred yards. His mind began to envision for him a horrible agonizing death. Lying comatose in this stinking jungle, he would be promptly tenderized by the vile black ants, and then be eaten by a giant tiger. In twenty-four hours all that would remain of Bud Cotter would be a putrid pile of tiger shit. Poor Margo and his family would never know what happened to him.

Still walking fifteen minutes later, however, Bud was positive beyond any doubt that he was very near death. His anguished mind now formulated a new plan. He would fall on his K-Bar and bring a quick end to this wretchedness, but the Honcho saved him when he ordered Monster to call in an extraction helo.

Twenty-five minutes later, Bud staggered into the hooch and dropped his weapons and gear onto the floor. Eaton walked in behind him. "Cotter," he said in a friendlier tone than he had used at anytime previous. "You did one hell of a job out there last night. Congratulations."

Bud gave the Honcho an exhausted, sad smile and peered at the SEAL through red swollen eyes. "Lad, I think I am going to die at any moment. You can have my .45, but do me one favor, will you?"

"What's that, Cotter," Eaton said, amused.

"Don't tell my wife what a tulip she married."

Laughing quietly, Eaton slapped Bud's back. "Okay, Cotter. It's a deal. But don't under rate yourself too much. You cost me twenty bucks tonight."

"I did? How's that?"

"I bet Mouse a twenty that you'd never make the night without an early extraction. Heh, heh, heh."

"Well, if you want to know the truth, I damn near caved a couple of times. Hey, listen, Lad. Thanks for everything. I really appreciate what you guys are doing for me."

"No problem, Cotter. You're making our job easy. By the way, you do want a shower don't you?"

"Jesus, yes, but what do I do about the no soap rule?".

Eaton handed Bud a bar of soap wrapped in an OD green wrapper. "Use this. It doesn't have any scents or perfumes in it."

"Jesus, thanks, Lad."

"No problem, Cotter. Get yourself some rest. I'll see you later."

"Okay, thanks."

"Oh, and one other thing," Eaton said, grinning, "don't wash those cammies with detergent, just rinse 'em out in water. You've got 'em scented just about right."

Bud glanced at his filthy uniform pants and blouse. Both were caked with mud, sweat, slime and unidentifiable stains. Bud slowly shook his head, "Holy shit, what a way to make a goddamn living."

Showered and unbelievably refreshed, Bud fell into the deepest sleep he could remember short of his time on the Comfort when he was in a coma. The combinations of a day change from Hawaii, and the intensive non-stop physical and mental exertions to which he had been subjected left his body and mind fully drained and fatigued.

He awoke at 1630, foggily remembering where he was. He sat up on his cot. His body ached terribly from head to toe. He believed that even his hair was hurting. Painful irritated welts and lumps speckled his legs, some topped with white heads of pus. He squeezed one of the festering welts and winced as pus and blood burst forth painful as the jab of a knife. Bud rose from the cot very slowly. His feet were sore and tender. Stiffly and painfully, Bud grabbed a towel and staggered naked into the shower. Eaton was waiting for him when he returned.

"Feeling better, Cotter?"

"Yeah, the sleep helped. I had one hell of a case of jet lag."

"No shit, Cotter," Eaton grinned. "Ever thought about giving the SEALs a shot? After the way you hung in there through yesterday and last night, I'd say you'd have a good chance of making it. We can always use pilots."

"You've got to be shitting me, Lad," Bud snorted, pulling on skivvies. "I'd die the first week, the first day! You guys are nuts. You do realize that don't you?"

Eaton laughed. "Believe it or not, Cotter. We love this shit."

"I believe you do, Lad. I really believe you do."

"Don't bust open those bites," Eaton said, examining Bud's ravaged legs. "You'll get one hell of an infection in this climate. I'll take you over to see Doc. He's got some stuff that kills the pain and itching and dries them up in a day or so."

"Thanks, I could sure use it."

"How about some chow? We can go over tonight's operation while we eat."

"Okay, Lad, sounds great. I'm starved."

That night Seal Team Bravo One One minus Bud Cotter was inserted into the Fishhook around midnight. Eaton, Monster and Mouse spent the night reconnoitering the area to find a suitable spot to set up a daylight OP for Bud. The Fishhook was a fever of activity that night. Truck convoys and caravans of elephant burdened with supplies moved east toward multiple distribution points in the area. The team located a complex of hooch factories that were turning out weapons, ammunition, rice cakes and gauze battle dressings. As a bonus, huge stores of Russian made self propelled rockets were hidden under netting. A steady stream of trucks, elephants and men carried the wooden crates containing the rockets away in the darkness.

The team located a ridge fifteen hundred yards west of the hidden manufacturing complex. Several hours of meticulous searching revealed a large overhang of rock along the face of the ridge. Two large hissing Cobras occupied and defended the cave-like area under the overhang of rock. Mouse disposed of the serpents with precision lightning-quick swipes of his razor sharp machete. Sitting under the low rock overhang, the team had a clear view of the hooch's and nearby supply trails. The Honcho had Monster call for the insertion of John Wayne, the radio call sign and nickname the SEALS had given Bud. The team located an LZ for the helo on the opposite side of the ridge. Monster called in the coordinates.

Forty-five minutes later Bud jumped clear of the helo and scurried off into the jungle led by Mouse. Today Bud carried only his camera, pistol and the K-Bar knife. Moving cautiously, the pair endured nearly an hour of sloth-like climbing in order to breach the ridge and slither downhill to a point near the OP. The climb was especially strenuous for Bud as he huffed and puffed along behind the SEAL. With an all clear signal from the Honcho Bud and Mouse joined Monster and the Honcho.

The first pale light of dawn found Bud awe struck at what he was observing through the powerful scope. The North Vietnamese had created a self-sufficient manufacturing and supply center in the Cambodian jungle. The traffic of people, vehicles and animals was a continuum. The NV brazenly moved supplies into and out of this center with no fear of intervention by the US. Bud wondered how many setups like this there were in Laos and Cambodia. He observed and photographed the hooch complex and trails until he had had expended three rolls of 35 mm film.

He had been peering through the scope and snapping pictures for over an hour. He took his eye away from the instrument and turned his painted face to Eaton.

"Show me exactly where we are on the map," Bud whispered.

The Honcho unfolded a plastic covered grid map and marked an X with a black Navy issue ballpoint. "We're here, four miles and about two clicks inside Cambodia," the Honcho whispered.

"This is unbelievable," said Bud. "The gooks must have setups like this from North Vietnam all the way down to the Mekong . . . Jesus."

"No doubt about it," the Honcho whispered in reply. "So far, we've located over a dozen similar operations between the Parrot's Beak, Angel Wing and up here in the Fishhook. It's hard to say how many more there are that we haven't located."

Bud shook his head. "Look, Lad. I've seen enough. Let's get the hell out of here."

The Honcho nodded and lifted the canvas cover off the face of his wristwatch. "We've got to locate another LZ. No way are we going to use the one where you came in. Now that it's daylight, zipper heads will be crawling all over the other side of this ridge looking for us."

"Okay." Bud nodded.

The Honcho glanced at Bud's buttoned holster. "Got a round in the chamber of your weapon?" Bud shook his head.

"Better chamber one."

A streak of fear jolted through Bud as he took out his Colt and ran a round into the chamber. The Honcho's usual matter of fact attitude was one thing. Being told to lock and load his weapon told Bud all. They were in deep shit out here on this ridge, and everyone on the team must have known it except him. Now he knew. With shaky hands, Bud checked his spare clips. The three SEALS were carefully checking their weapons and gear. Five minutes later, the Honcho signaled Mouse to take the point. Methodically, at a maddeningly slow pace, the team began to move out.

They moved down and away from the ridge at oblique angles. By observing the position of the sun, Bud knew they were moving in a generally easterly direction, but at a snail's pace. Several times they heard voices and observed men carrying AK-47's along jungle paths. The team negotiated most of the thick jungle obstacles by going directly through them, never using an animal or human foot trail. Bud's hands and face were scratched and burning from the scrapes of thorns and razor sharp leaves. The insects were wicked, but today, somehow, he was able to mostly ignore them. Slithering through places he would not have believed a man could go, Bud fixed complete and total faith in the silent determination of the three SEALs. Even the huge tiger paw marks they saw in a pathway did not rattle him, not as long as Honcho, Mouse and Monster were with him.

Standing at its noon zenith, the hot tropical sun baked the humid jungle below the layered umbrellas of trees. The team silently waded across a sluggish river thickly studded with cajuput trees. When they emerged on the opposite bank and were in secure cover, the men checked each other for leeches. Deep inside a massive vertical netting of tangled leafy vines that reached into the treetops, the Honcho signaled the team to rest and take water. Eaton took out his map and studied it. Five minutes earlier the team had watched a dozen NVA soldiers on patrol walking in the jungle. The soldiers were jabbering, laughing and smoking. Their weapons were slung haphazardly across their backs. The Honcho whispered to Bud that the patrol was probably looking for them. Apparently these NVA soldiers were of the opinion that their patrolling was a waste of time. They knew not how close to death and how very fortunate they were. Under normal circumstances, the SEALS would have killed all but a couple of the patrol. Those spared would be taken prisoner and interrogated back at Tay Ninh.

Two hours before dark and approaching the border of South Vietnam, the team came to a much used jungle road that lay fifty yards in front of them. Taking out his map, the Honcho pointed to a spot on the chart. They were very close to the border. The Honcho pointed to another spot inside Vietnam. If the area was secure, that would be their extraction point. Not far to go now. Mouse low crawled and slithered like a snake toward the road, when he was nearly there, a truck was heard coming from the left. Mouse seemed to melt into the jungle. Truck past, Mouse low crawled to the road and meticulously studied the forest on either side of the road. After what seemed an eternity to Bud, Mouse rose from his hiding place, scampered across the road and disappeared into the jungle. Bud and the two SEALs lay motionless for ten minutes until Mouse signaled to the Honcho that the area was secure. Bud never saw Mouse signaling. By now, however, Bud was no longer amazed. These guys did things, saw things, heard things, sensed things and knew things that Bud was convinced he could never learn in a hundred years.

The Honcho signaled to Monster. He low crawled ahead until he was at a spot where he could clearly observe the road. Satisfied after a long scrutiny, Monster scrambled across the road and vanished into the foliage at a place different than where Mouse had entered the forest. Now it was Bud's turn. The Honcho patted his back and Bud began to crawl through the jungle toward the road. He approached to within one hundred feet of the road when another truck came rumbling up the road. Bud quickly low crawled to a big tree and lay flat behind the thick trunk. A five ton Soviet built truck approached, slowed, and stopped one hundred and fifty feet in front of Bud and to his right.

Four men sat on crates in the bed of the truck smoking and talking. Four AK-47s were leaned into the front right corner of the bed. Bud heard the metallic rasp of the parking brake being set. With the truck idling noisily, the driver jumped out of the cab, lit a cigarette and walked into the woods a short distance where he relieved himself against a tree. The four men in the back of the truck jumped down. Three of them began to relieve themselves. The fourth man opened a metal box behind the cab of the truck and removed a handkerchief size piece of scrap cloth. He said something to the others and walked into the woods, oblivious to danger.

So frightened that he began to tremble, Bud nevertheless had the presence of mind to remember Eaton's words. "Do everything you possibly can to keep cover between yourself and the enemy." He slowly wriggled his body to keep the tree trunk between himself and the unsuspecting NV soldier. With quivering hands, Bud carefully took out his K-Bar knife. "Surely he's going to stop before he gets close to me," Bud thought. But the man must have been overly modest. When he did finally stop, he was five feet from Bud's position. The man looked back toward the truck and, still not satisfied, the soldier took a few more steps to put the tree between himself and the truck. He looked around and prepared to drop his pants. It was at that moment that he saw Bud lying no more than six inches from his feet.

Gripped in a blind haze of mortal fear, Bud dropped his weapon and struck like a snake, grabbing the NV soldier's ankles and jerking them out from under him. The soldier wasn't very large, probably weighing no more than 130 pounds. He landed on his back with a thud and a grunt. The noise of the running truck engine muffled the sounds of the man's fall. The others were standing in the road behind the truck smoking and talking. Bud was on top of the soldier in an instant. The oriental features of the NV soldier's round face were deformed by terror. Seconds passed as the soldier struggled and Bud, in a near state of panic, tried to decide what to do. Bud grabbed the K-Bar. He hesitated a second and then rammed the K-Bar into the man's mid section just below the ribcage. The soldier opened his mouth and screamed aloud for an instant until Bud could get his hand over the soldier's mouth. The soldier's breath reeked like a sewer. The soldier was jerking and bouncing wildly, desperately struggling to get away. When Bud withdrew the knife, the soldier's blood spurted all over him. Appalled at what he was doing, Bud stabbed the soldier again, this time in the upper chest just below the collarbone. More blood gushed out, spurting a thick, dark red geyser, but the soldier continued to thrash and struggle and did not die. Untrained in killing techniques and in a state of panic, Bud didn't realize that he had to hit the heart to kill the man instantly. This was a gruesomely messy, bloody business. The soldier's eyes, wide with incomprehensible pain and terror, looked into his assailant's hideous green face and battled to push Bud away with ever weakening arms and body thrusts. Suddenly the Honcho was there and dropped his body over the soldier's thrashing legs.

"Stick the knife upwards under his breast bone," he hissed.

Bud guessed where the soldier's breastbone should be and rammed the knife through his shirt upwards into his chest. The man stiffened, his eyes widened, his body shuddered and fell limp. He died in horror, staring at Bud Cotter's hideous green painted face. Bud began to notice a foul odor. The soldier's bowels and sphincter had released. Slowly, Bud removed his left hand from over the man's mouth. His hand was bleeding. In his struggle and terror, the soldier had bitten deep into the fleshy side of Bud's hand. Only now did Bud begin to feel the pain. His entire body began to tremble uncontrollably. The combined repugnant odors of blood, feces and urine suddenly seemed overwhelming. Aghast at what he had done, he gagged and vomited violently. Literally covered with the soldier's blood, he moved off the corpse. Kneeling, sitting back on his feet, still gripping the bloody

K-Bar, Bud stared at Eaton with wide distressed eyes. The Honcho laid a hand on Bud's shoulder, "Cold-blooded, man, cold blooded, really hard core."

The other NV soldiers were scattered on the road behind the truck, lying in pools of black congealing blood. When they had realized that something was happening to their comrade and began to react, Mouse and Monster quickly neutralized the four soldiers with silent fire from their Hush Puppy pistols. Monster appeared out of the bush and quickly attached timed C-4 charges under the truck; in fifteen minutes the truck would disappear in a hellish explosion. Hopefully there would be a lot of bad guys around when the stuff went off.

The Honcho poured water from his canteen across the wound on Bud's hand. He took out a small can and sprinkled yellow sulfa powder on the wound. He placed a sterile, OD green dressing on Bud's hand. Still trembling, Bud wiped the bloody blade of his K-bar on the dead man's pants.

On a signal from Mouse, the Honcho and Bud moved quickly, crossed the road and vanished into the forest. The Honcho was strongly concerned about Bud's hand wound. More importantly, he had to quickly find an extraction LZ. Once the NV found the bodies on the road or when the truck exploded, all hell would break loose. Every zipper head in the Fishhook would be out looking for them. The Honcho located a place on the map north of their position. He briefed the team in whispers and they moved out.

Fifteen minutes later they heard a loud muffled explosion in the distance as the C-4 exploded. Forty minutes later, in the southernmost portion of the Fishhook, the team jumped into a Huey extraction helo escorted by two bristling Marine Cobra gunships. Moments later the trio of helos crossed the border into Vietnam.

On the ground at Tay Ninh, Bud was hustled to sickbay where "Doc" Welsh, the team corpsman, gave him a sedative for the shakes, cleaned out his hand wound and sutured it with eight sutures. While the corpsman worked on his hand, Bud fought to erase the abominable picture of the NV soldier's death mask. When Bud rammed the knife into the man's heart, a loathsome dread had overwhelmed him as he watched the light of life fade from the soldier's eyes. The reality that he had actually killed a man with his own hand fully descended upon him. Somewhere this young man had a family, a mother, maybe a wife and children. The soldier died because he had to take a crap and wanted a little privacy. The entire episode was just too incredible to believe. It was as though this was all a ghastly loathsome dream. He had killed another human being, and he would never know the man's name. This wasn't anything like strafing trucks and infantry with a Skyraider. Killing people from a speeding aircraft is impersonal, likened to watching a movie, or a TV program. Killing the soldier with a knife was personal, very personal, an in your face up close kind of personal.

When the corpsman finished, Bud and Eaton walked over to the hooch area. A dozen or more SEALs including Mouse and Monster were sitting on old NV wooden mortar round boxes drinking cold Pabst Blue Ribbon beer. The group surrounded a thirty gallon drum filled with ice and cans of beer.

"Hey, John Wayne, how's the hand," said Mouse, punching triangular holes into the top of an icy can of beer with a church key. He handed the beer to Bud.

"Thanks, Mouse," said Bud, accepting the beer. "It's not too bad right now, still pretty numb from the stuff Doc Welsh used."

"That zipper head really bit the shit out of you."

"Yeah, he did."

That was the last word spoken in reference to operations. The men spent the rest of the evening talking about home, women, sports and everything but their life and work in Vietnam. The SEALs were aware that Bud was from CINCPAC, and they knew the story of what had happened on the two combat rescue operations in which Bud had been injured. Tonight they treated Bud like one of their own, even a couple of the "hard cores" seemed to accept him now. It made him feel good. Bud drank seven or eight beers before staggering off to the hooch and collapsing on his cot.

The next afternoon at 1500, Bud climbed aboard a Huey helo to make the hop from Tay Ninh to Tan Son Hut for a meeting with Navy intelligence and SOG personnel. Armed with indisputable evidence that North Vietnamese forces were wantonly violating Cambodian territory, CINCPAC could now recommend an appropriate military response to CNO, and thus to the White House. Removing this major enemy threat so close to Saigon would save countless American as well as South Vietnamese lives.

The SEALs of Bravo One One honored the stalwart Naval Aviator by standing in a line to shake his hand before he boarded the Huey bound for Tan Son Hut. This outsider who looked like any other non-hacker at first glance had definitely been born again hard during the past three days. John Wayne was going to convey the fruits of their dangerous and deadly labors back to the Honchos in the world. Scuttlebutt had it that the new Commander in Chief had a real pair of balls, and that he was a pretty tough guy who didn't give a shit about anti-war protesters or those lying scum-sucking media maggots. Well, they would just have to see about that.

Leaving Tay Ninh on this hot muggy afternoon, Lieutenant Bud Cotter, a once spoiled, carefree, young man from Nashville Tennessee had unconsciously and unintentionally, been transformed into a warrior worthy of a horseman of Attila The Hun. Baptized in the fires of war at Khe Sanh, steeled and honed by his bloody agony over the A Shau Valley, and again, quite by chance, he had become an executioner in the rain forest of Cambodia. Such steel and cold-blooded resolve was quite extraordinary in a pleasant and naive lad that Bud Cotter once had been.

Staring out the door at the jungle racing by below, the disquieting thoughts of war and death began to fade into sweet thoughts of Margo. This had been their first separation since the wedding. The loneliness was much worse than he had imagined it would be, but now, in a few hours, his beloved Margo would be back in his arms. He sat back in the web seat and began to hum, *Together At Twilight Time*.

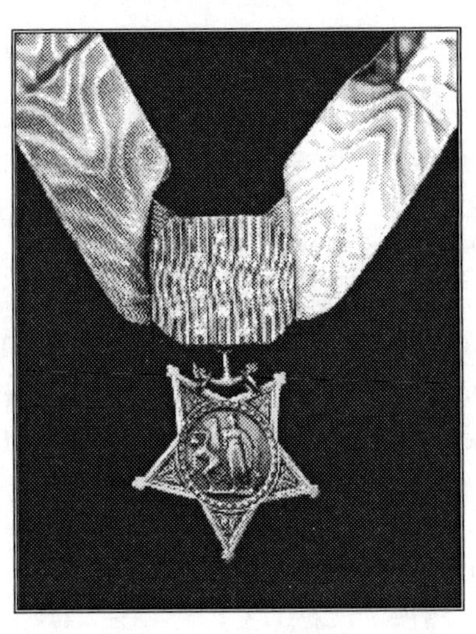

Congressional Medal of Honor

COTTER, TOLAND M.

Rank and Organization: Lieutenant, Navy Composite Squadron VC-110.

Place and Date: A Shau Valley, South Vietnam, 6 August 1968

Entered Service at: Nashville, Tennessee

Born:17 October 1945,Nashville,Tennessee

Citation:

For conspicuous gallantry and intrepidity at the risk of his life above and beyond the call of duty. On that date, Commanding Officer of Squadron VC-110 was on the ground and under attack by 1,000 North Vietnamese Army regulars. Hostile troops and heavily armed vehicles were moving on a road and through heavy jungle toward the position where Commander Ferguson awaited extraction by a Search and Rescue Helicopter. Other hostile troops had established anti aircraft positions to the immediate south of Commander Ferguson's position. The tops of the 1,500-foot hills were obscured by a 1000 foot ceiling, limiting aircraft maneuverability and forcing pilots to operate within range of hostile gun positions, which often were able to fire on the attacking aircraft. The rescue helicopter was hit by enemy 23 millimeter fire and sustained damage to its fuel tanks forcing it to egress the area. Lieutenant Cotter and three other VC-110 pilots were providing interdicting fire on the enemy troops and vehicles placing themselves in perilous danger of automatic antiaircraft fire. In the belief that a replacement search and rescue helicopter could not extract Commander Ferguson before enemy troops would reach his position, Lieutenant Cotter announced his intention to land his aircraft on a muddy road close to Commander Ferguson's position. The three other VC-110 aircraft continued to strafe enemy troops and vehicles to cover Lieutenant Cotter's extraction of his Commanding Officer. Although aware of the extreme danger and likely failure of such an attempt, Lieutenant Cotter elected to continue. Directing his own air cover, he landed his aircraft and taxied to Commander Ferguson's position.

While effecting a successful rescue of the downed pilot and a North Vietnamese prisoner, Lieutenant Cotter's aircraft was damaged by heavy ground fire with nineteen 23 millimeter bullets striking his aircraft and severely wounding Lieutenant Cotter. In the face of severe bleeding and with the capability of using only one arm, Lieutenant Cotter managed to fly his aircraft for a period of twenty-five minutes to Danang Air Base, South Vietnam. Lieutenant Cotter's profound concern for his fellow airman, and at the risk of his life above and beyond the call of duty are in the highest traditions of the U.S. Navy and reflect great credit upon himself and the Armed Forces of his country.

To those who have fought for it, freedom has a flavor that the protected will never know. (Sign at Khe Sanh, 1968).